In the
Face
of Death
We Are
Equal

THE PRIDE LIST

MU CAO

In the
Face
of Death
We Are
Equal

TRANSLATED BY SCOTT E. MYERS

LONDON NEW YORK CALCUTTA

THE PRIDE LIST

EDITED BY SANDIP ROY AND BISHAN SAMADDAR

The Pride List presents new as well as classic works
of queer literature to the world. An eclectic collection of
books of queer stories, biographies, histories, thoughts,
ideas, experiences and explorations, the Pride List does not
focus on any specific region, nor on any specific genre,
but celebrates the fantastic diversity of LGBTQ+ lives
across countries, languages, centuries and identities,
with the conviction that queer pride comes from its
unabashed expression.

Seagull Books, 2019

© Mu Cao, 2019
First published in English translation by Seagull Books, 2019
English translation © Scott E. Myers, 2019

ISBN 978 0 8574 2 698 7

British Library Cataloguing-in-Publication Data
A catalogue record for this book is available from the British Library.

Typeset by Seagull Books, Calcutta, India
Printed and bound by WordsWorth India, New Delhi, India

CONTENTS

TRANSLATOR'S NOTE

Throughout this translation, I preserve the Chinese units of measurement used in the source text. One li is equivalent to 500 meters; one jin is equivalent to 500 grams; one mu is 666.67 square meters. Chinese currency is referred to variously as yuan, kuai, or RMB depending on the word used in the source text. One mao is 1/10th of one RMB; one fen is 1/100th of one RMB. Throughout, I preserve the Chinese naming convention of placing family name before given name, though most characters are known only by nicknames. For readers not familiar with the rules of pinyin, the "Qing" in character Ah Qing's name is pronounced similar to "Ching."

In the
Face
of Death
We Are
Equal

ONE

1

Those who know me call me Old He, and they also know that I've worked at a crematorium for my entire life. Few people have had enough contact with me to call me a friend. As a child, my greatest ambition was to become a musician, but a turbulent political campaign came along and left me an orphan. I chanted the slogans of Chairman Mao just like everyone else, then went off enthusiastically to join the labor force by working at a crematorium. I feared neither hard work nor getting tired and dirty, so my walls were quickly filled with certificates of merit.

A female corpse lingers in the morgue, no family to come and claim her. Nor has anyone stepped forward to pay the cremation fee. In just a few short days it will be my sixtieth birthday and day of retirement. What, I have been asking myself, will I do once I leave this place? I've come to regard the crematorium as my home, and my work unit has given me a two-room apartment that's just as old as I am. I was but twenty when I began working, and everything I had done up to that point had been executed with such enthusiasm. And yet, the day I entered the crematorium, I regretted it. The baneful stench of rotting flesh held me in its grip, but I never cried—I just burned one body after another. As for all the young lives prematurely cut short—they've made me understand the importance of life.

In my apartment I flip through old photographs from the days of my youth. I look at a picture of myself with Xia Nanshan, just as I have done a million times before. This photograph is thirty years old.

Xia Nanshan was a handsome young man with an odd personality and unusual interests. From the day he stepped into the crematorium to join the world of work, I secretly desired him. Again and again I expressed my admiration to him, and sometimes I would intentionally press my body against his. I wanted to know if he kept me in his heart.

"Get the fuck off me, He Donghai—stop bumping up against me!" This Xia Nanshan, five years younger than I, sometimes turned hostile.

I was deeply unhappy. I did my best to think about women, about bad women, whorish women. And yet, my gaze remained glued to Xia Nanshan's body as I watched his every move. Carrying corpses with him each day, going in and out of the morgue and cremation room—this was my happiness.

Nighttime fell and the sky grew dark as it always does. All the crematorium workers who had ended their shifts and returned home—perhaps they were holding their wives as they slept at this very moment. Only two people working the night shift remained, and they were asleep at their work stations. Xia Nanshan grabbed a set of keys and quietly opened the door to the morgue; inside was a female corpse releasing a foul odor. It was so late; why had he gone in there? After all, the woman was not one of his relatives or loved ones. It was then that I realized there had been many occasions when I had seen him enter that area of the crematorium, not to resurface for some time. On the surface, Xia Nanshan appeared to be a quiet, gentle, and educated young man, but he was in fact much bolder than I. The first time I ever lifted a female corpse, I took one look at her face and was so horrorstruck that I pissed my pants. Those with even less guts than I circumvented the crematorium when walking near it.

I grabbed a flashlight and stepped softly into the dark and gloomy morgue. There I was stunned to witness a scene that nobody would believe and which made my skin crawl and my hands tremble. "Xia Nanshan!" I shouted. "You animal! You're worse than a pig or a dog! You—"

"Brother He!" he cried, "I'm begging you, don't tell a soul about this . . . whatever you want from me, I'll do it!" He knelt before me, tears streaming down his cheeks.

I looked at Xia Nanshan and felt anger, hatred, sadness! How could an exceptional young man like him be a necrophile? Ever since I had revealed my sexual orientation to him I had been unable to raise my chin with dignity. I myself would have liked to dive headlong into the cremation chamber, so great was my self-hatred. Even when Xia Nanshan yelled at me I still idolized him. How could I love someone like that? He was sick, and I wasn't normal either!

"Xia Nanshan!" I shouted. "Get the fuck up! I'll keep my mouth shut about this, but promise me you'll never do this kind of insane thing again!" This was the first time in my life I had spoken to someone as though I were a "leader."

After that, Xia Nanshan started cozying up to me, endlessly offering me cigarettes and that sort of thing. When another corpse arrived the next day, he rushed to lift the upper half of the body, giving me the lighter end. When these things happened, my feelings for him only grew stronger. Joyfully I carried corpse after corpse with him into the cremation room, and to each of these bodies I silently thought: "Better to be miserable and alive than happy and dead!"

2

Snowflakes filled the sky, dancing as they fell. Fires burned in stoves everywhere, emitting a glowing warmth that caused the frozen people to feel as though they were being sent to paradise. Snow piled up outside doors bore the traces of footprints; slowly it started to melt and turn into spring streams. Willow trees lining the water spit shoots from the crevices between their roots, turning the ground into a stretch of green.

I stepped out of the crematorium with Xia Nanshan. We walked for some time before coming across a grove of peach blossoms, which took us by the hand and led us into spring.

I was thirty then; Xia Nanshan was twenty-five. We were two contented bachelors.

"Hey Little He, play the flute for me!" Despite my being older than him, Xia Nanshan had never regarded me as his "Big Brother." In those days everyone called me Little He. The leaders at my workplace called me Little He, my coworkers called me Little He, and Xia Nanshan called me Little He, too.

"Sure," I replied. "I'll play the flute—your meat flute! Which song do you want to hear?" Anytime I was in high spirits I liked to joke around with Xia Nanshan, and often attempted to provoke his sexual desire. Again and again, his cold and detached demeanor left me heartbroken.

I blew into the flute—blew into the lonely spring night!

"Why aren't you attracted to women, Little He?" Xia Nanshan gazed, perplexed, at tufts of clouds on the horizon as they drifted farther and farther away.

"Why are you attracted to dead women, Little Xia?" I sat very close to him, but emotionally we pushed each other away.

I took Xia Nanshan into my arms and pressed my lips against his. He gave no reaction, so I started to caress him. Every organ in his body froze and it seemed as though I myself were attempting to make love to a corpse. Was I a necrophile, too?

"Xia Nanshan!" my heart cried. "Do you know how much I love you? Why don't you love me, too? Why are you not moved by my love? Am I really less appealing to you than a female corpse?"

Xia Nanshan grabbed a key and went into the morgue. Seeing that there were only three male corpses inside, he quickly came back out. Soon after, though, a woman in her fifties was carried in. This woman, dead from sickness and dried up like a piece of firewood, caused Xia Nanshan's hands to linger affectionately for some time.

"Dammit, Xia Nanshan, if you fucking do this again I'm reporting you for necrophilia!"

"Go ahead and fucking report me, He Donghai! Why don't I report you for sodomy while we're at it?"

When we were done cursing each other out, we carried the corpse to the room where the cremation chamber was housed. There, we placed the body in the retort and reconciled. Together we washed our faces, washed our feet, washed the stench of death off our bodies. Together we ate, drank, and used the bathroom. Together we carried the dead.

When Dr. Hua was not yet a doctor, a case of smallpox had turned her into a pockmark-faced girl. Her face also had five black moles on it, the one closest to her mouth sprouting several hairs. She was as big and tall as any man. People were terrified when they saw a woman like that, so at the age of twenty-eight Dr. Hua was still not married.

Dr. Hua had put all of her energy into her studies, and before graduation she had the greatest achievements of any student at Zhengzhou Medical School. Never satisfied, she promised herself that she would become the best surgeon in the country. After she began working at Zhengzhou People's Hospital, she wanted even more medical knowledge, so she asked for a few days off so she could visit the famous professors working at Beijing People's Hospital. There, an aged professor took a liking to her and wanted to make her his daughter-in-law. But when his son set eyes on her he felt as though he were looking at an old witch, and stayed away for several days to avoid his father's wishes.

Dr. Hua's self-esteem took a blow from this, so she spent the day wandering the streets and cursing the heavens for making her so ugly. She walked aimlessly, endlessly, until she had no idea where she was. That's when a big red apple fell from the top of a twenty-floor building she was passing and slammed right on top of her head. In an instant, the world went black and she passed out on the ground.

A young passerby saw that a woman had fallen. He was eager to be the chivalrous hero who saves the damsel in distress, but when he saw the woman's face he took off running. Along came another passerby, but he took one look at her, shook his head, and continued on his way.

A few moments later, a young lady walked by. "This poor woman!" she cried. "Dying right here on the street, and no family coming to help!" She sighed and walked away.

Finally, an old man riding a flatbed tricycle lifted Dr. Hua up off the ground and took her to the crematorium.

"Another corpse with no one to claim it?" I mumbled to myself as Xia Nanshan and I lifted the still-limp body and carried it into the morgue.

The sky grew dark and it would soon be time to get off work. The only people in the crematorium were myself and Xia Nanshan; together we ate shelled peanuts and drank double-distilled sorghum baijiu. Suddenly and for no apparent reason, Xia Nanshan started calling me "Big Brother" and raised his glass to me repeatedly. I was thrilled by this sudden outpouring of attention. Before long I was drunk, and lay on the bed and fell into a deep sleep.

When Xia Nanshan saw me sleeping like a dead pig, he gleefully grabbed the key to the morgue and went inside. He removed the woman's clothing, kissed her breasts until her body grew warm, and got on top of her, his body trembling as he panted. He entered her, and just as he was climaxing she embraced him.

Throughout Beijing the news spread like wildfire: a dead person at the crematorium had come back to life.

The woman who had come back from the dead was this very Dr. Hua. In the moments when she was regaining conscious-ness, she perceived that a man was kissing her. Never in her life had she enjoyed the love of a man—and this man, who believed himself to be defiling a corpse, succeeded in giving her an orgasm. Dr. Hua fell in love with Xia Nanshan right there in the morgue. She regarded him as a personal savior whom she wanted to repay.

"I love you, Xia Nanshan. I want to marry you!" Her eyes burned with tears and her heart erupted like a volcano.

"I . . . I . . . " stammered Xia Nanshan. "I have nothing! I can't bring you happiness. If you marry me, you'll regret it . . . " He did not want to be uncouth in his rejection of this woman who had given him a fleeting night of passion. He was, in fact, terrified of her.

"Whatever you've done in the past," Dr. Hua replied, "I don't care. All I care about is that we're together now. All I need is for you to give me a sincere heart—you're my first love! You're my first man and I will love you forever!" Impassioned tears dripped from her pockmarked face.

Xia Nanshan resisted Dr. Hua's advances. Could it be that he simply considered her too ugly?

"Marrying a woman as ugly as that would be worse than death!" he told me. When I saw him hiding in the bathroom, I couldn't help but laugh.

"Little He, do me a favor and go see if that woman's left yet." Xia Nanshan had been squatting on the toilet for more than two hours.

I left the bathroom and found Dr. Hua sitting outside in the courtyard. She was no longer pinching her nose, for she had become accustomed to the stench of dead bodies surrounding us.

"Aiya!" she cried. "Big Brother He, why hasn't Xia Nanshan come back to work yet?" Her voice was sweet and tender, like a bee gathering honey.

3

At last Xia Nanshan emerged from the bathroom. He stood face to face with Dr. Hua.

"Nanshan," she began, "I'm certain that I'm pregnant with your child!" She blushed and the five moles on her face twinkled like stars. "Let's get married, quick!"

He nodded. His family was not well off, so he and Dr. Hua went to Zhengzhou, where they got married. It wasn't long before Xia Nanshan's work was transferred to Zhengzhou as well. During their honeymoon, the newlyweds went to the seaside, where they found a heart-shaped stone on a sandy beach. The stone was red and had been rubbed down by ocean water until it was smooth and shiny.

"Nanshan," Dr. Hua said, "think of this heart as representing your own heart. Give it to me as our wedding gift so I can wear it around my neck forever." She closed her eyes and waited for his kiss.

Xia Nanshan rolled the heart-shaped stone around in his fingers until its temperature matched his own. "Is this heart a gift to us from the ocean?" he wondered. When they returned from their honeymoon, he drilled a hole through the stone, then threaded it with a red string. On the back of the stone he used a chisel and mallet to engrave the word "love." He placed the heart around his wife's neck for her to wear against her chest.

Xia Nanshan watched as his wife's belly grew bigger each day, and yet each day he became more and more melancholy. "What kind of child is this?" he asked himself. "Was it conceived when we had sex in the crematorium morgue?" He began having dreams in which he would see his smiling mother walking toward him. She leaned into his ear and said, "I'm going to be reincarnated!" Then she would disappear.

Soon enough, Dr. Hua gave birth to a plump, pale boy. The child very much looked like Xia Nanshan. Each day, the mother took her precious son into her arms, humming and singing lullabies as she waited for her husband to return from work.

Holding the month-old baby in his arms, Xia Nanshan stepped outside and into the courtyard of the home he shared with Dr. Hua. Just as he was entering the courtyard, he heard a hoarse voice calling his name. "Xia Nanshan!" it cried. He looked all around him but didn't see anyone, then he heard the words again: "Xia Nanshan!" The voice sounded like that of his own mother. He looked in every corner of the courtyard to locate the source of the sound, and then he heard the cry once more, this time very clearly: it was coming from the lips of his own child! Alarmed, he flew back inside and told his wife what had happened.

Holding the child in her arms, Dr. Hua looked at her husband skeptically. The child looked up at his mother's face and laughed. Dr. Hua made faces at the child—she wanted to scare him so he would stop—but this only made the boy laugh with even greater delight.

"Our child is so strange!" Dr. Hua exclaimed. "He hasn't cried once since he was born; he just laughs and laughs. So odd! What should we name him?" She pulled out a breast as she spoke, and stuffed a nipple into the child's mouth.

"We can't raise this child," Xia Nanshan said. "Let's give him to another family to adopt!" He lowered his head somberly as plumes of smoke drifted from his mouth.

Just then, a hoarse sound arose from before Dr. Hua's chest. Xia Nanshan threw down the cigarette butt in his hand and jumped up excitedly. "Listen! Did you hear it? The child spoke again—he called your name!"

Dr. Hua had, in fact, heard a hoarse voice emitting from her son's lips; in quick succession it called out first her name, then her husband's. The image of her and her husband having sex in the morgue flashed before her eyes. "My god!" she thought. "How could we have conceived our child in a cursed place like that?"

"Did you hear it?" Xia Nanshan was beginning to choke up. "This inauspicious child is still saying our names!"

Dr. Hua held the child close and began to cry. When the boy heard her sobs, he laughed.

The cold wind howled as snowflakes fell like banknotes from the afterlife. It was dusk outside, but there suddenly appeared bright rays of light that looked like daybreak. Head lowered, Xia Nanshan walked ahead as Dr. Hua moved with

11

heavy footsteps behind him, the child resting in her arms. They arrived at Zhengzhou Railway Station, where only a few people could be seen looking like snowmen as they walked through the desolate streets. With tears in her eyes, Dr. Hua removed the red, heart-shaped stone from her neck and placed it around the neck of the child, who was sleeping sweetly, bundled in thick rolls of cotton clothes.

"Let's dump this child and get out of here! We can have more children later, lots of them!" Xia Nanshan pulled the infant from his mother's arms and placed him on the snow-covered ground.

With an aching heart, Dr. Hua picked the child back up from the snowy ground so that she could see her own flesh and blood one last time. Tears streamed down her cheeks. Her child was so adorable! How could he be some kind of freak? She kissed his face; even in slumber he still smiled! What was he dreaming of? Gently, she placed the child back on the ground below the eaves of a shop near the railway station. "He's my child!" she thought as the tears continued to fall.

Xia Nanshan took his wife firmly by the hand and away they walked, not daring to turn around one last time to look. The shattered snowflakes chased them in the wind as a voice from behind cried out for Mama.

My life became dull after Xia Nanshan left. A year after he had moved away, I received a letter from him; he said he was now a history teacher at a primary school in Zhengzhou. I wrote him a reply immediately, using the written word to convey how much I missed him. When I did not receive a second letter from him, I wrote him again—but again, still nothing. There was nothing I could do but let go of my feelings.

Someone in my work unit introduced me to a woman; we only met a handful of times before getting married. I was with her for five years, but we never had children and when we slept together her spine grew cold. Following a friend's suggestion, we went to a hospital to undergo an examination; it showed that my wife was unable to conceive. Still, I never raised the issue of divorce, and actually became somewhat kinder to her upon learning that she couldn't bear a child. But she wanted a divorce, insisted on it in fact, so there was nothing for us to do but end the relationship. I never remarried.

By day I continued burning corpses, and in the evenings I read books that I borrowed from the library. Sometimes during those long, lonely nights, I would write lyrical poems or play the flute. Slowly, time passed.

4

When I was forty-five years old, I published a few articles and, with the money I received, arranged a visit to Zhengzhou. While I was in a small bookshop making a purchase, I unexpectedly bumped into Xia Nanshan. He was forty now and had gained quite a bit of weight. He invited me for a drink at a bar, where he informed me that he was now the history teacher and assistant principal of a middle school. He took me to his home, where I saw his wife, Dr. Hua. She was completely unrecognizable. The five moles had vanished and her entire face had undergone some kind of cosmetic procedure that made her look prettier. She told me that she worked at Zhengzhou Hospital as an attending doctor in the surgical department. She was also hospital vice-director.

Again and again I raised a glass to my old friend! In the course of our conversation I learned that they, like me, had no children. We moved from the topic of marriage to kids and the mood in the room grew gloomy as we sighed sadly to each other. Dr. Hua told me that she had given birth to a son, but when she took him to a park one day she was careless and he slipped out of sight.

"Maybe you'll find him one day!" I offered in an attempt to console the husband and wife.

"He'd be fourteen this year," Dr. Hua replied with a sigh. "He's got to be in middle school by now!"

When our visit was over, I stepped out of the magnificent apartment building where Xia Nanshan and Dr. Hua lived. On the road back to Beijing, I kept thinking about my own identity and status; a sense of inferiority transported me back to the crematorium, back to my life as an ordinary worker.

At the age of fifty-five, I inadvertently stumbled upon a gay park, where I met a number of tongzhi—comrades, fellow gays. They all called me Old He. Before long I couldn't enter the park without seeing one or more familiar faces. I had many wild times and experienced intense passion with that group of young people, who made my life feel more youthful with each passing day. I started looking forward to Sundays, for this was when I usually saw them. Sometimes I would invite a few money boys out to eat, or I would invite them back to my place to fool around. I was ripped off on a few occasions, and one bastard tried to blackmail me. And yet, my lonely heart continued to cruise the park, loving these young men when the opportunity presented itself, touching them as gently as a dragonfly skimming across a pool of water. Increasingly, after each encounter I became unable to say goodbye to them. I was more than willing for some ugly kid to con me out of the money in my pocket if he was hungry and needed to eat. Those homeless kids—their tears, their emotions, their hopes and dreams of home—whenever I think about them, my heart aches.

At the gay park I got to know a young music teacher with whom I had many hobbies and interests in common. Thirty years old, his surname was also Xia, and indeed he looked just like Xia Nanshan. Each weekend before seeing him, I took a trip to the barbershop and did my best to look a little younger.

My heart, as light and happy as a butterfly, would flutter to the school where Teacher Xia taught. There I would find him completely lost in the piano as the clouds outside the window floated alongside the sound of the music he made. I'll never know if I started taking piano lessons with Teacher Xia because I fell in love with him, or if I fell in love with him because I started taking piano lessons with him. In those days, we often sat together in Sunday classrooms, a hundred empty seats and desks before us, sharing passions so powerful that one felt young again.

It wasn't long before my many years of yearning for Xia Nanshan was redirected toward Teacher Xia. When we were in bed together, I would excitedly grab his swelling, reddening cock.

"It's huge!" I would exclaim.

Sometimes I would joke with him about it. "Your features are so delicate and handsome, but this thing of yours is so thick and coarse. It doesn't go together at all!" Then Teacher Xia would pull that treasure out and stuff it in my mouth.

I started having dreams that he and I were having sex together in the morgue. Teacher Xia's face would morph into the face of Xia Nanshan as my soul drifted away from my body. Turning to look at myself, I discovered that my own face had transformed into the pockmarked visage of Dr. Hua, the five moles twinkling like stars.

By day, I cared for Teacher Xia like a father; by night, I ensnared him like a whore. We went on this way for a year. One day, Teacher Xia came to see me at the school, where I was practicing piano. We left together and went to a quiet wooded area; the look on his face told me something wasn't quite right. I wanted to comfort him, so I spoke gently.

"Uncle He," he said after a long period of silence, "let's just break up!"

"Why? Why do you want to break up? What's the point?" My voice trembled and I suppressed the anger rising in my heart.

"I'm thirty, Uncle He—I can't keep going on this way! I want to get married, have a child. That's the only way people will see us as normal!" His eyes were moist.

I sighed helplessly.

Teacher Xia left, and I remained standing in the black night, feeling as though my heart had been torn from my chest. Silent tears streamed down my cheeks.

Unwilling to give up, I went to see him, but we only stood in silence, neither of us uttering a word. When I got home, I wrote him a letter saying that I hoped our feelings would continue as before. Even if it meant seeing each other only once a month, I wrote, I would be willing to keep the arrangement for the rest of my life. But time passed and he never replied. Alone, I went to the nearest bar and drank a glassful of sorrow.

One month later, I heard that Teacher Xia was to be married. I bought him a Western-style suit to congratulate him.

The last time we saw each other was on his wedding night. I got drunk and he took me home, holding me up by the shoulders as we walked. When we arrived at the grove where we had rendezvoused in the past, I embraced him frantically and began to sob, stripping off my clothes as I begged him to let us make love one last time. Teacher Xia also began to cry. His cock refused to get hard; I got on my knees and bit into it ferociously. In pain, he punched the top of my head with his fist so hard that I saw stars. Releasing his bloody dick from my mouth, I knelt on the ground like a wild animal emitting its last hopeless cry.

Teacher Xia pulled a handkerchief that I had once given him from his pocket and wiped the blood off his cock. Then he tossed the bloody cloth to the ground, turned his back to me, and walked away.

When I crawled up from the ground, my eyes met a bright, full moon illuminating the night sky. I walked with the moon by my side until I arrived at a stone bridge that stretched across a gleaming body of water. Reaching out, I lunged forward.

I should have died that night, but the water was too shallow. By the time I crawled out of the mud and onto the riverbank, my stomach was full of sewage. After regaining full consciousness, I recalled that during day I had often seen dead rats floating in the water. The memory made me vomit.

Morning on an autumn's day. I was returning from the vegetable market with an assortment of plastic bags of various colors hanging from my fingertips. Just as I entered through the front door, I heard the comforting sound of the telephone. There was no time to stop in the kitchen first, so I went directly to pick up the phone; sure enough, it was my kids. I told them excitedly that I had picked up a bunch of their favorite things to eat. The instant I hung up I picked up the dozen or so plastic bags from the floor and started to get busy in the kitchen. One thing was certain: I wanted all the food to be ready before they arrived. When I thought of those lovable kids opening up their little red mouths and greedily eating the food I was about to cook, happy notes leapt from the bottom of my heart.

Just as I was preparing the stir-fried beef and mushroom, I heard a knock at the door.

"Hello, Uncle He! Happy sixtieth birthday!" Ah Qing entered with a smile.

I received the two bottles of alcohol that Ah Qing had brought with him. "Aiya, my little angel!" I said. "Have a seat and rest for a while! I was just whipping up the beef-and-mushroom dish you love so much. Do you want me to add a lot of chili peppers?"

"Sure, go ahead!" Ah Qing walked over to me. "But this is too much for Uncle He to do on his own. Let me be your assistant!"

Ah Qing was a true, born-and-bred farm child with the simplicity and goodness of the countryside. He didn't look a day over twenty-five, and he was also a talented poet.

Three years ago I went down to a city in the south to participate in a poetry and prose writers' symposium. Passing through Zhengzhou along the way, I decided to stop at Xia Nanshan's place to pay him a visit. While taking a pleasant, solitary stroll through the city, I entered Zijing Mountain Park, where I chanced upon a young man named Ah Qing, who looked very much like my first love, Xia Nanshan. And yet, there was also something about his demeanor that reminded me of Teacher Xia, whom I had also loved deeply.

It was dusk on a summer's day and very muggy. Ah Qing sat alone on the grassy bank of Gold Water River, a forlorn expression glued to his face. The park served as home base for all the gay guys of Zhengzhou. Handsome young men walked back and forth in threes and fours. I approached Ah Qing and made a deliberate effort to ask him the time; he pointed toward the big clock hanging outside Zijing Mountain Department Store. We started talking about literature and soon hit it off, so I invited him out for a bite to eat.

At a night market not far from Zhengzhou Railway Station, Ah Qing and I sat facing each other at an outdoor restaurant. The waiter brought us a menu and I invited my guest to order. Ah Qing looked at the menu for a while, then handed it back to me without ordering a thing.

"No need to be polite! Go ahead and order a dish that you like." I pushed the menu back across the table to him.

"No, let's have Uncle He order! We'll get whatever you would like. I can eat anything; I've never been picky with food!" Ah Qing looked at me earnestly, and seemed embarrassed by my attempt to put him in charge.

I went ahead and ordered. "Home-style tofu, fried mushrooms, red-braised fish . . . " Food was much cheaper in Zhengzhou than in Beijing, so I ordered copiously.

"Oh, that's enough! That's more than what two people can eat." Ah Qing took the menu from my hands and passed it back to the waiter.

The waiter swiftly delivered our food to the table, along with some large bottles of beer. Ah Qing and I clinked our glasses together and drank. Often he looked lost in thought, his eyes revealing a kind of secret melancholy.

"No need to stand on ceremony—go ahead and eat!" I seized a chunk of meat with my chopsticks and put it in Ah

Qing's mouth. He was surprised by this token of affection, but opened his red lips to accept it.

"You have a very high-bridged nose—it's quite handsome! When I look at you, you make me think of a friend from long ago." I looked at him tenderly.

"Thank you, Uncle He, for the compliment." He lifted his glass cheerfully, then swallowed its contents in a single gulp.

"How about another bottle?" I asked, turning to look for the waiter.

"No, Uncle He, we've already had five!" He wiped the corners of his mouth with a napkin.

I paid the bill and took him to the Jinxin Hotel.

Inside our room, I drew a bath, carefully adjusting the water temperature. "Ah Qing," I said, "come take a bath!"

"Uncle He should go first!" He sat on the couch and watched a TV show.

I walked over to the couch, then took Ah Qing in my arms and kissed him. We took off our clothes and got into the bathtub, where we playfully splashed each other with water to ignite our arousal. Before long, Ah Qing was hard. His cock was long and thick, a full nineteen centimeters with a big, red, bulbous head that looked like a budding flower.

The faucet shot forth pearls of water. They landed on Ah Qing's smooth, glossy skin and on the budding flower, which was by now throbbing and pulsing. Glistening and transparent, some pearls fell to the floor, disappearing among the clouds of soapsuds that had fallen from the tub.

Ah Qing closed his eyes, enjoying the feel of water on his skin.

In the mirror I saw my skin had lost its elasticity. Age spots marked my limbs, the soles of my feet were covered in wrinkles, and all of my skin sagged toward the earth. My shrunken cock hid in the chaotic mound of hair that surrounded it, and I noticed for the first time that my pubic hair had lost its glossy black sheen. I looked at this young man, who ignited every ounce of jealousy, madness, and foolish passion in me—and even then I couldn't get it up. Truly, I was old.

"Let me scrub your back, Uncle He." Ah Qing wrapped a hand towel around his palm and moved it toward me.

"Thank you! What a nice fellow." In gratitude, I turned my back to him, doing my best to push my ass up against his pulsating flower bud.

Two indescribably warm hands moved across a stretch of skin in which I had long ago lost confidence. Those hands made my heart race and the blood in my veins pulse faster. I felt as though a little fawn were racing about inside my body. At last! My cock stood up from that withered mound of grass.

"Good boy . . . let me scrub your back, too." I turned around, determined to show Ah Qing that I wasn't just some useless old codger.

He laughed as he placed the towel in my hand, then turned around obediently. His shoulders were broad and his waist was narrow; one could easily discern the outline of his bones. I glided my hands up and down his body with great care, as if I were afraid I might puncture his strong, beautiful skin. I ran the towel along his body, unable to resist the urge to follow the cloth's path with my tongue. Greedily, I kissed this flower-like young man as he lay enveloped in the warm embrace of the water.

"Uncle He, the food's about to burn!" Ah Qing rushes over to me with blood-red fish scales caked to his hands. A strange burning smell hits my nose and the memories in which I have been lost are abruptly interrupted.

I quickly grab the frying pan by the handle and lift it from the stove. "Oh, no! We can't eat this! I'm going to make it all over again. This is Little Fairy's favorite dish!"

"The fish is all washed, Uncle He. You should take a breather and let me make it!" Ah Qing grabs a towel and wipes the sweat from the top of his head, then pushes me out of the kitchen.

I look at the clock on the wall: nearly twelve. A knock at the door—and there they are, my little angels! Little Fairy, Little Thing, Little Jade, Little Tough, and Little Devil pour into my apartment, all shouts and greetings. They throw down the things they've brought, then wrap their arms around me tightly as they press their lips against my cheeks. Here they are, my greatest joy!

TWO

1

Dancing snowflakes filled the sky. Ah Qing walked through the railway station, feeling lonely; he wanted to buy a ticket home, but not a single kuai of money lined his trouser pockets. Cold and hungry, he curled up under the eaves of a nearby restaurant as the snow fell more heavily with each passing minute. He lifted his head and suddenly saw a beautiful woman in white walking toward him; behind her, a vast expanse of willow trees sprouted light yellow buds.

"Mama!" He shouted in excitement.

The woman in white cast him a warm smile as she called out, "Ah Qing! Aaaaah Qing!" Then her voice grew faint.

Ah Qing reached out to embrace the woman, but all he got was an armful of dancing snowflakes. And he cried! He yelled out: "Mama! Mama! Don't abandon me!"

Ah Qing awoke from the nightmare, his entire body covered in a cold sweat, and sat up in bed. Inside the pitch-black dormitory his classmates slept like rows of piglets. He closed his eyes and his mind raced as a powerful sense of fear gripped him.

In tears, a fifteen-year-old Ah Qing exited the office of his Chinese-language-arts teacher.

Ah Qing knelt beside a coffin, the inside of which was as black as night, a white filial piety cap on his head. The room was full of activity as men and women entered and exited. Ah Qing looked at his father, who sat outside the doorway of the main room of the house with drooping eyelids, a cigarette dangling from his lips.

A pile of cold loess buried his mother.

Ah Qing knelt before the grave, tears hanging at the corners of his eyes. The darkness of the sky pressed downward as white snowflakes fell from its depths. The more they fell, the bigger they grew. The sound of Ah Qing's sobbing grew more and more distant.

He entered the small courtyard where he lived, a basket of dry, withered-up leaves on his back. His father sat outside the main doorway of the house, smoking a cigarette; clouds of smoke obscured the expression on his face. Ah Qing carried the basket into the kitchen, struck a match, and lit the leaves in his hand. He was making a fire and was going to cook.

"Big Brother, what are you making? I want youbing!" Ah Qing's nine-year-old sister ran into the kitchen, a schoolbag on her back, then squatted beside her older brother. She had always loved his sesame-seed pancakes.

Ah Qing reached out and lovingly patted his little sister on the head. "Alright," he said. "Big Brother will make you youbing. Now go and do your homework. Don't make Dad get angry and hit you again."

Ah Qing brings food to a small wooden table saying, "Dad! It's time to eat!"

Ah Qing leads an old cow along a small country road.

Ah Qing enters the field to pick cotton.

Ah Qing lights a fire and cooks in the kitchen.

Ah Qing gazes at the snowflakes falling outside the window.

Ah Qing, shirtless, harvests wheat with his father.

Ah Qing carries a sprayer on his back and sprinkles pesticide on seedlings.

Ah Qing leads an old cow in a village at dusk.

Ah Qing gazes at the snowflakes falling outside the window.

Ah Qing had grown to be a tall boy. Setting the food before his father, he said timidly, "Dad, I want to go to Zhengzhou and find a boss to work for. I'm seventeen now."

His father heaved a heavy sigh. "If you want to go, then go! It's not that Dad doesn't want to keep you in school; it's just that ever since your mother passed away, all of the household burdens have fallen on my back. I've worked myself to death raising you. I can't afford to keep sending all three of you kids to school."

Ah Qing kept silent. He watched as a billow of smoke escaped his father's nostrils.

Their home was a tile-roofed house with three rooms. Short and squat, it had weeds that pushed their way out from between the tiles. In the courtyard, two jujube trees with crooked necks crawled with little yellow flowers that were just beginning to blossom. Under one of the trees lay an old ram. Two lambs that had just completed their first month of life jumped about in a world that was still new to them.

Ah Qing walked to Little Jade's home. Little Jade's mother had tears in her eyes and her voice choked with emotion. "Children," she sobbed, "you're only seventeen! It's not easy going out into the world. The two of you are like brothers; you have to take care of each other. When it's cold out, be sure and put on some extra clothes. The city is full of all kinds of bad people; the two of you need to be upright and decent. Don't go turning into a couple of thieves!"

"Don't worry, Shenzi," Ah Qing said to the woman. She wasn't his aunt by blood or marriage, but this is what he called her. "I'm going to take good care of Little Jade." His heart ached a little.

"Ma! Me and Ah Qing better get going." Little Jade's eyes fogged up.

"Wait, Little Jade! Ma hasn't packed the eggs she boiled for you!" Little Jade's mother secured the boy's backpack to his back, then ran into the kitchen and returned with a bowl of eggs. "Child, if you can't find work, come back right away. And don't go hungry because you don't want to spend any money on food!"

"Ma! I'm going now." Little Jade waved goodbye as he stepped out of the courtyard gate.

"Little Jade, is your money secure? Don't let pickpockets get you!" Little Jade's mother followed close behind.

Little Jade patted his belly, where his underwear was pulled up high, and laughed. "The money is in my underwear! Don't worry, Ma, I won't lose it!"

Little Jade's mother stood outside the courtyard gate wiping her eyes with one hand and waving with the other. With one hand suspended in the air, she watched the outlines of Little Jade and Ah Qing as they receded farther and farther into the distance.

Near the entrance to the village stood a stone half-buried in the earth with the words "Dragon Gully Village" carved into it. Just outside the village in a muddy ditch, a few pigs covered in mud shoveled muck with their noses in search of something to eat. Ah Qing and Little Jade walked, periodically turning their heads to look behind them. They didn't want to say goodbye to the village where they had grown up, to the tile-roofed houses of varying heights, to the aged locust trees. Uninterrupted hosts of chirping sparrows flew overhead.

The two boys squeezed onto a hard-seat local train along with throngs of other migrant workers who had left their villages and were headed to cities in search of employers to hire them. The train had long since filled to capacity, the luggage racks piled up high and the spaces beneath the seats stuffed with bags of all sizes. Ah Qing and Little Jade had no choice but to stand with their backpacks still tied to their bodies in an aisle that was just as overflowing with people as the seats themselves. Some of the rural laborers smoked; others took off their shoes or ate melon seeds or chatted or called people sons-of-bitches. The smell of cigarette smoke and the foul stench of feet and sweat permeated the cabin.

Ah Qing didn't mind all this too much. He looked out the window at the patches of barren farmland flying by.

At last they arrived at Zhengzhou Railway Station. They got off the train, backpacks securely tied, and made their way out of the station exit. The large square out front was saturated with the sound of cars coming and going. They asked an elderly newspaper seller for directions to their destination—the outdoor hiring site—and then walked to the T intersection where Erma Road and Jiefang Road met. Cars, some parked, some moving, lined the streets. Small groups of men and women of all ages sat, stood, squatted or lay on the ground. Employers, too, squeezed their way through the crowds.

"*This* is the hiring site?!" Little Jade cried in distress when they got there. "It's dirtier and more chaotic than a cattle market!"

"I hope we can sell for a good price!" Ah Qing said with a sardonic laugh.

It's autumn, 1991.

A fat guy covered head to toe in grease spots approached the boys. Looking them up and down he asked, "So, you're together, huh? What kind of work do you want to do?"

"Yes, we're together, boss. What kind of work do you want us to do?" Ah Qing fixed a suspicious gaze on the man's eyes. The only thing he wanted to know was whether this person was reliable.

"It's a restaurant—odd jobs. You want it? The monthly pay is—" the fat guy raised a fist, then extended his index finger and thumb.

"Eight hundred?" Little Jade's jaw dropped. "Great! We'll do it!"

"Not that much, kiddo! What can you do? Can you cook? Even our cook only makes two hundred a month." The fat guy opened up his big mouth and laughed.

"You mean eighty? That's not enough! Can't you go a little higher?" Ah Qing's backpack pressed downward, causing his body to curve under the weight.

"Not enough?" the fat guys asked. "That's already a lot! You guys can make some money and learn a new trade at the same time. After six months, if one of you can learn to cook, your pay will go up to two hundred! Where else are you going to find such a good job? We also provide room and board. See those two guys over there? One look and you can tell they're not honest! They wanted to come with me, but I didn't want 'em!" The fat guy pointed at two disheveled youths standing at a distance. They were frail and skinny with faces encased in worry.

"Give us a hundred!" Little Jade haggled. "We'll work hard for you!"

"You guys seem alright, so I'll bump it up ten kuai. If that's not enough for you, then forget it, I'll go and find someone else." The fat guy acted like he was about to leave.

"Ninety? We'll think about it. After we've given it some thought, we'll let you know." Ah Qing followed with his eyes as the fat guy made his way back into the crowd.

2

No one could say exactly when the two young migrant worker women quietly appeared by Ah Qing and Little Jade's side. But they did, and at just that moment a woman with curly hair, penciled eyebrows, and a thick layer of red lipstick stepped out from the jostling crowd, her extremely high high-heeled shoes clicking and clacking as she walked. Behind her trailed a wretched looking man with a gaunt face. He wore a suit and tie and looked very much like the Guomindang spies one sees in the movies. The curly-haired woman brought her high-heeled leather shoes to a standstill in front of the migrant worker girls, then pulled out a pack of cigarettes from her snakeskin-patterned purse. No sooner had she extended her long fingernails to pull out a cigarette than the gaunt man reached into his pocket and produced a lighter, which he used to light her cigarette as he bent over slightly, a fawning smile glued to his face.

The curly-haired woman faced the crowd of migrant workers and blew smoke rings at them disdainfully. She turned to the two girls and looked them up and down. They retreated a few paces, timidly.

The curly-haired woman frowned, then flicked a coil of sizzling red ash with her long fingernails. "So you two girls have come out to work for a boss, eh? What do you think of hotel work?" She seemed to be doing her best to sound aloof and indifferent.

"We . . . we don't want to work at a hotel," one of the girls replied after gathering her courage. "We want to work at a clothing factory."

A sneer erupted from the woman's nose. "A clothing factory?! You'll work yourself to *death* in one of those! Sometimes you don't even get paid! You can make more money at a hotel, but not everyone is suited to it. Go ahead and decide for yourselves!"

And with that, the curly-haired woman squared her shoulders arrogantly and moved to another group of migrant worker girls.

A middle-aged man with a half-smoked cigarette dangling from his lips approached.

"Wei! Where are you guys from? You have identity cards? What kind of work you want to do? How about odd jobs at a restaurant? It includes room and board. We're not a big outfit—I can give you eighty kuai a month each. What do you say—you guys want to do it or not?"

The middle-aged man spit the cigarette from his mouth, then lifted a grease-covered leather shoe to extinguish it.

The sky grew dark as the shops lining the streets lit up.

"Are you hungry, Little Jade? Let's get something to eat. We haven't found any work today, but there's always tomorrow!" Ah Qing took Little Jade by the hand.

"The bosses here are something else!" Little Jade sighed. "Their clothes are filthy! If the bosses are this dirty, just imagine how dirty we'd get doing odd jobs at a restaurant!"

They approached an outdoor food stall stationed at the hiring site. An old lady was busy ladling noodles for a few young migrant men. Four tiny wooden tables standing before the stall were seated almost to capacity.

"How much is a bowl of noodles?" the boys asked. "How much is a salted egg?"

The old lady smiled warmly. "Noodles, five mao for a large bowl; salted eggs, two for five mao!"

They ordered two bowls of noodles and four eggs, then found a place at one of the wooden tables and began to eat their dinner.

"Ah Qing, where are we going to sleep tonight?" Little Jade asked, a look of worry on his face. "At a travel hostel? I've heard a lot of those places are black inns. In the middle of the night they'll kill you, then take your money and steal your valuables!"

"Do we look like we have a lot of money?" Ah Qing laughed. "We'll tell the hostel boss that we're not businessmen, we're out here selling our labor. It'll be safer that way. My clothes are a bit shabby and make me look like a worker. But Little Jade, your mom just made yours—you look like a dandy!"

Little Jade laughed loudly as he and Ah Qing got up to leave the food stall. They were walking under the flickering lights of the streets when two boys covered head to toe in dust walked past them, backpacks on their backs.

"Wei! Hello, brothers!" Ah Qing greeted them. "Where are you from? Where've you been sleeping at night?"

"We're from Zhoukou. I'm Little Wave and this is Little Tough. Where are you guys from?"

"We're from Dragon Gully Village in Zhumadian. I'm Ah Qing and this is Little Jade."

"It's so hard to make money working for bosses in Zhengzhou!" Little Wave continued. "Little Tough and I have been here for over two months. We worked at a restaurant for one month—that was one evil boss! He didn't pay us a single kuai and even blamed us for ruining one of his tables! Fuck! If that black-hearted boss ever shows his face at the hiring site again, we're going to give that son of a bitch a good beating!"

"Where have you been sleeping at night?" Ah Qing repeated.

"Me and Little Tough and a bunch of other people from our hometown have all been sleeping in the ticket lobby of the railway station."

"Ah, I see."

"Well, see you tomorrow, brothers!"

The illuminated signboard hanging outside Bright Promise Hostel shined brightly. Ah Qing and Little Jade paced back and forth near the front door, unsure of whether or not they should enter.

"It's not that cold outside. We could sleep in the railway station, too!" Ah Qing removed his hands from his pockets.

"I can't sleep well if it's not in a bed!" Little Jade replied in anguish. "If we sleep in the railway station our clothes will get all dirty and we won't have anywhere to wash them! If we're wearing dirty clothes tomorrow it'll be even harder to find work!" He paused, then asked, "Ah Qing, when you left home, how much money did your dad give you?"

"Twenty kuai! I . . . " Ah Qing lowered his head in embarrassment.

"He's not even your real dad—no wonder he doesn't act like one! That's just ruthless. If we don't find work you won't even have enough money to get back home!" Little Jade threw out the words in anger.

Ah Qing's face turned white and lifeless; he bit his lower lip.

Little Jade took hold of Ah Qing's ice-cold hand. "I'm sorry, Ah Qing. I shouldn't have said that. All I meant was . . . okay, don't be upset. We'll find work, earn lots of money and take it back home with us. We're going to make sure that your dad and my mom know they didn't raise their sons for nothing!"

30

"I'm not upset," Ah Qing replied. "Having the opportunity to leave our village and work for someone has put me in a much better mood than I was at home."

"Let's go inside the hostel and ask how much a dormitory room is for one night. My mom gave me a fair amount of money; let me pay for tonight and after you've made some money you can pay me back!"

They entered the hostel and went to the registration window.

"Excuse me," Little Jade said to the girl working there. "How much is the dorm per person per night?"

"One bed in an eight-person room is three kuai per night," the girl replied. "Six kuai total for two people."

Little Jade passed the money and two identity cards through the window. The girl grabbed a big set of keys, which jingle-jangled loudly as the boys followed her through a dark and dingy hallway. Inside the room, the lamp light was a pale, dull yellow and the floorboards underfoot were damp. There were eight beds lined up in a neat row, three of them already occupied. One of the men slept heavily, snoring loudly.

Ah Qing lay down on one of the beds and stared fixedly at a few winged insects crawling on the ceiling. Little Jade lay on his side and gazed at the red string around Ah Qing's bare neck and shoulders.

"Ah Qing, you still wear the stone heart that your birth mother left you! Mothers really are most loving people in the world! As soon as I left home, I started to miss my mom. I wonder if she's gone to bed yet!"

"I've always worn it," Ah Qing replied. "It's just an ordinary stone, but I have very strong feelings for my mother. And for my adoptive mom, too. It was hard for me when she died. She wasn't my birth mother, but she's the one who raised me so I've always seen her that way!"

"Who knows?" Little Jade said in excitement. "Maybe you'll find your birth parents while we're out here selling our labor! Maybe you'll bump into them just like they do in the movies. For all you know, your birth father is a millionaire! When the time comes, don't forget about your brother Little Jade!"

"I was only a few months old when I was abandoned by my birth mother. Even if she suddenly appeared before me I might not recognize her! And she—she would only recognize me if she remembered this stone heart around my neck. Her son is already seventeen! Maybe she's already dead; for all I know, she died even earlier than my adoptive mom!" Ah Qing's voice began to shake.

"Oh, Ah Qing, I've really put my foot in my mouth," Little Jade said apologetically. "I was really just talking about my own mother—I didn't mean to make you start thinking about yours. Anyway, it's okay, my dear brother! Think of my mom as your own; she's always loved you, ever since we were little." He reached out a comforting hand and placed it on Ah Qing's chest, where he felt a red, heart-shaped stone.

3

Early the next morning, Ah Qing and Little Jade arrived once more at the hiring site, their backpacks firmly strapped to their backs. Jiefang Road and Erma Road were deserted, with only a few cars occasionally speeding past, spitting out black and white exhaust. The doors of big shops and little ones were all shut tight; beneath the eaves of one of them was a thick cotton quilt, and inside that thick cotton quilt was a bundled-up person. A foot swathed in a frayed sock stuck out and a worn-out pair of leather shoes lay on the ground at the side. Motionless, the person slumbered heavily, as if their dreams had whisked them away to paradise.

A middle-aged street-cleaner woman with a big broom whooshed her way forward along the road. Sunlight gripped flying specks of dust and bounced off aged wutong trees, whose greenish-yellow leaves swayed in the wind like the outstretched palms of beggars.

More and more people arrived at the hiring site, assembling in numbers even greater than the day before. Signs made of wooden planks and cardboard lay strewn about on the ground or were held in the hands of migrant workers. They were a variety of sizes and thicknesses, and had words written on them: cook, painter, breakfast, renovation, noodles, electrician, nurse attendant, pan-fried bun wrapper, sewer repair, beautician, liangpi noodle processing, driver, tofu pudding, tailoring, electric welding, lamb noodle soup, professional tire repair, assorted cold dishes, printer . . .

Amid the bustling crowd stood a boss with a beer belly who was looking for a cook. He spit globs of phlegm to the ground and spoke glibly in non-standard Mandarin. Around him swarmed a group of working men, each one eager to know whether meals were included in the job. A middle-aged woman sitting on a large bag closely inspected and occasionally scratched at a fungal infection on her feet. A little girl with a face full of freckles gnawed on a piece of sugarcane, periodically spitting bagasse to the ground beside her feet.

Just then, a fat woman carrying a backpack emerged from between Ah Qing and Little Jade, then farted with a loud "boom!" as she passed. Little Jade raised his hand to cover his nose and mouth; Ah Qing laughed while covering his. The whole thing caught the attention of the surrounding crowd and people turned to look at them.

The fat woman found a place amid the crowd to let her feet fall, then slid the bag under her big fat butt. She pulled a wrinkled handkerchief from the pocket of her maroon-colored jacket, raised it to her garlic bulb of a nose and, with a loud honking noise, deposited a river of snot into the cloth. She calmly stuffed the handkerchief back into her pocket and began to wait for her very own boss to appear. Suddenly a slender young woman with glasses on her nose and a book in her hand approached her.

The slender woman lowered her head and looked down at the fat woman's ample form. Her demeanor was courteous and genteel. "Pardon me, Big Sister!" she began. "Are you looking for work?"

The fat woman looked up with a smile and laughed. "Yes, I left my village to come out and find work. Doesn't matter how hard or dirty it is—whatever it is, I can do it!"

The slender woman smiled. "Has Big Sister looked after children before?"

The fat woman patted herself down, then stood up. "I've had four children and I raised 'em all! They're big enough to run all over the place now—the first and second ones are already in primary school. When the first girl was born, her father named her Beckon A Brother! The idea being she was supposed to help make the next one be a boy. But the second one was a girl, too, so we named her Beckon Again! Well, who would have thought the *third* one would be a girl, too? *She* got the name Beckon Anew! By the time the fourth one came along, we were out of hope and there was the only thing to call her: Stop Beckoning!"

The surrounding crowd guffawed loudly and the slender woman covered her mouth as she laughed. "Big Sister, you are so funny!"

Suddenly the fat woman opened her eyes wide and her face grew serious. "Whether it's baked buns, steamed buns, dumplings, or meat pies," she said, "I know how to make 'em all!"

"Oh! You've misunderstood, Big Sister. What I mean is . . . "

The fat woman seemed to be growing anxious. "Whatever work it is, I can do it . . . whatever the work, I can do it."

The slender woman was growing anxious, too. The book in her hand fell and dropped to the ground: *The Birth of Tragedy* by Friedrich Nietzsche. The fat woman picked up the book in a hurry and placed it back in the slender woman's hand.

"Thank you, Big Sister!" the younger woman said politely. "I can tell you're honest and reliable. I'd like to ask if you can help take care of my child and cook for my husband. I'm going to be leaving the area to pursue a PhD. With Big Sister watching over my family, I would be very relieved!"

"Okay, okay, okay," the fat woman said.

The slender woman led the fat woman out from the mass of people gathered around, then called out to a taxi. The new hire got into the vehicle, then craned her head to look back at her brethren, smiling happily as she disappeared into the distance.

After the women left, a middle-aged man in a somewhat wrinkled suit and tie approached Ah Qing and patted him on the shoulder. "Did you come out to work all alone?" he asked.

When Little Jade overheard the middle-aged man's inquiry, he moved closer to Ah Qing.

"The two of us are together!" Ah Qing said, and he took hold of Little Jade's hand.

The man scrutinized Little Jade's face, which was as white and delicate as porcelain. "You'll get dirty doing the job I'm offering," the man said. "I'm afraid this one can't handle it!"

Little Jade looked at the man disdainfully and took a few steps to the side.

The middle-aged man in the wrinkled suit turned back to Ah Qing. "I only need one person. You coming or not? We provide room and board and the pay is a hundred kuai a month!"

"I'm not going," Ah Qing replied. "We're together. If I go, we both go. If I don't go, neither of us goes."

"Shifu, what kind of work is it?" A thin and frail young man with a backpack stepped up to the middle-aged man, blocking any departure route he might have wanted to take.

"It's keeping watch over a boiler. Think you can do it? You'll have to shovel out boiler slag each day. Think you can do it?" The middle aged man repeated himself while looking the young man up and down.

"That's nothing, shifu! I can do work that's harder, more exhausting, and dirtier than that!" The frail young man's eyes flashed brightly.

"How old are you? Where are you from?"

"Sixteen! From Xinyang!"

The middle-aged man led the frail youth out of the crowd. Ah Qing watched the new hire as he disappeared and wondered whether he himself would have been able to get accustomed to that kind of work.

"Ah Qing, there's another big pile of people gathering over there. Let's go and see what kind of work it is!" Little Jade took Ah Qing by the hand and they made their way to another area of the hiring site.

They tried to make their way into the dense crowd, but there were too many people squeezed tightly together. They had no idea what kind of work was being offered, nor could they even see a boss anywhere. Standing on the tips of their toes in hopes of catching a glimpse of whatever was going on, they watched as a young man with a shaved head made his way out of the crowd, scratching his scalp.

"What kind of work is it, brother?" asked a curious Little Jade.

"Nothing for us, that's for sure! He wants to hire a man, but he wants you to do women's work! It's nursing some sick old half-paralyzed guy. Every day you have to wash his face and his stinking feet, you have to empty his bedpan, you have to wash his clothes and cook for him. You tell me, is this a man's work? And on top of that, for something that filthy, that tiring, that aggravating, he's only paying eighty kuai a month! You'd starve on that! You won't see me waiting on a living corpse!"

4

Little Jade grabbed Ah Qing by the hand, then turned on his heel to lead him to a different spot. That's when they heard a male voice call out, "Catch him! Don't let him go! He didn't pay me my wages!"

In great alarm a balding fat man jumped over a migrant worker who was sitting on the ground; two outraged young men lunged forward in pursuit. In his panic, the balding boss accidentally trampled the leg of another migrant worker, who proceeded to give him an angry push, causing him to fall to the ground, where he lay, panting and out of breath.

The two young men who had lunged at the balding boss grabbed him tightly by the collar. Turning to face the crowd, one of them yelled, "This black-hearted boss cheated us! We worked for him for over a month, but he came up with an excuse not to pay us and told us to hit the road! Come on, guys, let's give him some payback!"

Fury erupted from the crowd. "Beat him to death! Kill the son of a bitch!"

The young men raised belligerent fists and began repeatedly hitting the balding boss.

"The police are coming!" a woman's voice screamed.

Everyone within earshot dispersed. Some of the men lowered the fists they'd been brandishing and returned to the larger crowd. The balding boss lay on the ground, his face a bloody mess. His trousers had been ripped in the brawl, causing a pair of floral printed underwear to become visible through the tear. His two front teeth were knocked out and blood trickled from his nose and mouth. A relentless stream of moans—"Aiya, aiya!"—escaped his thoroughly misshapen lips.

Two police officers dismounted their motor trikes, yelling loudly for everyone to disperse. "Move along, people, move along!" Then they walked over to the balding boss on the ground.

"What happened? Who did this to you? Can you stand up and talk?"

Staggering, the balding boss crawled up from the ground and scanned the crowd in search of the people who had beaten him. Just as he was raising a finger to point in the direction of a familiar face, his trousers fell completely to the ground, revealing two fat thighs and a pair of floral printed underwear.

The police officers guffawed as laughter erupted from the crowd. "Ha ha! That's disgusting!" the officers shouted.

After things had settled down, Ah Qing and Little Jade stepped under the canopy of an outdoor food stall and ordered two bowls of lor mee braised noodles. When they finished the noodles, they asked for two cups of complimentary tea.

"What if *we* have a run-in with a black-hearted boss like that?" Ah Qing asked.

"Beat him up! Just like they did today!"

"What good would it do just to beat him up? We came out into the world to make money, not get in fights. We need to stay smart—we need to be absolutely certain about a boss before we go with him!"

"Ah Qing, after we earn some money, I want to learn a skill. What do you think I should study?"

"I want to learn to cook," Ah Qing replied. "For starters, if you're a cook you'll never go hungry!"

"I don't want to be a cook. It's too dirty working in a restaurant! Just look at how many unemployed people are holding up 'cook' signs—they're everywhere! And every one of them is wearing greasy, dirty clothes!"

Ah Qing furrowed his brow. "What skill do you want to learn then?"

Little Jade smiled mysteriously, then moved his lips close to Ah Qing's ear. "I want to go to beauty school, and after that I want to open my own salon!"

Ah Qing said nothing in response. He was too busy silently weighing the relative advantages of these two trades.

In the little courtyard of a farming family in Mt. Mang Village, a woman just over twenty years of age held her three-year-old treasure in her arms. Outside the courtyard gate, a minivan-taxi horn could be heard as the little treasure's father stepped out of the vehicle. He was followed by Ah Qing and Little Jade. The little treasure's father paid the cab fare and the driver made a U-turn and drove away.

Ah Qing and Little Jade followed their new boss upstairs to a room on the second floor. There they found a double bed and a desk on top of which sat a reading lamp. A few traditional Chinese ink wash paintings hung on the walls.

"What do you think, brothers?" the boss asked. "This room's not bad, eh? My little brother and his wife used to live here, but six months ago they moved to the city to open up a restaurant and this room's been empty ever since. Anyway," the boss continued, "you guys rest for a while. I'm beat, too, and tomorrow we start work. Your pay starts from tomorrow! Room and board, plus eighty kuai a month each. Alright, brothers! I'm going downstairs now. If you need anything, just give me or my wife a holler! Big Brother's going downstairs now!"

"The boss and his wife are very hospitable!" Little Jade exclaimed as he sat on the bed, visibly at ease in the new space.

"The boss said we're a little more than thirty li from the city," Ah Qing replied. He wanted to relax, so he sat on the bed, too.

"It doesn't matter where we are—work is work! I think it's going to be pretty comfy working here! There are mountains, rivers . . . hey, Ah Qing, let's go look at the Yellow River tonight! What do you think?"

"What?" Ah Qing exclaimed. "The Yellow River? Tonight? No way! It's already dark outside and we won't be able to see anything. Besides, this is our first time here so we don't know the way."

"It's not far!" Little Jade insisted. "Didn't you hear what the boss said? He said just walk two li north and we'll hit the bank of the Yellow River."

"Let's do it another day! We just got here to start a new job; if we go running around on the very first day, our host family isn't going to be very pleased!"

The two boys lay on opposite sides of the bed. Ah Qing remained perfectly still, his mind swirling with thoughts and worries. Little Jade pulled a book from the nightstand drawer; it was a Chinese translation titled *The Collected Works of Shakespeare*. He flipped through the volume, looking at the illustrations inside.

Ah Qing shut his eyes and, before long, seemed to be asleep. Little Jade, however, put the book down, then stuck out a finger and began gently scratching Ah Qing's foot. This made Ah Qing giggle as he withdrew his straightened leg, an act that prompted Little Jade to grab him by the leg as if he were planning to drag him across the bed. Ah Qing fought back. He gripped Little Jade by the foot with one hand, then began scratching the sole of his foot with his finger. Finally, Little Jade loosened his grip on Ah Qing's foot, then scuttled over to Ah Qing's side of the bed to go to sleep.

Little Jade turned off the light and looked at the moon outside the window as it cast its sweet light into the room. Unable to fall sleep, he tossed and turned, then watched Ah Qing's sleeping face for a while. Gently, he stretched an arm across Ah Qing's chest, then slowly moved his hand downward. Ah Qing's lips began to tremble under the thick cotton quilt; he abruptly rolled over and pressed Little Jade beneath him. When he took Little Jade's tongue into his mouth, it sounded just like an infant suckling a breast.

5

Early the next morning, Ah Qing and Little Jade got up and washed their faces and brushed their teeth. The boss's wife got up and washed her face and brushed her teeth, too, and she also combed her hair. The boss was last to get up, and he washed his face and brushed his teeth as well. Steamed buns, rice porridge, and vegetables were spread out on the dining table. After Ah Qing and Little Jade had eaten breakfast with the boss and his wife, they went to the room where liangpi noodles were made. There, the boss showed them everything they needed to know: how to knead the dough, separate the gluten, strain the starch, boil water, spread oil on an aluminum plate with a brush, and scoop out the starch paste. When all was said and done, there finally appeared before their eyes numerous round sheets of liangpi noodles.

After receiving their instructions, they got to work. Ah Qing rolled up his sleeves and began to knead dough in a large ceramic bowl. In a separate ceramic bowl, Little Jade rinsed the dough that Ah Qing had just kneaded. As Ah Qing held the bowl under the faucet to let more and more water pour in, the gluten gradually separated from the water, which grew starchier by the moment. After the starch settled to the bottom of the bowl, Little Jade poured off the excess water that had risen to the top. Meanwhile, the water in the wok on top of the fiery burner jumped and swirled as it came to a boil. Little Jade grabbed a brush and applied cooking oil to the base of the thin aluminum plate; Ah Qing then quickly set the plate atop the boiling water, where it floated. White smoke and hot air filled the room, and the boys became so busy that not just their foreheads, but their entire heads were covered in sweat.

The boss, meanwhile, busily served freshly prepared liangpi noodles to customers.

Day by day, time passed.

Summer arrived quickly and a great rain fell, flowing downward in seemingly endless droves. The boss entered the workroom, a cigarette dangling from his lips. He saw that Ah Qing and Little Jade were still busy at work.

"Take a break when you're done with this batch of liangpi!" said the boss. "With rain like this, tourists aren't coming out for sightseeing and street peddlers aren't setting up their spots, either. We won't have customers until the weather clears! You guys have been hard at work for days, so get some rest." Having spoken, the boss turned on his heel and walked out of the workroom.

"This rain is great!" Little Jade said, looking outside as he rubbed his aching waist. "When it's like this we don't have to work ourselves to the bone!"

Ah Qing removed his trousers, which were covered in patches of flour. "I hope the old man in the sky has mercy on us and makes it rain two days and nights a week!"

41

"We've been working more than twelve hours a day!" Little Jade added. "I've never worked this much! Being home with a mom to take care of you really is the best!"

"Do you miss home, Little Jade?"

"I miss my mom! I wonder if it's raining back home, too."

"Listen!" Ah Qing said with wonder. "The sound of the rain is so beautiful! Little Jade, let's go climb the mountain together. In the rain, the Mt. Mang scenery will be gorgeous!"

Wearing matching white T-shirts and red shorts, Ah Qing and Little Jade descended the stairs of their new home. Barefoot and carrying a big black umbrella, they walked toward the mountain. A light rain pitter-pattered overhead and glittering crystals of water dripped from tree branches. They stood in a pavilion at the top of the mountain and gazed out at the turbid waters of the Yellow River flowing into the distance. Mt. Mang was still being developed for tourism and many of the scenic spots were overgrown with weeds. A few couples appearing deeply in love walked romantically in the misty rain.

Supporting each other by the shoulders, Ah Qing and Little Jade descended low-lying Mt. Mang, then climbed up a small hill, at the top of which grew the saplings of a variety of planted trees. The hill was connected to another hill by a drawbridge, which the boys crossed; they continued a bit further until they reached and then ascended the Pavilion of the Floating Sky.

"Look, Little Jade—there's a bunch of people gathering around something over there. What are all these people doing here on a rainy day like this?"

"Wow, there's a police car, too!" Little Jade opened the umbrella. "Let's go take a look!"

They ran toward the crowd of people, where a police officer was lifting the corpse of a young man into a police vehicle. The officer drove off and all the lovers and vacationers who had been gathered around dispersed.

"Oh, dear!" one person in the crowd sighed. "It was a university student—he killed himself over lost love!"

"What a dreadful way to die!" a middle-aged woman continued. "The policeman said he took sleeping pills. There was a suicide note in his shirt pocket along with a picture of him and his girlfriend!"

Chills ran down Ah Qing's spine and he grabbed Little Jade by the hand. "Come on, Little Jade, let's go back!"

"Yes, but slow down!" He gripped Ah Qing tightly. "We don't want to slip and fall!" They walked as raindrops rolled off the umbrella and onto the ground.

THREE

1

It was a winter's night, the kind with icy winds that blew so hard they tore into one's pores with a cold that was enough to make any lonely heart freeze over. There, in the park, a ghostly young man drifted, a wandering soul with no family or friends to rely on. His black eyes flashed beneath murky gray rays of lamppost light. He watched me as I walked toward him.

"This late and you're not going home yet?" I patted one of his hunched-up shoulders and he made an obvious effort to smile. His lips were turning purple and they trembled. He looked as though he wanted to explain things, to give me a good impression so that I would take him home with me.

"I'm waiting for a friend," he said, "but he might not come. It's too cold out." The words were directed at me, but the young man gazed into the distance as he spoke. He seemed to be telling me that if his friend were to show up now, it wasn't me he'd be leaving with.

"What's your name? How old are you?" I reached out and took hold of one of his frozen hands. "Are you going to keep waiting for that friend?"

"My friends in the circle call me Little Fairy. I'm twenty."

"Little Fairy?!" I laughed.

"Listen, Uncle. Can you host? If so, I'll go home with you right now." Little Fairy opened his bright, black eyes and looked at me.

I wasn't sure that I wanted to host, but I couldn't bear to lie to this child, who so desperately needed warmth.

"Yes, Uncle can host. He'll take you home now." I opened up the right side of my coat and held Little Fairy tightly against me as we stepped out of the park.

I took him home with me.

"I bet you're hungry, Little Fairy!" I said, holding up two packages of instant noodles. "One pack or two?"

"Two, please, Uncle He!" Little Fairy stared at the noodles with hungry eyes.

I stepped into my small, narrow kitchen and lit the gas burner, then began to prepare the noodles in a wok. When the water came to a boil, I cracked two eggs and dropped them in.

The noodles were barely cooked when Little Fairy picked up a bowl and stepped toward me. In quick succession he ladled the noodles into the bowl, then into his mouth.

I sat down and turned on the TV.

"Are the noodles okay?" I asked, smiling as I craned my neck to look at him.

"They're good . . . good!" He chomped on the noodles and gulped down enormous mouthfuls of broth. By the time the words were out of his mouth, the noodles had completely vanished. He hurriedly drank down the rest of the soup, displaying the great, pitiable hunger he had endured for so long.

My heart ached somewhat as I watched Little Fairy eat. I stood up and walked in his direction, then pulled two more packages of instant noodles from a cardboard box and returned to the kitchen. They were ready in no time. Little Fairy ate like he really was a magical little fairy. He waved his chopsticks before my eyes and the noodles disappeared, leaving the wok's interior bone dry. I made him a third batch of noodles.

"I'm sorry, Uncle He! It's just that I was so hungry today, and Uncle He's noodles are so good!" Little Fairy had eaten several bowls of instant noodles at that point and his face was now flush.

I suddenly recalled my own childhood days of hunger. In those days, there was nothing that wasn't an object of my appetite. I used to watch earthworms ingesting mouthful after mouthful of dirt and envied their good fortune.

"There's nothing good on TV, Uncle He. Let's go to sleep!" Little Fairy's eyes turned from the TV screen, where an endless stream of medicine commercials was being shown.

The day I met Little Fairy, I had been knocking around the public park for half a year. I was fifty-six.

I held Little Fairy tightly in my arms as we lay in bed together. I didn't want to have too much contact with his flesh yet, as my hands and feet were very cold. Only after my limbs warmed under the blanket did I begin to touch and caress the skin of this heartbreaking little fairy. It was then that I suddenly realized that he was wearing a wig and the skin beneath his clothing was as coarse as tree bark. When I touched Little Fairy's penis, he cried out like a bird. In haste I pulled my hand away like a child who had been caught doing something wrong.

"My hometown is Zhangjiajie, in Hunan Province," Little Fairy began. Lying in my arms, he told me his story.

In your first year of middle school you had a classmate named Little Wei. Your families lived in the same residential area. On Sundays, you and Little Wei would play together, do your homework together.

Little Wei's father was a driver who was on the road hauling and delivering goods almost all year long. This Uncle Ma rarely came home, but when holidays came around he would drive his big blue truck into the small square at the center of the residential area where Little Wei lived. With a solemn look on his face and dressed in clothes that were always neat and tidy, Uncle Ma would descend the vehicle with two bottles of liquor in his hands. Only after he stepped off to the side would the neighborhood kids lunge forward to encircle his big blue truck and begin touching it everywhere.

Once when you were very little you had a high fever. Your mother went out looking for your father; she found him gambling at a restaurant. He cursed her out brutally, so she put you on her back and carried you to the hospital with tears in her eyes. It had just rained and the streets were covered in mud. Your mother was frail and weak and she moved through the mire with heavy steps, nearly falling on several occasions. You almost passed out in your feverish state and you had no idea if it was daytime or night. Then, in a faint haze, you seemed to hear your Uncle Ma's voice. You wanted to open your eyes to see him, but your eyelids wouldn't lift. Your head rested heavily against your mother's shoulder. A big pair of hands lifted your head and a wide forehead pressed against your face.

"This fever is high—he needs to get to the hospital right away! Isn't the child's dad at home? Why isn't he worried about him?"

"That bastard!" Mother replied. "Out drinking and gambling all day long—doesn't concern himself with a thing at home! Go ask him yourself. He'll either beat you or yell at you!" Her voice choked with sobs. By the time a teardrop had fallen from the corner of her eye, your Uncle Ma had hoisted you up and onto his shoulders, which were as thick and sturdy as a horse's back. Ma. The name meant "horse."

From then on, you fantasized that your mother was a bad woman, that she had seduced Uncle Ma and become pregnant by him, and that you were the offspring of this union.

2

During the summer vacation of your fourteenth year, you stole a cigarette and learned to smoke like your Uncle Ma.

Not far from the residential area where you lived, a utility pole stood at the side of the road. Next to it a streetlight shined brightly, illuminating the missing-person poster attached to the pole. You hadn't seen a trace of the imbecile of a child who had wandered off; his father had scrawled onto the poster that there was a five-thousand-yuan reward for anyone who brought him home. Each time you saw that missing-person sign, you daydreamed that you would be the one to find that stupid child and bring him back to his father. You would be rich, and you'd buy lots of toys and sweet fruits.

You caught a glimpse of someone walking toward the public toilet. You could only see him from behind, but—yes!—it was Little Wei's father! There was the Uncle Ma about whom you had been dreaming for so long. It had been more than a month since you had seen that warm and loving smile. "Uncle Ma!" you wanted to cry out, but your feet moved faster than your mouth and the next thing you knew you were following him. You waited outside the entrance to the toilet, where the sound of gurgling piss met your ears and made your heart race. Suddenly the thought of catching a secret glimpse flashed through your mind and you charged into the toilet. When Uncle Ma saw you, he smiled and nodded as the splashing sound of cascading urine continued. It was the first time in your life you saw a big, dark cock, right there in front of you. This was a big man's treasure. One day you would grow one just like it.

You had made many friends at school, and on Saturday nights you began staying overnight in the school dormitory despite the fact that it was very close to your home. At first your parents asked you where you had been. When they found out you were sleeping at school, they didn't concern themselves with it again.

One Sunday, you brought a classmate named Little Jie home with you to play. Little Jie was the child of a migrant family. He told you he didn't want to go home that day. As you neared the front door of your home, you heard the familiar sound of your parents fighting. You were used to it, but it was embarrassing to have a classmate hear it. You were still deciding whether to take him inside or run back out to the street when you suddenly heard your big sister crying. You lowered your head and your palms broke into a cold sweat. Little Jie took you by the hand and the two of you went back to the street. Neither of you felt like talking; you just kept walking farther and farther away from home. Before long the sky was completely black. You went with your classmate to a convenience store, where you bought two packages of instant noodles. Together you sat beneath a streetlight and ate them dry. Little Jie told you that his parents fought a lot, too; this was the main reason he stayed away from home on Sundays. Perhaps it was Little Jie's story that made you feel your destinies were intertwined. You became good friends.

"Come back and stay with me at school tonight!" Little Jie's thin, dark face was heavy with loneliness.

"I want to go home," you said. "But I'm also scared!" You quickly added, "Alright, I'll go home a little later. How about I walk you back to school first? The main gate will be locked if we get there too late."

"Alright! Let's take People's Road. It's a little longer, but there are lots of streetlights." Little Jie tightened his belt.

Side by side, you and Little Jie walked back to school.

You were still unbearably hungry. The instant noodles were like air in your belly; you couldn't feel a thing. You didn't know if your parents were done fighting yet—perhaps they had finished making dinner and were now eating? You knew that if you didn't go home they wouldn't wait for you to eat. Father was cruel to you, and Mother at times would suddenly become like a stranger. Their entire lives, it seemed, were spent in regret—did it have something to do with you? You knew that your mother had given birth to you because you looked very much like her, but were you really your father's? You knew you were supposed to be, and yet it also seemed as though maybe you weren't. You thought back to the time when you were little and the ground was covered with mud, when you had a high fever and your mother carried you on her back. As she walked on the road to the hospital, you leaned your head against her shoulder and you thought you would die. A big pair of hands lifted your head and a wide forehead pressed against your face. "It's Uncle Ma!" you remembered thinking. His voice had been so comforting. You crawled onto his shoulders, which were big and broad like a horse's back. The rain fell endlessly in the dark night and a large black shadow pursued you. You flew upward, you stretched your arms out toward a light.

"Be careful!" Frantically, Little Jie dragged you from the middle of the road.

A car zipped past you, headlights flashing brightly. You hadn't paying any attention to the road. You were almost hit by it.

"Fuck! Driving that fast? We'd be screwed if he hit us!" There was no reproach in Little Jie's voice. He held your hand. He showed concern for you, his face appearing even thinner and darker than usual, enveloped as it was in night shadows.

You had just about arrived at Zhangjiajie Middle School. The main gate wasn't fully shut yet and the shifu who served as night watchman sat beneath a twenty-five-watt light bulb, an old bald-headed guy by his side. The late-spring night breeze blew and the delicate fragrance of flowers drifted toward you from inside the campus.

Little Jie disappeared into the shared sleeping space of the dormitory and you exited the campus gate, thinking about the helpless and resigned way he had laughed when telling you the story of his parents. Your heart filled with compassion; if you hadn't been quite so hungry you might have stayed with him through the night. You had already spent the last bit of change in your pocket. Now your parents were in a fit of rage; you were going to have many more days without any money.

As you walked back to the residential area where you lived, you began to pray. The lights in your home were still on but the sound of fighting had ceased. You held the door key in your right hand and gently knocked with your left.

"Fuck, you're back?" Your father opened the door with eyes that were red and a face that reeked of exhaustion. His voice was low and weary. In your experience, this meant that everything was going to be okay, that you weren't going to be beaten or yelled at. You lowered your head and cautiously made your way through the living room. Cutting through the kitchen, you grabbed a youbing and began taking huge bites.

After seeing Uncle Ma's thing in the public toilet, you began to see a big, dark cock in your dreams at night. You fantasized that the next time you encountered Uncle Ma in the toilet, it would be dark outside; nobody would be able to see what you were doing. Uncle Ma would hold you tightly in his arms; surely he would also kiss you madly. But when you actually stood face to face with Uncle Ma, your face would flush red. When you actually stood face to face with Uncle Ma, you would be filled with desire yet refuse his kisses and his embrace.

News of Little Jie becoming lovebirds with a girl in his class spread rapidly throughout the school. At an assembly the principal and head teacher criticized them mercilessly and made them write self-criticisms that were open for all to read. For a time, everybody at school was talking about the scandal behind their backs; some students said that the girl was pregnant. Later on, she killed herself: her body was found hanging from the steel-frame basketball hoop on the playground. Little Jie dropped out of school; later, some people said he had become mentally unstable. You never saw him again, and the whole affair made you dislike athletics. In an instant, male and female students started keeping each other at a distance.

You didn't know why, but being near female classmates always filled you with an intense fear.

What you longed for day and night was a pair of big, broad shoulders.

One day, you thought you saw Uncle Ma walking toward the public toilet on the side of the road. You followed him as if involuntarily. Only after entering the toilet were you able to see that it wasn't Uncle Ma at all.

During the summer vacation of your fifteenth year, all of your waiting finally paid off. It was just the two of you inside the toilet. You didn't know if you should stand up and pretend to piss or squat down and pretend to shit. Disobediently, your little chicken began to swell. You were getting so hard it hurt and you wanted nothing more than to hold on to Uncle Ma and have a good cry. Uncle Ma seemed to notice your rapidly stiffening little chicken and his face suddenly turned as red as if he had been drinking. You watched as the last drop of piss fell from his body; his big, dark cock grew larger and larger. You squatted down, body swaying, and suddenly felt the four walls of the toilet spinning around you. You opened your panic-stricken eyes wider; your mouth, too, opened wide, eager to swallow something down.

The expression on Uncle Ma's face grew opaque. It was like something burning in a dream.

You don't quite know how it happened that you were brought inside Uncle Ma's home with his arms wrapped firmly around you. Little Wei and his mother and younger sister had disappeared the way people disappear in dreams. Your breathing became rapid and your body went limp.

Your face pressed up tightly against Uncle Ma's face. He kissed your delicate skin with his burning lips and you suddenly felt that you had come home. You recalled that your father had never kissed you; he only yelled at you and beat you. Your heart palpitated wildly and your frozen limbs seemed to be floating.

This was the happiest night of your life. You had yearned for this day for a long time; never could you have imagined that such a beautiful day would come. Your little chicken swelled even more wildly than before and you couldn't help crying. Lovingly, Uncle Ma touched you with his big hands and asked you if there was anywhere that didn't feel good. Father had never showed this kind of concern for you, nor had he ever touched you this way. Teardrops fell in heavy clusters. You wondered if Uncle Ma had touched Little Wei like this in the past, if he had made him drift into sleep each night like a little boat floating on a bay, giving him dreams that were sweeter than candy! You started to envy Little Wei. Cursing, you hoped that he and his mother and little sister would never return from his grandma's.

Every organ in Uncle Ma's body called out to you!

As if in a trance you answered the call. You felt that Uncle Ma's skin and flesh was so hot it might scald you. You wanted to sleep, but you were gripped by insomnia. Under Uncle Ma's kisses your little chicken stiffened again and a liquid that looked like egg whites shot out in volumes greater than in dreams.

It became harder and harder for you to be away from Uncle Ma. When you were alone, you often masturbated while fantasizing about him.

Uncle Ma, too, was kinder and kinder to you each day. Sometimes you daydreamed that you and Little Wei had switched fathers.

You had never seen what Father's cock looked like! Nor did you know precisely what he had done to make you be born. You were lonely. Standing before your father you felt that he was a stranger. You had always believed that your mother couldn't have been a good woman because she had married a man who didn't care for you. "That man is a bastard!" came a scream from deep within your heart.

You spent the summer in secrecy with Uncle Ma. He took you in his big blue truck to go have fun in another city. Sitting in the front seat beside him you felt the cool, refreshing wind against your cheek; outside the window was rich green scenery. You pulled down the zipper of Uncle Ma's trousers and pulled out his cock, which was as big as a banana, and held it in your mouth. The car moved forward excitedly.

"It's so funny!" Uncle Ma said with a laugh. "Little Wei's mom is starting to suspect I have a woman on the side, but she can't find any proof!" When you heard this, you thought it was a little scary, but also funny!

When Little Wei and his mom weren't home, Uncle Ma would open up the window on the second floor and place a red teacup on the windowsill. This was how you communicated for the purposes of clandestine lovemaking.

"I'm going over to Little Wei's to play," you would say to your family, you would say to everyone you knew. You didn't know how many times you'd told this lie.

One day when you saw the red teacup, you ascended the staircase to the second floor and knocked on the door.

Uncle Ma took you into his arms and pulled you into the bedroom. A few articles of women's clothing were folded up neatly on one corner of the bed. You enjoyed looking at women's pretty clothing, but not at pretty women.

You could smell Uncle Ma's body odor; it was a very nice smell that wafted out of his armpits. His broad, wide shoulders pressed down on you. You were like a little tortoise that had finally found its shell. You embraced the heavy weight pressing down on your body. This was the sense of security you had longed for.

"Kiss me again, Uncle Ma!" you panted, eyes closed, and your face flushed red.

Uncle Ma's tongue glided from your ear to the nape of your neck, then flickered down to one of your nipples, which was just the size of a soybean, and down to your trembling belly button. The tiny hairs on your body seemed as if on fire. Sweat poured, semen shot, and before long, tears flowed, too.

When others bullied you, you pushed your tears down into your stomach. When your parents beat you or yelled at you, you pushed them into your heart. Uncle Ma made living happy. When he made you come, the tears that had been trapped inside finally got to come out, too.

"I love you, Uncle Ma. I'll love you forever, Uncle Ma." Your tears mingled with his sweat.

"Time goes by so fast," Uncle Ma sighed. Reluctantly, he released you from his arms and pulled up his trousers.

You left Uncle Ma's place, counting your footsteps.

You left your place and went to the foot of Uncle Ma's building. You looked up in search of the red teacup, but it was nowhere to be found.

In a dream, you stood at the foot of Uncle Ma's building and looked up. Ever so gently, the window opened and a red teacup magically appeared on the second-story windowsill.

On a mid-autumn Sunday, you had just stepped out of your building when you spotted Little Wei's mom exiting the residential area with a bag in her arms. You rushed to the foot of Little Wei's building, looked up and saw the red teacup; a white mist seemed to be rising from it. You and your Uncle Ma both tore your clothes off. He kissed you madly, then mounted you; he was a tortoise shell growing on your back. His cock entered you and your anus convulsed in pleasure. Just then, Little Wei's mother entered the bedroom. She stared at the two of you in shock, then began screaming and crying. She howled like a rabid dog and threw things across the room.

Utterly gripped by terror, you threw on your pants and bolted out the door. It was only while running down the stairs that you realized you had left your underwear on the bed. You didn't dare return home. Instead, you ran endlessly, feeling as though there were countless pairs of eyes mercilessly digging into your back, an unbroken stream of frightful faces cursing you. If your parents knew about this! No tears fell from your eyes; you felt that you were a bad child and bad children weren't allowed to cry! Full of hateful regret, you paced back and forth at an intersection in the dark.

To continue going to school, to repent and reform, you braced yourself and returned home. In your heart you prayed: perhaps Little Wei's mom would think this too shameful to speak of, perhaps it would cause her to lose so much face that she wouldn't even tell your family. Hadn't she gone out to do something? Why had she suddenly come back? Did she already suspect something, or had she forgotten something at home and only learned of these scandalous acts when she came back to get it? You wanted to turn into a mouse and disappear into a crack in the wall.

You never would have expected that Little Wei's mom would march straight to your home and make a huge scene over what had happened. She pointed right at your parents' noses and hurled insults at them. Then she went to find others in the neighborhood and described to them all the vile things she had seen. When your father saw you, he pounded you with his fists until your nose twisted out of shape, your lip split, and you were covered in blood. You spit out one of your teeth and your entire face was bruised and swollen. You didn't have time to cry, didn't have time to moan and groan. A single kick knocked you to the ground and you felt your father's foot kicking you again and again. Blood flowed from your nose and from your mouth, but no tears fell from your eyes. You closed your eyes and discovered that you were willing to be kicked by your father, one blow at a time, all the way to death.

"I'll kill you, you filthy animal! I'll kill you, you filthy animal!" Father's voice became more and more remote; the sound of spectators trying to stop the fight became more and more remote; the sound of Mother's sobbing became more and more remote, too. The buildings around you began to spin and the earth beneath your feet seemed to be floating in the air like a boat on water. You couldn't see yourself. The black night pressed down on you like a toppled steel tower.

After being kicked out by your father, you no longer went to school. Nor did you seek refuge with other family members or with friends. You couldn't face anyone, so great was the shame. In the daytime you slept under a bridge, at night you foraged through the streets looking for food. You wouldn't steal and you wouldn't beg; instead, you ate from piles of garbage. When you couldn't take it anymore, you returned home, knelt at your mother's feet and begged her to take you back. She hadn't seen you in more than ten days, yet she wouldn't hold you. When she saw the condition you were in, all she did was cry. Your father still wouldn't forgive you; he screamed at you for causing the entire family to lose face. When he grabbed a leather shoe to beat you again, your older sister threw her arms around you and pushed you out the front door. With tears in her eyes, she tried to give you twenty kuai so you could buy something to eat. You didn't take your sister's money. You laughed in the face of this family that had abandoned you and thrown you out like so much trash. You puffed up your chest and descended the stairs.

Counting your footsteps, you went to Little Wei's building. When you reached it you stopped and raised your head to look up. You no longer saw a red teacup on the windowsill. You saw the window, which was now tightly shut, and you laughed. Suddenly the window opened and a familiar face appeared. Uncle Ma saw you smiling at him; he returned your gaze with a look of surprise and was seemingly at a loss as to what to do. You turned and left, counting your footsteps as you walked.

The first time you stole something, it was half a container of gasoline from a driver. It was only half a container, and you wanted a full one. What you wanted was a very large container of gasoline. You walked with the half-full container of gasoline to a pile of rubble at a demolition site. All the old buildings that were to be torn down had been torn down, but the high-rise buildings that were to be built hadn't yet been built. All that remained was a stretch of silence, a silence desperately needed by the dead! What you really wanted was to turn to ash, but you only had half a container of gasoline, so now you thought: just burn to death and that will be good enough. You opened the lid of the half-full container. The gasoline splashed onto your clothes; the last remaining drops you let fall on the top of your head. There really wasn't enough gasoline. You wanted to die quickly, but your shoes were dry and your hair wasn't soaked through. You didn't know how long you would have to burn before you would die. You looked for the matches. You wanted to strike the match in your hand just like the little match girl in the Hans Christian Andersen story.

Suddenly you saw a man running toward you. When the man came closer you saw that it was Uncle Ma.

"Don't come near me! Don't come near me!" you shouted, and you wept.

Uncle Ma moved faster. When he was only a dozen paces from you, he tripped on a rock and fell to the ground. He raised his smashed face and yelled at the top of his lungs: "Don't do anything stupid! Stop!"

"Strike the match! Strike the match!" You seemed to hear a little girl's voice calling in your ear. With lightning speed you struck the match and in an instant you saw yourself light up. The world around you was on fire, countless insects biting at your skin.

5

You were in the hospital for a week before you opened your eyes. The first thing you saw was Uncle Ma's face, which was thin and haggard from grief. His eyes were red and his lips were dry and cracked. When he saw you open your eyes, a tiny smile appeared on his lips and his eyes welled with tears. Half the skin on your body had been burned off, as well as a large section of the hair on your head. All that was left was a face that you no longer wanted, a face that continued to exist incompletely for this world.

Your parents never visited you at the hospital. Your older sister came a few times. She would stay for a while and then say goodbye, rubbing her eyes as she left. Only Uncle Ma stayed by your side.

After you got out of the hospital, you and Uncle Ma moved into a rented apartment. It was only later that you found out that your Uncle Ma had left his wife for you.

When Uncle Ma told Little Wei's mother that he wanted a divorce, she cried for some time, then clenched her fists and said, "Fine, we'll get a divorce. But the child stays with me. The apartment and all our savings stay with me, too."

Uncle Ma agreed to each of Little Wei's mother's demands, and he left their home with nothing to his name but a few articles of clothing. To provide you with medical care, he borrowed money from friends. He never did tell you how much he had paid for your hospital stay and medical expenses.

Your hair never grew back, so you wore a hat each day. Even with the hat, you no longer wanted to go out and live. On your sixteenth birthday, Uncle Ma bought you a wig and you finally saw your handsome face in the mirror. When the two of you walked in the street together, you feared that a strong wind would come along and blow the wig off. You didn't go to the public bathhouse anymore, for the skin beneath your clothing was uglier than a toad's. Sometimes you went into the bathroom and tried to masturbate, but your cock remained flaccid.

You crawled on Uncle Ma's back and cried because you were no longer able to ejaculate. He kissed your tears; no longer were they trapped inside your stomach, trapped inside your heart. With Uncle Ma at your side, you cried anytime you wanted. He made you promise that no matter what happened, you would keep on living. You began to put on weight. Uncle Ma, however, got thinner and thinner.

To make a living, Uncle Ma resumed driving his truck, eternally hauling and delivering goods.

When you were alone, you would lie in bed and sleep. When you woke up, you would eat the candies that your Uncle Ma bought for you. They really did smell good and they were very sweet. You ate them standing at the window, you ate them when you went outside. You ate them while sitting down, you ate them while lying in bed. You ate them endlessly, and endlessly you put on weight. You knew the taste of sweetness.

Three years later, Uncle Ma bought a two-bedroom apartment. Although your new home hadn't yet been renovated, you moved in. One time when the two of you were lying in bed, you reached out and touched Uncle Ma's cock. For the first time in three years, he didn't stop you. In the entire previous three years, Uncle Ma had had no sexual contact with you.

"Wait till I've done a few more long trips and made a little money. I'll take you traveling to every corner of the country!" Uncle Ma held you in his arms.

"Don't do any more trips, Uncle Ma! You're always gone for more than two weeks at a time!" Lovingly, you stroked his emaciated face.

Your Uncle Ma wouldn't listen. He was determined to continue making long-distance trips so that he could earn more. Each time before stepping out the door, he gave you wonderful things to eat and told you to wait for him to come back. On several occasions, he encouraged you to go back to school, but each time you shook your head resolutely and said no. As long as Uncle Ma kept taking care of you, as long as you were together, there was nothing that you wanted, nothing that mattered.

You started smoking and drinking. When you were nearly at the point where you had forgotten how to cry, Uncle Ma had an accident.

One of Uncle Ma's coworkers came to comfort you. Whatever he might have said, the words had no impact on you.

You didn't believe that your Uncle Ma was really gone. He was going to come back! You didn't cry. You were sure that fate was playing a big joke on you.

In dreams you saw Uncle Ma driving his truck with you sitting right beside him, the wind blowing past your face. A cold wind blew in the darkest, deepest place of the black night.

"Ma Shifu was really unlucky! The car fell into a valley. Just before he died, he asked me to take care of you." Uncle Ma's coworker appeared once more. He placed a hand on your shoulder to comfort you.

"Go away! Go away!" You wanted to push away anyone who came near you. "Go die! Everyone, just go and die! My parents can go and die, too! The only ones who shouldn't go and die are me and Uncle Ma!" You sobbed loudly.

You stood outside the doorway, waiting for your Uncle Ma to come back.

In dreams you saw Uncle Ma come back for real. He walked toward you, carrying sweet fruits in his hands.

You stood in the wind. You stood in the rain. You waited for your Uncle Ma to come back.

In dreams you saw Uncle Ma come back for real. His big, warm hands enveloped you.

You stood in the interminable black night. You stood and stood.

Little Wei's mother came to claim the apartment. Little Wei was with her. As the relative of the deceased, he had the right to inherit the property. But you were nothing. The relationship between you and Uncle Ma had no legal protection. You didn't care about the apartment. You didn't want anything. You only wanted your Uncle Ma.

You became a drifter after that, leading the life of a vagrant. You took the wig Uncle Ma had given you and went from city to city, sleeping in parks, in railway stations, under bridges and in tunnels. No matter how cold the dark night was, your Uncle Ma kept living in your heart.

Little Fairy finished his story and fell asleep in my arms. I wasn't his Uncle Ma, but I felt I could love him just as his Uncle Ma had.

FOUR

1

Snuggling close together, they slipped into dreamland. The sky lightened as quickly as it had darkened, however, and once again they got to work—Ah Qing kneading dough and Little Jade rinsing gluten. They remained busy at work until the sun went down.

The half-moon outside the window slowly became round.

"Little Jade, have you noticed that the boss and his wife don't seem quite right lately?"

"Yeah, it does kind of seem that way. Maybe it's because business hasn't been very good lately and we haven't been working as much. But they can't blame us for that! When there's a lot of work to do, we do it! So when there's not that much to do, we should get some rest time!"

"Mid-Autumn Festival is in just a few days! Is the boss going to give us some time off? We're almost out of flour and I haven't seen them go out to buy more!"

"You're right!" Little Jade replied. "If we get a vacation, let's go home for a visit. I really miss my mom!"

At breakfast there were two more dishes than usual on the table. One was scrambled eggs, the other stir-fried pork.

The boss's wife spoke with a smile. "Ah Qing, your work performance has been great! Same goes for you, Little Jade. I barely realized it's been quite a few months since you came to our house and started working!"

"Yes, Saozi!" said Little Jade. He and Ah Qing had addressed her as "saozi"—"older brother's wife"—since their arrival. "It's been five months since we came here!" His chopsticks paused midair.

"Really?" she asked with exaggerated surprise. "Has it been five months? It doesn't seem that long! I bet you guys miss home, huh?"

Ah Qing looked first at the boss's wife and then at the boss. But he was unable to understand what was going on inside their heads. "Yes," he said, "we've been here working for five whole months. We do miss home a bit."

"When we're done eating, let's have Saozi calculate your wages," the boss said evenly. "Mid-Autumn Festival will be here soon and you guys should go home for a visit because it's going to be the off season. If you want to come back and work next year, give me a call ahead of time and I won't go to the hiring site to look for anyone."

Ah Qing and Little Jade nodded.

The boss held a cigarette between his lips; plumes of smoke obscured his expression. His wife went into the back room for a moment, then quickly returned and sat down at the table directly across from Ah Qing and Little Jade. The smile on her face was relentless. "Five months—that's three hundred fifty kuai each!" she said triumphantly. "Go ahead and count it to make sure it's right!"

Ah Qing's face suddenly reddened. "No, that's not right! Saozi, we agreed it was eighty each per month and that it included room and board. It should be four hundred kuai each!"

"That's right!" Little Jade added, lengthening his neck. "Saozi must have calculated it wrong!"

"No, no," the boss's wife replied. "I didn't calculate it wrong—you guys are *thinking* about it wrong! You know that business has been awful these last two months. We've made less in the last two months than we normally make in a single month—and on top of that, we have to make sure you guys get to eat every day! I counted the last two months as one month, so that's four months total. And how much is four months?" She looked at her husband.

"That's a hard one!" The boss said as he blew a cloud of smoke from his mouth. "Four months at eighty is three twenty! Three hundred twenty kuai!"

The boss's wife leaned in with a fake smile. "That's right! It's supposed to be three hundred twenty kuai each, but I'm giving each of you an extra thirty kuai. You see? Your Saozi hasn't treated you like outsiders! Let's just say this extra thirty kuai is a gift from Big Brother and Sister for your travel expenses when you go home!"

Little Jade remained motionless with downcast eyes. Ah Qing bit his lip and pushed his rage down into his stomach, but he didn't say a word.

The boss's wife cast her husband a look as if she was giving him a secret signal. He threw his cigarette butt to the ground, then stuck out a foot and stomped on it ferociously.

"Hurry up and take it!" he said impatiently. "You tell me, when have we ever treated you unfairly? For goodness sake, we eat at the same table as you! We share a courtyard and a house with you! You guys are young; I only took you in to work for us because I felt sorry for you! If you had gone off with one of those black-hearted bosses, forget about three hundred fifty kuai—you wouldn't even see five kuai! Now take it, brothers!"

Ah Qing picked the money up from the table. "Here, Little Jade, take it! Let's go find some work!"

Biting his lip, Little Jade took the money and stuffed it into his pocket.

They took a bus back to the hiring site. "I want to go home, Ah Qing," Little Jade said. "I've never had this many pent-up frustrations."

"I don't want to go home, Little Jade. It wasn't easy for me to come out to work; after all this, I want to stay out here and keep making money!" Ah Qing sighed deeply.

Little Jade leaned against Ah Qing's shoulder as the bus rushed forward. Outside the window, trees seemed to fall backward as they flew past.

"I'm not going home to celebrate Mid-Autumn Festival," Ah Qing continued after they had descended the bus. "Here, take this money and give it to my dad. Tell him I'm doing just fine in Zhengzhou!" He slipped a wad of cash wrapped in paper into Little Jade's hand and together they walked from the hiring site to the main entrance of Zhengzhou Railway Station. "Alright, then! We're not very far from home—just one day on the train and you'll be there. Have a safe trip, Little Jade!"

"It would be wonderful if we were going home together!" Little Jade gripped Ah Qing's hand, seemingly unwilling to say goodbye. "But one day we'll come out together to work again, right?"

"Hurry up and get inside the station, Little Jade! I need to get back to the hiring site to find work. As soon as I have stable work, I'll write to you." Tears suddenly filled Ah Qing's eyes.

Little Jade disappeared into the station and Ah Qing went by himself back to the hiring site. There, he sat among the crowd of people, scanning the market in search of a boss.

Once again the sky grew dark. Ah Qing was hungry, so he returned to the outdoor food stall where he and Little Jade had once eaten; there, he ordered a bowl of lor mee braised noodles. Then he paced back and forth outside the entrance to Bright Promise Hostel, periodically squeezing the money at the bottom of his pocket. Instead of going into the hotel, though, he turned around and headed back to the railway station, where the public square out front was full of people mostly sitting on the ground. There were peddlers, migrant workers, vagrants, beggars, thieves, prostitutes, and swindlers. All kinds of lights flashed; all manner of noises could be heard. The night grew colder as it got darker. The gentle mid-autumn breeze blew against one's face, blew against one's heart.

Ah Qing saw migrant workers fast asleep on the cotton quilts they had rolled out.

Ah Qing saw migrant workers getting ready to pass the night on their woolen blankets.

Ah Qing saw migrant workers lying and resting on spread-out pieces of newspaper.

Ah Qing saw people lying on newspapers, and it occurred to him to do the same. He walked past the many peddlers clustered outside the square, eventually stopping at one of them to buy a newspaper from an old man for five mao. Then he returned to the assemblage of sleeping people, opened up the newspaper and sat on one page while reading the advertisements and news articles of another.

Exhaustion was written on Ah Qing's face. He spread out all the pages of the newspaper and lay on top of them, using his backpack as a pillow.

The night wind clung to the ground, causing the corners of the newspapers to flutter in the breeze. Ah Qing closed his eyes.

The moon watched over the midnight square outside the railway station, its light shining down as if roasting dried radishes spread out on the earth.

In greater and greater numbers, the homeless filled the square; it grew colder as the hours crept past midnight. In the chilly wind bodies began to curl into balls. This made them shrink, and opened up new beds in the square!

2

The sky went from black to gray and gray to daylight. Ah Qing walked along the street looking for a place to wash his face, but no matter how many streets he walked, he wasn't able to find a water faucet that could be used for free. Finally he gave up on the idea and returned to the railway station, where he spent two mao to enter a pay toilet where there was a sink he could use.

A sign hung above the door of a breakfast vendor; on it was written "Authentic Pepper Spice Soup from Xiaoyao Town in Xihua County." Customers sat at a long and narrow red table eating baked sesame cake shaobing and drinking pepper spice soup.

"Hey boss," Ah Qing asked. "How much is a bowl of pepper spice soup?"

"Five mao per bowl!"

"And the baked sesame cakes?"

"Two for five mao!"

"Give me one soup and two baked sesame cakes." He sat on the narrow red bench at the table.

"One soup, two baked sesame cakes!" shouted the boss. On his head he wore the white, rounded taqiyah of the Hui people.

The boss took hold of a big wooden spoon and ladled a bowl of pepper spice soup from the red, fiery pot. A little girl took the bowl from him and delivered it to Ah Qing, who lifted the white ceramic spoon propped up against the inside of the bowl and gently stirred the liquid to break up the sesame oil and vinegar that had gathered at the center. The little girl then darted from the long, narrow table to two young workers who were busy making baked sesame cakes. She grabbed a couple of round, golden-yellow shaobing dotted with sesame seeds and brought them over to Ah Qing.

Ah Qing took a big bite of baked sesame cake, then a big mouthful of pepper spice soup. All alone he passed the Mid-Autumn Festival in this way.

Many girls still wore skirts on those mid-autumn days in Zhengzhou, but the vagrants of the hiring site, those drifters who had long suffered hunger, disappeared into their cotton-padded jackets even during the daytime. Were they still cold?

Ah Qing wore a long-sleeved white shirt whose white collar had long since become a black collar. He was already familiar with the topography of the hiring site—it was just a street full of cheap migrant workers whom no one cared about.

Another afternoon had arrived. A man with hair that was parted in the middle and very small eyes entered the hiring site carrying a rod-shaped object made of aluminum alloy—no one could tell exactly what it was. The small-eyed man constantly moved his small eyes about in an effort to catch a glimpse of the bulging breasts of all the migrant worker sisters. When he found a girl he wanted to talk to, she flashed him a look of contempt and turned her narrow waist in the other direction. Feeling snubbed, the man with the small eyes walked away, but it wasn't long before his small eyes resettled on a seductively dressed woman's ass.

When the seductive woman turned around she bumped her head right into the head of the small-eyed man. "Aiya!" she cried, "Why don't you watch where you're going?!"

"Excuse me, Little Sister, are you looking for work?" the small-eyed man asked, offering a face full of smiles. "What kind of work does Little Sister want to do?"

The seductive woman straightened her back and looked right at him. "You looking for trouble?" she asked him. "Do I look like a migrant worker girl to you? This guy!"—she looked around as if pointing him out to the crowd—"his eyes are so small he can't tell the difference between a boss and a worker!" The seductive woman walked off, cursing and rubbing her head.

Holding the aluminum object, the small-eyed man was still searching in the crowd when he suddenly stopped before Ah Qing and looked him up and down dispassionately with his small eyes. "Hey guy," he began, putting a serious look on his face, "you lookin' for work? You want to be an apprentice?"

"What kind of apprentice?"

"Printing! Making signs for stores. It's not hard work and you can make good money with it. Learn my trade and you'll make eight-hundred to a thousand a month! But look at you now—right now, you can't do anything! Not to worry, though—just learn with me. I don't pay apprentices for the first three months, but I cover room and board. After three months, you'll get paid this much per month." The small-eyed man opened his right hand to indicate five hundred yuan.

Ah Qing's eyes brightened. "Alright," he said, "I'll go with you. Where is the shop?"

"Let's go. I'll take you to there. Shifu and apprentice can walk and talk!"

"Shifu, let me carry that for you!" Ah Qing reached out a hand.

"Oh, this?" he laughed. "This isn't heavy; it's what I use to make signs—it's very expensive! Let shifu carry it himself, okay?"

The pair walked, one in front of the other.

"Shifu, where is the shop?"

"The shop my apprentice opened is on Datong Road and mine's on Dehua Street. Do you know Dehua Street? It's the most prosperous street in Zhengzhou!"

"Yes, I know Dehua."

The small-eyed man led Ah Qing away from the hiring site, past the railway station and onto Datong Road. He pointed out numerous shop signs along the way.

"You see all this?" he asked. "This is all the work of shifu and his apprentice! All the bosses of the major streets here in Zhengzhou know me! I have so much work that it's never done. Come on, let's cut through the wholesale clothing market on Dunmu Road."

They walked a good deal, until Ah Qing's forehead was sweating profusely. On Dunmu Road there were a great many people buying and selling clothing. Racks of clothes stood in rows outside the stores; beside these, even more clothes were spread out on blankets on the ground. Mixed among all the people coming and going were food vendors who lined the streets shouting out the names of the items they were selling. Ah Qing squeezed through the crowd alongside this small-eyed shifu, who, he could see, had no interest in buying clothes. Instead, his small eyes moved up and down along the bodies of the pretty young women moving about in the street. Ah Qing was beginning to lose confidence in this shifu, but he followed him pessimistically deeper into the crowd.

The man with the small eyes squeezed his way out from between two girls wearing identical skirts. One of the girls cried out a loud "aiya!", then twisted her neck and looked down at her behind, where she saw a small hole in her skirt, and, worse, right on one of her buttocks. "Stop!" she cried. "That man up ahead—you right there—*stop*! You've ruined my skirt!"

When the small-eyed man heard the girl's cries, he realized that the disaster had been caused by the aluminum object in his hand. Pretending not to have heard her, he disappeared into the sea of people.

The girl with the hole in her skirt went after him without skipping a beat. When she reached him she began pulling at him. "How can you just keep walking?" she shrieked. "You've ruined someone's skirt! Here I am calling out to you, and you just keep walking! You tell me what I'm supposed to do now? Take one good look at this skirt I just bought!"

The small-eyed man lowered his head and looked at the hole, which was roughly the size of a mung bean, in the girl's skirt.

"Ha ha, so it *is* ripped!" he exclaimed cheerfully. "But a hole this small is nothing! You can still wear the skirt just as before! Oh yes, you can still wear it just as before!" The small-eyed man offered the girl a wide smile.

The second girl, who did not have a hole in her skirt, stepped forward, then placed one hand on her hip while pointing at the small-eyed man's nose with her other hand. She went into a tirade, sounding very much like the old ladies who go shouting through the streets.

"Look, everyone! Everyone come over here and look! We just bought these new skirts, and before you know it, this man right here ruins one of them by poking a hole in it! Look at the size of this! And right on her butt! How is she supposed to wear this now?" As she spoke, the girl with the hole in her skirt stretched the fabric of her skirt to make sure that everyone gathered around saw the mung-bean-sized hole. It was as if she wanted to make it even bigger so that everyone would be able to get a better look at it.

"Buy her a new one!" A man's voice called out.

"Tell me, how much should I compensate you?" The man with the small eyes squared his shoulders.

"I'm not going to try and squeeze extra money out of you, okay? We bought these skirts yesterday and they were eighty kuai each. If you don't believe me, we'll go back to the store right now and buy one!"

"See, here's how I see it," the man said. "I'll give you a few kuai. I mean, look how small this hole is—just make do and keep wearing it!"

"What?!" the girl cried. "What did you say? Give me a few kuai so I can 'make do and keep wearing it'? Do you have eyes? This is a brand-name skirt made in a proper factory! Now it's got a hole in it because of that toy in your hand! Just look at this—it's bigger than your eyes!"

At that the crowd roared with laughter and Ah Qing's face went red. As the companion of the small-eyed man, he too had to endure the ridicule.

"Hurry up, then!" the girl continued. "Eighty kuai! One kuai less and you're not going anywhere!" She stuck out her hand.

"Why aren't you paying her?" the girl with no hole in her skirt demanded. "We're not lying to you—these skirts really did cost eighty kuai!" She persisted in pointing at the man's nose.

The small-eyed man was growing nervous and began to sweat. He reached up to wipe his forehead.

"I've already spent all the money that I had on me," he said. "I can't give you that much right now!"

"Then borrow it from someone else!"

The small-eyed man turned to Ah Qing with an exasperated sigh. "Apprentice! Go ahead and pay the eighty kuai for shifu and I'll pay you back later!"

Ah Qing stared at this small-eyed man, whose shop door he hadn't even entered yet! He thought back to all the big talk this shifu had made on the road, and it became obvious that he was not a reliable person. Ah Qing shook his head.

"I'm a worker," he said. "I don't have any money on me."

"Give me that thing you're holding," one of the girls said, "then go home and get the cash! Where do you live? Is it far?"

"Yes, yes—I'll go home and get it. I live nearby. I can be back in ten minutes!" The small-eyed man placed the aluminum rod into the hands of the girl with the hole in her skirt, then turned to Ah Qing. "You stay here and keep an eye on these two; this is worth much more than the skirt!"

"Okay, I'll wait for you." Ah Qing's face flushed red.

The crowd of onlookers dispersed, but the street continued to bustle with people coming and going.

To survive, an unlucky peddler had destroyed his vocal cords from yelling. A middle-aged shampoo seller held a microphone, doing his best to imitate popular songs from Hong Kong and Taiwan. An aged woman with dark skin carried a huge rack of bras on her shoulders. A short, slender man in a woman's skirt stood upon a chair, wriggling his ass to attract business.

"It's been twenty minutes and not so much as a trace of his shadow!" The two girls in skirts glanced at their wristwatches, and they also glanced at Ah Qing's backpack. "Wei!" one of them suddenly shouted in Ah Qing's direction. "What's that small-eyed guy's name? What's your relationship to him?"

"I don't know his name!" Ah Qing replied. "I just met him at the hiring site; he hired me to work for him."

"Work for *him*?" they exclaimed in unison. "Can't you see what a disgusting pervert he is, leering at all the girls like that? A guy like that is a real piece of work! He doesn't even have eighty kuai on him but he wants you to work for him? Definitely a scammer!"

"It's been almost half an hour and Small Eyes hasn't come back yet!" said the girl with the hole in her skirt. "Do you think his thing is really worth eighty kuai?"

"How much did he buy this thing for?" the girl with no hole in her skirt asked Ah Qing.

"I don't know," Ah Qing replied. "When I first saw him, it was already in his hand."

"What are we doing with this thing, anyway? Let's ask someone. We'll sell it for however much it's worth."

A few men who appeared to be migrant workers walked past the girls and Ah Qing. The girl with the hole in her skirt approached them promptly. "Hey, brothers! Do you guys want this?"

"You selling?" they asked. "I'll give you two kuai for it."

"What?! How can this thing be worth so little?" The girls threw up their arms in exasperation and stomped off in the other direction.

3

Ah Qing walked the streets until he found an isolated spot. There, he changed out of his dirty clothes and into clean ones. Then he returned to the hiring site.

Ah Qing waits for a boss, standing.

Ah Qing waits for a boss, squatting.

Ah Qing waits for a boss, sitting on the ground.

A boss came by, but he didn't even cast a glance at Ah Qing. Instead, he walked right past him with two girls at his sides.

Another boss came by. This one, too, completely ignored Ah Qing, walking right past him with yet another girl at his side.

Ah Qing took a few steps until he was standing in the most conspicuous spot he could find. Right away he saw another person who appeared to be a boss walking in his direction. This time, Ah Qing stepped forward to meet him. "Hello, boss! Are you looking for someone to work for you?"

Ah Qing saw a woman with disheveled hair sitting at the foot of a wutong tree, coughing interminably and seemingly suffering a nasty cold. A filthy infant child rested in her arms. The child stretched out a pair of blackened hands and pulled at its mother's thin, hollow breasts while using its mouth to suck and bite.

Nighttime fell and Ah Qing drifted alone through the dark streets until he grew tired, then he returned to the square in front of the railway station. All of the vagrants who were there sleeping like dried radishes now slowly curled up their flesh, which had been denied warmth. By now Ah Qing was accustomed to lying among them at night, and he quickly fell asleep just like them.

The night wind stuck close to the ground, making all the corners of the newspapers pressed beneath people's bodies flutter in the breeze. Ah Qing felt as though he were an insect sleeping in a windmill.

He dreamed that he was walking in an empty railway station when he suddenly saw two five-mao coins twinkling on the ground before him. Happily, he squatted to pick them up, then looked up to find more shiny coins blinking at him. He picked them up excitedly and before long his hands were overflowing with spotlessly clean coins. Just then, snowflakes began fluttering down from the sky; they were soon falling heavier by the second. Ah Qing lifted his head and saw a woman in white clothes walking toward him. She had long, tousled hair.

"Mama!" He called out in joy.

The woman in white gave him a warm smile and replied, "Ah Qing! Aaaaah Qing!" In an instant, her voice grew faint.

He reached out to hug the woman in white, but succeeded only in hugging a sky full of snowflakes. And he cried! "Mama! Mama! Don't abandon me!" he yelled into the swirling snow.

Ah Qing paid two mao to enter the public toilet inside the railway station. There, he washed his face, then returned to the Hui breakfast seller, from whom he ordered a bowl of pepper spice soup and two baked sesame cakes. After breakfast, he returned to the hiring site.

Before his eyes there appeared a familiar face. Ah Qing moved closer, then patted the boy's shoulder. "Little Wave!"

"Hey, it's you! Your name is . . . "

"Ah Qing!"

"Right! I remember—you're from Zhumadian! Where's your buddy?"

Little Tough saw that Little Wave was talking with someone, so he moved closer to join them. When he saw Ah Qing, he giggled foolishly.

"Little Jade went home before Mid-Autumn Festival." Ah Qing sounded a bit sad as he conveyed the news.

"Well, that's okay! At home you can rely on your parents, but out here in the world you can rely on your friends! Anytime a brother has a problem, I do my best to help." Little Wave took Ah Qing by the hand.

"What kind of work have you and Little Tough done these last six months?"

"We did three months of work at a moving company, two months at a food-processing factory, and one month of odd jobs at a restaurant. Fuck! We made three or four hundred kuai from the first job, but the ones after that didn't give us a single fen—all that work for nothing!"

Once again the sky went dark and the three fellows walked together along the main road, backpacks securely tied to their bodies. They stopped at a tiny outdoor restaurant with a clear plastic sheet draped over a small wooden table. Little Wave bought three bowls of noodles; Little Tough bought three eggs, and, at another tiny outdoor restaurant, Ah Qing bought six vegetable buns. They sat close to one another under the plastic sheets, filling their stomachs and talking about the future.

Nighttime in the square outside the railway station. The three young men pulled crumbled newspapers from their bags and flattened them, forming a single bed of paper on the ground. Little Wave lay down, Little Tough lay down, Ah Qing lay down, and all the vagrants around them lay down, too.

"How old are you, Little Tough?"

"Sixteen!"

"What about you, Ah Qing?"

"I'm one year older than Little Tough. You?"

"I'm two years older than Little Tough and one year older than you!"

Absentmindedly, Little Wave began to sing: "I am a wolf from the north . . . in the boundless wilderness I walk . . . the sorrowful northern wind cries . . . "

In the night sky above them, dark clouds concealed the moon.

Raindrops startled Ah Qing out of his dreams. He sat up on the newspaper and awakened Little Tough and Little Wave with a nudge, then in a great hurry the three boys gathered up their paper bedding. The rain fell faster, more impatiently, and it took just moments for the ground to become completely saturated with water. Reluctantly, all the sleeping people in the square lifted themselves up from the ground and made their way toward the ticket lobby. The large, open ticket lobby inside the railway station quickly filled with slumbering people.

The three guys stuck close together as they moved away from the square toward the main building of the railway station. Once inside, they made their way toward the ticket lobby, where they too lay down for the night.

"It's much warmer here than in the square!"

"Will they let us sleep here?"

"Don't think about that. Even if we only sleep for a while, it's still better than nothing!" Little Wave yawned loudly.

"Sometimes the police don't let people sleep here, but maybe they'll let us because it's raining!" Little Tough's nose dripped endlessly from the cold.

Ah Qing's mind raced with worried thoughts for a while, then he closed his weary eyes and went to sleep. He wasn't asleep long, however, before he was kicked awake by someone. Opening his eyes in a panic, he saw that it was a police officer. Immediately, he crawled up from the ground.

"Get up! Up! Up! Outside! You can't sleep in the ticket lobby!"

Tears formed in the corners of Little Tough's eyes as he placed a hand on his lower back where he had been kicked. With his other hand he pushed himself up from the ground.

After the ticket lobby was cleared out by the police, the unemployed vagrants of the migrant-worker tribe went outside and stood under the eaves of the railway station. The heartless rain continued to fall, heartlessly.

As soon as the police left, however, the ticket lobby became filled with garbage all over again, and this garbage all fell into a deep sleep. Surely they were dreaming of their own mothers, who held them tightly in a warm embrace.

4

The streets were soaked with a night's worth of rain and the wind caused dry leaves that were the shape of outstretched palms to float silently downward. Very few people remained in the hiring site and completely gone were the old, weak, sick, and disabled. Before the eyes of those migrant workers who did remain appeared a new batch of job-seeking competitors, their black eyes open wide.

"You guys looking for work?" A man walked by.

"Yes, sir! We're looking for work. How many people do you need? There's three of us."

The man looked at Little Wave, looked at Ah Qing, looked at Little Tough.

"Alright, I'll take all three of you! It includes room and board. Monthly pay is a hundred kuai each."

"Sir! What kind of work do you want us to do?"

"Selling breakfast!" the man replied. "You can eat whatever you want. Trust me, you won't go hungry!" At that, he led the three boys away from the hiring site.

On a northern section of Shakou Road, a ground-level living space consisting of three rooms, each with its own door leading outside, was full of tables, chairs, bags of flour, pots, pans, ladles, and basins. Just out front was a shed whose roof was made of corrugated cement tiles; in one corner sat two stoves made of iron sheets and a couple of oil drums.

Out in the shed, the new boss began to teach the three boys their new job.

Little Orchid was the boss's daughter. Eighteen or nineteen years of age, she had long hair and a round face. She remained wordless as she washed vegetables and prepared food. When she was done with her work, she sat off to one side with a Chiung Yao novel, which she read just as wordlessly as when she had been working.

"Little Orchid, is the food ready?" her dad called out. "If so, let's eat!"

"Yes, it's ready!" She closed her book absentmindedly.

The boys ate several more steamed buns than usual and had two extra bowls of soup.

"Which of you is gonna wash the dishes?" Little Orchid asked rather rudely. She returned to her book without even waiting for a reply.

Ah Qing and Little Tough took the initiative to wash dishes while Little Wave moved closer to Little Orchid. "What are you reading?" he asked.

"A book by Chiung Yao. Why aren't you washing the dishes?"

"Ah Qing and Little Tough are already doing it. We don't need that many people to wash five people's dishes, do we?"

"Go!" she said impatiently. "Get over there! Stop disrupting my reading!"

Little Wave returned to Ah Qing and Little Tough, periodically turning his head in Little Orchid's direction to watch her read. She sighed deeply, then clutched the book against her chest as a look of contentment spread across her face.

Soon it was time to go to bed, so they all returned to the main building. Little Orchid slept in the northern room, her father in the southern. The room in the middle was piled high with miscellaneous objects. Large planks of wood separated the southern, northern and middle rooms from one another.

The three boys shared a bed made of wooden planks that had been placed in the middle room. Ah Qing and Little Tough slept with their heads to the north and their feet to the south, while Little Wave slept between them with his head to the south and his feet to the north. Little Wave propped his head up high and gazed toward the north, wondering what Little Orchid was thinking about on the other side of the thin wooden wall.

From the darkness one periodically heard the shrill sound of trains calling in the night.

The sun had not yet risen when Little Orchid's father shouted for everyone to wake up. The clock on the wall indicated 4 a.m. on the dot. Reluctantly the boys put on their clothes and looked up at the clock, mumbling to themselves and to one another: "We have to get up *this* early?"

Little Orchid was already dressed when she heard Little Wave grumbling his way out of the middle room. "You don't have to work in the afternoon," she said. "You can sleep all you want then!"

Little Orchid's father used a long iron awl to pry open the tightly-sealed door of the stove, then began to direct the day's work. Little Orchid put soaked soybeans into the soymilk processor as Ah Qing kneaded dough in a large ceramic bowl. Little Wave and Little Tough placed all the tables and chairs in their proper places.

Little Orchid's father placed a big pot on the stove's flickering flame, then began to make pepper spice soup. After letting it stew just the right amount of time, he poured the liquid into two large metal containers, thus freeing up the pot so he could make a second batch. Little Orchid and her three helpers, meanwhile, set themselves to task making millet congee, soy milk, tofu pudding, and tea eggs. Little Orchid's father placed a frying pan on the burner of the second stove. The oil heated and, step by step, he showed Ah Qing and Little Wave how to make pan-fried youbing.

Gradually the sky lightened. White smoke rose from the tiled shed and an eye-catching white wooden board with red characters was placed out front. The sign read "Authentic Pepper Spice Soup from Xiaoyao Town in Xihua County."

Nearly every city in Henan Province had signs that read "Authentic Pepper Spice Soup from Xiaoyao Town in Xihua County." Having pepper spice soup for breakfast had become the custom of Zhengzhou's migrant-worker tribe.

Another day dawned and all the people working the early shift came once more for breakfast. Ah Qing's and Little Wave's four hands moved at the speed of light. Little Orchid ladled soup and cut pieces of youbing for customers, her eyes as quick as her hands. Little Tough ran here and there, busily wiping tables and clearing away bowls, spoons, and chopsticks.

By 10:30 a.m. or so, customers were no longer coming into the shop. With a cheerful smile, Little Orchid's father called everyone to breakfast; after eating, they cleaned all the tables and stools and washed the pots, basins, bowls, and spoons. The doors of both stoves were completely sealed with ash.

"Alright, everyone! This is how we work each day. In the afternoons, if you want to sleep, sleep. If you want to go out and have fun, go out and have fun. There's just one thing you need to remember: don't cause me any trouble!" Little Orchid's father stretched his back as he spoke.

It was nearly dusk and the three boys went to the railroad tracks. When a train flew past, they raised their arms in the air and shouted excitedly.

Night fell and they squeezed into the wooden bed they shared and closed their eyes, ready for dreams. Again the hour hand of the clock on the wall ticked steadily to four.

"Get up! Get up! Time to work!"

Already accustomed to the drill, the boys got out of bed. Hurriedly they got to work, each doing his job.

Gradually the sun rose and all the people working the early shift came for pepper spice soup and youbing.

Two shady-looking youngsters entered the shop. One of them had a mole at the corner of his mouth, and he patted Little Orchid's father on the shoulder. "Looks like business has been pretty good, old man!"

"Yep, not bad! What would you two fellas like to eat?" Little Orchid's father asked with a smile.

The one without a mole at the corner of his mouth snapped his fingers twice. "Two bowls of pepper spice soup, two youbing, and four tea eggs!" he yelled.

"Little Seven's gonna be in for a while." The one with the mole approached Little Orchid. "He won't be out for almost a year! If Little Orchid needs anything, you just come find your Brother Mao." He flashed her a lewd smile.

Little Orchid smiled coldly. "I couldn't possibly inconvenience you."

The two young men sat down and began to eat. "Hey, Little Orchid, bring us some napkins!" the one without a mole called out when they were finished.

"I'm in the middle of something! Little Tough, go get them some toilet paper!" Little Orchid gave the two customers a contemptuous sidelong glance.

Little Tough paused his dishwashing, then brought a roll of toilet paper that had been chopped in half to the two young men.

"What the—?" one of them shouted. "*This* is what your restaurant uses for napkins? What the fuck? This is toilet paper for wiping your ass! This is a roll of toilet paper that's been cut in half—that's what you're using for napkins?"

Little Tough was so taken aback by these words that he retreated to one side and resumed his dishwashing. Ah Qing and Little Wave stayed where they were, stifling their laughter and doing their best to stay focused on the job at hand.

"You've never seen anyone wipe their ass with it, so how can you be so sure we don't use it as napkins?" Little Orchid asked with a sneer.

The guy with the mole whispered something into the other guy's ear. They cast Little Orchid shifty glances from the corners of their eyes, then got up and swaggered out the door without paying.

"Finished eating? Well, take care now and please come again!" Little Orchid's father accompanied them to the door, a wrinkly smile on his face and seemingly unaware that they hadn't paid.

The following morning, the clock on the wall struck four as always.

"Get up! Up! Time to work!"

Little Orchid's father came in from outside, yelling angrily. "Little Wave! Go clean up those two piles of dog shit out in the shed!"

Little Wave ran out to the shed, then quickly ran back in.

"Sir! That's not dog shit! That's human shit!"

"If I say it's dog shit, it's dog shit!" Little Orchid's father seethed. "Only a dog would just crap wherever it wanted. Damn mongrels."

Little Wave grabbed a shovel and went to pick up the two piles of feces. When Little Orchid saw what was going on, she ran to his side and hissed, "This is definitely the work of those bastards from yesterday! Fuck those guys! I hope they get anal warts and die a terrible death!"

5

One afternoon, a thin, dark-skinned youth in a black leather jacket walked along Shakou Road. Reaching his destination, he lifted his head and saw the familiar sign: "Authentic Pepper

Spice Soup from Xiaoyao Town in Xihua County." Feeling content, he lit a cigarette and stepped into the cement-tiled shed. Seeing that Little Orchid wasn't there, he continued to the storefront.

"Little Orchid!" he shouted. "I'm back!"

Little Orchid was lying on her bed reading Chiung Yao's novel *Last Night's Lantern*. When she heard Seventh Brother's familiar voice, she threw the book to one side and jumped up.

"Seventh Brother! Are you back?!"

"Yes, Little Orchid, it's me!" Seventh Brother said as he entered her room. "Did you miss me? I thought about you every day!"

He pulled Little Orchid into his arms and gave her a passionate kiss. That's when Little Tough came in from outside and unconsciously glanced into the northern room. The instant he saw what was going on, he turned on his heel and went back out, crashing into Ah Qing and Little Wave, who were entering the building at that very moment.

"What are you in such a hurry for?" Ah Qing asked.

Little Tough's face turned red but he didn't say a word. Together, the three employees stepped into the middle room they shared.

"Dad hired those three guys to be his assistants," came Little Orchid's voice from the northern room. She pushed Seventh Brother away from her.

Seventh Brother poked his thin face into the middle room and his mouth broke into a wide smile. He pulled a pack of Scattered Flowers–brand cigarettes from his pocket. "Here, guys," he offered politely. "Have a smoke!"

The three boys lay on their wooden bed and practiced Seventh Brother's hooligan way of smoking, while Seventh Brother himself stayed in Little Orchid's room. Suddenly, however, the girl's father entered the middle room and gave two dry coughs. This caused Seventh Brother to get up immediately. He stepped out of Little Orchid's room and into the middle room, where he pulled out a cigarette and gave it to the older man. Little Orchid's father took the cigarette from him and popped it into his mouth. Seventh Brother took out a lighter and lit the man's cigarette. All five men were sitting on the wooden bed in the middle room now.

"You sure got out fast!" Little Orchid's father remarked. "Wow, look at you, mister moneybags—smoking Scattered Flowers now?"

"When you have connections, anything can be done! My oldest brother and second brother work at the Public Security Bureau, my third brother and fourth brother are at a government administration organ, and my fifth and sixth brothers . . . anyway, when you have connections, there's nothing that can't be done! I'd barely gone in when I got out again!"

"Yes, well, you'd better start walking the right path or there's going to come a day when you won't get out!"

Little Orchid and Seventh Brother were taking a walk along the railroad tracks.

"My dad doesn't want me to marry you," Little Orchid began. "It's not the fact that you're eight years older than me that bothers him. It's that you don't have a legitimate profession. If you really care about me, then find a job!"

"Little Orchid, come with me! I've lost too much face to stay in this city. Come with me to Xinjiang Province. We can work the land, we can do business, we can . . . "

"No! I'm my dad's only daughter and right now it's just the two of us. Back home, my mother is sick and my little brother is still in school. Dad can't be without me right now." She shook her head, paralyzed with grief.

"You sure have a lot of sympathy for your dad, Little Orchid! How about thinking of me for a change? No matter what, I'm definitely taking you away with me . . . " Seventh Brother pulled at her hand; he was growing angry.

Little Orchid pushed him away and ran off in tears.

At nine o'clock in the morning, the pair of hooligans returned to the shop. As soon as they walked in, the one with the mole at the corner of his mouth gave Little Orchid a rough pat on the shoulder. "Hey boss! Give us some soup!"

Little Orchid had been ladling pepper spice soup into a bowl for a customer. When she was patted on the shoulder, the bowl slipped from her hand and tumbled into the pot. Scalding hot soup flew into the air and splattered across the customer's eyeglasses.

The customer removed his glasses angrily. "Is this how you do business?" he shouted. "Good thing I had my glasses on! If I hadn't, my eyes would have been burned either by the temperature or by the pepper!"

Little Orchid seethed at the young men. "Can't you see I'm serving a customer?! Keep your hands to yourself!"

"What are you yelling at me for, girl? You obviously dropped the bowl because of your own carelessness!"

Little Wave approached the two hooligans in anger. "Get out of here, or you'll see just how unfriendly I can get!" he warned.

Ah Qing and Little Tough put down their work and went to stand beside Little Wave. Little Orchid's father restrained his mounting anger. "Alright, alright!" he said. "Go on and get out, you two!"

"Get out? It won't be that easy for you."

"What are you gonna do, you small-time thugs?" Little Orchid's lips trembled.

Humiliated by these words, the youth with the mole raised his leg and kicked a table stacked high with bowls and plates. It fell to the floor with a loud crash, taking numerous dishes with it. Several customers put down their chopsticks and moved to the side to watch the spectacle. Just then, from out of the crowd, someone stormed forward. He grabbed the young man with the mole and punched him in the head no fewer than a dozen times.

The youth looked stunned. "Seventh Brother! How did you get out so fast?!"

"Fuck! If I want to get out, I'll get out! Let me tell you two turtle spawn loud and clear: Little Orchid is my girlfriend! If you guys wanna die, come find me!"

"We won't ever come here again, Seventh Brother! We wouldn't dare!"

"Get the hell out of here!" Seventh Brother shouted. He kicked the youth with no mole squarely on the ass and the two hooligans scampered out the door.

Ah Qing followed Seventh Brother into a square courtyard surrounded by four houses—a traditional siheyuan. Up a two-meter-high wooden lattice coiled with metal wire, a series of winding grapevines climbed like snakes.

"These two were originally my eldest brother's," Seventh Brother said, pointing to two of the buildings. "After he bought another place and moved out, he gave them to my second brother. When my second brother bought a place and moved out, he gave them to my third brother—and so on until my fourth and fifth brothers moved out of the compound, too." Seventh Brother pointed to the south-facing main building. "My sixth brother and his wife live in that one."

Ah Qing looked around the courtyard at the oddly shaped potted landscapes on the ground. When Seventh Brother saw him looking at the penjing, he continued.

"My father left all these when he died. He was a penjing designer; he passed away before I finished primary school. Sometimes I like to just gaze at these potted landscapes and get lost in thought! Why do so many cultured people like these kinds of decrepit trees, trees that can't even stand up straight? These should be growing out in nature!"

"The same tree will have a different fate in two different places," Ah Qing said thoughtfully. "If a tree doesn't blossom or bear fruit, it doesn't matter how green its leaves are—if it's in the countryside it's going to be chopped down for firewood.

But if the same tree were to grow along Chang'an Street or in a public park, its life would be protected."

"Well, I don't have much of an education," Seventh Brother replied, and he remembered the brawl he'd had with the two hooligans earlier that day. "And when I see someone I don't like, I want to fight them!"

Seventh Brother loosened the string of keys at his waist. His right hand was wrapped in gauze, so he had to use his left hand to push open the door of the fourth building.

"Come in, Ah Qing. This is the one I live in. It's not very big, but when my sixth brother and his wife buy a new place and move out, this whole compound will be mine!"

Ah Qing sat in a chair.

Seventh Brother handed Ah Qing a pack of Butterfly-brand cigarettes. "These are terrible!" he said. "If you don't like them, I'll go out and buy something else." He paused as if mustering the courage to say something. "Ah Qing," he began. "Your Big Brother Seven needs your help with something."

"What is it?" Ah Qing asked. "If it's something I can do, I will certainly help!"

"I'd like you to help me write a letter—truth is, I guess you could say it's a love letter!" Seventh Brother held up his injured right hand for Ah Qing to see.

Ah Qing nodded in agreement, and then, line by line, Seventh Brother spoke as Ah Qing wrote.

Later that day when no one else was in the breakfast shop, Ah Qing took advantage of the opportunity to pass the letter to Little Orchid. The following day, Little Orchid also found the chance to slip a letter between Ah Qing's fingers. When Seventh Brother received the letter from Ah Qing, he hugged him in excitement.

"My brother! Thank you . . . "

Later while everyone was having dinner, Seventh Brother arrived at Little Orchid's house carrying a portable radio cassette player. He was in extremely high spirits. "Look, Little Orchid!" he said excitedly. "I bought you a boom box!"

Everyone got up from the table and gathered around the portable music player to take a look. Seventh Brother turned it on and a song by Taiwanese singer Zheng Zhihua flowed from the device. "Ah, youth! Youth!" the lyrics cried out.

Before there was even time for the Zheng Zhihua song to finish, a police vehicle stopped outside the shop and two officers came in and took Seventh Brother away. "Little Orchid!" he called out wildly to his girlfriend while being escorted to the police vehicle. "Wait for me!"

Little Orchid hid away in her room and cried. Her father ran after one of the police officers.

"Comrade Police Officer! What did he do this time?"

"Peddling pornographic books and magazines!"

When Little Orchid's father found out she was pregnant a few days later, he beat her. She knelt at her father's feet and cried loudly.

"Can't you give this old man even a little face?" her father yelled. "Look at you—not even married and your stomach is growing!" After his grief subsided, he took Little Wave aside and told him that he was arranging for his daughter to have an abortion.

Little Wave agreed to his boss's plan. Posing as Little Orchid's husband, he went with her to the hospital for her to have an abortion. Little Orchid lay on the operating table and screamed at the top of her lungs.

"What are you screaming for?" asked the increasingly impatient, middle-aged female doctor. "You should have thought of this when you were still feeling well!"

After being discharged from the hospital, Little Orchid lay in bed for several days and wouldn't talk to anyone. One day, Little Tough brought her a bag of apples. "Sister Orchid," he said, "have some apples!"

Little Orchid lay in bed, tears drenching the tips of her long eyelashes.

"Are you ever going to get back to work?" her father would ask her, visibly annoyed. "Just lying here day and night—you trying to piss me off or what?"

The clock on the wall indicated four on the dot. "Get up! Up! Time to get to work!"

Little Orchid and the three boys all climbed out of bed to work their respective jobs.

Spring Festival and the Lunar New Year were rapidly approaching. Little Orchid's father paid the young men their wages, and he did not cheat them. He also bought them some new clothes, saying that he hoped they would come back to Zhengzhou to work for him again the following year. Dressed in their new clothes, the three young men went off happily to the railway station.

"Bon voyage, Ah Qing!"

"I hope we'll be together again when we come out to work again next year, Ah Qing!"

Ah Qing embraced his friends tightly as he said goodbye.

FIVE

1

"I haven't eaten yet! Can you take me out to eat?"

Little Thing gripped my leather belt tightly, seemingly afraid that I would leave the instant I pulled up my trousers.

I looked at the pitiable little thing before me and laughed. "Don't worry," I said. "I will definitely take you out to eat."

On the floor were strewn crumpled-up balls of soft white tissue that had just been used to wipe up semen.

I pulled up my trousers and led Little Thing by the hand out of the public toilet, where the bright sun nearly blinded us as it shined in our faces. I took him to Sichuanese restaurant and we stepped inside.

With no regard for manners, Little Thing ordered a tableful of food and began to eat ferociously. After paying the bill, I let him keep the couple dozen kuai in change that the server gave me.

Two months later, I bumped into Little Thing again in the public toilet. When he smiled at me, I grabbed the little thing and led him out of the dark, stinking toilet.

"Do you come here a lot, Uncle He?" he asked me as we walked outside.

"Oh, no! I don't come here much. I usually go to bars or parks." My ears grew hot and I suddenly felt as though some invisible person were cursing at me.

I took Little Thing to a public bathhouse, where the water flowed ecstatically from the faucets onto the tops of our heads and from the tops of our heads onto the ground.

As a child, you had been raised by your maternal grand-mother—your Lao Lao. Your parents never gave you a proper name; they just called you "Little Thing." Behind her back, they called your Lao Lao "Old Thing."

When your parents married, your father went to live with your mother and her family. This turned tradition upside down, since it was usually the woman who went to live with the man and his family. When you were little, your parents often went on about how they were going to get a divorce; sometimes in the middle of the night, the fighting turned into hitting. All the neighbors bullied your family, and you were terrified of going to school because of the way the group of degenerate children there knocked you to the ground and rode you like a horse. Your parents rarely looked after your health. For as long as you could remember you felt that you were a child whom no one needed, a child who had been overlooked for so long by the people around him.

When you were little, when your parents weren't home, your Lao Lao would play with you by shaking her thin, hollow breasts at you. Sometimes when you were especially disobedient and wouldn't stop throwing tantrums, she would tell you ghost stories. Upon hearing these, you became so frightened that you wouldn't dare go on making a fuss. Obediently, you would crawl under the old, worn-out quilts and go to sleep. Again and again you woke up, startled, from your nightmares, and tightly clutched Lao Lao's emaciated, shriveled-up breasts.

When you were little, your face once became so puffy and swollen that you could barely open your left eye. Your Lao Lao put you on her back and went from house to house beg-ging the neighbors for cactus. She cut off the spines with a razor blade, then used a wooden stick to mash the flesh into a green paste which she wrapped in a piece of paper and pressed against your face like a baked sesame cake. One half of your head was wrapped in a cotton cloth; it held the flatbread in place until the swelling went down.

When you were little, you were always sick. If it wasn't a cold, it was diarrhea or a bloody nose. You were plagued by an outbreak of head lice and when winter came your entire body began to itch all over; your Lao Lao seemed always to be scratching you. When summer came, you had sores on your scalp. You would run around barefoot and your feet and legs would be cut by shards of glass from broken bottles. When the wounds got infected, they would start to leak a yellow liquid and white pus. For the entire summer, red and purple mer-bromin and gentian violet was smeared across your face, hands and feet. With herbal plasters stuck to your legs, you would limp about looking for sweet things to eat.

When you were little, you loved eating sweets. Sour dates, rotten pears, bad apples, putrid oranges; melons yellow, green and white; fruits that were round or long or crushed—you ate them and ate them constantly! When autumn came, you and some other kids ran into the corn fields and feverishly gnawed the corn stalks for the sugary juice they yielded. You climbed date trees like a monkey who was finally able to pluck the last sweet red date from the highest branch.

When you were little, huge rains appeared out of nowhere, and they fell until the entire village was afloat. Nothing made you happier than running with the other kids into the ditches at the sides of the roads to catch little fishes and loaches. When the fishpond at the northern end of the village was filled to capacity, the water surged and streamed toward the fishpond at the southern end of the village. All the fishponds and ditches were full of golden, glistening water that overflowed and rushed toward the village. The adobe brick walls of the houses began to collapse, giving villagers shortcuts when they wanted to stop by one another's homes to chat.

2

Your stomach hurt again—surely there were roundworms in it, you told your Lao Lao. Early in the morning, she carried a bamboo basket to the market to sell eggs. The bottom of the basket was padded with golden yellow wheat straw. Over twenty white- and red-shelled eggs lay in the basket, fat and sleeping heavily. Each egg sold for five fen; Lao Lao used the money to buy salt for the family. This time, after buying salt, she went to the pharmacy, where she bought you deworming medicine.

You held in your hand the deworming medicine—pills that were pink, pale yellow, and the color of powdered milk; they were sweet in your mouth, just like chocolate. Lao Lao made you go hungry before you ate the pills, saying that this was how you completely killed the roundworms. You liked eating the deworming medicine, but dreaded shitting afterward.

You pulled down your elastic waist pants and hung your ass over the pit latrine. It was full of cow shit, goat shit, chicken shit and human shit, with black plant ash mixed in. A single roundworm fell from your anus and your forehead began to sweat. You didn't dare look at the worms as they discharged from your belly. They had eaten so much that they were plump and white, and glistened like noodles as they fell. Anytime you saw noodles after that, you immediately thought of those frightening worms.

"Lao Lao . . . " you began to cry loudly. A big roundworm came out, but only half way. Still alive, it wriggled frantically as it struggled to get back inside you. Nothing, it seemed, would make it come out.

Lao Lao extended her long fingernails, then clutched the chopstick-length roundworm and dragged it out of your ass.

Sometimes when you were shitting, chickens would congregate around your backside waiting for roundworms to eat. One time, a rooster was unable to wait any longer and began pecking at your ass viciously. You covered your bleeding skin with your hands and cried loudly, "Lao Lao!"

Holding a big stick, your Lao Lao came running toward you, shouting at the chickens to shoo them away. Then she watched as all the remaining shit and worms exited your body.

"Little Thing, Lao Lao will fry you an egg," Lao Lao smiled. "You're still so skinny! Hurry up and grow taller and put on some weight. After you get big and tall, no one will dare bully you!"

One time, you grabbed a live snake and threw it at a boy who was half a head taller than you. He was so frightened that he began crying loudly. From then on you were a bad kid and no one dared bully you again.

3

You were fifteen when you entered your first year of middle school. Among your classmates, there were those who were a couple of years younger than you and those who were a couple of years older. It was the best middle school in the town. Three classmates squeezed together at each derelict old desk. Three people sitting on one long, wooden bench, reading and writing, arms bumping against one another. All the characters the students wrote were crooked, but it didn't matter, since instead of writing characters one could always draw. One could always draw the face of the teacher with big huge glasses on it and a nose as crooked as the characters.

In wintertime, the road home was frightfully dark and sometimes it was covered completely in mud. Step by step you moved forward, knowing that if you weren't careful you would fall and be late for school. Not a single streetlight lined the three li of road separating the school from your home, so when returning in the evening there was nothing to do but carry a flashlight as you walked. Later, you went to live in the school dormitory. You stepped into the room for first-year students, a quilt in your arms.

In the upper berth of a bunk bed you slept beside a sixteen-year-old classmate. In the lower berth slept two thirteen-year-olds. In the middle of the night, your sixteen-year-old classmate would crawl on top of you and begin to squirm. The only thing separating you was two layers of underclothes, and before long your underwear was soaked through with semen. Sometimes you crawled on top of him, too, and after crawling off him you continued to hold him as you slept. Sometimes the two of you practiced kissing like you had seen men and women do in the movies. The tip of his tongue was cool. Without warning he coughed. You pulled the blanket up and covered his naked shoulders.

You heard iron bunk beds squeaking in the night. In darkness you searched for the sound, sensing that two classmates were holding each other, their bodies rubbing up against each other. The sound was coming from the bunk at the left; soon it came from the right, too. Suddenly your bunkmate woke up, his stiff thing hidden away in his underwear, and pressed his body tightly against yours and started rubbing against you. You felt his underwear getting wet, and before long yours was, too. You looked in many books, but nowhere could you find information about how to wash semen stains out of underwear. Layer after layer of dried semen encrusted your underwear like paste. In stealth you threw the underwear away, then went to buy a new pair.

Conditions in the dorm room were very poor, and when the lights were off you couldn't see a thing. Although there was a toilet outside, a plastic bucket was placed near the door; classmates needing to piss would feel their way through the dark to find it. They were always able to, but usually missed the target and the piss splashed to the floor anyway. In wintertime after everyone had gone to bed, no one wanted to put their clothes back on, search for the keys, open the door, and walk the dozen or more meters to the bathroom. Sometimes, when a classmate forgot to crap before bed, he would hang his ass over the piss bucket in the middle of the night and shit right there. When the feces fell, it dropped into the piss pot with a loud splash, causing urine to splatter against his buttocks; the rest of the feces he would simply let fall outside the bucket. When the other classmates woke up the following day no one would know whose crap was on the floor. Then they would bitch and moan, and eventually take turns cleaning up the mess.

One classmate had a quilt that was torn; in stealth, someone had pulled cotton out of it to wipe his ass. Sometimes the piss bucket would be filled to capacity before daybreak, so classmates would just stick their dicks in the iron pipes of the bunk beds and piss. Everywhere and at all times the stench of urine and feces permeated the dormitory. When the school year started, that classmate had arrived with a quilt, but by the time he went home for winter vacation it had turned into a bed sheet.

One winter night, the head teacher picked up a flashlight and went off to do a night patrol. When the beam of light shined in through the broken window it illuminated the bottom berths, where the head teacher saw all the prepubescent classmates deep in sleep. Things on the upper berths, however, were different. There the iron frames banged against one another. Classmates lay on top of one another, their asses wriggling about, quilts pushed off to one side. Utterly stunned, the head teacher kicked the dormitory door in anger. The dorm leader was awakened by the angry sound of the head teacher cursing outside the door; hurriedly, the dorm leader opened it up. When the head teacher stormed in, he tripped over the piss bucket and fell to the floor. With a loud splash, the contents of the bucket toppled to the floor, covering it with urine. Pairs of hands ran along the walls but no one could find the hanging string that turned on the light.

"Why won't anyone turn the light on?!" the head teacher shouted in anger.

"The string is broken, Teacher Wang," replied the dorm monitor.

One of the classmates lit a candle and the head teacher got up from the floor, his big hands soiled with mud and piss.

Teacher Wang looked around the room in search of the two bad students he had seen on the upper berth, but he was so agitated that he couldn't clearly remember which bunk they had been in. Everywhere one looked there were beds, and on each narrow one there slept two or even three classmates.

"Nobody puts on their clothes! Every one of you, come outside!" Teacher Wang howled at them.

With coats draped over shoulders, you and your classmates stepped out of the dormitory and onto the sports field, where you lined up in an orderly row before the teacher.

"Who was it? Which two of you weren't sleeping? Which of you were pressed on top of each other and causing trouble?" Teacher Wang moved the flashlight back and forth across the students' faces. Snowflakes began to fall and a student sneezed. Then two students sneezed, then three. Before long, all the students were sneezing.

Alerted to the ruckus, the school principal arrived on the scene and asked the head teacher what was going on. But Teacher Wang's mouth suddenly froze up and he was unable to describe exactly what it was that he saw.

Once a week, the school underwent a thorough cleaning. Students whose families lived nearby would go home and return to school with brooms and shovels on their shoulders.

The food in the cafeteria was terrible, too, and not a single drop of oil could be found in the vegetables boiling in the pot. Breakfast was rice congee, lunch was noodles, and in the evening it was salty soup with floating, leftover congee and noodles. Many of the classmates took their meal tickets off-campus to buy food, and before long there was a big street in the area where the tickets went into circulation. When students ran out of meal tickets, they notified their parents, who rode their bicycles to school with bags of wheat to trade for more tickets. With meal tickets one could buy sunflower seeds, candy, and plenty of other things on the big street. You traded meal tickets for a new pair of underwear.

Word spread that cadres from the county or perhaps district offices of the Ministry of Education would be visiting the school for an inspection. Under the supervision of the school principal, the cooks in the cafeteria started making food for students that would be up to standard. Meals were half vegetable, half meat, and drops of oil now floated in the salty soup like plump flowers. The price of meal tickets didn't go up and students were now able to buy large bowls of fatty meat. Many students who hadn't tasted oil in a long time ingested so much of it that their stomachs grew big and round and they had to make frequent trips to the toilet.

After the visit from the Ministry of Education, your school was designated by upper-level leaders as an educational institution of excellence, innovation, and health.

4

When you were seventeen, you finally managed to earn a middle-school diploma. You did not, however, want to pursue further study, and your parents wanted you to find work quickly to help ease their burden. You left school with your schoolbag still strapped to your back, and the pages of your textbooks became toilet paper for the entire family.

You left home and went with a group of grownups to work on a construction site in the city. Before long the palms of your hands were covered in blisters, and the blisters soon turned into calluses. When there was no work to be done at the construction site, you went to restaurants with some of the drunkards to consume booze and meat. Listening to their dirty language made your heart as happy as if you'd been eating candy.

A young guy who looked like a university student approached you, an architecture design in his hand. He looked at you and gave you a gentle smile. You looked right back at him and giggled foolishly—you didn't know why. It just seemed like the polite thing to do!

"Wow! Look at all these calluses on your hands!" this university student, whose name was Little Jian, exclaimed approvingly as he took hold of your hand.

You laughed, noticing how good his hand felt on yours.

Little Jian took you to his office, where he showed you pictures of all the buildings he had designed. He was only in his twenties, but he was already an architectural designer.

"Do you like these buildings?" He held your hand and the two of you sat on his bed.

"They're great! It's just too bad that I'll never be able to live in a place like these for as long as I live!" you replied pessimistically.

"As long as you work hard, you'll be able to." Little Jian spoke reassuringly. He gazed at you gently and his eyes settled on your nose. "How old are you?" he asked. "Have you hit twenty yet?"

"Me, I'm seventeen," you said, then paused. "People from the countryside age quickly." You seemed to be seeking an explanation.

You stayed at Little Jian's place that night, and you slept with him. When your flesh entered his body, you felt for the first time that you had truly grown up. Your body was getting stronger and stronger, but your heart was still cowardly and weak. Sometimes you were afraid of Little Jian because he had read more books than you and he was a few years older than you. He understood more things than you. You feared that he might suddenly do something to hurt you.

You went back to continue working at the construction site. One day Little Jian came looking for you to ask if you wanted to continue your studies; you shook your head to say no. You climbed the tall iron scaffolding and watched as the people below turned into ants. You weren't afraid of ants, not even ants that were bigger than the ones you were looking at now. You looked at the ant-sized people at the foot of the building and laughed. You unzipped your pants and took a leak.

Again Little Jian came looking for you. The truth was that you missed him a bit, but you weren't willing to let the words come out of your mouth. Even less were you willing to take the initiative to go see him.

"My dear Little Thing, have some candy!" Little Jian popped a piece of unwrapped candy into your mouth.

Little Jian held a piece of candy in his mouth and told you to bite the part that was sticking out. The syrupy sweetness made your lips stick to his.

You didn't know if Little Jian liked you or liked your cock. He was good to you—more and more so all the time. And yet, you never felt any gratitude. You regarded everything that was transpiring between the two of you as a game.

Little Jian was to be transferred to a city in the south for work. He asked you for a mailing address; without thinking much of it you gave him the address of your family home. You were certain that he'd forget you before long. Cities in the south were surely very beautiful; he'd have no trouble finding even more friends down there.

You didn't see Little Jian off when he left. He, however, gave you an exquisite diary and fountain pen, asking you to write in it whenever you missed him.

You used the diary to keep track of your personal finances. There, you wrote down all your expenditures for things like socks, shoe insoles, toothpaste, shampoo.

You missed your Lao Lao, so you wrote a letter home. Your older sister wrote back to you right away. She told you that your Lao Lao had slipped and fallen on a rainy day, breaking her pelvic bone.

You went to see the foreman at the construction site and asked him for your wages. He only gave you enough for the trip home. You rushed to get there, but when you saw your parents they just reprimanded you for giving up a paying job to come home. Seeing your Lao Lao in bed on the verge of death made your eyes fill with tears.

Lao Lao lay on the bed, hair disheveled, mouth drooping to one side, the corners of her eyes encrusted with discharge. Her hands and fingers were soiled with her own feces. A bucket for urinating was on the floor at the foot of the bed and traces of shit and blood could be seen on the walls. It was the seventh month of the lunisolar calendar, but Lao Lao was so cold that she curled up into a ball. Beside her pillow sat pills of red, yellow, and white. You asked your parents why they hadn't taken Lao Lao to the hospital. They said the doctor's opinion was that there was no point because she wasn't going to get any better. Her pelvic bone was broken. She was too old. The bone would never heal and she wasn't worth treating anyway.

Your Lao Lao became a disposable person. No longer was she able to wash clothes and cook for the family.

Your parents, however—they were in great spirits. No longer did they fight. Instead, they talked endlessly about burying Lao Lao.

You grabbed a hand cloth, dampened it with warm water and wiped Lao Lao's face and hands. You brushed her grayish white hair, then braided it and set it in a bun. You spoon-fed her, first medicine, then egg-drop soup. Tears fell into the soup as she ate; she wasn't able to finish the entire bowl. You stayed by Lao Lao's side, and you held her as she got up from the bed to urinate and defecate. Before long, her face regained some color and her mouth no longer drooped to the side. At night, she moaned endlessly when she slept.

"I can't wait for this old thing to die! She's driving me to the grave!" This was Lao Lao's flesh-and-blood daughter speaking. This was your own mother speaking.

The heat of the seventh month was unbearable, and yet your heart was growing colder. You hoped your Lao Lao would get better, but you were powerless to help her. You could clearly see that she was out of medicine, but your father pretended not to notice. The truth was that your parents didn't want to go to the hospital and spend any more money. There was no doubt that they hated you, this stupid child whom they had birthed and raised and who was now preventing them from letting Lao Lao hurry up and die. If Lao Lao were to die quickly, the family would save half a bowl of food that much faster.

You looked at your parents and saw people who were becoming more and more like strangers to you each day. You held your Lao Lao in your arms; she was withered and dried up like a piece of firewood. Your heart was broken. You cursed all the men and women who kept having babies. "Do you really think your children are going to love you?" you wondered.

You were just a stupid child, needed by no one. No one needed your Lao Lao, either. You couldn't bear to see her go. You wanted to give her just a little more love, let her leave that place with just a little bit of warmth. You stood in the rain and your tears fell.

Your Lao Lao died. She had smiled at you that very morning. It was dusk on a windy rainy evening when you found her. She looked a wreck, her face yellow like a crumpled-up piece of paper. Her mouth drooped to one side and her own feces was caked under her fingernails.

You stood before your Lao Lao's grave as the night wind blew past.

5

In half a year's time, you received ten letters from Little Jian as well as two pictures. Only after looking at the pictures did you realize that he was in fact quite handsome! Little Jian said that he missed you very much and that he wanted you to visit him down south in Suzhou. You wrote him a letter saying that you didn't have money for a ticket. Almost instantly, he came up with two hundred kuai for your ticket; you promptly used it to get drunk at a bar. After drinking you went home and became explosive with your parents. You were all grown up now; you had grown from a stupid child into a big, bad man. Your parents didn't dare lift a hand to hit you now, and if they did you would have knocked them to the ground. Instead of wearing your older brother's tattered, second-hand clothes, now you went out and bought a steady stream of fashionable items. All of your time you spent in the company of a bunch of little hooligans. Together you went to prostitutes, stole things, got in gang fights, got drunk, got disorderly.

Everyone who knew you feared you and did what they could to stay out of your way. You rounded up some of your buddies and went crashing into your neighbor's home to make them pay for having bullied your family when you were little. On a few occasions you were arrested and taken to the local police station. They put you in handcuffs as they yelled at you and roughed you up. When you got out of jail you went back to tormenting others just as you had been tormented in the past.

Little Jian wrote to you again asking why you hadn't gone to visit him, but you didn't feel like writing back to him. It was only after you got in another fight and the police came after you yet again that you finally bought a ticket to Suzhou.

You hunted down Little Jian and the two of you began living together. He said he loved you very much and that you didn't have to get a job or do housework. As long as you stayed at home and waited for him to return each day, everything would be fine. When he got off work he came home and made you dinner. When he got paid he took you to the mall and bought you things. He bought you beautiful new clothes even as he couldn't bear to spend money on himself. Each night you were able to satisfy Little Jian's sexual desire, and if you were ever upset about anything you would use his money to go get drunk. Little Jian never uttered a nasty word to you; he showed his love for you in everything he did. To this love you quickly became numb.

In the five years that you lived together, Little Jian brought you a lot of happiness. When he wasn't home, your felt that your life was boring. The reality, though, was that you couldn't bear the idea of being supported by anyone. More and more, you lost respect for yourself.

You started hanging out at a public park, where you unexpectedly fell in with a group of gay guys. You had sex with other people behind Little Jian's back; when he found out, he went into a fit of screaming and yelling, then started crying. One comrade who was a money boy said guys like you and him should take advantage of their youth. Make some money to prepare for retirement—that's what you should do! This money boy had a seemingly endless supply of stories from the gay circle and you felt that all the things he had said made sense. After all, if Little Jian liked you, it was only because you were still young. Just wait until you came down with an illness or couldn't get it up anymore and you'd see how quickly he'd abandon you! Nowadays, you reasoned, people can't even rely on their own children. What about Little Jian—could you rely on him? Not even heterosexuals had true love anymore—

could there be true love between members of the same sex? The more you thought about it, the more frightened you became. You became convinced that Little Jian would abandon you and abandon you fast. You had nothing!

A middle-aged man from Hong Kong said that he liked you quite a bit. He took you to a hotel and then, after playing with you all night, gave you money. You put it in a bank account, then started looking—in parks, bars—for more opportunities to make money. But you weren't able to find another man who was quite so generous. You started to hate Suzhou, and became determined to go to Hong Kong. You'd make better money there.

You and Little Jian had lived together for five years, and yet it suddenly seemed to you that you had gotten nothing out of it. You told him that you had met an old guy from Hong Kong, that this old guy wanted to take you back with him, that this old guy said he was going to give you lots of money.

Little Jian became enraged when he heard this. He raised a hand to hit you, but you didn't threaten to hit him back because you knew you had done him wrong. Little Jian suddenly began to cry, then ardently begged you not to leave. You didn't want to deceive him. Only when you brought up the idea of breaking up with him did you realize that you really did love him after all and that you could no longer accept the idea of being supported by him without giving him anything in return. You wanted to live for yourself and for everything in life that was yet to come. Only by making lots of money would you have a sense of security when you were old. You felt sad; your teardrops fell on Little Jian's face. Each time you thought about leaving him the pain in your heart got worse. And yet, you did leave. You left the home that you and Little Jian had shared for five years.

You went back to the hotel to look for that old guy, the one from Hong Kong whom you didn't like one bit. He took you to back to Hong Kong with him right away. A week later, he passed you on to some other old guy. When that old guy was finished playing with you, he handed you off to yet another.

A year later you decided that you had endured enough hardship, so you went back to Suzhou to look for Little Jian. When you got there, however, Little Jian's landlord told you that he had moved out the year before, so you went to his workplace in hopes of finding him there. One of his coworkers told you that he had returned to his hometown in Henan Province, where he now worked as a schoolteacher. There was nothing for you to do but clench your teeth and go back to the park and work as a money boy. After making enough money for a ticket, you took a train to Little Jian's hometown.

You arrived at Kaifeng in Henan Province and went straight to the primary school in the countryside, where you saw Little Jian. He had given up a five-thousand-kuai-per-month job in Suzhou and returned here to work as an ordinary schoolteacher with a monthly salary of just eight hundred! And all this was brought about because of you! You hoped that Little Jian would be able to forgive you.

Little Jian faced you coldly. He had only one thing to say to you: "I don't love you anymore."

But you were unrelenting and determined to get him back.

Little Jian pulled some cash out of his pocket. "This is all I can give you. I hope you'll be able to find a good place to go."

You embraced Little Jian and cried loudly as you related to him everything that had happened to you, all of the difficulties you had seen. You wanted him to know that you truly loved him, that you knew you were wrong, that you were full of regrets. You begged him for a chance to atone for your mistakes.

Little Jian turned and walked toward the railway station. You followed closely behind.

He bought a train ticket and pushed it into your hand, heartlessly instructing you to leave.

Right there in front of all the passengers buzzing about the station, you fell to your knees before Little Jian and banged your head violently against the ground. Blood dripped down your forehead and rolled off your nose.

For a moment he began to cry, but then restrained his tears and rushed to a fruit-vendor stall, where he grabbed a knife and began ruthlessly cutting his own arm.

"Are you going or not?! If you don't go, I'll keep cutting myself!" Blood flowed from Little Jian's arm and dripped to the ground. When the drops touched the dirt, they formed blood-red pearls.

Your heart died forever that day.

You picked yourself up from the ground and went far away.

Looking and feeling like a walking corpse, you made your way to Beijing. Each time you walked in the streets, or went through an underpass, or entered a public park or a toilet—at each of these moments you realized that you had always been a roundworm, a gluttonous little roundworm that pined after sweet things. Shit out from the asshole of love, you were dead forever in the toilet bowl of human life.

Little Thing's story left me speechless. I knew that my love was powerless in the face of all that he had described, and I suddenly felt old. Water in the public bathhouse continued to flow as his saturated skin grew white and puffy. Later, he fell into my arms and slept. I remained motionless, a pile of feces lingering in the cracks of time.

SIX

1

A train rushed toward the south. Outside its windows, the winter cold hung heavily in the air as villages flew past, labyrinths of low walls and gray tiles.

Ah Qing made his way through the dusk, his backpack securely tied to his body. Hardly a pedestrian was on the street. He gazed off into the distance at the plumes of smoke rising from the many chimneys flecking the village, then quickened his pace. In the fields, frost draped the shoulders of wheat seedlings, reflecting a cold, pallid light.

"Ah Qing, I'm so glad to see you're back!"

"Little Jade, my dad told me you're engaged to be married to Little Xiang. Little Xiang is the prettiest girl in the village!"

"I don't like girls!" Little Jade exclaimed. "I don't know why, but I've always dreamed of being with a boy. Also . . . when I have wet dreams I'm always dreaming of boys."

"That's impossible, Little Jade!" Ah Qing answered in surprise. "Don't go freaking me out like that!"

"But it's true, Ah Qing! I . . . " And Little Jade pressed his lips against Ah Qing's.

Ah Qing accepted his kiss.

"Tell me the truth, Ah Qing. Do you love me?"

"I love you a lot, Little Jade, but sooner or later we're going to have to get married and have kids! We're both men. Spring Festival is in just a few days. After that we're both going to be eighteen, and then in two years we—"

"After Spring Festival I want to leave the village and find a boss to work for, and I don't want to come back!"

"What? Little Jade! You should think of your mom. Your dad died young and your little sister is still just a kid. It's not easy for your mom! Do it for her, Little Jade. You have to get married!"

"Getting married is just a way of showing respect to your parents! I really don't want to—it'll never bring me happiness. Why would I want to fall into that trap?"

"What is going on with you, Little Jade? Why didn't you think about this a few months ago before you and Little Xiang got engaged?"

"Ever since I got engaged, I haven't been sleeping well. I've been thinking about it nonstop—this is hard for me!"

"It's okay, Little Jade. Maybe the idea of being engaged is still new to you. Once you get used to it, it'll be fine!"

"Ah Qing," Little Jade looked at him imploringly. "Why can't you and I love each other?"

Little Jade's mother stepped into Ah Qing's home. "Ah Qing," she said, "Shenzi is going to be a matchmaker for you!"

Ah Qing's face went red. He stood and offered Little Jade's mother his seat.

Ah Qing's father was all smiles as he smoked a cigarette. "We're relying on you completely, Ah Qing's Shenzi! Ah Qing and Little Jade are like brothers—and here they are, eighteen years old in the blink of an eye! I heard through the grapevine that Little Jade and Little Xiang are engaged to be married. Aiya! Little Xiang is a good girl! Even prettier than her sister Big Xiang!"

Little Jade's mother laughed heartily. "You're not outsiders to me, so I'm not going to hide things from you. The girl I'm introducing Ah Qing to is even less of an outsider—she's my own niece, one of my brother's daughters!"

"Well, that's wonderful! She must be just as pretty as you are!"

"Me? I'm old! But Little Na—now she's just gorgeous!"

"Well, that's fine!" Ah Qing's father said in earnest. "In that case, we'll entrust the entire matter to you!"

Outside the village, Ah Qing and Little Jade walked along a riverbank, their shoulders nearly touching.

"Now we're really going to be relatives, Ah Qing! My cousin Little Na really is pretty—much prettier than Little Xiang!"

"I may not be too promising as a husband," Ah Qing said. "If Little Na and I get married, I'm afraid that one day she won't be satisfied with me!"

"It's hard to say," Little Jade replied. "You're going to have to make an effort with her since there are a lot of people chasing her. I can't promise she'll always be faithful! But the feelings between you and me . . . those won't ever change."

Ah Qing looked at the icy river water and sighed.

"They won't change, right, Ah Qing?" Little Jade persisted. "All I said was one sentence and you suddenly got sullen and quiet! Don't worry, okay? You and me, we're like brothers! I don't care about people's business. I only care about what's going on with you, and any burdens you have you can unload on me. I'm going to say good things about you around my uncle and cousin!"

"Little Jade, when Spring Festival is over I want to leave the village again to sell my labor. But this time I want to save a little money so I can learn a trade!"

"Do you still want to study to be a chef?"

"Not necessarily. I'll learn whatever trade allows me to make some money!"

"When Spring Festival is over, we'll go out to sell our labor together, okay?"

"Fine, as long as you're willing to go through some hard times with me!"

"Let's look for work in the south, okay? It's not as cold down there."

"Which city should we go to, and which province—Guangdong or Hainan?"

"There are tons of us Henanese working in Guangdong, Ah Qing, especially in Dongguan. People who come back from there say you can make five or six hundred a month. Any job you could find at the hiring site in Zhengzhou pays, at most, a hundred!"

"Guangdong is so far away! And if we can't find work there, we won't be able to come back. Also, down there they eat more rice than noodles—they eat rice three times a day! Will you be able to take it?"

"You can get used to anything! We'll go down there and find a factory to work at. We can stick it out for a year, and after that we'll have enough money to open our own factory!"

One snowy day, a family from the village hired some workers to build them a house. The workers were shirtless and sang work songs as their rammers beat the earth. The sound of their voices traveled far and made the snowflakes melt into sweat.

Spring Festival was right around the corner. The front doors of all of the homes were plastered with images of gods and couplets written in black ink on red paper. When New Year's Eve arrived, firecrackers exploded throughout the countryside.

Ah Qing took his younger brother and sister to visit their mother's grave. With his back to the wind, he lit a candle for her, then made an offering of a cut of pork, a bowl of steamed buns, a stack of joss-paper money, and a long string of firecrackers. Ah Qing lit the fuse and the sound of rapid explosions merged with the racket of firecrackers exploding at other tombstones. He knelt before his mother's grave with his two younger siblings, and together they burned the money and prayed.

"Ma!" Ah Qing said, "I've come with little brother and sister to wish you a happy New Year!"

At that very moment, Little Jade and his younger sister were also kneeling at a grave and praying. "Dad," Little Jade said, "Little Sister and I have come to wish you a happy New Year!"

In the distance, graves glowed with flickering lantern candlelight. Lanterns glowed in homes throughout the countryside.

And this is how the living and all of their dead relatives spent a wonderful New Year's Eve together!

2

Ah Qing and Little Jade took a train to the south. In the large square in front of Guangzhou Railway Station, oceans of people milled about and the cars were so numerous they dazzled the eye.

"Ah Qing, is that south or north?" Little Jade raised a finger and pointed at an overpass.

"I don't know! We should buy a Guangzhou city map." Ah Qing rubbed his eyes.

Just as Ah Qing and Little Jade were sitting in the square studying the map, five young men who looked like migrant workers approached them. The young men encircled them.

"What do you guys want?" Ah Qing lifted his head and asked timidly.

One of the youths mumbled something in a dialect that Ah Qing and Little Jade couldn't understand while the others grabbed hold of them and began searching them from head to toe. Little Jade was so frightened that he pulled his arms together in front of his chest as if trying to curl into a ball. One of the youths pulled some cash from Ah Qing's pocket and another did the same to Little Jade. The remaining three weren't content to leave it at that, for they proceeded to open the boys' backpacks and look for anything of value.

Ah Qing saw a police officer in the distance. The officer appeared to be walking toward them. "Stop—thief! Stop—thief!" he shouted.

The young men fled in disorder, but the police officer seemed not to have heard Ah Qing's cry, for he now moved farther and farther away.

"What are we going to do, Little Jade?" Ah Qing asked in distress. "This city is so scary!"

"If we had known it was going to be like this, we wouldn't have come to Guangzhou! They took all the money we had on us!" Little Jade was just as dismayed as Ah Qing.

"Don't be upset, Little Jade," Ah Qing said, then he lowered his voice and added, "I still have fifty kuai hidden in my backpack. It'll be enough for us to eat for a few days."

Ah Qing and Little Jade began walking as they continued looking at the map. In the advertisement section they came across an employment ad: "Such-and-such Company seeks ten warehouse porters. Please call such-and-such number . . . "

They entered one of the many small shops in the area that kept phones on their counters for customer use. They picked up the red receiver and dialed the number. When the boss answered the phone they spoke to him in standard Mandarin. He gave them an address, which they jotted down, and in just moments they were jumping on a bus to go see him. They met the man with whom they had spoken on the telephone; he was a short fellow who hired them on the spot. Right there and then they joined a group of workers carrying boxes on their shoulders from a freezer warehouse to a freight truck parked outside. Day and night the workers shuttled back and forth, filling one truck after another with boxes. When it was break time, they sat outside the warehouse and ate the boxed lunches they had purchased from nearby food vendors. When it was nighttime, everyone slept together in a pitch-black storage room.

"Is your stomach any better, Little Jade?" Ah Qing asked with concern one night as they were lying down to go to sleep. They had been working at the warehouse for several weeks at this point, and Little Jade had begun complaining of stomach pain. "If it still hurts, I can ask the boss to give you some time off."

Little Jade's face was thin and wan. He curled up under his cotton quilt and looked miserable.

"He's not acclimated to the new environment," a worker brother said. "Medicine won't help a problem like that!"

The following day, Ah Qing stepped into the boss's office. "Manager," he said—most of the workers addressed the boss as "Manager" because it sounded more polite than "Boss"— "Little Jade is sick. He's not acclimated to the new environment here, so I want to take him back to our hometown."

"You can go if you want to," the boss replied. "But you haven't even worked here a month yet, so how am I supposed to calculate your wages? Imagine if all of the workers did this! What's a manager like me supposed to do?"

"I know we're not supposed to do this, Manager, but Little Jade is really sick and it's serious! What if he . . . " Ah Qing implored.

"Alright, alright, say no more. If you guys want to go I'm not going to force you to stay. But I'm only paying each of you for ten day's work."

"But Manager, we've worked here for twenty-five days! We've even worked on Sundays!"

Having nothing more to say about the matter, the boss pulled out a pen and rapidly filled out two wage collection forms. Utterly powerless, Ah Qing took the slips of paper and went to collect the four hundred yuan that he and Little Jade had collectively made from ten days of work.

Ah Qing helped Little Jade stay upright as they entered Guangzhou Railway Station, where they boarded a northbound train for the twenty-six-hundred-li trip back home.

"Wake up, Little Jade!" Ah Qing said, shaking his travel companion awake. "We're in Zhumadian!" Little Jade had been nuzzled up against Ah Qing's chest, fast asleep.

Little Jade awoke with a contented look on his face. When he saw the familiar scenery outside, his eyes filled with tears.

"If you want to cry, Little Jade, just go ahead and let it out. Let your tears flow onto our native soil—it will make you feel better!"

Little Jade held onto Ah Qing tightly and cried.

When nighttime fell, the boys entered a restaurant, where they ordered two bowls of lamb noodle soup.

"Eat up, Little Jade, you haven't had a thing in days! These are the noodles of our home region—if one bowl isn't enough, have another!" Ah Qing picked up a piece of meat with his chopsticks. "Open wide, let me give you a few bites!"

Obediently, Little Jade opened his mouth and accepted the chunk of lamb from Ah Qing's hand. Gradually, Little Jade's hands began to feel the warmth of his native place. Picking up his own pair of chopsticks, he continued to eat mouthfuls of meat and soup.

"You need to eat, too, Ah Qing. I'm feeling better already!" Little Jade laughed with tears in his eyes.

Ah Qing took Little Jade by the hand and they entered a travel hostel, where they rented a double room for the night.

In the morning, Ah Qing got up from bed first. "Little Jade," he asked, "are you feeling a little better? Should we go home first? Then we can—"

"No," Little Jade interrupted, "I'm fine now. Now that I've eaten a meal and slept for a night in our native place, I really am feeling much better!" Completely naked, Little Jade crawled out from the blankets and danced around the room, making Ah Qing roar with laughter.

"Ah Qing, do we have enough money to make it to Zhengzhou?"

Ah Qing produced all of the money in his pocket and began to count. Zhengzhou was four hundred li away.

"We have thirty-six kuai left, Little Jade. It's enough for two train tickets to Zhengzhou, but—."

"But if we can't find work right away, then it's going to be tough. Well, if it's tough, it's tough! It can't be any worse than when we were working in Guangzhou. We've only been away from home for one month. If we go back to Dragon Gully now, the entire village will laugh at us! Instead of going home, let's go back to the hiring site in Zhengzhou and find work there!"

Once again Ah Qing and Little Jade boarded a north-bound train. Outside the window they saw bright-green wheat seedlings and willow trees that had already sprouted light-yellow buds.

In the Zhengzhou night, Ah Qing and Little Jade walked along the familiar streets.

"Little Jade, we only have five kuai left! What are we going to do tonight?"

"Didn't you say that last year you slept in the square outside the railway station for an entire week? Well, tonight I'll sleep there with you—it will give me a taste of what it's like to sleep in a square!"

"No, Little Jade. Last year when I slept there it was mid-autumn and the temperature was still high! It may be spring now, but when the sun sets it's just as cold as winter!"

"Then what should we do?"

"Let's go to the night market and walk around. Who knows, maybe we'll come across a boss who's looking to hire!"

"Sure!" Little Jade laughed. "Walking will increase our body temperature, too!" Despite facing the prospect of home-lessness, he was able to remain cheerful.

From inside a seedy movie theater—it was the kind that operated outside the supervision of the Film and Television Bureau—there drifted the sound of howling, acrobatic fighting, and weapons clanging against one another. The name of the martial-arts film that was playing was written on a chalkboard outside; at the lower corner was written the words, "Stay all night, one yuan." Ah Qing and Little Jade paid two kuai and entered the dark, cavernous space and searched for a place to sit. The boys watched the dim screen on which men and women in historical costumes fought and killed one another, until finally they fell asleep. No one could say exactly when the sound of fighting was replaced by the kind of moaning one hears in the bedroom.

Ah Qing opened his eyes wide and his sleepiness evaporated in a flash. He nudged Little Jade, who was sleeping beside him but quickly woke up. Little Jade rubbed his eyes and sat up straight, then looked at the screen before them, where a man and a woman were in the throes of sexual passion. Ah Qing suddenly felt that the world around him was spinning and the thing below his waist was becoming so hard that it began to ache. Little Jade stretched out a hand and placed it on the stiffening mound, which he began to rub. Then he opened Ah Qing's zipper. Ah Qing pulled Little Jade's cock out of his pants, too, and there in the theater they masturbated each other until they both ejaculated into the darkness.

3

Little Wave and Little Tough entered the hiring site, where a short, fat man approached them.

"What kind of work are the two of you looking for?"

"As long as it pays, we'll do it!"

"Do you guys have identity cards? Will you do odd jobs at a restaurant?"

"Yes, we have identity cards. How much per month?"

"One hundred! What do you think? Not bad, eh?" The short, fat man gave them the thumbs-up sign.

"No way, that's too little! Boss, surely you know that workers' wages have been rising this year!" Little Wave waved his hand in the air to express his discontent.

"Give me a number, then."

"Bump it up fifty more!" Little Wave said.

"One hundred fifty kuai!" Little Tough echoed the proposition. "Yes or no?"

"Brothers, you're asking for too much. This is just a small shop! There's rent to pay, administrative expenses, public sanitation fees. Also—"

"Okay, okay, we get it! What do you want to go down to?"

"Listen, brothers—one hundred twenty kuai per month plus room and board. If that's not good enough for you, I'll just have to go and find somebody else!"

And so Little Wave and Little Tough trailed behind the short, fat man. After a while, they asked, "How much farther is it, boss?"

"Not far, not far at all!"

They continued to trail behind him.

"Boss, how come we're not there yet?"

"Any minute now! It's just up ahead." The short, fat man's forehead dripped with sweat.

Still following him, Little Wave and Little Tough crossed through one intersection, then another.

"This boss is a real penny-pincher!" Little Tough grumbled in a whisper. "Look at him—completely covered in sweat but he still won't spend a little money for a taxi!"

"Hey boss! Really, how much farther is it? Ten li? Twenty li?" Little Wave was growing impatient.

"Almost there! Just three li left!"

"What? Three li?! We're not going! Our feet are about to turn into blisters!" Little Tough halted.

"You go ahead, boss, we're not going to work for you!" Little Wave said with a frown. "If we did, you'd work us to death!"

"Brothers! Am I walking too fast? If you can't keep up, I'll go slower." The short, fat man wiped the sweat from his forehead and flashed them a smile.

Little Wave grabbed Little Tough by the hand and began walking in the opposite direction.

"Wei! Where are you going?" the short, fat man shouted. "Come back! I'm not trying to trick you! We really are almost there!"

"This guy is sick in the head!" Little Tough grumbled, ignoring the short, fat man's shouts. "We've been walking all day for nothing!"

Suddenly Little Wave stopped, a look of happiness stretched across his face. "Look, Little Tough!"

Little Tough's eyes moved in the direction indicated by Little Wave's finger. On the glass window of the Zijing Flower Hotel before them was a red paper banner on which was written the following: "Zijing Flower Hotel is recruiting outstanding servers! Requirements: male, at least 170 centimeters in height, pleasant and normal-looking face, between eighteen and twenty-two years of age, unmarried." In haste, they walked to the entrance of the building, leaving the short, fat man behind.

Dressed in identical uniforms, Little Wave and Little Tough began working each day at the Zijing Flower Hotel. They clocked in at 9:00 in the morning and worked all the way until 10:30 at night! The work was exhausting but they made three hundred kuai a month—much more than one normally made from jobs found at the hiring site!

Little Wave carried a serving tray up the stairs as Little Tough carried one down. They bumped into each other on a staircase landing.

"Are you tired, Little Tough?"

"When I see all the delicious-looking food on these plates, I forget about being tired. All I know is that my mouth starts to water!"

"Well, go ahead and let it water, then! Let it drip onto the plate, maybe it will give it some extra flavor!"

Little Wave and Little Tough stayed busy going up and down the stairs. Then they bumped into each other again in the washroom.

"I want to stay here in the washroom for a while! I've been running around so much my feet are killing me!"

"And I'm starving! We have to wait till 10:30 for dinner!"

"The manager doesn't let us eat the customers' leftover food. All this chicken and fish that's barely been touched by a pair of chopsticks—straight to the garbage! It's a real shame how much food this hotel wastes every day! This manager, he doesn't realize there are still people out there who haven't solved the food-and-clothing problem!"

"On the surface of things our hotel seems so generous! All this leftover fish and meat, they throw it in the garbage right in front of the customers! But behind the scenes they're so cruel to the employees. Sometimes we can't even get fresh vegetables to eat!"

At that very moment, they heard the swishing sound of a toilet flushing, followed by the thud of a bathroom stall door opening. Out from the cubicle came the server Xiao Jiang carrying a serving tray. Little Tough's and Little Wave's hearts jumped in their chests.

"I thought we were the only ones in the bathroom!" Little Wave whispered. "Do you think this guy's going to rat us out to the manager?"

"That's so bizarre! Why would he bring a tray into the washroom?"

"Come on, let's get back to work! We'll be in a lot of trouble if the manager finds us slacking off in here!"

The boys continued to ascend and descend the staircase, transporting plates of food in an endless series of roundtrips.

One evening after all the customers had left, Little Wave was busy returning serving trays to the kitchen while Xiao Jiang cleared the tables. Quickly before anyone else had a chance, Little Wave grabbed a lighter from a table and dropped it into his pocket. Xiao Jiang cast him a look, then grabbed two plates full of leftover red-braised beef and five-spice chicken; these he placed on his serving tray before rushing off. Seeing what was going on around him, Little Wave snatched some vegetable remains and leftover soup and ran behind Xiao Jiang.

Little Wave followed Xiao Jiang into the washroom, where he gingerly pressed his ear against the closed door of a stall. What he heard, however, wasn't somebody taking a crap, but the beautiful sound of teeth crushing food! After he slipped back out of the washroom he couldn't help but laugh. He laughed until his stomach hurt, until there were tears in his eyes, until the laughter was harder to bear than the crying.

After work when they were outside on the road, Little Wave told Little Tough everything.

When the cook Xiao Liu got off work, he pulled his jacket off the kitchen clothes rack. Barely was he out the back door of the Zijing Flower Hotel when a security guard stopped him. Xiao Liu followed him to the manager's office.

"Manager Wang! What did you call me in for?"

"Xiao Liu," the manager began. "Is the hotel not feeding you enough?"

"N—n—no! M—m—manager Wang . . . " Xiao Liu was thrown off guard by the manager's question. Sweat began to pour from his forehead and he started to stutter.

"Someone has reported you, saying that each night when you get off work you take things from the kitchen. I would like to inspect you to find out whether this is true!"

Manager Wang cast a look to the security guard, who reached a hand into Xiao Liu's pockets and produced four eggs and a piece of dried beef. In anguish and shame, Xiao Liu lowered himself to the floor, held his head in his hands and began to sob.

"Manager Wang, I know what I did was wrong, but please don't fire me—don't fry my squid! My mother is in the hospital, Manager Wang! Honestly, I didn't even want to do something like this, but . . . Please, just don't . . . "

Xiao Liu didn't return to work the following day.

From Zijing Flower Hotel management came the urgent announcement: a group of provincial- and city-level cadres would be dining at the hotel. Armed with this knowledge, employees of every department redoubled their efforts and busied themselves with preparations. When the fat, pasty old men arrived, they were led to the most splendid dining hall in the hotel. With smiles on their faces, servers of both sexes carried serving trays and alcoholic beverages as Manager Wang ran back and forth giving orders. When the fat, pasty old men were ready to leave, Manager Wang personally accompanied them to the ground floor and saw them off.

After the cadres left, the servers began clearing the items left on the tables.

"These old officials are so weird!" exclaimed one worker. "Their chopsticks barely touched the fish and meat, but they ate a ton of vegetables!"

"Yes, and you know why?" Xiao Jiang piped in. "Those old officials have eaten so much fish and meat that they're sick of it!"

Xiao Jiang turned on his heel and walked off with an entire fish. Little Wave and Little Tough followed closely behind, but not before grabbing some roast duck and braised chicken for themselves. Furtively the three boys stepped into the men's washroom, where they entered three separate toilet stalls and closed the doors behind them. In an instant the lovely sound of teeth crushing into meat was heard. Little Wave was taking a big bite from the duck's tail end when a greasy hand suddenly appeared under the partition. "Little Wave," a voice whispered, "let me try some of that duck!"

Little Wave tore off a chunk of duck meat and pushed it into Little Tough's hand.

Little Wave threw bones into the toilet as he ate.

Little Tough threw bones into the toilet, too.

And Xiao Jiang threw bones into the toilet as well.

A week later, a sanitation worker stopped by the manager's office. "Manager Wang," he began. "The washrooms on the third floor—both the men's and the women's . . . eight toilets are clogged!"

Customers squeezed into a bustling clothing store on Dehua Street. Inside the store hung a horizontal banner on which was written: "The customer is God!" Outside the front door a vertical blackboard stood erect. On it in white chalk was written: "Hiring male and female salespersons. All ages and education levels."

Little Lotus and Little Chrysanthemum stepped into the clothing store, where they were met by a warm and enthusiastic boss.

"Welcome to the two young misses, honorable customers both! May I ask, are the two misses buying clothing for themselves or for family and friends?"

"Are you the boss?" Little Lotus smiled. "Little Chrys and I have come to apply to work here as salespeople."

The boss led them into the backroom of the store. "Tomorrow morning before 9 a.m.," he said, "come here to report for duty!"

Little Lotus and Little Chrys left the store.

"How strange, Little Chrys!" Little Lotus exclaimed when they were outside. "He didn't ask about our education history, he didn't ask us our age, he didn't look at our identity cards, he didn't even write down our names! None of that, and tomorrow morning he wants us to come to work!"

"Maybe he wants to try us out for a day!" Little Chrys replied. "Let's see what he says after tomorrow."

"As long as we have a job! I don't even care if it's full-time or part-time. Let's just make sure we're here on time tomorrow morning before 9."

The following day at 8:30 a.m., Little Lotus and Little Chrys went back to the clothing store. When they arrived, they saw that a dozen or so men and women of varying ages were already gathered near the door. None of them seemed to know one another.

"Wow!" Little Lotus exclaimed. "How can there already be so many people here? Are these people all customers?" She approached a girl standing near the front door. "Excuse me, are you here to buy clothes or to apply for a job?"

"I work here two days a week!" the girl replied. "Thirty kuai a day! I've worked here six days now."

"Oh! Are you a salesperson? When I was here yesterday I don't think I saw you working."

"It's your first day—you still don't get what the boss wants us to do. When we leave here at the end of the day, we don't know one another. Just watch what we do and follow along and everything will be fine!"

At 8:55, a young man on a motorcycle arrived and opened the front door. Soon after, the boss from the previous day showed up, too. He pulled out a small composition notebook, the kind that primary-school students use, and asked everyone to write down their names. As they were doing so, eight more people, six young women and two young men, approached the store. Unlike the first group, they didn't stop to sign in, but walked directly into the shop and got to work while the notebook continued to circulate; Little Lotus and Little Chrys were last to sign in. When everyone had finished writing their names, the boss took the notebook from them, then led everyone inside. The shop was officially open for business, and the boss began welcoming customers with a smile.

Little Lotus took Little Chrys by the hand, but she had no idea what to do! They moved closer to the girl to whom Little Lotus had spoken outside. She was trying on a jacket and seemed to be shopping. Meanwhile, all of the other people who had been outside were now haggling over prices with the sales staff. Neither Little Lotus nor Little Chrys could tell who was a real customer and who was not. They went to talk to the boss, who really did seem to regard anybody who was not behind the sales counter as a god.

Little Lotus grabbed Little Chrys by the hand and quietly dragged her out to the street. "Little Chrys!" she cried. "I've figured it out! The boss hired us to pretend to be customers!"

"How deceptive! Should we do it or not?"

"Why not? It's not easy to find work! As long as they're paying I'll do anything, even be a decoy!"

They returned to the clothing store and Little Lotus asked a salesperson to take a women's jacket down from a rack. She and Little Chrys both tried it on and her face flushed red with excitement. "Oh, this is so pretty!" she exclaimed. As this was transpiring, two young women shoppers walked by. When they heard Little Lotus say the word "pretty", their eyes moved toward the jacket in her hand. Then the young women shoppers asked a salesperson to take an identical jacket down from the rack so that they too could try it on, too.

Little Lotus and Little Chrys saw that this was their opportunity to drive the deal home.

"That jacket's gorgeous, Little Chrys! The boys are going to be all over you if you wear it. Let's get one each!" She turned to a salesperson. "Excuse me, how much is this jacket?"

"The original price is one hundred twenty yuan, miss. Today we have a special price of eighty." The salesperson gave a practiced smile.

"Alright then, we'll take two!" Little Chrys began to pull the money from her wallet.

The two young women shoppers were intent on buying the jacket, too. They wanted to haggle over the price with the salesperson, but they had just watched as Little Lotus and Little Chrys wore the garments, which were sure to make other girls jealous, right out the door. Seemingly afraid that the lovely item would suddenly sell out, the two young women shoppers forked out the money without hesitation! The boss cast them a smile as they walked out the door with their new jackets. "We welcome the two young misses to visit us again!" he said gleefully.

Dusk fell as Little Lotus and Little Chrys walked along the street.

"This job is a lot of fun!" one of them said. "It's not tiring work at all! The only thing you have to move is your mouth. I feel like a movie star acting in a movie!"

"My only worry is that we won't be able to do it for long!" replied the other. "What if the boss is arrested? Do you think we'll be implicated, too?"

As they spoke they neared a motorized passenger tricycle operated by a disabled driver. It was Xiao An. He was sitting in the driver's seat, waiting for a passenger.

"Hey, it's Brother An! How's business today?"

Xiao An lifted his head and saw Little Chrys walking toward him. She was with his younger sister, Little Lotus. "Oh, not bad!" he replied.

"Brother An, I'd like to set you up with someone. Are you interested?"

"What? Me being like this, who would want me?" Xiao An laughed.

"Big Brother!" Little Lotus suddenly interjected. "What Little Chrys says is true, we want to set you up with someone! The woman is from Guizhou and she has a three-year-old daughter. She lives in the same residential compound as Little Chrys—they share a courtyard. If you're interested, we'll take you to meet her!"

Xiao An parked his motor trike inside Courtyard No. 8, a small cluster of buildings surrounding a courtyard connected to Shangcheng Street by a narrow, nameless winding side street. After he came to a halt, Little Lotus and Little Chrys emerged from beneath the weather tarp covering the wide passenger seat behind the driver. Xiao An lifted the prepackaged cake he had bought, then twisted his disabled foot and followed Little Lotus and Little Chrys into the center of the courtyard.

"Landlady Nai Nai!" Little Lotus called out to an old woman living in Courtyard No. 8. "I brought my Big Brother Xiao An with me!" Landlady Nai Nai—"Grandma Landlady" —was what everyone called her.

Nearly eighty years of age, the old landlady had a head of silver-white hair. When she saw Little Chrys bringing Little

125

Lotus's older brother in with her, she laughed and welcomed them.

The old landlady began to tell the story of the woman they wanted to set Xiao An up with.

"This woman's fate has been just awful!" she began excitedly. "First, she was tricked by her own cousin into leaving Guizhou Province and going up north to Hebei. When she got there, she was sold to an old man in the countryside, and she even had his child! Their little girl was only three when the old man died. His daughter from a previous marriage took the woman and sold her all over again, this time along with her child, to a scrap collector in the outskirts of Zhengzhou. Now this scrap collector actually had a lot of money, but he abused her and the girl. The woman had no choice but to bring her daughter into the city. The two of them have been staying at my place for over three months now. They haven't given me a single fen in rent, but I don't have the heart to make them leave. I've been wanting to help her find a decent man who will treat her and her daughter well. Little Chrys tells me you're still a bachelor, yes? Your legs are a little messed up, but that hasn't prevented you from making money, now, has it? Who's perfect? No one!" The old landlady smiled, revealing a row of gleaming white dentures.

The following day, Xiao An bought the old landlady a gift and, after giving it to her, took the unlucky woman and her daughter home with him.

"I have a sister-in-law now, Big Brother! I'm so happy for you!" Little Lotus exclaimed. "Now that things have changed, I can't keep living here all squeezed in with the three of you, so Little Chrys and I have rented a place together." Little Lotus started to pack her bags.

5

After Seventh Brother got out of prison, he went looking for Little Orchid. When he found her, she quickly became pregnant and married him without her parents' permission. Little

Orchid's mother grew sicker and sicker, leaving the girl's father with no choice but to close his shop and go back to his hometown.

As Little Orchid's stomach grew bigger and bigger, Seventh Brother did whatever he could to earn money so that he could raise a family. He sought out his father's old classmate, with whose help he found a job as a gardener at Zijing Mountain Park. Seventh Brother worked hard at being a good father and did overtime at work each day. Using his shears, he trimmed all the pine trees and cypresses in the park into all kinds of animal shapes.

On June 1, Children's Day, kids went to Zijing Mountain Park, where they saw green tigers, green monkeys, green pandas, green horses, green deer, green wolves, and green pythons. All of the animals were green in these little friends' eyes.

On that very day, Little Orchid gave birth to a baby boy and named him Little Dragon. Little Dragon got fatter and fatter; Little Orchid, meanwhile, got thinner and thinner. Seventh Brother's heart ached, for he knew that his wife was struggling.

"Let me buy you a skirt, Little Orchid!" Seventh Brother said, holding the money he'd just collected from his job. He wanted to do something nice for her.

"Oh, don't do that!" Little Orchid replied. "My skirt from last year is still wearable. Why don't you buy our Little Dragon a toy car instead?" She changed the boy's wet diaper as she spoke.

Seventh Brother lowered his head and smoked a cigarette in silence.

"Stop smoking!" Little Orchid reached out to pull the cigarette from Seventh Brother's mouth. "It'll harm the child's health!" She tossed the butt out the door.

Little Orchid held her child in her arms and sang to him a lullaby that her own mother had sung to her when she was small; before long Little Dragon fell sweetly into sleep. Seventh Brother had already taken off his clothes and gotten into bed, where he waited patiently for Little Orchid. After she had lulled the child to sleep, she got to work on an item of clothing she was knitting for him. Seventh Brother reached out a hand and took hold of one of Little Orchid's breasts, which he began to stroke and fondle.

She removed her clothes and lay down, then took her husband's flesh inside her. Seventh Brother breathed heavily on top of her and the bed began to sway. Just then Little Dragon started to cry. Little Orchid pushed her husband to the side, walked over to the boy and began singing a lullaby. Seventh Brother lost his erection, then rolled over in annoyance, doing his best to fall asleep.

He went into the bathroom to masturbate. When he returned to the bedroom, he saw Little Dragon lying in his wife's arms, lips wrapped firmly around her nipple and looking quite content as he drank her breast milk. Little Orchid put the sleeping child down, then went into the kitchen to cook. The instant she left the bedroom, Seventh Brother gave the child a hard whack on the butt. Little Dragon began to cry and Little Orchid rushed back into the bedroom to hold him. Her hands were caked with flour, so she asked her husband to go and cook. Seething with rage, he banged a spatula loudly in the kitchen.

When there was no work for him, Seventh Brother stayed home, where he watched TV and slept all day. One time, Little Orchid took Little Dragon to a nearby shop so that she could make a phone call. From the call she learned that her mother's sickness would require a great deal of money, so she asked Seventh Brother to take care of the child while she went out to look for work. That's when she met an old landlady living in Courtyard No. 8 off Shangcheng Street. Little Orchid began working as her maid.

Seventh Brother went back to the park to work, leaving Little Dragon with Little Orchid. Each day, Little Orchid put the child down to sleep, then jumped on her bicycle and rode to the old landlady's place, where she would cook for her, wondering all the while whether her own child was hungry! Once, when she went out to buy medicine for the old landlady, she took advantage of being away from Courtyard No. 8 by taking fifteen extra minutes to ride home and check on her son. She found him alone in his bed crying, and her heart ached and tears poured from her eyes.

Little Orchid used her husband's wages to buy daily necessities, and mailed her own first month of wages to her parents back in her hometown. She saw her husband off to work, put her child to bed, then jumped on her bicycle and rode off to the old landlady's place. She returned home that evening when the sky was already dark. Little Dragon was lying in bed crying; her husband sat off to the side smoking.

"You don't take care of our own child, then go off to someone else's house to be their maid?"

"Well, *you've* been here, haven't you? Why aren't you holding him?"

"I just got off work! Look how late it is and I haven't even eaten yet!"

"Then make yourself some dinner!"

And Little Orchid and Seventh Brother would begin to fight.

Little Orchid was at the old landlady's place washing clothes when Seventh Brother suddenly appeared with a crying child in his arms. She took the child from him lovingly, then began to yell at him. Having deposited the child with his mother, Seventh Brother turned on his heel and left. Little Orchid chased him. Little Dragon cried loudly, then Little Orchid cried, too. The sight of Little Orchid with a kid in her arms caused the old landlady to feel greatly annoyed. She walked over to Big Sister Plum Blossom's Hair Salon.

"Ah! Auntie Landlady is here! Welcome! Welcome!" Sister Plum Blossom smiled and offered the old landlady a seat.

"Little Plum Blossom, how's business been lately?" the old landlady asked, revealing a sparkling row of white dentures.

"Please, Auntie Landlady, don't worry. Even if business goes downhill again, I'd never miss rent."

The old landlady ignored what Sister Plum Blossom had said, opting instead to complain about her new maid.

"That Little Orchid, she's so careless! When she's cooking, she'll take the things I want to eat and give them to the cat—then cook the cat food for me! Just today her husband came to drop off their kid! You tell me, Little Orchid: Are you my maid or not? You can take care of your kid when you get home!" The old landlady sighed. "And yet," she continued, "when I see Little Orchid crying, I don't have the heart to fry her squid!"

"Oh, Auntie Landlady is so kind!" Sister Plum Blossom gushed. "Otherwise, how could you live to be eighty and still be in such good health? Really, I envy Auntie Landlady for having two such filial sons. One of them a Public Security Bureau director, the other the head of a news agency! During Spring Festival and other holidays they always drive here to see you, and they bring you such nice things!"

"Only good people get good rewards!" the old landlady enthused. "If I hadn't accumulated so much virtue with all my good deeds, my sons never would have gone this far! You know, a monk came to my home and informed me that I have good luck and good fortune, so I spent five hundred kuai on a statue of the Buddha to bless and watch over the whole family! Then a Taoist master came to me and said the same thing as the monk, so I spent another five hundred kuai buying all the medicine he advised me to get. On New Year's Day and again on the Lantern Festival, I always burn incense to the Bodhisattva Guanyin. Sometimes I even donate money to Christianity!"

"So which god does Auntie Landlady really believe in?"

"As long as they're a god, I believe in them! And as long as someone's a good person, I'll help them." The old landlady's tightly clenched lips formed a righteous smile.

At that moment, Little Orchid entered the hair salon. "Nai Nai, the food is ready," she said. She turned to Sister Plum Blossom and nodded politely.

SEVEN

1

A public park at dusk.

I was chasing a young guy. Short, with a white, round face, his small red lips pouted like he'd suffered some terrible offense. He looked as though he'd been cloned from a pile of dolls. He circled me, then lured me in by climbing up an artificial hill, then climbing back down again. From a thicket of trees he darted into a public toilet, then darted out of the public toilet and back into the thicket of trees.

Green pine trees hugged one another as they grew bigger while downy wild grasses stood on tiptoe, peeking out from the cluster of trees. The sound of crickets chirping rang out like cell phones. Anonymous wildflowers blossomed silently, their fragrances pulling at spider webs.

"Good boy—come over here!" I called out to the little devil.

Obediently he moved to my side, then blew a big bubble from his pouting red mouth. When it exploded, the bubble gum stuck to his lips.

"You're so adorable!" I removed my hand from a pine tree and placed it on his head. He laughed.

I leaned in to kiss his cheek but he ducked under the pine branches, causing several dozen needles to fall and poke at my old and utterly shameless face. "Aiya!" I cried out, and the little devil laughed even more happily than before.

"Don't lift it so high!" he whispered, patting my ass.

I lowered my jutting ass and felt his cock push against my upper thigh.

"Your ass is too high!" The little devil slapped my butt anxiously.

It occurred to me that there was a full twenty centimeters' difference between my height and his, so I bent over further to relax my sphincter and take his banana of a cock.

Little Devil—that's what I decided to call him—spread my ass cheeks with his hands. "I still can't get it in," he said plaintively. "The way you're standing is too high up!"

By this time, my forehead was covered in sweat, my waist was twisted to the point where it started to hurt, and my asshole needed to be satisfied. I began moving my feet around in the darkness, seeking a depression in the ground so my legs would suddenly become twenty centimeters shorter.

"Wait a sec, I'll be right back," Little Devil reeled in his hard cock, pulled up his pants, and disappeared into the grove of trees.

Squatting, I spit a glob of saliva onto my fingers and gently rubbed it into my asshole for lubrication. That way, the convulsing area would be as soft and lithe as a flower in full bloom!

Carrying two big bricks in his hands, Little Devil returned from the grove. When he placed the bricks on the ground and stepped on them, the little devil grew into a big devil. Beads of sweat hung from his thick black eyebrows. I kissed his face lovingly, then unzipped his pants and pulled out his cock, which I proceeded to hold in my mouth. It was like I was playing a magical flute!

Before long, Little Devil's hot blood synthesized and became one with my old bones. I was happy as a little boat, and Little Devil was my oar. Together we rowed, shaking the moonlight from a night that was as deep and dark as the blackest sea.

"Did that feel good, Uncle?" Little Devil asked as he pulled up his pants.

"Yes, it felt great! Thank you—good boy!" I was getting ready to make my way out of the grove of trees.

"If you enjoyed it, then please pay me. I'm an MB—a money boy." Little Devil stretched out his hand and placed it in front of my face.

"How much do you want? I'll pay you, I'll pay you . . . " My hand trembled as I felt around in my pocket; in my heart I was starting to loathe this boy. I figured if I gave him one or two hundred kuai I wouldn't be shorting him. This is a money society, and no one's going to serve you for free. Ah, youth! Youth is wonderful, it's the greatest wealth! Me, I'm just an old man now. An old man who knows that the day he can no longer consume is the day he'll be ready to die!

"Come on, pay up! I haven't had dinner yet!" Little Devil grumbled.

"I'm sorry, I'm so sorry!" I said after feeling around in my pocket. "I took a friend to lunch today and spent all the money I had on me! Wait till next time," I continued somewhat awkwardly. "Next time, I'll bring a lot of cash for you."

Little Devil took off, pouting. Feeling ashamed, I watched his back as he walked away.

One week later Little Devil and I bumped into each other in the park again. I had already walked a number of full laps around the park. There were a few old guys like me; I had no interest in them. There were a few deflated-looking middle-aged guys; I had no interest in them, either. There was one extremely effeminate young person dressed in bright, flamboyant clothes; even less was I interested in him. I thought about how I still owed Little Devil money from our previous encounter. Although I was disgusted by this kind of money-boy behavior, I couldn't help but be seduced by it, for anytime a beautiful boy pulled out his big pink cock, my blood would rush straight to my head. My rickety old bones would become soft and I would practically lose my balance as I walked. My ass would shake involuntarily and my anus would bloom like a withered, dried-up old flower opening its petals to meet a fresh spring breeze.

"Still want it, Uncle He?" Little Devil's feet came to a standstill and he cast me supercilious look.

"Yes, I still want it," I laughed, "and this time I will definitely pay you. I'll give you the entire five hundred kuai in my pocket. Does that work?" I flashed him a smile like a prostitute no one wanted.

Little Devil pouted with his little red mouth, then blew a scrotum-sized bubble with his chewing gum. When it exploded, he brought the gum back into his mouth and resumed his non-stop chewing.

I took him by the hand and walked with him in the beautiful dusk.

We made our way to the familiar grove of trees. Here and there the downy grass at our feet was littered with crumpled pieces of tissue. It went without saying that all of these were masterpieces left behind by people like us. I could practically smell the hormones in the air. Yes, bring it! Moisten me with your semen; it sprays me like cologne. My love would eternally refuse to grow old. My love would forever be a child who pines for candy.

"Where did those two bricks go?" Little Devil lowered his head and searched at the foot of the trees.

"We don't need them," I replied, pulling down my trousers and getting on my knees in the grass.

Little Devil spit saliva mixed with bubble-gum juice into his hand, then smeared the whole mess gently onto his stiffening cock. It vibrated as it searched for a warm hole in my flesh. Listen! You can practically hear the whole thing enter at once.

As the evening wind blew, the pine trees held one another and swayed.

2

Little Devil stopped fucking me; he was panting.

He pulled his moist cock out of me and in an instant my ass was empty and deserted.

"It's time to pay me, Uncle." Little Devil held his hand out before my chest.

My heart was still palpitating rapidly. I reached into the pocket where I had placed the money: empty! I felt inside my other pocket, and that was empty too. Where had my money gone? Where was my five hundred kuai?!

"It must have been stolen by a pickpocket when I was on the bus—I had five hundred kuai!" I tried to explain to Little Devil, but explanations were useless. I already owed him from the last time.

"You old fraud! Always trying to eat for free!" Little Devil pointed at my nose and cursed, then disappeared into the pitch-black grove.

My face grew insufferably hot, but my ass retained the memory of pleasure.

"That fucking thief, making me lose face like this!" The profanities fell from my mouth as I retreated to the trees, a pathetic bastard. I was terrified of seeing Little Devil again; there was no way I could lift my face in his presence. The only thing I could lift, and half-heartedly at that, was my ass, and even this would soon be cold and desolate! There was no doubt that this little devil would tell other MBs that I was an old thing who was always trying to eat for free!

Oh, but it's hard to avoid one's enemies! Some days later, my anus started itching again, so I went to the park, where I again bumped into Little Devil. I smiled recalling how pleasurable it had been the first two times.

Shaking my ass, I walked past him. But he ignored me, so all I could do was shake my ass away from him in search of a new cock. Each time I saw those impotent men in public toilets, their mouths open even wider than mine as they waited for something . . . there were no words! They were just as ugly as I was, and just like me, their way of life was utterly shameless.

Lonely, I sat on an evening rock.

Lonely, I waited for the hand of Death to pull me away.

Lonely, I saw Little Devil, who paced back and forth, every bit as lonely as I was. I felt the thick wad of bills in my pocket; the old men on the notes laughed at me. In the dusk, I was getting older and older.

"Want me to fuck you?" Little Devil jeered. He held a disposable bowl of instant noodles in his hand. I could hear the clear, sharp sound of him chewing.

"Yes, I want you to fuck me—I want you to fuck me to death!" I offered a sheepish smile as my heart leapt, a vague confession of the shame I knew I should feel.

"Let's go! Same place." Still eating his instant noodles, Little Devil began walking toward the grove of trees.

Suddenly animated, I jumped up from the stone. Once again my ass started to shake as I walked, excited but somewhat skeptical, behind. This time I was definitely going to pay him! I touched the money in my pocket again. Oh, Little Devil! Just fuck me to death—don't let this old guy suffer such a meaningless life!

The evening wind blew. The evening wind belonged to me. Did spring belong to me, too?

I got on my knees in the grass, my asshole opening to welcome the bullet that was about to explode in my flesh.

Little Devil spit a glob of saliva on his hand and my asshole suddenly became wet.

Oh, Little Devil! Why have you not yet dropped your pants and pulled out that delicious ham intestine! Wait, no, not a ham intestine—a tender melon! No, no, not a tender melon—but a sweet banana!

Little Devil exploded in laughter. "You old thing," he exclaimed, "always wanting to eat for free! I'll give you something to eat! Eat some chili powder!" He laughed once more and ran away.

All at once my asshole was on fire and I thought I was going to die. Little Devil had stuffed an entire packet of instant noodle seasoning straight up inside me: salt, MSG, sugar, chili pepper . . . this was something not even Freud would have encountered!

My eyes filled with tears as I ran home in a panic. When I got there I removed my trousers, then shoved a plastic tube inside me and turned on the bathroom-sink faucet. My large intestine filled with water, which then flowed out of my ass with a gurgling sound. I put the tube in again, and again the water shot out of my ass. The water flowed from of my rectum, flowed from my stomach, flowed from my heart.

It was wintertime and all the wet areas on the ground outside had frozen over. I wobbled along the road, paying close attention to the people around me. Handsome young faces populated the crowd; some were clear, others indistinct, and some retreated into the distance. Some moved toward me, then quickly passed me by. Winter was so cold, and colder still with no one to love! Though my heart no longer seemed to be beating, my body still moved, greeting another endlessly long spring.

Suddenly I slipped and fell. I wanted to get up but I was in so much pain that I couldn't move. There was nothing I could do but lie there and wait for a kind-hearted person to come and help me up. A man looked at me as he walked by, but he kept walking. A woman did the same. This went on with one person after another until I had been lying on the ground for half an hour and hundreds of people had walked by, not a single one of them willing to stretch out a warm hand to help me up. I began to lose hope. I was waiting for Death to come take me away.

At that moment, a young guy with a smile on his face approached me, then lifted me up from the ground. When I saw that it was Little Devil, my eyes filled with tears. He took me to a hospital, where I stayed for two days. After I was discharged, it was Little Devil who took me home and stayed by my side for a week. I recovered from the fall, and Little Devil and I, despite our age difference, formed a friendship.

Little Devil lay on top of me. I unpeeled a bright red tangerine and fed him pieces of the fruit as I broke it apart.

"This one time I was in the park and I met this old guy," he began, talking with his mouth full of fruit. "He told me he liked me a lot, then he said he ran a shop that sold cell phones. He had five really nice cell phones in his pocket, and he said he'd give me one if I could get him off. I was so happy to hear this! So I went with him into a public toilet where we did some hand jobs and oral. After he pulled his pants up, he really did give me a cell phone, a really nice one! I pressed a button and heard 'Happy birthday to you, happy birthday to you . . . ' I showed that phone off to all my friends! It was only when I went to the telecommunications office to get a number and a SIM card for it that I found out it was a toy phone you could get for five kuai!"

I laughed and patted Little Devil on his lovely head. Then I listened to his story.

3

Wearing the new pair of jeans you had just bought, you trailed behind a middle-aged man. This rustic, uncouth middle-aged man wasn't willing to part with the money it took to ride a bus, so he walked along a river filled with filthy sewage water with you close behind. Reflected in the filthy water you saw a streetlight glowing like clear moonlight. A grassy lawn lined the riverbank; cut short, it looked like a man's crewcut and you enjoyed walking on it. The fact was, you didn't like this middle-aged man one bit, but if you didn't go with him you'd have no choice but to spend your own money to sleep at a travel hostel. When a person leaves home on their own, they should save every kuai they can!

It was Zhengzhou's worst, cheapest hostel, just ten kuai per night for two people to stay in a single room. The room was eight square meters and had a big, worn-out bed and a short, squat table. Two plastic basins sat on the floor; it was unclear which was for pissing and which was for washing one's face. There were no bathrooms on the upper floors and the light bulb in the stairway had gone out, so anything that had to be done had to be done in the eight-square-meter room. The middle-aged man washed his ass in one of the basins; you pissed in the other.

You hadn't gotten any decent rest in days. You took off your shoes, and when the middle-age man did the same you saw ten yellow-gray toenails tearing through a pair of reeking socks. Covered in dead skin and mysterious crumbs that fell to the floor, they were the most disgusting feet you had ever seen in your life. Your stomach felt queasy.

You undressed, then crawled under the dank, clammy quilt. The noxious smell of urine floated up from under the quilt and crawled into your nose like a caterpillar. The middle-aged man's mouth came near you and you smelled his breath; it reeked of garlic and leeks. For the rest of the night you endured him, thinking to yourself: "Just make it through till morning—then we settle the bill!"

You slept, and when the rumbling in your stomach was no longer bearable, you opened your eyes. The sun was up. The middle-aged man was gone.

"Fuck!" you yelled. "Another free-eater—gone!" Spewing curses, you jumped out from under the quilt and went to grab your clothes. That's when you saw that your new jeans were gone, too! In their place lying across the bed was an old pair of filthy trousers covered in grease spots, dirt smudges, and cum stains. This shameless middle-aged man had run off with your brand-new jeans and eighty percent new sneakers. When you remembered his stinking toes, one hundred percent of you did not want to do what you knew was unavoidable: wear the shoes he had left behind.

With no money and no friends to turn to, you slept under bridges and in tunnels. For drinking water you ducked into the public toilet at the railway station.

It was in the park that you met Little Fairy. He had once tried to kill himself and up until that point had worn a wig. His entire body was covered with burn scars; his cock was burned, too. He was tragic at the park, for no one was ever interested in him. He couldn't top, and when he tried to bottom, any dick big or small would go limp the instant it touched his scar-covered ass. Little Fairy was a sweet talker: anytime he saw a money boy he would call out, "Hey, Big Sister! Hey, Little Sister!" When you were able to make a little money selling yourself, you would invite Little Fairy to eat. Sometimes when the two of you slept in the park, the cops would do sweeps to drive you out.

It was hard to find work, and when you did find it, it was even harder to get paid. When you did have work, the pay was only enough to fill your stomach. The streets were always plastered with help-wanted signs. Every shop, it seemed, put up the same sign: "New Owners, Looking for Skilled and Unskilled Workers." Every employment agency ripped off unemployed workers. All those movie directors looking for a limitless supply of extras—they ripped people off, too. There was the registration fee, the cost of taking a picture, the cost of training. Everywhere one looked in China there were con artists: from village to city, from provincial capital to the capital of the nation! They lied; they spoke through masks. Each person lived shamelessly.

To make a living you scrapped the self-respect that a man should have. Everyone threw their self-respect out of the window. Everyone lived a mean existence.

Every city regardless of size had plenty of money boys. Back when you were hustling in the parks of Chengdu, even guys who looked like Andy Lau or Aaron Kwok couldn't sell for more than twenty or thirty kuai! And for a guy like you, ten kuai, max! Things were even worse in Zhengzhou, where five kuai was considered too high a price! Some people derided you, saying you were too short. In fact, you were two centimeters taller than Deng Xiaoping! One fat old guy with glasses—he told you he was a retired cadre and a Communist

Party member—said his place wasn't an option, so he took you to the public toilet in the Zijing Mountain Department Store. You fucked him and he gave you just five kuai! Even in the countryside you'd get ten kuai for a fuck! Human beings—they really really were cheap cheap cheap cheap fucking goods.

You and Little Fairy went to many cities together. Finding someone to love was so hard, and each time you met a new gay comrade it never progressed beyond a one-night stand! Even if you didn't take their money, they would act like they didn't even know you after fooling around. So you may as well take their money—think of it as compensation for spiritual losses!

When the two of you couldn't find work and were not able to sell yourselves, you went hungry. Sometimes you contracted venereal disease. Homeless and without money to see a doctor, there was nothing you could do but steal the medicine you needed.

Once you and Little Fairy robbed a house. Little Fairy kept watch as you slipped in through a window. The place was as big as a palace. You walked around looking for stuff. There were so many nice things in that house, you had no idea what to take! The TV was too big to carry, as was the refrigerator and the washing machine. There were vases, potted landscapes, works of calligraphy and art created by famous people . . . you figured this must have been the home of some big, greedy bureaucrat. Suddenly, on a large table placed at the center of the entrance hall, you spied an object wrapped in yellow silk. It reminded you of the great seal given to the Yellow Emperor that you had seen in the movies! You unwrapped the yellow silk and found a carved, golden box of considerable weight. You bit it and discovered that it wasn't very hard. This was definitely a box of pure gold, and inside there would surely be a stash of priceless jewelry! All you had to do was take this gold box and never again would you have to worry about finding food, water, or a place to sleep. In haste you picked it up and slipped out of the house just in time to see the owner's domestic servant returning from a shopping trip. The servant was carrying bags full of all kinds of delicious-looking food. He didn't notice you and you and Little Fairy were able to run off.

Stealing was dangerous in the daytime, but a friend had once told you that the more dangerous a place was, the safer it would be. He said that he had once robbed a bank in a crowded urban area in broad daylight! With a masked face and a gun in his hand, he shot and killed two police officers wearing peaked caps. Then, with a bag of money on his back, he calmly slipped into the crowd outside and got away without incident.

You and Little Fairy wrapped the gold box in clothing, then walked until you came to a scarcely peopled alleyway, where you ducked into a public toilet.

"This box is so damn heavy!" Little Fairy said as he wiped sweat off his forehead. "Let's open it up and see all the good stuff inside!"

With your sleeve you wiped your forehead, too, then pulled the box out from the cloth. "Little Fairy, we're rich! This is from the house of a big, greedy official—there's going to be a ton of jewelry in it!"

Full of surprise, happiness and fear, Little Fairy looked toward the door of the bathroom, seemingly afraid that someone might suddenly walk in. You lowered your excited voice to a whisper and began thinking of a way to open the gold box. Together you tried prying it open with your hands. When that didn't work, you hit it repeatedly. When that didn't work, you banged it first against the porcelain toilet and then against the wall. You stomped on it and beat it with your fists. Fuck! At last, the lid of the gold box cracked open just as tortuously as if it had been a tortoise shell.

"Oh my god," Little Fairy exclaimed, "it's an urn! There's nothing in here but ashes!" His face went as white as a sheet of paper and he ran out of the door, the damp, tiny hairs on his body standing on end.

You were full of fear, too, so much that your teeth chattered. With trembling hands you closed the lid of the box, then gently placed it beside the squat toilet bowl and ran outside.

As you were running out of the door you crashed headlong into old ragpicker.

"Sorry, sorry!" you shouted as you reached down to help the old man up off the ground. He stood up and laughed, then carried his big garbage bag into the toilet.

You and Little Fairy waited for the old man to come out, waited for something to happen. When he didn't, you gathered up your courage and took Little Fairy by the hand. The two of you quietly approached the toilet entrance, then craned your necks around a corner to catch a glimpse of the old man, who was opening the gold box in delight. He poured the ashes into the toilet bowl and swiftly placed the empty box into his bag. Then he stepped out of the bathroom, a look of contentment on his face.

4

You and Little Fairy began stealing bicycles near the park.

On the side of the road, you saw a lovely bike with a heavy lock on it. You weren't going to pry the lock open; instead, you would wait. If the owner didn't return, and if a taxi van drove by, you would flag down the driver, tell him you lost the key to your bicycle lock, then have him take you to a bike repair shop. Every taxi driver hated the patrol officers, who routinely stopped their vehicles so they could find some excuse to give them a ticket. The only thing drivers cared about was whether they could pull in some money. Pretending not to know that the bike was stolen, they would drive you to some faraway repair shop, then take your money and leave. And the bike-repair shifu? Well, it wasn't easy for them to make money, either! With one eye open and the other closed, they would help you pry open the lock, charge you a fee, and send you on your way.

You and Little Fairy rode your bikes, wildly, joyfully, through the streets.

Eventually you sold all those nearly brand-new bikes to petty bargain-hunters who were always looking for a way to get something cheap and easy. They'd pay fifty to eighty kuai for a bike, then happily jump on it and ride home.

One Sunday, you were stealing yet another bike from outside the park when you were nabbed by a cop and taken away. Your heart raced as you sat in the police vehicle, telling yourself that it was over.

The police officer who had picked you up was very handsome. He was just as big and tall as all the handsome cops one sees in the movies and on TV.

He was poised and relaxed as the police car raced forward, causing peddlers on the side of the road to scamper off like so many frightened rats. How ugly they all were! This big-brother cop at your side, however—he was so debonair, so handsome! Your cock began to stiffen.

The handsome police officer didn't take you to jail; instead, he took you to a cozy home. He offered you an alcoholic drink, something to eat, and let you take a shower. Then, benevolently, he gave you an education: he kissed you, caressed you, comforted you, loved you, protected you. This handsome big-brother cop even said he would find you a job.

He grabbed a condom, then used his mouth to unroll it down the length of your cock. After lubing his asshole with an oil-based cream, he squatted on top of you like the Bodhisattva Guanyin mounting a lotus. You became so full of emotion that you cried! Together the two of you rocked and swayed . . . keep rocking, wonderful, big-brother cop! You felt that your four limbs were trembling. A mirror crashed to the floor and shattered, crying out in excitement.

If only cops and robbers the world over were like this! Would not all places under heaven be filled with peace and tranquility?

You were hungry again. And again and again you circled the park.

A child who was selling flowers walked toward you. He was only seven or eight years old. "Uncle," he said, "why don't you buy a rose?"

You shook your head and kept walking.

A ragpicker child walked toward you. With eyes fixed on the plastic water bottle in your hand, he was waiting for you to finish it and throw it away. This ragpicker child had lips that were dried and cracked; you wanted him to drink, so you stretched out your arm and gave him the bottle. This boy, just twelve or so years old, took it from you gleefully, then removed the bottle cap and poured the water onto the ground.

The ragpicker child ran off with the bottle.

Your heart began to sting!

That ragpicker child ran through the park day and night. He spotted a pregnant woman with a large, protruding belly, then grabbed a rock and threw it directly at her stomach. He yelled as the rock flew through the air: "Bad woman! A woman with a big belly is a bad woman!"

You watched the woman as she held her stomach and lowered herself to the ground. There she sat crying out for help, and you suddenly thought of your own mother.

Mother was a bad woman who had become pregnant with you without even being married. You had always known that you were a bastard, a seed who had been sown in the wild. You yearned for a father: a father who was big and tall, a father who loved you dearly, a father who would spank your bottom. He would be a father who came home often, a father with a cock, a father who'd make sure no one ever called you a bastard again!

Mother held you in her arms as she spread a blanket on the ground to sell socks. She didn't say a word. Day after day dusk fell as you watched one big, tall man after another pass by. These men carried children who were the same size as you on their shoulders—those kids looked so happy! They were happy because they had a father.

You hated your mother, who never should have left you without a father. You hated all women who divorced men. You hated menstruating women, women who had sex, women who were pregnant. Brutally, you bit into your mother's breast. After that, she smeared chili oil all over it!

You were fast asleep in your mother's arms when she seduced a man, a soldier whom you called "Uncle." She did it for you. This soldier uncle was big and tall, and each day he came to buy socks from your mother. It wasn't long before he became your father. The day you ate your mother and father's wedding candy, you were six years old.

5

"Daddy, hold me!" It was your first time acting like a spoiled brat.

"Daddy, kiss me!" Your face was tickled by Daddy's scratchy whiskers.

"Daddy, I'm hungry!" You were growing taller.

"Daddy, I'm afraid of dogs!" You were getting braver and braver.

"Daddy, I'm afraid of the dark!" Your eyes were getting brighter and brighter.

"Daddy! Daddy! Daddy, I love you!" Your father left home; your father came back; you were full of joy.

Your family had always been poor. Your parents couldn't afford to buy you toys, and sometimes they didn't have money to buy you candy either. But as long as you had a dad and a mom, your heart was full of sweetness. When you were in primary school, your parents went off to a factory to work. You always did as they said and your grades at school were always good; your teacher praised you often. After school, you helped your mother with the cooking and washing; you helped your father with the hauling and the cleaning. But just as your love for them was deepening, your father left you and your mother. He had stolen things from the factory and been taken away by the police.

Each day you waited for your father to come home. For two years you longed for him day and night; finally, he returned. He couldn't find work after coming home, though, and fought with your mother constantly. Crying, you tugged at your father's hand, and asked him to stop hitting your mother.

"He's not your daddy!" your mother yelled as she pointed at his nose. She kicked him out.

Your crying intensified as you wrapped your arms around your father's legs so that he wouldn't leave. He really did stay because of you. He found a job sweeping streets and cleaning toilets. Everyone looked down on him; your classmates at school made jokes about him. Once again, you wrapped your arms around his legs, this time so that he wouldn't clean toilets anymore. He really did stop cleaning toilets because of you.

Father started stealing again and the family finally had some money. He would buy you the sweetest candy, and mother the prettiest clothes. He began inviting his friends over for meals that consisted of meat and alcohol. These men and women, whom you called "uncle" and "auntie," all praised you for being a good boy. The next time father went out to steal things, mother dressed herself head to toe in military clothing and went with him. You wanted to go with father, too, to be his helper. He kissed your face and said, "Good child, listen to grownups. Stay here at home, don't cry, and wait for Daddy and Mommy's safe return."

Home was cold and desolate, full of nothing but the sound of rats fighting each other. You looked at the black night outside and your young heart began to pray: "Old man in the sky, please bless my dad and mom so they can steal lots of things and come back home. Please make them come back home soon!"

You crawled on top of the table in front of the window and went to sleep. In your sleep you perceived two big hands wrapping themselves around you. When you opened your eyes the sun was up and your father was sleeping beside you. You heard his loud snoring and couldn't help but reach out and pinch his nose.

When you were twelve years old, your father and mother were arrested and taken away. Your maternal uncle took you to live in his house. You cried all the way there.

You started getting sick all the time, and awoke crying from nightmares each night. Your uncle and his wife didn't like you; secretly they ate with your cousins while you were asleep. One summer when you were taking an afternoon nap, you awakened with a start and heard your uncle and his family eating watermelon loudly like a bunch of pigs. When no one was home, you ate their eggs, and when they found out, they locked all the eggs inside a cupboard. You began stealing scraps of copper and iron, which you sold to a recycler. Once when your cousin broke a hot-water thermos, he told your uncle that it was you. Your aunt scolded you brutally, and your uncle beat your ass with a shoe until it was purple and blue. The lesions became infected with blood and pus, and when you lay down at night you couldn't fall asleep. You cried thinking about your father in prison. Although he wasn't your real father, he had always loved you and taken care of you, and he had never hit you.

Sores developed on your buttocks, but your uncle and his wife paid you no mind. They neither took you to a doctor nor gave you medicine. Clenching your teeth, you waited for the day when your dad and mom would come to take you home.

Uncle and his family were going out. Just before leaving, your aunt inspected everything in the house, hiding this, locking that, and taking with her other things still. All that was left behind was you, this thorn in their side—a thorn with a sore-covered ass who crawled atop a wooden stool, mouth half-open but saying nothing.

You wanted to leave that place, and you wanted revenge.

You went into the kitchen, pulled down the huge steel family wok and drilled holes through it, holes that were as big and numerous as the sores on your behind. You left their home with a smile on your face.

For two months you drifted in the streets, leading a vagrant life, stealing here, digging things out of the garbage there. You were never very far from your natal home, though, and in the end you finally saw your withered- and spent-looking mother return to the area.

"Why didn't Daddy come back, too?" you asked, holding her hand as you walked.

"He'll be back in a few days." She held your hand and took you home.

"She's a bad woman, a shameless woman!" The older women in the neighborhood pointed at your mother and spoke behind her back.

Mother couldn't find work, so she spread a blanket on the ground to sell socks again. You wanted to help her but she knocked you on the side of the head, telling you to go back to school, study hard, go to college and vindicate her. You went back to school with tears in your eyes. Each day you saw how overworked your mother was, and each day you longed for your imprisoned father. Your heart was broken.

When your father was released from prison, he didn't come back home. He had formed a gang with some of the other prisoners and gone off to do business in another city upon release. He sent a letter saying that he would come back after making a lot of money. You began writing letters to your father telling him that you missed him, telling him that you would always love him.

You didn't know why your father had gone and killed someone. He promised that he would come back home to see you!

Mother took you with her to claim your father's body; you cried all the way there. The sky was black and a cold rain fell, soaking her hair and your clothes. You were so cold you shook. Your broken heart cried out, "Daddy, I want to take you home!"

Stumbling forward, you ran with uneven steps, your feet planted in the mud—deep one moment, shallow the next, though you were so exhausted you were barely able to move at all. Breathing heavily, your mother followed closely behind until you arrived at an execution ground, where you couldn't see a thing. On this stretch of undeveloped wasteland on the outskirts of the city there lay more than a dozen corpses with no family members to claim them. You and your mother moved your hands along the stiff bodies, searching for your father; you touched a misshapen face and your hand was drenched with putrid blood. You were so terrified that you began to cry, and your mother cried with you. The raindrops continued to fall; in the cold, your consciousness grew weaker and weaker.

You and your mother continued to feel among the corpses, but still you couldn't find your father. Suddenly your mother fainted. She was covered in mud and blood; you cried out in despair. Never again would your father hear your voice.

You supported your mother as you walked toward a faint light in the distance.

You stayed the night at the travel lodge that was closest to the execution ground.

You woke from a dream in tears, then closed your eyes and tried to go back to sleep. You dreamed of your father; his face was covered in blood and his half-open mouth called out. You lost your voice. It was all cried out.

At last it was daybreak. The sun crawled out from the coffin-like darkness and spit up a mouthful of blood.

You and your mother returned to the execution ground. Only five of the bodies that had been there the night before remained. All of their trousers had been removed, their reproductive organs—including those of your father—gone.

Again you cried, saying you had done your father wrong because you'd failed to keep watch over his cock.

EIGHT

1

A great fire shook the city. Overnight, the Zijing Flower Hotel was reduced to ashes.

"Oh, dear mother!" Little Wave cried in horror when he saw the ruins before him.

"Great, we're unemployed again!" Little Tough sighed.

And so they returned to the hiring site, where they found more unemployed migrant workers assembled than ever before. Two weeks passed and still they were unable to find work. Xiao Jiang, the server from the hotel, also appeared at the hiring site in search of a job. Little Wave and Little Tough saw him talking to another boy.

"The Zijing Flower Hotel fire case has been solved!" Xiao Jiang explained excitedly. "They say it was an inside job. A female server named Xiao Xia did it!"

"Wow!" the boy replied. "That girl's out of her mind! Why did she do it?"

"Vengeance! Xiao Xia did it because she wanted revenge against the manager! Good thing she set the fire after we got off work. If she hadn't, we might have burned up just like the building! Listen, Xiao Xia used to be my girlfriend! But ever since she and Manager Wang got together, we've drifted apart. Some say she got pregnant but Manager Wang wouldn't divorce that faded old wife of his. His wife comes from a powerful family, you know! One of them is on the Communist Party Central Committee!"

"I'm sure that bastard Manager Wang gave her a big belly, then decided he didn't want her anymore!" the boy stated confidently. "That's why she did it!"

"What about Xiao Xia?" Little Wave interjected. "Was she arrested?"

"She's dead!" Xiao Jiang replied. "She used gasoline to set herself on fire! Manager Wang owned that hotel—she used her own death to destroy his property! That sure was stupid of her."

Little Tough wasn't entirely satisfied with this explanation. "Well, what happened to Manager Wang?" he asked, knitting his brow. "Why didn't Xiao Xia kill him?"

"I heard he went to a different city to open up a new hotel!"

"How can he be that loaded?"

"He's got connections out there. When you have power, you have money!"

Another week passed and Ah Qing and Little Jade returned to the hiring site, where they bumped into Little Wave and Little Tough.

"You've lost weight, Ah Qing!" Little Wave said as he tugged at Ah Qing's hand warmly. "We haven't seen you in two years. Where have you guys been?"

"Little Jade and I went to Pingdingshan, Beijing, and Suzhou. It didn't take us long to learn that crows are equally black all over the world! Everywhere you go, it's illegal factories and black-hearted bosses. We've done odd jobs at restaurants and bookbinding at a print shop. We've worked as cleaners, movers, salesmen, servers, and security guards. We never got paid. All we ever got to eat at those black factories and all the other places was a lot of bitterness and injustice!" Ah Qing gave Little Tough a friendly pat on the butt.

"The four of us should split up and go look for work in the streets," said Little Wave. "Me and Little Tough have been standing here at this hiring site for more than twenty days. Every day there are fewer and fewer bosses, but more and more workers!" With a smile and a wave of the hand, he led everyone out to the street.

The four young guys headed off in different directions. North, south, east, and west, they traversed the city of Zhengzhou for an entire day. When darkness fell, they reunited at the agreed-upon spot: the February 7 Memorial Tower. Ah Qing, Little Jade, and Little Tough were the first to show up.

"All three of us have come back empty-handed!" one of them lamented. "Now we just have to wait for Little Wave to come back with some good luck!"

Little Wave approached the memorial tower with a bundle of rolled-up papers in his hand. "Oh man!" he exclaimed. "That was exhausting! How did it go? Did you all find something?"

The three boys shook their heads.

"Look you guys, look at these employment ads! They were posted on walls and lampposts." With a big laugh, Little Wave unrolled the paper advertisements and gave the boys a page each.

"These are all the same!" Ah Qing exclaimed after reading the ad. "You only needed to tear down one, Little Wave. Why did you get so many?"

"You don't get it!" Little Wave replied. "If I didn't tear all of them down, someone else would get the job! They were all wet when I swiped them! I ran all over the place—every time I saw one, I grabbed it!"

Little Jade read the ad aloud: "Red Plum Clothing Factory seeks ten sewers and six garment pressers. Skilled workers preferred, male or female. Address: Shakou Road."

"But we've never done that kind of work!" Ah Qing laughed bitterly.

"What's so hard about being a garment presser? Isn't it just ironing clothes with an iron?" Little Wave rolled the papers back up. "Anyway, I've already called the factory. I told them there's four of us and that we've all worked in garment factories."

The following day, the four boys showed up at Red Plum Clothing Factory. It was a privately owned factory run by a fat female boss in her early fifties. She had two sons that were just as fat as she, and they took turns supervising the workers. In order to get the job, the boys obediently handed over their identity cards. There were more than sixty workers there, male and female, and all of them were new arrivals. Few had any real skill in their jobs, and many of them were apprentices.

Along with the other new hires, Ah Qing, Little Jade, Little Wave, and Little Tough started working as junior pressers, gluing heavy strips of interfacing to collars, cuffs, and other parts of clothing items to give them weight and structure. After Ah Qing and Little Wave had done this for a few days, the boss moved them to another workroom, where they began pressing clothes with a steam iron.

Unless they worked overtime, all of the workers got off at midnight. That was when they would lay on their beds with sore waists and aching backs. After lying down, no one wanted to move again.

At 8 a.m. each morning a buzzer sounded, telling them that it was time for breakfast. Rubbing their sleep-deprived eyes, the sixty-plus workers would step out of the dormitories, then turn on the water faucets to wash their faces and brush their teeth. After that, they grabbed their meal tickets and metal food boxes and proceeded to the cafeteria to eat. The cook was a young guy around twenty years of age whom everyone called Xiao Gong. Each day, he prepared steamed buns, boiled vegetables, and made rice congee in a great big pot. The instant the minute hand passed 9 a.m., breakfast was no longer served.

There was no dining area inside the cafeteria, so after getting their food, some workers would return to their dorm rooms to eat. Others would go outside to an open lot beyond the factory door. There, they placed their bowls on the ground and squatted as they ate.

For breakfast the staples were steamed buns and deep-fried youtiao dough sticks. There was a limit on the number of youtiao workers could have—they could only use their meal tickets to get two each. Steamed buns were more plentiful, but sometimes the steamed buns that Xiao Gong made were hard and dark and grew sticky in one's mouth. Lunch staples were rice or noodles; these came with dishes like vermicelli with radish and bok choy. Occasionally, there would be a few small pieces of pork. When evening came, each worker had only a few bowls of boiled noodles. But although the food left much to be desired, at least the workers didn't go hungry.

Each morning when the workers lined up for breakfast, Xiao Gong would use his big ladle to fill their meal bowls with rice porridge, always with a smile on his face. Sometimes the female workers would call out "Enough! Enough!" When this happened, Xiao Gong would invariably continue to fill their bowls with his ladle. But if the male workers said this, Xiao Gong would stop immediately, laughing to himself as they walked away.

Breaks were very short, with hardly even enough time to engage in flirtatious banter.

2

"Girls, get to work!" the boss shouted as she walked into the sewing room.

"Guys, get to work!" the boss shouted as she walked into the ironing room.

"Boss, we have too much work to do! It's too much for two people!"

"That's right, boss! We couldn't even finish yesterday's work and today there's more coming at us. Give us one more person to work with us!"

"Pretty soon we'll hire some more workers for the factory —then you'll have some extra hands!" The boss turned and left.

Next, the boss entered the cutting room, where a fabric cutting machine screeched as it sliced ten layers of cloth. Three fabric cutters were hard at work, their foreheads drenched in beads of sweat.

"You need to use this time to work!" she called out. "Workers in other rooms are waiting for something to do!" She turned on her heel and returned to her office, where she burned a stick of incense to the God of Wealth.

It was 2 a.m. on the dot. The older of the boss's sons was in the workshop supervising workers who were doing overtime.

"I'm going to the bathroom!" Little Jade put down the iron he'd been using.

"Me too!" Little Tough put down his iron, too.

Ah Qing entered the bathroom, where he found Little Jade and Little Tough squatting on a couple of toilets, dozing. They looked terribly uncomfortable as they tried to sleep; Ah Qing wanted to wake them but didn't have the heart. He was also afraid that the boss would come in, catch them in their slumber and give them a round scolding. So he watched them sleep. Before long, however, he leaned against the bathroom door and himself nodded off for a while.

Together, Little Wave, Ah Qing, Little Jade, and Little Tough stepped into the boss's office.

"What is it?" She furrowed her eyebrows. They looked like leek leaves.

"Boss, there's something I need to take care of at home. Let me go back." Tufts of messy hair fell across Little Wave's weary forehead.

"Boss, there's something I need to take care of at home, too. I'm going back with Little Wave." Little Tough's eyes were red.

"Boss, I don't want to work anymore! It's too hot and I can't sleep at night." Ah Qing's voice was hoarse, his lips dry and cracked.

"Boss, I miss my mom! I want to go home!" Little Jade looked aggrieved and his nose twitched.

Angrily, the fat female boss jumped up from her seat and slapped the top of her desk with one hand while pointing at their noses with the other. Then she went into a tirade.

"*You*," she began, "were the ones who wanted to come here to begin with. I sure didn't ask you to come! When you got here you said you'd do *anything*. Turns out you *won't* do anything! I knew the four of you couldn't find work and weren't able to feed yourselves. I only took you in because I felt sorry for you! How could I have known you would be this ungrateful? So you want to go, huh? Go ahead, go! Go home! Go on, get out of here, I won't stop you!"

"Give us our wages, then we'll go!" Little Wave was getting so worked up that his face reddened.

"And our ID cards!" Ah Qing looked at the boss in anger.

"What? You're telling me you want your wages, too? I didn't even ask you for an apprentice fee! Not to mention the cost of you eating here every day!" The fat female boss grew increasingly explosive.

"How you can you be so black-hearted!" Little Jade said as he took a step toward her.

Little Tough gritted his teeth. "If you don't give us our wages and identity cards, we'll call 110!"

The fat female boss slammed her hand down again, causing the God of Wealth figurine on her desk to shake.

"How dare you? How dare you?" she shouted. "The four of you don't know a thing!" But then she suddenly grew calmer and tried reasoning with them. "Boys, try to see the position I'm in. Just when I need people the most, you decide you want to go! I'm not trying to stop you from going, but what can I do? If some go today, then some go tomorrow, what's going to happen to this factory? So stay here, guys, okay? Auntie begs you! Work here till the end of the year and I won't give you one less fen than you've earned. Okay? Alright?"

The boss patted their shoulders with a fat hand as she spoke, like a mother patting her precious sons.

In room 301 on the third floor, eight workers slept naked in their beds. Mosquitoes buzzed overhead, descending periodically to bite them.

"Fuck!" shouted Little Wave, swatting at the mosquitoes. "If we don't die from this heat, we'll be bitten to death by mosquitoes! That vampire of a boss still hasn't given us an electric fan!"

"I want to go home!" exclaimed Little Tough from the berth below Little Wave. "I can't take it anymore!"

"Me and Little Wave, our noses have been bleeding the last few days," exclaimed Ah Qing, who lay beside Little Wave. "Mine has bled twice today. If it keeps going on like this, there'll be no more blood left!"

"You and Little Wave should drink more soup," said Little Jade from the berth below Ah Qing. "Drinking soup helps reduce internal heat!"

"I already drink more than enough rice porridge, soup, tea, and water every day!"

"Ah Qing," Little Wave said. "Tomorrow morning, let's go get some sugar water from Xiao Gong!"

"All the sugar is reserved for management's food. Do you think Xiao Gong will give us any?"

"He'd better—if he doesn't, we'll knock him around a bit!"

It was early morning and breakfast was about to be served. Ah Qing woke up, his nasal passage and throat unbearably dry, arms and legs blistering with mosquito bites. He gave Little Wave a shove to wake him up.

"Hey!" Ah Qing said. "There's no one around. Now's our chance to ask Xiao Gong for some sugar!"

With light footsteps, Ah Qing and Little Wave slipped through the backdoor of the kitchen. The air swirled with big white clouds. There, on the other side of the kitchen, was Xiao Gong, the honest and hardworking young bachelor, jerking off into a pot of rice porridge. Ah Qing was about to yell something, but Little Wave covered his mouth, then pressed his lips against Ah Qing's ear. Ah Qing listened and nodded, and Little Wave exited the backdoor and ran to the boss's office.

Ah Qing was dumbstruck as he watched the smoke curl upward and Xiao Gong's purple cock continue to swell. Suddenly his own cock got hard. Without waiting for Little Wave to return with the boss, Ah Qing ran out of the kitchen and into the bathroom.

The boss entered the kitchen with Little Wave, and then walked toward Xiao Gong. Just as the boss reached him, the Red Plum Clothing Factory cook moaned loudly and ejaculated into the porridge.

3

"I don't know why, but not only did the boss not fire Xiao Gong—she gave him a raise!" Ah Qing lay on the bed, utterly perplexed.

"Let's leave this clothing factory today," said Little Wave. "If the boss still refuses to give us our wages and identity cards, we'll leak the information about how Xiao Gong let his bear fly into the porridge!"

The four boys stepped into the boss's office. "We're leaving!" they announced.

"Fine! Go!" the boss replied. "We won't force you to stay! But wages aren't calculated until the end of the year. That's our factory policy! Come back for them then." Her two sons stood at her side with arms folded.

"First give us our identity cards, then we'll talk!" Little Wave stuck out his hand.

"What identity cards? When you guys came here, I saw with my own eyes that we gave them back to you!"

"No you didn't! You locked them in a drawer!" Ah Qing pointed at the boss's desk.

"Fine then, I'll open the drawer and let you look for them yourself!" She unlocked the drawer, then pulled out dozens of identity cards, which she began going through one by one. "I told you they're not here, and they're not! You guys lose them, then come over here and try to blackmail me!"

Little Wave smashed his fist on the table. "Give us our wages and identity cards right now!"

Like a couple of wild dogs, the sons grabbed hold of the four boys and pushed them out the office door while the boss hurled abuses at them like a shrew.

In anguish, Ah Qing and the others ran out of the clothing factory and toward a newsstand, where they used the little red phone perched at the window to dial 110. When the police answered, Ah Qing told them that a boss had withheld his wages and identity card. The person on the phone told him to go directly to the local police station. Out of the corner of his eye, Ah Qing suddenly spotted the telephone number for a news hotline printed on a copy of the *Zhengzhou Daily*. Instead of going to the local police, he hung up the phone, then lifted the receiver again and dialed the hotline number.

"What news ya got?" A journalist answered the phone.

"We're working at a clothing factory and the boss has withheld our wages and identity cards!" Ah Qing shouted into the phone.

"That's not news, it happens all the time!" the journalist replied. "Go talk to the Labor Bureau!" He hung up.

Ah Qing put down the receiver and paced back and forth along Shakou Road. Just then, he spotted a familiar figure walking toward him.

"Seventh Brother!" he shouted.

When Seventh Brother saw Ah Qing, he grabbed him happily. Ah Qing could smell the alcohol on him. The boys told Seventh Brother the entire story of how a clothing-factory boss had withheld their wages and identity cards.

"Fuck! They have the nerve to open a black factory on my doorstep? Let's go! If they don't pay up I'll burn their factory down!" Seventh Brother tugged at Ah Qing's shoulder and off they all went.

Seventh Brother was a local ruffian—the boss's sons actually knew him! When they got back to the factory with him, the boss admitted that she herself had lost the workers' identity cards. She gave them one hundred yuan each as compensation, and said that at the end of the year Seventh Brother could come and collect their wages on their behalf. Finally, the boss gave them a wage advance of one hundred yuan each so that they would be able to return home. The boys left the factory and walked along the street holding two hundred yuan each. The money had been hard-won only by suffering a good deal of humiliation.

"Hey Ah Qing, Little Wave, Little Tough, Little Jade," Seventh Brother said warmly. "Come to my place for dinner!"

To thank Seventh Brother for his help, the boys stopped to buy him a few gifts on the way to his home.

"Little Orchid!" Seventh Brother shouted the instant they walked through the door. "Look who's here!"

"Hey, it's you guys!" Holding Little Dragon in her arms, Little Orchid smiled as she held open the door. "Welcome!"

The four unlucky lads returned to the hiring site, where they waited among the tightly packed crowd. Finally, a boss approached them.

"Wei! You guys looking for work?"

"Yes! What kind of workers do you need?"

"We're a moving company. How many of you are there? You have identity cards, yeah?"

"There's four of us, boss," one of the boys replied.

"Boss!" exclaimed another. "About our IDs. When we left home we forgot to bring them. But we're all honest and we've all worked at moving companies."

"The four of you are together?" the boss asked skeptically. "How could not a single one of you have brought your ID?"

"Look at us, boss—do we look like bad people? We really did forget our IDs!"

"Try us out for a few days, boss. We are absolutely reliable!"

The boss shook his head and walked away.

"That damned factory boss has really screwed us over! Without identity cards no one will hire us." Ah Qing watched the boss disappear into the crowd.

Little Jade sighed grimly. "Forget it, Ah Qing. Let's go home."

"Now is not the time to go home! The wheat has just been harvested. It doesn't make sense for us to go home right now!"

"I agree," Little Wave said with a squeeze to Little Jade's hand. "Besides, we haven't made any money. "For better or worse, we have to make it to the end of the year. Then we can finally go back to that black factory and get paid." He gripped Little Jade's hand tightly.

"I no longer have faith in coming out to work," Little Tough said. "There's not a single boss out there whose heart isn't black as coal. If we find work, we're slaves. If we don't, we're human scum." He lowered his head and gazed at his dirty feet.

"Don't be so pessimistic, Little Tough," Ah Qing said, doing his best to console him. "We're still young, and youth is capital. Youth is hope!"

At that moment, a young beggar walked by and stretched out a filthy hand. "Big Brother," he said, "please pity me. I can't find work and I can't get home. I haven't eaten in days."

"Go, get out of here!" Little Wave shooed the beggar away. "We don't have work either!"

The young beggar gave no indication that he intended to leave, but continued pestering them in the most abject way. Eventually Little Jade's heart went soft. He pulled a half-eaten piece of leftover bread from his bag and gave it to the beggar.

Just then, the crowd surged forward and surrounded two people, a man and a woman.

"Wei! Hey boss, what kind of workers are you looking for?" someone from the crowd called out.

"Workshop workers," replied the male boss.

"Workshop workers!" repeated the female boss.

"What do you mean, workshop workers?" everyone asked. "What are the job requirements?"

"Workshop workers are workers who work in workshops. We're looking for young people."

"Excuse me, boss, but where is the factory?"

"Western outskirts of the city!"

"Hey, boss!" Little Wave said, stepping forward. "Our identity cards were withheld by a black factory we worked at. Do you really need them?"

"As long as a person is honest, it's okay not to have an identity card!" the female boss said with a smile.

Ah Qing, Little Jade, and Little Tough stepped forward to join Little Wave. The female boss looked at the four boys, the smile never leaving her face. "You guys sure look ready to go!" she said cheerfully. "We'll take every one of you!"

"Anyone else want to come and be a workshop worker?" the male boss called out. "Twenty kuai a day! We welcome Sichuanese brothers, as well as anyone who can work hard and tough it out!"

"We provide room and board! Each person gets twenty kuai per day! Step right up and sign up!" The female boss's voice rang out sweetly, seducing the hungry crowd.

Ah Qing took hold of Little Wave's hand and pulled him to one side. "Little Wave, do you think they could be con artists, too? Jobs from the hiring site don't go for more than two hundred a month!"

"Good people are few and far between these days," Little Tough replied with eyes that were only half open. "There are a lot of bad people out there, but they're not going to advertise that they're bad! You have to guard against others. I don't have any faith in these two either, but even if we end up as their

164

slaves, it would be better than staying here and being beggars and human scum!"

Ah Qing laughed. "Don't be so fucking pessimistic, Little Tough! Working at a black factory has really worn your spirit down. If you end up at another one, it could make you crazy!"

"At this point, I wish I would go crazy! I'd be better off that way!"

"If you really want to go crazy," Little Wave said with a pat to Little Tough's butt, "then take off your pants and run around the hiring site naked!"

"I'm not going to go streaking through this cattle market!" Little Tough laughed bitterly. "If I was going to streak somewhere, I'd do it in Tian'anmen Square!"

4

Xiao An drove his motorized trike, specially designed for disabled users, into the railway station. A police officer shouted out to him, then brought him to a halt.

"Are you aware that the city has a new regulation?" the officer demanded. "You can't drive this kind of tricycle in the railway station anymore."

"Okay!" Xiao An replied. "I won't come in again!"

"Not so fast!" the officer said sternly. "First you pay a fine, then you can go."

Xiao An got off his vehicle and hobbled over to the officer. With a big smile, he offered the man a cigarette.

"Don't give me that routine!" the cop scoffed. "Pay the fine, right now!"

"How much is it, Comrade Police Officer?" Xiao An looked at him imploringly.

"A hundred yuan!"

"A hundred yuan?! Comrade Police Officer! I don't make that much in two weeks! I'm disabled—please take that into consideration!"

"Fine! I can see you're in a sorry state. Just give me fifty, then. And remember, don't come driving this kind of vehicle into the railway station ever again!"

"Right, right! Next time I won't come in!" Xiao An handed the officer fifty yuan, then stuck out his hand for a receipt. The officer turned on his heel and walked away.

"Comrade Police Officer! You forgot to give me a receipt!" Xiao An called out anxiously.

The officer turned around. "You want a receipt? If you want a receipt then give me a hundred!"

Xiao An hurriedly climbed back onto his motor trike and sped off.

Inside a room, a woman with a face covered in fly shit held an emaciated child with whom she played now and then. A fuming Xiao An sat on the bed. He launched into a tirade about the police officer.

"If you can't make any money with your passenger trike," his new wife said when he finished his rant, "we need to think of another way!"

"I'm disabled!" he cried. "Apart from driving my tricycle, what can I do?" He lowered his head in anguish.

"Listen," the woman began. "Back when I was sold to that village in Hebei Province, the villagers always spoke of a place called Happy Village. People went there to buy counterfeit money. One yuan of real money bought ten yuan of fake money. I know where Happy Village is. It's in a very remote area. No one takes care of the crops anymore so the fields are a wasteland, and yet all the families there are rich! No one farms anymore; instead, everyone's bought printers so they can secretly print one-yuan and five-mao notes. The largest denomination they make is two yuan. Anything larger than that is hard to spend."

"If you get caught doing that you'll go to prison!" Xiao An exclaimed.

"You won't get caught if you're careful! And even if we're caught, buying isn't as big a crime as printing! The counterfeiters at Happy Village print money day and night and they're not afraid, so what is there for us to be afraid of?"

Xiao An passed the child to his younger sister Little Lotus, then went outside and drove his motor trike to Happy Village, his new wife pointing the way.

Happy Village was seemingly deserted with not a single person in sight. A group of dogs roamed freely and howled, happily copulating in the streets.

Xiao An's wife knocked on each door in the village. Finally, a woman answered.

"Who are you looking for?" the woman asked.

"We've come to barter," Xiao An's wife replied. "We want to trade the contents of this burlap sack!"

"Are you sure you're not lost?" the woman asked, incredulous.

Xiao An intervened. "Let's go, wife!"

The woman persisted with her questions. "Where are you from?"

"Henan."

"Go into the cornfield," the woman said, pointing. "You can look over there." Then she shut the door.

Hobbling along on his crippled leg, Xiao An followed his wife, who kept leaning back to whisper in his ear.

In the unkempt cornfield, weeds grew with straight backs. Four or five women carrying baskets were busy cutting wild grass. Xiao An's wife carried her burlap sack full of pig feed and looked around, trying to find whoever it was that was supposed to meet her. Two migrant men from a different province held bags. They were engaged in some sort of transaction with a couple of women who also had burlap sacks.

The woman who had answered the door entered the cornfield. She, too, had a burlap sack.

"I'm over here!" Xiao An's wife whispered as loudly as she could.

The woman came over, the heavy sack secured to her back, and then dropped it onto the earth. "Did you bring enough money?" she asked quietly.

Xiao An's wife handed a thousand yuan of real money to the woman, who snatched it and began counting rapidly. Nonchalantly, she pulled a note from the stack and rubbed it against her face several times. Then she stuffed the entire wad into her undershirt pocket.

"This whole bag is for you," she said. "It's all two-yuan notes. If you want to exchange again, come back to this spot."

Suddenly, from deeper inside the cornfield, came the voices of several police officers. "Halt! Don't move!"

Everyone lifted their feet in flight as the cops spread out to chase them.

Xiao An's wife picked up the bag and ran through the cornfield, weaving in and out of the stalks. When she turned to look she saw a young policeman close to her heels. Hastily she threw down the bag, then dropped her pants, got on her knees and stuck her ass in the air.

When the young policeman saw Xiao An's wife's ass perched up high, when he saw that quivering asshole, he immediately closed his eyes and became unable to move! The cop couldn't help it; he squatted on the ground and vomited.

Again Xiao An's wife picked up the bag and ran, making her way into an even denser area of cropland. Before long she was back at her husband's side. They stuffed the bag into Xiao An's motor trike and sped off along the small country road. When the sun set, the stars and electric lamps were the only lights that remained.

"Nai Nai, I'm hungry, I want milk! Nai Nai, I'm hungry, I want milk!" A boy—a young man, really—cried outside for his grandmother. He was around twenty years of age.

Little Lotus pushed open the door and looked outside, where she saw a stupid-looking boy a little more than a meter and a half in height. The old landlady's door suddenly opened all the way. A large speckled cat meowed and jumped out.

"Oh, my Little Treasure!" the old landlady exclaimed when she saw the boy standing outside. "Nai Nai's good grandson! Come in! Nai Nai will give you some milk."

The boy hopped through the door of the old landlady's house.

"Hey, Little Chrys!" Little Lotus asked. "Who is this stupid boy?"

"The old landlady's grandson. Over twenty years old and every day he cries for his grandma to give him milk: 'Nai Nai, I want milk! Nai Nai, I want milk!' Their family must have done something really bad or they wouldn't have given birth to such an idiot!"

Little Lotus laughed. "Didn't you say you wanted a rich husband? I'll play matchmaker and set you up with him. In his family, money and power come easy!"

"Oh, drop dead!" Little Chrys punched her on the arm. "As if I would marry a stupid boy like this!"

After Little Lotus and Little Chrys became unemployed, they spent several days wandering the streets and looking somewhat halfheartedly for work. It was nighttime when they finally returned to Courtyard No. 8. As they passed the entrance to Sister Plum Blossom's Hair Salon, they saw that a light was on and music was playing.

They retired to the room they shared and lay on a double bed.

"I was with that guy two nights in a row and he never came back!" Little Chrys grumbled. "What do I do now?"

"It's not like you lost out from it!" Little Lotus replied. "He bought you clothes and gave you money, didn't he?"

"He was so generous; I thought he really liked me! That's the only reason I gave him my first time."

"Who cares? Just go find someone else! Listen, I've got it all figured out. Women will never make any money unless they learn to be bad."

"Let's go talk to the boss at Sister Plum Blossom's Hair Salon. She might be able to help us make some money!"

They went to Sister Plum Blossom's Hair Salon and overnight began living the life of a prostitute.

5

"Seventh Brother," Little Orchid said to her husband, "the old landlady told me that her son loves potted landscapes. He's the director of the Public Security Bureau! Let's pick the two best penjing that we have and give them to him. If we need anything further down the road, we can ask them for help!"

"Little Orchid," Seventh Brother replied, "I may be poor, but I don't suck up to anyone. My older brother and his wife look down on me—well, I look down on them too! It's just a little stinking money, right? What's so great about that? But I know you're working as a maid for the old landlady now, so I understand how you feel. If you want to give her son a couple of penjing, then go ahead."

With that, Seventh Brother hopped on his creaking bicycle and rode off to work.

After Little Orchid lulled Little Dragon off to sleep, she stepped out the front door, locked it, and then jumped onto the family's flatbed tricycle and pedaled her way to Courtyard No. 8. The old landlady had already made herself breakfast. When Little Orchid arrived, the old landlady acted as though she hadn't noticed and proceeded to feed the big speckled cat.

"I'm sorry I'm late, Nai Nai!" Little Orchid said, wiping beads of sweat from her forehead. "I heard Uncle Director likes potted landscapes, so I brought him two of ours. Seventh

Brother has been tending them for years—they're the best ones in our home!"

"Ah, Little Orchid! Have a seat and wipe the sweat off!" The old landlady's face switched from grim to cheerful. "Look," she continued, "I was just feeding the cat!" She stood with a smile and walked over to the open door to see the two potted landscapes sitting on the flatbed of the tricycle parked outside. Then she got her director son on the phone and told him to come pick up the gift.

"Little Orchid!" the old landlady said after hanging up. "I know you've still got a little one at home. If it weren't for all your life hardships, how could you possibly toss your own child aside to come out and be a maid? So listen, from now on, don't worry about coming here to make breakfast. I'll just go out and have a bowl of pepper spice soup or tofu pudding! When you come here, just help out with some clothes washing and cleaning, and that'll be enough!" She smiled, exposing two gleaming white row of dentures.

"Nai Nai, what kind of tree is this?" the stupid child called out from the courtyard.

"Don't bump into that, Little Treasure! That's for your father!" The old landlady lowered her small, bound feet to the floor and scurried out of the bedroom.

A police vehicle drove past the entrance to Sister Plum Blossom's Hair Salon. The driver slowed down and yelled out the window, "How's business, Little Plum Blossom, pretty good?" Sister Plum Blossom waved and cast him a smile, but said nothing in reply. A few minutes later, she watched in envy as the old landlady's Public Security Bureau director son drove off triumphantly with the two penjing.

"Sister Plum Blossom," Little Chrys began. She and Little Lotus were sitting on the couch of the hair salon. "The old landlady has raised two sons and both of them turned out to be officials. But she also has a stupid boy for a grandson—who knows what kind of horrible things she must have done to

171

deserve it?" Little Chrys shelled a long succession of sunflower seeds as she spoke. There wasn't a single customer in the salon.

Sister Plum Blossom sighed loudly. "Life is hard for people in our profession! No children to come visit you when you're old. So you'd better listen to what I say, Little Chrys and Little Lotus: As soon as you find a reliable man, marry him and have a kid! Don't be like your Sister Plum Blossom! I'm over forty now—no man is going to want me."

"But Sister Plum Blossom still looks young!" Little Lotus replied as she sat before a mirror to brush her hair. "You only look a little over thirty. Who knows? Maybe one day you'll meet a rich guy!"

The old landlady stepped into Sister Plum Blossom's Hair Salon, a speckled cat cradled in her arms. "Little Plum Blossom!" she called out. "Time to give me next month's rent!"

"Relax, Auntie Landlady, I would never fall behind in rent! I've got it right here for you." She reached into her wallet and pulled out the money as she spoke, then handed it to the old landlady, who immediately sat on the couch and began counting. Sister Plum Blossom reached out to pick up the speckled cat, whom she wanted to hold, but the creature suddenly jumped from the old landlady's knee onto the vanity dresser. There it spied a speckled cat in the mirror, which it began to woo with imploring meows.

"Come here, kitty! Meow, meow!" The old landlady placed the rent money in her undershirt pocket.

The speckled cat ignored the old landlady and instead pressed its face up against the mirror, causing the old landlady to laugh in amusement. When Sister Plum Blossom came over and slapped the top of the vanity dresser, the cat finally snapped out of its daydream. With a screech, it jumped off the dresser and onto the floor, where it began running about wildly, evidently scared out of its wits.

"Catch that cat, Auntie Landlady!" Sister Plum Blossom cried. "We're trying to do business around here!"

"Good kitty!" The old landlady said. "Now come back home with me." Slowly she bent down and implored the cat to listen to her.

Sister Plum Blossom was running out of patience, so she stepped into her personal living quarters in the back of the salon. There, she pushed open a glass door covered with bright, decorative paper and peeked inside.

Inside the room, behind a screen of white cloth, one shadow stirred atop another. Without warning, the speckled cat squeezed into the room from between Sister Plum Blossom's feet. When she accidentally stepped on its tail, it screeched and jumped into the air, then began crawling up the white screen. She tried to catch it, but the animal took a flying leap and landed directly on a bare ass which had by now stopped moving. From behind the screen, one heard the voice of a man cursing, then one of the shadows jumped up off the other and a naked man came running out. When he saw Sister Plum Blossom and the old landlady standing in the doorway, he retreated to the other side of the screen to put some clothes on. As he turned his back to the two women, they saw that his buttocks were covered in large, red scratch marks from the cat's claws.

Sister Plum Blossom couldn't help but burst into laughter. It only took the old landlady a moment to figure out what was going on; when she did, she laughed, too.

"Damned cat! Get out of here!" From behind the white cloth screen came the voice of Little Chrys.

An old man stepped into Sister Plum Blossom's Hair Salon.

"Welcome, customer!" She greeted him. "What kind of service do you need, sir?"

"I want to get my head buzzed and my face shaved!"

"I'm sorry, sir, but our clippers are broken today and we haven't had time to repair them!"

"Well, in that case, I'll just get a shave."

"I'm truly sorry, sir! But we also need to sharpen our razor. I'm afraid you'll have to go to another salon."

"I'm not in a big hurry," the man replied. "Take your time sharpening the razor and when you're done I'll get the shave."

"Sir, I really am very sorry, but the shifu who sharpens our razor isn't coming today!"

The old man got up from the salon chair in a huff and left.

"Geez! Damn old-timer!" Sister Plum Blossom fumed when he was gone. "Thinks all he has to do is dish out a few kuai and this old broad will wait on him all day long? Hell no!"

Little Chrys and Little Lotus were walking along the street when they noticed that a long line of people had formed outside the entrance of a newly opened pharmacy.

"How can there be so many people there? Is there some kind of cheap medicine they're buying?" Little Lotus craned her neck to get a better view of the front door.

"Go ahead and get in line, girls!" An old lady with white hair beamed at them. "National Day is right around the corner —to celebrate, this pharmacy is giving everyone a free box of medicine!"

All manner of people stood in the long line: young guys and gals, middle-aged folks, some with glasses, some without, old men and women with hair that was completely or partially white.

"But what kind of medicine is it?" Little Chrys asked. "If we don't need it, there's no reason for us to get in line!" She squeezed her way to the front.

"Who cares what kind of medicine it is?" Little Lotus replied, and she pushed Little Chrys forward. "If we don't need it, we can give it to someone else!"

Disorderly cries erupted from the crowd.

"Hey, stop pushing!"

"Ow! Someone stepped on my shoe and it fell off!"

At this point, there were still about a dozen people ahead of the girls. An elderly gentleman who was panting rather heavily pressed up against Little Chrys's back. The line behind him was still quite long.

A young man emerged triumphantly from the pharmacy, a box of medicine in his hand. Little Chrys and Little Lotus watched as the people in line ahead of them grabbed boxes that read, "Golden Gun 'Keep It Up' Pill." Exploding in laughter, they quit the long line of patients and continued on their way.

NINE

1

When your Lao Lao become pregnant with your mother, your mother already had four older sisters. When Lao Lao's father-in-law saw that his daughter-in-law had given birth to yet another girl, he beat her. It wasn't long before the old man went crazy and died off, and it was all because your Lao Lao had failed to give the Hu family a son. By the time your mother was born, her oldest sister had already married. Your oldest aunt's son was just one year younger than your mother.

Just when your mother was old enough to start remembering things, she stepped into the main room of the family's thatched cottage and found her paternal grandmother hanging from the ceiling, her tongue sticking out of her mouth. Your mother's childhood was a nightmare, and so was your father's. After your parents married and had you, your life was a nightmare, too.

You recalled from childhood that your parents had gone against tradition: After marriage, your father went to live with your mother's family, instead of she going to live with his. In those days and in that village, men who did this were looked down upon. To avoid being looked down upon, your father went here and there helping people however he could, always speaking with sweet words. But he never gave you a happy childhood. In your dreams you saw your parents fighting. Their fights tore your dreams to shreds.

Once when your parents were fighting, your father picked up a bottle of fertilizer with one hand and grabbed hold of you with the other. With tears in his eyes, he cried out, "My poor child! Your father is going to die now. I can't bear to leave you!"

Your father never did try to kill himself, not even once, but he cried constantly. When your mother got angry she would hit her own face; you feared her. Her fierce hands would hit her face until it swelled up. When your father wasn't busy crying, he was always off helping people with a smile—relatives, neighbors or friends, people in the village he knew well, people outside the village he had just met. He gave all of his smiles to others, but when he came home he'd always enter battle with your mother all over again. He never raised a hand to hit her; nor did she ever hit him. Most of the time when she fell into a rage she just hit herself; sometimes she would hit you and your older sister, too.

Your Lao Lao had extremely low self-esteem, and your Lao Ye—her husband—was constantly afflicted with ailments. She was already seventy by the time you were able to remember anything, and her tiny bound feet were wrapped in layers of blue cloth. Sometimes you watched Lao Lao as she unwrapped the cloth, revealing a set of disfigured toes that looked like tiny clamshells.

Lao Lao said that when she had been married off to Lao Ye, her parents did not give the groom's family a dowry. She had been given away when she was little, more or less like the child brides one saw in the movies. Lao Lao said she had a younger brother who had once been pressganged and dragged off by the Guomindang army; she worried about him even as she lay dying. Lao Lao said that she had given birth to a son, but the boy died when he was just two years old. She wanted to cry, but her husband wouldn't let her; he said there was no reason to cry, for his younger brother's wife had given birth to a son right around the same time. Your Lao Lao hated this nephew and kept all of her tears locked inside. Lao Lao also told you that she and your Lao Ye had arranged your mother's marriage. This caused your mother to hate them for the rest of her life.

Your mother was a seamstress and a real village powerhouse. Her feet were huge: she wore size-forty shoes just like your father. Your mother's shifu had been the wife of the village hospital director. This director's wife had taken in several female apprentices, but your mother was the only one who learned the trade well enough to strike out on her own, for she had attended school through the fifth grade. Her sister apprentices, on the other hand, had almost no education whatsoever. Back in those days, there was never enough to eat!

2

The sun was about to set on another dying day. You were resting against Lao Lao's breast, listening to her stories as you gently drifted into the world of dreams. You didn't like your paternal grandmother—your Nai Nai—and her sister, you thought sleepily as your Lao Lao held you in her arms. Before long, however, you were awakened by shouts and cries. At first you thought it was your parents fighting again, but you soon realized that it was your third aunt and her husband arguing as they returned to Lao Lao's house. Your mother's third older sister had been given away when she was little, so when you were born your mother's fourth older sister became your third aunt. This third aunt had sung opera for a few years, snagging the female lead in a stage production of *The Jade Bottle of Desired Temperatures*. She began to cry; the sound of her crying was much better than that of her singing, but you didn't like hearing it in the middle of the night. You would have preferred to hear her cry during the day.

"Have some apple, Little Tough!" With a smile, an old woman handed you several big, round apples from a bamboo basket.

"Little Tough, hurry and take your great aunt's apples." Your Lao Lao laughed sweetly.

You took an apple from Lao Lao's sister—you called her Lao Lao, too—and ate it with big bites.

After you ate the apple you went with your two Lao Laos past a field and then past a small river, beyond which you saw a patch of weed-covered graves. Your Lao Laos started to cry, and as soon as they did you became frightened. They told you that these were your great-grandparents' graves.

Once again it began to rain, causing water to leak from the roof. Tables as well as the floor were covered with basins, jars, and bowls for capturing water.

After the rain, your parents went into the fields and got to work picking cotton, then brought gunnysacks packed with soft white tufts encased in protective shells back to the house. The cotton inside the black and somewhat rotten husks were of a gray or pale yellow color; day and night, the entire family was at work breaking them apart with fingers and thumbs. You watched as the oil crept closer to the base of the bottle; father filled it up again. You hated this endless work and often cried to go to bed because you were only five or six years old. Your mother, however, cleverly concocted a way to keep you working: she promised that for every bamboo basket of cotton shells that you broke apart, she'd give you two fen. And so, in order to earn Mother's money, you kept breaking them apart. After an entire day and night of work, you finally managed to earn one mao. Sometimes, however, your mother didn't make good on her promise, or she paid you less than the agreed upon amount, and this made you cry. When Mother was angry, not only would she not pay you, she'd hit and scold you too.

You had been afraid of the dark since you were little, but you also hated lamplight, which reminded you that you were expected to work. You looked forward to rainy days and hoped it would rain forever so that the cotton in the earth would become soaked and mushy and you wouldn't have to do a thing. You loved winter, loved snowy days, because as soon as snow fell you knew that winter had arrived, and when winter arrived Spring Festival would be coming soon, and when Spring Festival came you were given New Year money without having to work for it. Ever since you were little you had loved money; when you slept you dreamed of long rows of coins in the streets which you would bend down to pick up.

When you were seven, you attended elementary school.

The school bell rang, alerting the village that class would be starting shortly; you remained standing in the doorway of your home pestering your mother for money to buy a pencil. A pencil cost only two fen in those days, but your mother still made you beg for it and it was only after you had bawled many times that she finally gave you the money.

"You still haven't used up the pencil you have now!" she scolded. "You want to destroy a pencil after just a few days— why don't you go break your own fingers instead?"

Your father never asked you how things were at school, nor did he pay any attention to the household finances.

It rained once more and once more the school and streets were deluged with mud. Everywhere you looked, parents holding umbrellas were bringing their children to school, but not once had either of your parents seen you off or picked you up. When school was over you stood outside under the eaves of the building; when the rain subsided, you held your shoes in your arms and ran home barefoot.

"Ma, give me five fen, okay? I used up all the pages in my homework notebook."

"Show it to me," she demanded, looking at you sternly.

You knew that one lie was all it would take to get yourself whacked in the head. You pulled the notebook from your schoolbag and showed her all the crooked characters you had written for homework.

"The fronts of the pages are all filled up, but why haven't you written on the backs? Write on the backs of the pages, then we'll talk!" Mother turned and walked off.

"Our teacher doesn't let us write on the backs of the pages!" you cried out in tears as she disappeared.

From then on you wrote on the verso pages of the notebook. When you needed money, you'd pull the notebook out for your mother to examine, then she'd give you five fen to go buy a new one. You hid the notebook for the rest of the semester, pulling it out again and again to show her. Mother never remembered, as her mind was fixated on one thing and one thing only: making money. Night after night she worked overtime, sewing clothes for people.

Another autumn, another autumn rain. More gunnysacks of cotton were picked and brought home by your father. Your mother made you earn your own money to buy pencils and notebooks. You had no choice but to break apart enough cotton to fill two baskets; you hid the money that you made under your pillow.

In class the teacher lectured. You watched as the mouth at the front of the room moved, then put your pencil in your own mouth and bit it. Your grades at school had always been shit and you failed every exam. As long as you weren't at the absolute bottom of your class, your mind would be at ease.

Back home, you entered the bathroom after your mother came out, and you saw a roll of bloody tissues in the toilet. It scared you so badly that you ran out of the bathroom. You hated sharing a toilet with your mother, so you often ran out to the cornstalks at the side of the road to piss and shit. When your father saw the way you kept running outside to defecate, he scolded you, saying that you were giving away your shit for free.

So you began to force yourself to crap in the toilet at home. Why didn't your mother go bury her bloody tissues in the dirt outside? It was always your father who buried them for her.

You heard loud cries coming from the family dog in the courtyard, so you wiped your ass against the wall and ran out of the bathroom to take a look. When you saw that female dog with a male dog from another household, their two hinds stuck together as if growing out of one another, you picked up a big stick and went to beat the male.

Once when you were fourteen years old, you were climbing a tree when you suddenly felt all the cells in your body jump about in pleasure.

You went to Little Wave's house to play, and there it was that you found him all alone secretly playing with his chicken! He spit a glob of saliva into the palm of his hand and rubbed it all over his stiffening, swelling cock, then moved his hand up and down along the shaft. In stealth you ran to hide among the stacks of wheat straw outside the village to practice what you had seen him doing. That's how you learned to masturbate.

You and Little Wave lay in bed together jerking off, and decided to see who could shoot the farthest! Little Wave's semen flew into the air and splattered against the wall, startling a little gecko, which fell off the wall and onto the floor, then scampered away.

It was evening on a summer day and you hid once more among stacks of wheat straw to masturbate. Just as you were approaching the gates of paradise, you heard a cough; the sound pulled you back to this world. You looked up and saw your harelipped Nai Nai looking at you with eyes that were as hungry as a wolf's. "Little Tough," she screeched, "you listen to your Nai Nai! And if you don't, I'll tell everyone in the village . . . " A wave of terror came over you; you felt as though you had done something shameful. Lowering your head before your harelipped Nai Nai, you waited to see how she would deal with the offense.

"Little Tough is a good boy—now you listen to your Nai Nai!" This harelipped grandmother, forty years your senior, climbed right on top of you, then reached out her withered, dried-up tree-bark hands, grabbed hold of your penis and stuffed it inside her dark hole. Following her instructions, you lasted until the very end!

"Little Tough," she began when it was all over, "meet me here every Wednesday and Saturday night. And if you don't, I'll tell the entire village about the disgusting things you've done!" Your harelipped Nai Nai tied the drawstring of her waistband and disappeared, and you ran like the wind back home.

"Little Tough, wait for me here every Tuesday, Thursday and Saturday night. And if you don't, I'll tell the entire village about the disgusting things you've done!" Your harelipped Nai Nai tied the drawstring of her waistband and disappeared. Slowly you walked back home.

You started having nightmares about your harelipped old Nai Nai raping you. She said she'd let you go after you got married.

You were raped by your grandmother for two years. By the time you were sixteen, you despised her. You began looking for ways to get revenge.

After searching through eight villages in a ten-li radius, a woman matchmaker plucked a stupid wife for one of your son-of-a-bitch uncles—one of Nai Nai's sons. When the new couple went to get their marriage license, the official asked them how old they were. Wiping snot from her nose with a corner of her husband's Western-style wedding suit, the stupid woman replied, "My ma says I'm twenty-eight!"

On the day of the son of a bitch's wedding ceremony, Little Wave took you by the hand to go watch all the excitement. Your harelipped Nai Nai spotted you in the crowd, then grabbed a handful of the wedding candy that was everywhere to give to you. You rejected it, so she forced it into your pocket, then hissed in your ear: "See you tonight. Same place."

Children covered their ears as firecrackers exploded, waiting for a chance to pick up any unignited ones that might have been left on the ground. After a long, red string of them had burst, you rushed forward to grab a paper firecracker that was the shape of a tube and as thick as the handle of a shovel. Watching the gray smoke twist its way upward, you put the explosive into your pocket.

"Light the fuse, Little Tough, I want to hear it!" Little Wave ran after you.

"Not right now," you replied, and you handed him the candy that your harelipped Nai Nai had stuffed into your pocket.

"Why don't you want this candy?" he asked in surprise. But you didn't answer, you just ran off quickly.

Once again you arrived punctually at the place where you and your Nai Nai always met. You watched as she smugly untied her pants, then spread two big thighs that looked like a couple of toads as she waited for you to enter her. As if guided by a supernatural force, you pulled the tube from your pocket and stuffed it deep inside Nai Nai's dark hole, then lit the fuse. You turned and ran in the opposite direction just in time to hear the muffled explosion behind you.

Your harelipped Nai Nai was paralyzed and confined to bed after that. Her stupid new daughter-in-law attended to her.

None of the villagers knew what had happened, but rumor circulated that your Nai Nai had had a run-in with a ghost. You grew restless. The day you turned sixteen you got your identity card, then left the village with Little Wave to drift and work in the outside world.

4

After leaving the black factory, you went to work at a travel hostel. Each day, your job was to clean all the rooms with a broom and mop. Often you had to dispose of the many used condoms that were always left there.

The boss was terribly stingy. The travel hostel had three floors, yet you were the only service employee! You worked each day from early morning until late at night—no Sundays off, and no vacations. However, at the end of the month your wages were always paid on time: just two hundred sixty kuai per month. You figured you would work until the end of the year, then become a street peddler. You would spread a blanket on the ground and sell pirated books, or maybe shoes and socks; you could also sell things like fruits and vegetables.

You grabbed a set of keys and led a group of migrant workers upstairs, then unlocked an eight-person dorm room and told them to go inside. This, you told them, was your cheapest room!

After the migrant workers entered the room, one of the older ones detained you to ask a question. "Excuse me," he inquired, "how far are we from the city courthouse?"

"Go west and it's about three or four li away," you replied. You figured that they had probably come to the city to try and sue someone. Just about every day, the travel hostel received lodgers arriving with letters of complaint that they wished to deliver to the authorities. You grabbed the keys again and led a pair of new arrivals, two injured migrant workers, upstairs.

"There are no more big rooms available!" you told them. "Is this four-person room okay?"

"How much per person per night?" the injured workers asked, poking their heads into the room.

"Fifteen kuai!"

"That's too much! We don't have that much money! Can you do ten?"

"Go back down to the registration office and ask the boss." You followed the injured workers with your eyes as they walked back downstairs.

A few minutes later, they came back and stepped into the four-person room. You didn't know whether they had persuaded the boss to lower the rate, and you didn't ask. The men sat on the beds of their choice and proceeded to ask, "Hey brother, where's the courthouse? Is it far from here?"

"So you guys are here to sue someone too, huh?" you said in reply. "The courthouse is just west of here, about three or four li away."

You went back to cleaning the rooms, replacing dirty sheets and quilts with clean ones. You took all of the dirty items downstairs, then turned on the washing machine and put them in. After they were washed, you hung them on the iron clotheslines on the balcony to dry. You were hungry, so you made some food. Then, using a pair of tongs, you opened the stove, placed an eight-jin coal briquette inside, and placed a huge aluminum pot on the burner. When the water boiled you grabbed an iron ladle and began filling tall, colorful hot-water thermoses with piping hot water until fifty of them lined the floor in neat rows. You picked up a trash can and carried it out to the big dumpster outside.

You lay on the bed. Your lower back burned with pain, but when you closed your eyes you managed to drift off to sleep. The sun hadn't risen yet when the boss, who had been working the night shift, shouted at you to wake you up. Gritting your teeth, you commenced another eighteen-hour day of work. At least all of your meals had meat in them— much better than when you were at the clothing factory and the brick factory! What could you do? You weren't going to find work that was better than this.

Two drunk men with a couple of prostitutes came to the travel hostel. You grabbed the keys and led them upstairs.

"Attendant, bring us two hot-water thermoses!"

"Yes, sir! I'll bring them right now."

You carried the thermoses from the first floor to the third; as soon as you got there, the two drunk men started to vomit. Holding up his trousers, one of them tried to feel his way along the wall to the bathroom, but he was unable to find the door, so he dropped his trousers right there and shit on the floor. The prostitutes ran out of the room, pinching their noses.

"Ugh! These guys are disgusting!" One of them yelled.

"This really pisses me off!" said the other. "They still haven't paid us!"

The snowflakes fell and a year's worth of sorrow came to an end. With your bag on your back, you took leave of the travel hostel and went to rent a room with a family in an urban village. It was a four-story residential building; a chalkboard hanging out front announced that a single room was available to rent.

"Is the landlord here?" you asked.

"A single room is sixty kuai a month," a middle-aged woman said. "It includes water, but not electricity. I'll need twenty yuan for the deposit."

She took you to the fourth floor and opened the door to a room that was about eight square meters in size. An ancient-looking single bed was pushed up in one corner beside an old desk. You dropped your bag from your shoulder, then pulled the rent from your undershirt pocket and handed it to the landlady.

You went to a department store and bought a cotton quilt, which you brought back with you to the room.

You returned to the department store and bought a bed sheet, a quilt cover, a pillow, a pillowcase, and things like that.

You went back to the department store yet again and bought a basin for washing your face, a hot-water thermos, a teacup, a food bowl, and things like that.

The sun was swallowed by the black night like a baked sesame cake and the stars began to twinkle with flecks of light that looked like breadcrumbs. Smiling, you lay on the bed and inhaled the scent of newness that clung to the quilt and bed sheets. At last, you had a home! Even if it was only temporary, this was the first time in your life of vagrancy that you had your own little corner to come home to. You were going to enjoy your new life in this corner.

Just as the sun was rising, you got up from bed full of energy and vigor. You washed your face and brushed your teeth, then walked to the little street where breakfast was sold and ordered four youtiao and a bowl of pepper spice soup. With an empty bag you entered a wholesale merchandise market, then went from one stall to another, haggling with bosses along the way. The bag in your hand grew heavy and you exited the market with a sense of satisfaction.

Nighttime fell and thestreetlights lit up one by one.

You spread your tarp out on the ground at the side of the road. Socks, gloves, shoe inserts, underwear, hand towels—

more than twenty kinds of items were spread out before you. It wasn't long before others showed up to spread out their own blankets beside you. The crowd was full of people coming and going, late-night pedestrians moving in and out of the night market.

A man and a woman wearing red armbands walked past you. The man tore off a ticket and handed it to you, and you diligently pulled out five yuan and gave it to him. Then they moved on, endlessly tearing off tickets and giving them to other peddlers as they passed by their blankets.

On the evening of your first day you sold two pairs of underwear, six pairs of socks and ten shoe inserts. You made eleven kuai, but five kuai were eaten up by those hungry dogs in the red armbands. Still, you were happy: it was your first day doing business and you weren't leaving empty-handed! You gathered everything up, hopped on your squeaky bicycle and went back home.

Ah, to save money! To save money you no longer went out to eat, but instead bought a coal stove and some honeycomb coal briquettes. You also went to buy cooking utensils—wok, bowl, ladle, saucepan—and cooking staples like oil, salt, soy sauce, and vinegar. You were acquiring more and more things for your room! To prevent carbon monoxide poisoning, at night you placed the stove in the hallway outside your door. If the stove was not properly tended, it was hard to keep it burning. If the coal went out, you'd pick up one of your briquettes with a pair of tongs, then walk over to your neighbor's stove, where you'd swap it for one that was burning! Sometimes the neighbors on the third floor would come to your door, too, and take one of your burning coals, leaving you one of theirs in return. You didn't know why, but anytime you saw those burning coals, you always had the warm feeling of coming home!

You returned to the wholesale merchandise market with an even bigger bag on your arm. In the morning you went to the morning market, at night to the night market—all to make more money! When you had downtime during the day, you popped over to other peddlers' spots to buy books and read. Those pirated books were only two or three kuai apiece! They brought some joy to your life, and they went a long way in increasing your knowledge.

Each day you rode your squeaky bike through big streets and little alleyways.

Each evening you spread your blanket out at the night market for about three hours, and each day at the morning market for about two hours. The night market and the morning market weren't in the same place. Each time, you had to hand over five yuan, and if you didn't make any money, this meant a five-yuan loss. There were many gloomy, rainy days when you didn't make any money at all, and on those days you felt quite depressed! At times like these you sat alone in your room smoking, not even wanting to read.

At the morning market, you watched pedestrians as they walked by.

One Saturday afternoon, you hopped on your bicycle and rode to Zijing Mountain Park, a bag flung over your shoulder.

You rode your bike across the bridge that stood inside Zijing Mountain Park. Atop the bridge streamed a steady flow of pedestrians and vehicles, and below it was a filthy river which flowed from west to east and which the people of Zhengzhou called Gold Water River.

Your eyes darted around you as you scanned your surroundings for the best spot you could find. Peddlers continued setting up shop while you remained cautious and observant, just as you had observed the other peddlers do. You had learned a good deal from them.

As customers approached, you kept your eyes open all around you—to guard against thieves, to guard against the peaked caps, to guard against customers paying with counterfeit money. And to guard against the ever-present possibility of not being able to sell a thing.

Some old guy approached you to buy socks. Just as you were explaining with a smile the advantages of the various types of socks you had to offer, a blue city-management vehicle rolled up and two peaked caps got out. In a panic, all the peddlers wrapped up their items and ran from the north end of the bridge to the south. All around you was the sound of things flapping about, running footsteps, and the cries and curses of the peddlers whose wares were being confiscated. In haste you rolled up your blanket, then held it tightly against your chest as you left the bridge and ducked into a narrow, quiet alleyway.

Back on the bridge, the only people that remained were pedestrians. The peaked caps got back into their blue city-management vehicle and drove off.

One by one the street peddlers came back—who knows from where? The instant they returned to their spots, their blankets were back out on the ground. The number of people who had emerged from their homes to enjoy the park increased and the entire walkway was soon congested. But the peaked caps came again from the southern end of the bridge with rapid footsteps. Panic filled the air once more and the sound of people running, screaming, and cursing could be heard.

You could see the sky's color darkening, so you gathered up your belongings to go back home. Truly, setting up a peddler spot on any of the park's roads made one's blood curl. It reminded you of all those black-and-white movies you had seen when you were little, of the chaos left by the Japanese devils after wreaking havoc on a village. There was nothing to be done. In order to survive, the people at the bottom of society had to endure this kind of humiliation.

You hadn't quite packed up all of your belongings when a young man with dark skin walked by. He smiled as he looked at the toy dog you were selling, but he didn't pick it up, or ask the price, or seem interested in buying anything at all. Something about him rubbed you the wrong way, so you ignored him.

Suddenly all the peddlers began running in a panic as two peaked caps rushed forward at full speed.

"The devils are coming! Run!" the young man alerted you.

You picked up the tarp on the ground; a bag of socks and the toy dog fell to the ground.

Picking up the socks, the young man said, "I'll help you carry your stuff! Let's go!"

You ran with him to another street. Breathing heavily, you panted, "Thank you! Thank you, Big Brother!"

"No worries!" he said. "I used to have a spot here, too. Now I rent a stall in the vegetable market!"

The two of you began to talk. He said his surname was Geng.

"Are you free this evening?" Geng asked. "Let's go to my place and hang out!"

"I don't want to trouble Brother Geng!" you replied. "I'm going to go home and organize my stuff. I have to go back to the night market tonight and lay everything out again."

"Which street are you set up on?"

"It varies."

"Well, alright then! I'll just look for you on the bridge in the park."

You waved your hand. "Goodbye, Brother Geng!"

He waved back at you, then followed you with his eyes as you disappeared, seemingly unwilling to say goodbye.

After meeting Little Geng, you saw him every Saturday and Sunday on the bridge inside Zijing Mountain Park. You still didn't know him very well, so you were rather cautious about getting too close. Each time you saw each other it was mostly just smiles and hellos. He always stood beside you, watching you as you sold things. When the peaked caps came to confiscate peddlers' items, he would help you gather up your belongings, and then you would run off together. You began to feel a sense of gratitude toward Little Geng. You wanted to treat him to a meal, but at mealtimes he was never anywhere to be found.

One early summer day, Little Geng appeared by your side yet again.

"Business going okay, Little Tough?"

"Thank you for your help, Brother Geng," you replied, not directly answering the question. "I'd like to treat you to a meal, but whenever it's time to eat I don't see you anywhere!"

"My good brother!" he exclaimed. "It's not easy for you to earn money! Making you break the bank for me would be embarrassing! I make more money than you, so why don't I take *you* out instead?"

"Let Brother Geng take me out to eat?" you laughed. "I'm the one who'd be embarrassed!"

"Are you free this evening? Come to my place and hang out! You don't need to go home afterward. We'll lie on my bed and talk."

"Sounds good!" you replied. "Where should we meet?"

"Why don't you just come with me now? I'll make you dinner tonight."

"I should go home first. Let's meet here on the bridge at eight o'clock."

"Okay, see you here! Whoever gets here first, be sure and wait!" Once again Little Geng watched you as you left, always unwilling to say goodbye.

You rode your squeaky bike back to your place, then sat on the bed thinking: Should you go or not? Little Geng was so enthusiastic about everything. Surely, you couldn't go back on your word! And yet, you also felt that his enthusiasm was a little excessive. First, he tells you to come to his place to hang out, then he says you should stay overnight with him, lie on his bed and talk! Suddenly you remembered all the stories you had read in books and magazines. Did Little Geng want to go homosexual with you? Oh well, you thought. Letting someone else jerk you off is always nicer than doing it yourself!

You combed your hair and washed up a bit, then changed into some clean clothes and rode your squeaky bike in the direction of Zijing Mountain Park. Little Geng was there on the bridge, sitting on a pedal trike and waiting for you.

You went with Little Geng to the second floor of a building, where you entered an eight-square-meter room. There was a single bed, a dining table, and on the wall above the bed hung an image of the Bodhisattva Guanyin.

"Have a seat," he said. "I'll make you dinner!"

"Don't trouble yourself too much. We can just have whatever!"

Little Geng whipped up four vegetable dishes in a flash. "Little Tough," he asked, "do you drink alcohol? I'm Buddhist, so I never do!"

"Then I won't drink either!" you replied.

"I don't drink or eat meat, so I didn't make any meat dishes."

"No problem! A guest should go along with whatever is convenient for the host. I'm happy to eat whatever Little Geng wants."

You sat across from each other, talking and eating.

After dinner, Little Geng filled a large, portable tub halfway with warm water.

"Little Tough," he said, "take off your clothes and have a bath!"

You were a little bashful about the whole thing, but Little Geng came close to you, saying that if you were shy, he would help you undress. You were even more discomfited now, but obediently you removed all of your clothes, and, stark naked, jumped into the tub.

"Let me bathe you, Little Tough!" His hands moved lithely across your flesh.

You were laughing awkwardly and feeling a little shy when suddenly Little Geng took your cock into his mouth. At first you were nervous, but soon felt a pleasure unlike anything you had ever known.

Little Geng kissed every inch of your inadequate flesh as you closed your eyes and enjoyed the sensation of being loved by a member of your own sex.

TEN

1

The two bosses, one male, one female, quickly attracted the attention of a group of migrant workers who had nothing to eat and no place to sleep. The female boss looked at them tenderly, evidently unwilling to let them slip from her hands.

"Hey, you four—the ones without identity cards. You coming or not? We need to get a move on!"

"The job really includes room and board and you really pay twenty kuai a day?" Little Wave asked with some skepticism.

"Yes, it does, and yes we do! If you're afraid we won't pay you, you can get paid at the end of each workday. If we don't give you your money, then you can leave that very day. Our factory's economic performance is very strong—we never withhold anyone's wages!" The female boss gave the four fellows a kind, confident smile.

"What do you say, brothers? Do you want to go?" Little Wave turned to Ah Qing, Little Jade, and Little Tough. Apprehension was visible on their faces.

"Why don't we go to the factory and have a look?" Little Wave continued. "If it's no good, we'll just come right back!"

The bosses recruited twelve migrant workers that day. The man flagged down a taxi van and six of them hurriedly squeezed into the back. Then the woman hailed a second taxi van and Ah Qing, Little Wave, Little Jade, Little Tough, and two other boys who were seventeen or eighteen years of age all piled in. The vans rolled out of the city center, looking like two loaves of bread, carrying with them each person's hopes, and in some cases illusions, about what lay ahead.

On a stretch of highway leading to the western suburbs, a tanker truck sat parked on the side of the road. The two vans pulled up alongside the tanker and everyone got out. The bosses paid the taxi drivers, who turned around and drove off in the direction from which they had come.

"Boss! Where's the factory?" everyone asked as they looked at the two bosses in surprise.

"Don't worry, we're just not there yet! The factory director sent this vehicle to come and get you. Come on, everyone, get inside!" The female boss continued to grin broadly.

"What kind of factory is this, anyway?" one of the migrant workers demanded. "If you don't tell us, we're not getting in this tanker!"

"Open the back and put 'em in!" shouted the male boss.

Two men with coarse, dark skin jumped out of the cabin of the vehicle. One of them opened the back of the tanker and out of the darkness jumped six more men, all with vile and ferocious faces.

"Crow! Rat! Get them in there!" the female boss laughed grimly.

Little Wave called out for help, but his cries were met with a blow to the face. Blood spurted from his nose and he struggled to get away. Ah Qing struggled too; the sleeve of his shirt was ripped. Little Jade screamed loudly, "Let me go!" All the other migrant workers had their clothes ripped in the fight or had their faces beaten to a pulp. Only Little Tough stood in place, obedient and motionless. He was the first one to be pushed inside the rear of the tank.

Not one of the twelve worker brothers managed to escape. Their bodies had already been beaten down by life, not to mention the heavy bags they had been carrying on their backs. In an instant, the beautiful hopes and illusions they'd brought with them were transformed into a reality of blood and tears. One by one the dreadful villains herded them into the tanker and locked the door. Through the tiny crack, one could see just two centimeters of sky.

The two human traffickers discussed price with Crow and Rat. Crow stuffed a stack of RMB into the woman trafficker's hand and she counted the money.

"No way!" the female trafficker cried out. "Crow, this is only two thousand! We agreed on two hundred per person!"

"Oh for fuck's sake, Crow and Rat! Come on, cough up four hundred more!" The male trafficker stuck out his hand.

"Damn!" Rat laughed loudly. "Listen, Brother Fox, Sister Fox! Can't you leave your brothers a little booze money? It'll only take you one more trip to the hiring site to make another two thousand! I don't even make that much in six months!" He gave an ingratiating smile.

"Cough it up!" The female trafficker was growing confrontational. "The only thing you guys see is us getting paid. What you don't see is the risks we take. We can get our heads chopped off for this!"

Crow spit a cigarette from his mouth, then pulled four hundred yuan from his shoe and handed it to the woman.

The male trafficker cast the female trafficker a look; she removed fifty yuan from the wad of bills in her hand. "Alright!" she laughed sinisterly. "Brother Crow, Brother Rat! Here's a little cigarette money for you! Let's work together again!"

Crow took the fifty yuan from the woman, then yelled in the direction of the tanker. "Listen up all of you! If any of you starts to cry and make a ruckus, you're going to get a beating!"

Crow and Rat started up the vehicle and sped toward the west. The tanker truck turned away from the asphalt motorway and onto a narrow dirt road. It headed northwest, traversed a steep precipice with a river below, then climbed over a gray cement bridge and raced between fields of fresh, bright-green corn seedlings. The vehicle turned at a fork in the road, then began to descend toward a desolate region full of rolling hills. It was getting dark outside when the vehicle slowed down and finally came to a standstill on a low-lying stretch of earth. The back of the tanker opened.

The twelve terrified workers were forced out of the vehicle and into a crudely built shed. Their brutish captors followed closely behind with flashlights in their hands. Once inside the shed, they searched the workers, removing from their pockets and backpacks anything of value. After that, the sounds of beating and crying could be heard.

Outside, a bald-headed man squatted at the entrance of a cave, silently smoking.

Crow and Rat left the shed and walked over to him, their faces brimming with smiles. Crow offered the bald man a cigarette despite the fact that he was already smoking one. "Big harvest today, Factory Director! Twelve guys, and each one is young and strong!"

"How much did you pay?" Smoke coiled upward from the factory director's nose. It looked like a serpent's shadow.

"They wanted a little more this time," Crow replied, "because they're all so young and strong. Five hundred each—six thousand for the twelve of them."

"That's right!" Rat chimed in. "It wasn't easy for me and Brother Crow to get them to agree to a number like that! We're gonna have to make these fuckers work hard so we can get that six grand back!"

"Destroy their identity cards and other documents. Hurry up and break them in so they know how to work. Whatever you do, don't let a single one of them escape. If one does, all of us—including me, the brains of this entire operation—will have to move out of here. Also, take care of those useless guys we talked about. And do it clean."

In the middle of the night from sheds dotting the landscape came wretched sounds.

In terror, the twelve migrant workers curled up together. They were cold and hungry, their bodies swollen and in pain.

At daybreak, one worker carried vats of thin gruel on the ends of a shoulder pole while another worker carried two baskets of steamed buns.

"Fuck!" Crow yelled, whip in hand. "Get up! Time to eat! Time to eat and when you're done eating it's time to get to work! Anyone who doesn't listen—this old guy is gonna beat to death!"

"We don't have bowls," Little Wave complained to Crow. "How are we going to eat?"

The words had barely fallen from Little Wave's mouth when Crow's whip landed on his back.

"Listen up, each and every one of you! When you work, you work! And when you eat, you eat! If any of you doesn't listen, this whip will make you listen! And if any of you has the balls to try and run off, just know that when I get you back here I will beat you to death!"

Rat walked over to join Crow. "Fuck!" he shouted at the workers. "Didn't we tell you to eat? What are you waiting for? You want me to break off a piece and feed you by mouth? Listen up and listen good: you eat at 5:30 every morning and start work at 6." Rat lifted his foot and kicked a worker's backside.

Crow's whip lashed out at another worker. "Looks like you haven't heard what we said!" he shouted. "In fifteen minutes it will be 6 on the dot. You're working today whether you finish eating or not!"

2

Little Wave went to get a steamed bun and all of his worker brothers did the same. Half starved, they had by now forgotten any sense of shame and proceeded to eat like pigs and dogs. When there was nothing left, they ran their tongues along the edges of the bucket to lap up any remaining traces of gruel.

At another worksite not far from where they were, a group of barefoot migrant workers fought like madmen to get their hands on a steamed bun. Those weak, wounded, and disabled workers crawled on the ground to pick up pieces of food covered in yellow earth. One worker attempted to stick his entire head inside a bucket; he was violently pulled out by several pairs of hands behind him. A face full of gruel collapsed to the ground and in an instant was covered with dirt. Each man's face turned ferocious and ugly. Their mouths opened wide, became distorted, bit and tore at anything around them. Like pigs and dogs, they growled madly.

When six o'clock arrived, Crow stood atop a hill overlooking the worksite and blew a whistle. The machines began to howl. Barefoot, the workers picked up steel shovels and began dumping soil into brick extruder machines. More and more soil and water was added, and before long a row of bricks that had been squeezed out by the machine sat glistening on a wooden board. No sooner did one worker carry away a stack of bricks than another worker replaced them with new ones. A bit farther away on a stretch of sandy earth, piles of bricks that looked like toy building blocks baked in the sun.

Bricks that were fully baked were carted off to a cave on a flat-bed vehicle. The cave looked like a mausoleum; smoke rose in the air like banknotes from the afterlife. Holding whips in their hands, Crow and Rat supervised the worksite. If any worker's hand or foot was too slow, he received a brutal lash.

The bald factory director sat on the hill, looking like a bald eagle. His dark, almost blue face was hidden beneath a veil of cigarette smoke pouring from his mouth. Shirtless and barefoot, workers toiled on the low-lying land below him, an area of twenty mu in total. The sound of the whip lashing out was heard frequently; bloody marks were left on the workers' bodies.

Ah Qing clenched his teeth as he worked. He could barely tell north from south, east from west at this point, nor did he dare raise his head to look around. Little Wave worked while keeping one eye on the whips in Crow's and Rat's hands. Little Jade's face was twisted and distorted. Little Tough stared like an imbecile at Crow and Rat. His toiling hands paused frequently, and when the whip landed on his back he laughed maniacally. The sound of his laughter made the flesh crawl. It was enough to make his tormenters' whips go limp, at least for a few moments.

"Rat!" Crow shouted, pointing at Little Tough. "This guy's clearly an imbecile—get rid of him!" He turned on his heel and walked away.

After dinner, the sun went down and the sky went black.

"Ah Qing, I have to shit," Little Tough said.

"Me too. I haven't shit in three days."

"Let's all go shit together!"

The four brothers, who had suffered more than their share of misfortune, dragged their weary and pained bodies from the shed.

"Don't move! What are you doing?" Crow blocked their exit.

"We haven't shit for days!"

"Go do it over there!" Crow pointed to a stretch of weeds in the dark. "But I'm warning you: every way out of this place has a guard. If any of you are tired of living, go ahead and make a run for it!"

They squatted in the grass and tried to defecate. Little Tough began crying in pain—no matter how hard he tried, it wouldn't come out.

"Try harder, Little Tough!" Little Wave said. "If it doesn't come out, you'll die from it being stuck inside you!"

"Don't worry, Little Tough," said Ah Qing. "We'll wait for you!"

"Relax your asshole, Little Tough!" said Little Jade.

"I still can't make it come out!" Squatting on the ground, Little Tough cried louder.

"I'll help you, Little Tough. I'll dig it out with my fingers!" Little Wave wiped his index and middle fingers on his pants, and with trembling hands placed them inside Little Tough's anus.

Little Tough moaned in pain as blood and shit fell from his body.

The others held him up and together they hobbled out of the weeds and back to the shed.

"Little Tough, if you want to cry, just cry! Don't let your tears stay trapped inside your heart!"

"I won't cry, I won't cry! I have food to eat now, I have work . . . "

Coal burned inside the cave as bricks squeezed from yellow earth were burned into hues of red and gray.

Relying on the faint light inside the cave, the factory director played cards with Crow, Rat and a few other guards. Two scoundrels working the night shift walked back and forth with flashlights in their hands.

Another dusk, another freight truck. It rolled into the low-lying area and spit out ten more youths.

Another morning. Migrant workers carried buckets of thin gruel and steamed buns on poles. Everyone's appetite was increasing; the number of people was increasing, too. It didn't take long to learn that if one didn't fight for food, one's stomach would remain empty. On this particular morning, Ah Qing, Little Wave, Little Jade, Little Tough, and all the other migrant worker brothers fought over who would get steamed buns. In order to get the last one, Little Wave fought with another worker. Ah Qing held on to the bucket of gruel tightly. One worker stuck his head into the bucket and immediately pulled it out again. He choked on the substance and a mixture of snot and gruel spurt from his nose.

Six o'clock arrived and Crow went to stand on the hill. When he blew the work whistle, three brick extruders began to howl.

A young man, eighteen or nineteen years of age, had previously had a steamed bun snatched right from his hand by Little Wave. Now, while working, the young man refused to cooperate with him. Little Wave threw his shovel to the ground and pounced on him. When Ah Qing rushed forward to pull Little Wave off of him, the young man smashed his fist into Little Wave's body and face six times. Little Wave's nose split open and fresh blood spilled forth.

"Let go!" Ah Qing yelled at the young man. "He's off you now, so why aren't you letting go?"

The young man's fist continued crashing forward, so Ah Qing released Little Wave and pounced on him.

"Fuck!" Crow yelled, brandishing his whip as he walked toward the men. "Get back to work! No fighting when you're working! If you want to fight, wait till you're done working. Then you can fight to the death for all I care!"

Ah Qing's back suffered a vicious blow from the whip. He let go of the other man and crawled off of him with heavy breath.

Crow walked up beside the man lying on the ground and gave him a brutal kick. "Fuck!" he yelled. "Get back to work!"

Blood dripped from Little Wave's nose, so Ah Qing tore off a piece of cloth from his tank top, rolled it into a ball and stuffed it in one nostril. He supported Little Wave as they walked to the pool of water nearby; there, Ah Qing began to wash away the blood and mud that was stuck to Little Wave's hands and face.

"Fuck!" Crow cursed as he rushed forward. "He can wash his own fucking nose! Get back to work!"

"You have no sympathy! Look at the state he's in! Wait until I've washed him and then I'll work." Tears were in Ah Qing's eyes.

Crow looked Ah Qing up and down. "Huh! So you want me to sympathize, eh? Too bad you were born in the wrong body. If you were a chick I'd sympathize with you morning, noon, and night!" Crow suddenly saw something under Ah Qing's soiled tank top—it was a red, heart-shaped stone. He reached out a hand and yanked it from Ah Qing's neck.

"Give it back! Give it back!"

"Fuck! I thought this was going to be something of value! It's just some crappy stone—and look! For fuck's sake, the word 'love' is carved into it! Ha ha!"

Ah Qing reached out to snatch the necklace from Crow's hand. With a single foot, Crow kicked Ah Qing to the ground.

Ah Qing crawled upward and tightly latched on to Crow's legs, begging with tears.

"Give it back! Give it back! My birth mother gave this to me! I beg you to give it back to me!"

Crow put his foot down on Ah Qing's back. "Fuck! I never would've guessed you were this filial! Alright, I'll give it back. Go and get it!" Crow laughed cruelly as he threw the stone into the pool of water.

Ah Qing dove into the water and began madly hunting for the stone his mother had given him. With clothes soaked through and a face covered in mud, tears filled his eyes as he searched and searched.

3

One night there suddenly fell a great rain. Crow blew the work whistle into the darkness, then ran with the factory director and Rat into the shed, where they kicked the migrant workers awake.

"Fucking get up! This rain will turn the bricks to mud! Get some tarps and go cover them!"

The instant Ah Qing was awakened from his dreams he placed a hand against his chest. When he felt that the stone heart his mother had given him was still there, he sighed in relief.

Braving the rain, the workers ran out of the shed and into the darkness. Ah Qing held a water-resistant canvas tarpaulin tightly against his chest, but he couldn't see anyone clearly, nor could he see where the bricks were. He slipped and fell, then got up again. Thanks to the lightning, he was able to see the stacks of bricks as they collapsed and turned to mud.

"Where the fuck is the flashlight?" the factory director shouted into the rain. "Quick, shine the light!"

In chaos everyone ran, slipping and falling, then getting up again and calling out like wild dogs. Several bolts of lightning struck in rapid succession.

Ah Qing's entire body was soaked through with rainwater. He sneezed twice, then rushed back to the shed.

"Little Jade, Little Wave, Little Tough!"

No one answered.

In an instant Ah Qing realized that this was the perfect opportunity to escape. He wanted to rush out of the shed and flee right then and there, but the thought of his three friends stopped him in his tracks. Could they be out in the rain wasting time and doing something stupid like trying to rescue the bricks? He wanted to run into the rain to look for them, but he couldn't see anything clearly. That's when it crossed his mind: escape all alone! If he could make it out of there, he would go to the police and save the others.

Ah Qing turned and ran out of the shed and into the rain. Someone else was running in his direction, however, and the two of them crashed headlong and fell to the ground. Ah Qing quickly climbed back up.

"Fuck! Pull me up, now!"

When Ah Qing heard that the voice belonged to Crow, he hesitated before reaching out a hand.

"Where is everyone?! Where did they run off to?"

"I don't know!"

"Come with me! Nobody fucking better try to use this as an opportunity to escape!" Crow grabbed hold of Ah Qing's hand.

The rain stopped and the sound of thunder receded into the distance along with the sound of the wind. The factory director took hold of the flashlight and went from shed to shed, counting people.

"Crow! Rat! You two worthless pieces of shit! Eight workers have run off—did you know that?"

"They won't be able to get away, Factory Director! Rat and four or five other brothers are on their motorcycles chasing after them!"

Ah Qing gazed into the darkest part of the night and prayed.

Five o'clock came and went, then six o'clock. Nobody brought the food bucket or steamed buns, nor was Crow's work whistle anywhere to be heard. Mentally shaken, the workers came out of their sheds, then went to the grassy area near the worksite and sat down.

Rat was on a motorcycle, and close behind him was the tanker truck, that unforgettable prisoner vehicle in which the workers had arrived. Like a horse being spurred on, it rolled into the low-lying area surrounding them. As soon as the vehicle came to a halt, Crow jumped out of the driver cabin with the other scoundrels and walked briskly to the back of the tanker truck to open it up.

Ah Qing opened his eyes wide and watched as Little Jade, Little Wave, Little Tough, and four other workers were ejected from the back of the vehicle and onto the ground. Their hands and feet were tied, and they hollered in pain as they hit the earth. The factory director walked over to the action, a cigarette hanging from his lips.

"Factory Director," Crow said, "we've already grabbed seven of them. There's one left, and I reckon it won't be long before our brothers find him, too!"

The factory director squatted on the ground and grabbed Little Wave by the neck. The prisoner opened his mouth wide and breathed coarsely.

"So you want to run! Want to know what it tastes like when we catch you and bring you back?" The factory director removed the cigarette from his lips and stuffed the entire thing into Little Wave's mouth.

Little Wave spit it out, then yelled with a hoarse voice, "You . . . you fucking . . . you're not even human!"

"Beat them," the factory director said calmly, pointing to the seven people on the ground. "Beat every one of them. Beat them all over, beat them to death . . . "

The director's henchmen raised their clubs and whips in the air and began hitting the seven bodies violently. Little

Tough laughed like a man unhinged, but Little Jade, Little Wave, and the others cried as if they were being torn apart.

Ah Qing closed his eyes—what was happening was too horrible to look at—but still the tears fell. He squatted at the factory director's feet and begged. "Please stop, Factory Director! Please show mercy on them this one time! If they're beaten too badly they won't be able to work for you anymore!"

"No mercy!" the factory director yelled, kicking Ah Qing to the side. "I'm gonna kill one of them, but not in front of the others. Nope! If I did that, they'd be so scared they wouldn't work nice and hard for me!" The factory director pulled the leather whip from Crow's hand and looked at the guards. "You guys have beaten them enough. Drag 'em all out of here." He turned to the seven escapees. "Except this one," he added, pointing to Little Wave. "This one I'm beating to death. From now on, for each one that runs off, we kill one!"

Ah Qing watched in horror as the guards dragged six of the escapees away, leaving Little Wave alone on the ground. Memories of the many days they had spent together, both the joyful and sorrowful, flashed through his mind.

The factory director's whip lashed out against Little Wave's body. Blood gushed from his nose and mouth.

"Please, Factory Director, no more! I beg you to spare him!" Ah Qing howled in anguish as he crawled toward the director's feet.

Little Wave felt as though he were being bitten by a thousand venomous snakes. His throat was hoarse from sobbing. His body floated upward—he discovered he could fly! Out went his arms and he flew just like a little bird. He flew over young corn stalks that were more than a meter high and which undulated in the wind like the silken hair of a young girl. Little Wave flew past a small, flowing river. In the distance he heard the sound of wind chimes and the singing of a young girl.

Ah Qing held Little Wave in his arms as the latter lay dying, but no longer did Ah Qing cry. He closed Little Wave's eyes just as Crow and Rat pulled the boy away from him. They lifted Little Wave and carried him off to the cave as Ah Qing fainted and collapsed to the ground.

4

Ah Qing abruptly awakened from his nightmarish sleep. He immediately sat up and called out for his three friends, Little Wave, Little Jade, and Little Tough.

"Ah Qing, it's me, Little Jade! Little Wave is dead!"

Ah Qing turned around and threw his arms around Little Jade. Then he began to sob.

The next day when six o'clock came around, Crow stood atop the high hill and blew the whistle to signal that it was time for the prisoner workers to begin the workday. Little Tough toiled for a spell, but it wasn't long before he stopped, stood motionless and laughed like an imbecile.

Like all the other workers, Ah Qing's skin had turned as black as earth from exposure to the elements. None of the workers' hair had been cut in months—for some it had been even longer than this—so their locks were long and disheveled, making them look like ghosts wandering in hell. At this point, they were nearly used to Crow's and Rat's whips. When the whip lashed against their skin, their faces contorted, and over time they lost the spirit of resistance and struggle. Day by day, they grew number, weaker, and more and more devoid of hope.

Ah Qing tried to remember what the man who had escaped looked like, but as hard as he tried, he couldn't recall. He knew only one thing: that he had lost two full layers of skin—one layer from the whip, the other burned off by the sun. When Ah Qing went to the pool to wash his face, he looked into the water and saw a dark, emaciated man. If it weren't for the stone heart from his birth mother hanging at his chest, he wouldn't even have recognized himself.

Ah Qing was by now accustomed to going alone after nightfall to a desolate stretch of weeds to defecate. He was used to this stretch of weeds, but the world outside this low-lying area? No longer was he certain what that was like. On several occasions he wanted to crawl to the top of the hill so he could take a look, but each time he was overcome by fear and stopped. He was afraid that the factory director, along with Crow, Rat, and the others, would discover him and beat him to death. Little Wave's death made him feel grateful, though. At all times, he remembered Little Tough's words: better to be a slave than to be human scum! When you're a slave, as long as you have work you have food to eat. But when you're human scum, not only do you have nothing to eat—you can't find work, either!

Ah Qing often looked up at the stars, which blinked their eyes at him and filled the sky completely. The moon waxed and waned as time passed, icy cold and unfeeling. He wanted to talk to Little Jade, and yet he increasingly felt that his friend was like a stranger to him. When he reached out to touch Little Jade's face, he showed no reaction.

"Come on, Little Jade, let's talk," Ah Qing said one night.

"I'm tired, I want to go to sleep." Little Jade turned over; his voice reeked of exhaustion.

"Little Tough, look at the stars—don't they look like blinking eyes?" Ah Qing touched his shoulder.

"I don't want to look, I just want to sleep."

They snored as they slept. There was nothing Ah Qing could do but lie down. As soon as he thought about the following day's work he shut his eyes.

Ah Qing ran all alone. Behind him was deep, low-lying land and before him was a hill. He crawled up the hill like the wind; when he reached the top he looked down and saw a little path. He followed it like lightning until there appeared a crossroads that cut through a dense cornfield. He chose the dirt path on the right and kept running. Up ahead there was a large asphalt road, and beyond that a cement bridge. Hope flashed in his eyes. But suddenly, he heard the sound of motorcycle wheels spinning behind him; he turned to look and saw Crow and Rat on two motorcycles chasing after him. Ah Qing felt a great wave of fear pressed against him, and he almost started to cry. When he thought of the way he'd be beaten to death, the way his corpse would be tossed into the cave and burned to ashes, his flesh shook. He continued to run forward in helplessness. He felt as though his legs had become as heavy as iron and there was a great wind sucking him from behind like a magnet. The men on the motorcycles surged forward and grabbed him.

Ah Qing awoke from the nightmare and felt that his entire body was covered in sweat. He looked at the starry sky outside the shed and for a moment it seemed that the stars really were blinking at him. He lay down once more and closed his eyes.

Ah Qing ran all alone, unendingly it seemed. Behind him was a deep depression in the earth; in front of him a high hill. Quickly he ascended the hill and saw that below it there was a narrow path, upon which he ran like the wind. Ahead of him, he saw an intersection crossing through the pitch-black cornfields; he turned to the road on the left and kept running. Now there was a freight vehicle on the road ahead of him. Ah Qing chased it, caught up with it quickly, and called out for help. When the man and woman in the freight vehicle heard his cry, they stopped. The woman looked down at Ah Qing and said with a smile, "Get in! We'll take you home!" Ah Qing thought that she looked familiar, and that's when he saw clearly: It was the man and woman from the hiring site who had deceived them and sold them to the brick kiln! He turned and ran in the direction from which he had come, but the man and woman turned around, too, and pursued him with mad laughter. The woman jumped out of the vehicle first. With a smile she stretched out her hawk-like hand to grab Ah Qing; she succeeded. He struggled to escape her grasp, but now Crow and Rat were also driving a freight truck toward him. In despair, he began to cry.

"Ah Qing, wake up!" Little Jade shook him frantically.

He awoke and tears fell from his eyes. Tightly he held Little Jade as he sobbed.

Little Jade and Ah Qing held each other as they slept, and then, holding hands, they ran together. Behind them was a deep depression in the earth; in front of them a high hill. Quickly they ascended the hill and saw a narrow path below, upon which they ran like the wind. Before them was an intersection that crossed through the pitch-black cornfields. Little Jade said "Let's take that road!" but Ah Qing shook his head to say no. Little Jade took Ah Qing by the hand and started off toward the road on the right, but Ah Qing pulled him back. Little Jade pulled Ah Qing's hand so they could run off to the left, but Ah Qing pulled him back again. Anxiously, Little Jade asked, "Which road do we take? If we're caught by them, we'll be beaten to death!" Now they heard the rapid sound of a vehicle galloping behind them. They turned to look, and saw that it was Little Tough on a motor trike with Crow and Rat! They were coming toward them! In terror, Ah Qing and Little Jade ran together, but they didn't get far before Little Wave suddenly appeared before them. Little Wave didn't say a word; he just turned and leapt into the pitch-black cornfield at the side of the road, disappearing from view. Ah Qing took hold of Little Jade's hand and they, too, jumped into the cornfield, through which they ran, still holding hands. They ran for so long that they soon reached the city. The sky was completely dark, so they followed the streetlights, circumventing the hiring site. They ran into a large courtyard and shut the gate behind them. Then they entered a building and ascended a flight of stairs which led them to a room. The owner of the room looked at them, dumbstruck. That's when they were able to see clearly who the owner of the room was: Little Orchid!

"Wake up, Ah Qing! It's time to eat!" Little Jade nudged Ah Qing's shoulder.

Little Tough had already stepped out of the shed. He walked to the side of the pool, where he washed his face. Ah Qing and Little Jade also went to the water to wash their hands and faces. Two migrant workers carrying poles over their shoulders—one with buckets of thin gruel, the other with baskets of steamed buns—approached. Everyone went after the food like wild dogs.

The clock struck six and Crow stood atop the tall hill, where he blew the work whistle. The workers, who were really just prisoners, began another day of labor.

5

Afternoon. The sun beat down on their blackened skin as they silently worked. The factory director sat smoking at the foot of a tree. In straw hats, Crow and Rat held their leather whips as they paced back and forth, utterly bored to death.

Two workers were excavating earth with shovels to make a new hill. Soft soil that had just been dug out was hauled away by another group of workers one truckload at a time. Still others, including Ah Qing, Little Jade and Little Tough, transported newly formed bricks, their bodies drenched in sweat. That's when someone suddenly cried out, "Snake! Snake!"

Most of the workers remained glued to their spots, but the two men who had been digging dropped their shovels and bolted. The man who had shouted "snake!" looked at the others in terror as a meter-long snake slithered out of a hole in the dirt. It was the color of yellow earth and a forked tongue spit from its mouth. A second, even bigger snake crawled out right behind it.

"Fuck!" Crow yelled as he and Rat ran over. "Two snakes scaring you like this? Give me that shovel—I'll show you how I kill 'em!" A worker picked up one of the shovels and handed it to Crow, who began thrusting it toward the ground madly. In a flash the two snakes were chopped into eight parts that continued to wriggle on the ground.

"Alright, the snakes are dead! Fucking get back to work now!"

The two workers who had been shoveling lifted their tools and resumed their work, but when they thrust the shovels back into the earth a large chunk of soil cracked open and out from

212

the dark recess slithered a long procession of snakes. Once again they ran off in fear, and once again Crow and Rat came running, yelling and cursing with tools in their hands. When they saw the hundred or more brightly colored snakes pouring out of the mountain, however, they became so frightened that they dropped their weapons and backed away.

"Everyone, get over here and kill these snakes!" It was the factory director himself running over. After spitting out the order, he himself took the initiative to grab a shovel and began hitting at the snakes wildly. Crow and Rat picked their spades and shovels up from the ground and ruthlessly began killing the creatures. Then the entire group of workers rushed forward, lifting any instrument they could get their hands on and going after the snakes as if releasing some kind of pent-up grievance. Meanwhile, the creatures continued to pour out of the cave, seemingly intent on rushing toward the people.

Ah Qing turned to Little Jade and Little Tough. "This is it!" he said in a frantic whisper. "This is our chance to escape! Let's go!"

"I'm not escaping anymore," Little Tough said, lowering himself to the ground. "I don't mind staying here and being a slave till they work me to death."

"Don't be like that!" Ah Qing pulled at him anxiously. "Come on, let's go together. This time we're going to make it!"

Little Tough remained on the ground, motionless. Little Jade wanted to take this chance to escape, but he was terrified of being caught and beaten to death. He didn't know whether to listen to Ah Qing or to Little Tough.

"Little Tough!" Ah Qing pleaded with the boy on the ground. "Little Wave is dead—we can't die here, too! We're brothers and we've suffered the same hardships! I can't leave you here! Come on, get up! Get up!" He pulled Little Tough up off the ground as his eyes filled with tears.

The three of them ran to the edge of the depression, past the stretch of weeds where they had defecated together so many times, until they came to the foot of a steep, slippery slope. Ah

Qing took the lead in climbing upward, using his available hand to grab hold of Little Jade's arm. Little Jade used his free hand to tightly grasp Little Tough's, and they climbed the high hill breathing heavily. Behind them was the deep, low-lying land, and on that land was a group of panicked people yelling as they frantically tried to kill the snakes. Suddenly, however, Little Tough's feet came to a standstill and he freed his hand from Little Jade's grip.

"I'm not going!" he shouted. "I'm not going to try and escape . . . you guys go! I'm willing to be a slave! I'm willing to die from exhaustion here, and then go and be with my Big Brother Little Wave!" In tears, he slid back down the side of the hill.

Ah Qing watched in sorrow as Little Tough retreated back into the low-lying area. He recalled the three dreams he had had the night before, and all at once the very thought of Little Tough filled him with terror. Ah Qing pulled at Little Jade's hand tightly. "Let's go! Now! We can make it this time—we can escape!"

Ah Qing and Little Jade flew across the pathway before them. Two crossroads appeared, cutting through the pitch-black cornfields.

"Ah Qing! Which road do we take?"

The dreams and their three different outcomes surged chaotically in Ah Qing's mind.

"Little Wave," he pleaded, "if your wronged ghost is here with us, please show us which road to take!"

A wind blew past them and from a distant place they heard the sound of a motorcycle.

"They're coming, Ah Qing! They're going to kill us!" Little Jade cried out.

"No! They won't catch us this time!" Ah Qing pulled at Little Jade's hand doggedly and they dove into a dense mass of cornstalks that were more than two meters high. The stalks had already been pollinated, and tall, lanky clubs of corn stuck out from them. Panting heavily, they ran through the cornfield as the sky turned black.

A half-moon hung in the night sky as fragments of moonlight scattered about the cornfield. Little Jade was on the verge of collapse. Ah Qing supported him as they ran.

"I can't go any further! I can't run anymore," Little Jade said, gasping for air.

"Let me carry you on my back!" Ah Qing squatted to the ground.

Little Jade crawled onto Ah Qing's back. With great effort, Ah Qing stood up and began walking forward step by step. Little Jade's sweat-covered face stuck closely to Ah Qing's shoulder.

With Little Jade on his back, Ah Qing soon lost track of their direction. Arduously they moved forward, two black shadows lost in the weak rays of moonlight dusting the dark cornfield. They approached a dirt road, but just as they were about to step out of the cornfield and onto it their ears were hit with the rushing sound of two motorcycles. Quickly Ah Qing let Little Jade down and they retreated two paces. They collapsed to the ground, not daring to move a muscle.

The motorcycles shot forth pillars of light that stretched meters ahead. The lights swept across the cornfields and above Ah Qing's and Little Jade's heads.

The motorcycles passed them, then disappeared in the opposite direction.

"Let's get back into the cornfield!" Ah Qing said.

The sound of a cornstalk cracking shot into the night. While pushing through the vegetation, Little Jade had stretched it to its limit and it snapped, making a noise as loud as a gunshot.

"Be careful, Little Jade! We can't make any noise!" Ah Qing squatted for Little Jade to get on his back again, and they proceeded to an even deeper, darker place.

Gradually the sky lightened and the sun shined warmly on the cornfields. Ah Qing and Little Jade held each other tightly as they slept.

The sun rose higher and higher, and mottled flecks of sunlight scattered the earth. Ah Qing's eyes were open; he stretched out a hand and wiped the tears from Little Jade's face. Little Jade woke up, too. He pressed his face against Ah Qing's chest and listened to his heartbeat.

"Ah Qing! We're still alive! I was just having this dream that—"

"Don't tell me, Little Jade," Ah Qing said, covering Little Jade's mouth with one hand. He didn't want to hear about the dream, didn't want to hear anything that might be inauspicious. "Listen," he continued. "We're going to be able to escape!"

"It's already completely light out, Ah Qing. Where can we go?!"

"We got lost last night. The first thing we have to do is orient ourselves, then we'll continue."

They squatted and carefully eyed the position of the sun and their own shadows.

"First we go east, then northeast or southeast!" Ah Qing took Little Jade by the hand and they moved eastward, stepping through a diagram of interconnected cornfields.

Hours passed and the sun began to set in the west. They continued walking until they heard the sound of water flowing.

"Little Jade, do you remember? When we were in that tanker truck, we drove past a river!"

"The crack in the door was too small—I could barely see a thing!"

"Listen! If we can make it past this river and keep going straight ahead for another twenty or thirty li, we'll be saved!"

The gurgling sound of flowing water grew closer and closer. They slipped out of the cornfield and climbed toward the riverbank. Two tall rows of poplar trees lined the broad embankment; between the rows of trees ran a stretch of yellow road that had been pressed flat by tires. The boys saw the river water flowing below the embankment; their tongues touched their dry, parched lips.

"Little Jade, let's go down and drink some water first!"

"Ah Qing, look, there's a bridge!" Little Jade pointed.

When Ah Qing looked up, he became so frightened that his face turned white. Beyond the poplar trees, on a bridge about a hundred meters in length, sat two motorcycles with their engines turned off. On one of them sat Crow with his back to Ah Qing and Little Jade. Ah Qing could see that Rat was facing Crow. Quickly he grabbed Little Jade's hand; they slid back down the embankment and returned to the cornfield.

No sooner had they slid back into the cornfield than a motorcycle sped through the two rows of poplar trees.

In fear, they crawled into a thick growth of weeds inside the cornfield. They were certain that Crow and Rat knew they were there, and they did not dare move for fear of bumping into a cornstalk and revealing their exact location to the men.

A motorcycle rushed past the cornfield, just meters from Ah Qing and Little Jade. In a few moments, it returned; this time they could see that it was Rat sitting on the bike. Before long, Crow's motorcycle came rushing past as well. The two men rolled to a standstill on the riverbank and dismounted their bikes.

"Crow! I wonder if those two have crossed the river! We keep going back and forth—how long are we going to keep doing this?!" Rat pulled a pack of cigarettes from his pocket and placed a smoke between his lips.

"Fuck! All we wanted to do was kill some snakes, and now people are escaping! I don't care if it kills us, we have to find them. I'm not afraid of them running. What I'm afraid of is them reporting us! We've all beaten workers to death! If we get caught, I'd be shocked if they don't execute us by shooting. I have a feeling that they haven't crossed the river yet. All we have to do is guard this embankment and they won't be able to run!"

"What if they've hidden in the cornfields and don't come out? What will we do then?"

"Our brothers are stationed all over the place. They could never make it through one of these exits. Even if they've hidden in the cornfields, it's so hot that after a few days they'll die either from thirst or from hunger!"

"But one person has already escaped," Rat protested. "It's been more than two months and they haven't reported us!"

"Fucking shut up and quit being a pain in the ass! If we don't bring these two bastards back, how are we going to explain things to that bald-headed ass of a factory director?"

Crow and Rat got back on their bikes and went off to search in a different area.

Ah Qing and Little Jade breathed a sigh of relief.

"Ah Qing! We were really out of hope just now! I thought they had already found us!"

"Little Jade, your lips are so parched that you're bleeding! Let's find something for you to eat here in the cornfield!"

Holding hands tightly, they stepped deeper into the cornfield, then broke apart a thin cornstalk and pulled back its layers of skin. Inside was a soft cob that hadn't sprouted any kernels yet; they bit into it and began chewing. After that, they found a few wild melons and began to eat those, too.

"We can't leave the cornfields, Little Jade. If we go back to the road it won't be long before they catch us! We have to stick it out here in the fields . . . we have to endure . . . "

"Endure until *when*?!"

"Until *they* can't endure any longer."

Two days passed.

Ah Qing and Little Jade remained in the cornfield, hungry.

"I have such a bitter taste in my mouth! And my stomach has been growling constantly!"

"It's going to be okay, Little Jade! We just have to believe in ourselves. We're going to beat them! We are not going to die of hunger! There are lots of things for us to eat here. These cornstalks are good for relieving thirst, and these tender corncobs can relieve hunger! We also have these wild fruits! They're a little bitter, but it's better than eating weeds!" Ah Qing looked at Little Jade's lips, which were starting to turn blue.

Tears fell from Little Jade's eyes, and Ah Qing kissed them. "My dear brother! Don't cry! Neither of us will cry! We have to stay strong and keep living. We also have to save Little Tough and all the other brothers who are suffering!"

Late that night, a great wind blew, followed by a heavy rainfall. Ah Qing and Little Jade removed their shirts and trousers and hung them among the cornstalks for shelter. Then they held each other tightly to warm themselves.

Raindrops fell from the little cloth canopy they had made as rain beat against the leaves of the cornstalks, making a heavy rustling sound. Harder at one moment, lighter the next, the rain was unremitting as Ah Qing and Little Jade held each other, their bodies curled into a single ball.

ELEVEN

1

You and Ah Qing rented a commercial space on a narrow street in Zhengzhou, where you opened a barbershop. A year later when the street was expanded the shop was demolished.

The two of you started spending all of your time at Zijing Mountain Park.

Worried that Ah Qing was secretly hooking up with other guys, you hid in a thicket of trees hoping to catch him in the act of cheating on you. Ah Qing sat on a rock beside the river as a handsome young man walked back and forth before him. Ten or fifteen minutes later, this vile boy sat on the rock beside Ah Qing and you watched as he pressed his lips against Ah Qing's face. Angrily, you came out of the cluster of trees and approached them, thinking about how much you'd like to punch one or maybe both of them right in the face.

When the young guy saw you coming toward them he got up from Ah Qing's side and made his way into the dark cluster of trees. Ah Qing ignored you, seemingly on purpose, and followed him. You were so furious you could have died right there. You spotted a bicycle under a tree, its wheel-lock securely fastened. No one else was around and it was quite dark. You knew it had to be that that slut's bike, so you picked it up and threw it straight into Gold Water River, where it landed with a splash and settled into the filthy water as if falling into a deep sleep. The river was shallow; a handlebar stuck out of the water like an erect penis.

You turned and ran a few feet, then stopped abruptly and came back. You wanted to know what position Ah Qing and that slut were having sex in, and for how long. Just thinking about him betraying you was enraging. You waited thirty-six minutes until Ah Qing and that slut resurfaced, looking extremely tranquil. You felt as though your lungs were about to explode.

"You haven't left yet, Little Jade?" Ah Qing asked with a laugh as he patted you on the butt.

You ignored him. You wanted to know if the bike you'd thrown into the river belonged to that slut. If it wasn't, what a waste of time and effort it had been throwing it into the river! One thing was certain: that slut wasn't going to get away with this. Anyone who touched your Ah Qing was going to pay a price.

"Aiya!" the boy cried out like a slaughtered chicken. "Where's my bike?"

"Could it have been stolen?" Ah Qing asked with concern. "Little Jade, weren't you here the whole time? Have you seen his bike?"

"I haven't seen it, and I don't have time to stand here watching bikes all day!" Your face was red and your voice was loud. "Not just any old bike is going to get stolen! If something's a piece of crap, not even a scrap collector will want it!"

The boy looked at you, then ran toward the water. Park lights and the dazzling half-moon conspired to illuminate the stinking river water. The handlebar of the bicycle still poked out of the water, as stiff as a big cock. The boy cried out as though he were being raped.

"It was definitely him—he threw my bike into the water!" The boy pulled at Ah Qing with one hand and pointed at your nose with the other.

"Yeah, I threw it into the water—I thought it was junk that no one wanted!" You squared your shoulders and clenched your fists. Whatever happened, you knew that Ah Qing would stand by your side.

The boy curled his hands into fists and came charging at you. Ah Qing grabbed him and held him fast, then began with the sweet-talk to try and calm him down. Then, to your complete surprise, Ah Qing jumped into the river, causing his trousers to get soaked to the knees. He lifted the slumbering bike out of the filthy water as the boy rushed forward with outstretched arms to receive it. The boy then released the lock with a key and pushed the bicycle up the riverbank with Ah Qing by his side. They ignored you and you began to regret your rashness. You loved Ah Qing dearly. His trousers were wet. Would he catch a cold?

"Ah Qing! Come back!" you yelled loudly.

Ah Qing and that boy stepped out of the park. The streetlights shined brightly, but in your heart there was nothing but darkness.

You hurried back home, but Ah Qing's shadow was nowhere to be found, so you returned to the park. He wasn't there either, so you went back home again. Back and forth you went until you were the only person left in the park. You were alone, and helplessly lonely.

Just as the sky was beginning to grow light, you went back to the place where you lived. Was this still the home that you and Ah Qing shared? Your entire body felt icy cold. Just thinking about Ah Qing holding someone else in pleasure made your heart ache as though it were being torn apart. Exhausted, you closed your eyes, which were red from crying, to go to sleep. When you awakened from the nightmares, it was already dusk outside.

You hadn't eaten or had a drop of water all day. Your head was dizzy and heavy, and your heart wouldn't stop crying out, "Ah Qing Ah Qing Ah Qing Ah Qing!"

When the sky went black and the streetlights turned on you returned yet again to the park. There, you spotted Ah Qing on the riverbank; his eyes were red and in a single night his faced seemed to have thinned. The two of you sat on a cement balustrade, neither of you saying a word. Ah Qing hadn't come home the night before. It was he who had done you wrong; you wanted him to apologize. You hated him for saying sweet words to someone else, for having sex with someone else, and for putting you through hell the night before. You wanted him to hang his head low and recognize that he had been wrong. Your heart was still bleeding. You wanted him to tell you that if he was ever with anyone else, it was just messing around because the opportunity was there; no matter what, he would never truly get involved.

"Where did you go last night?" Ah Qing opened up his parched, cracked lips to speak. He didn't seem to have slept well the previous night, either.

"Get off pretty good last night?" you asked with a sneer.

Angrily, he stood up to leave. You didn't go chasing after him. You hated him. Not one bit had he shown you that he knew he had screwed up, that it was he who had first done you wrong! You were determined to get revenge on him, determined to show him what it felt like to be abandoned by love.

Some guy from out of town said he liked you, liked your craziness. He hailed a taxi, and just as the two of you were getting in you saw Ah Qing walking in your direction. He looked at you with regretful eyes. You seemed to be moving very slowly; you were still waiting for him to apologize to you. As long as he gave you a little face, said some nice-sounding words to you, you would forgive him. You would return to his side.

The taxi lunged forward, but Ah Qing's red eyes remained glued to you. You couldn't hear his voice, and as the cab drove off your broken heart drifted far away.

2

When Little Jade got to this part of the story, his eyes filled with tears. It was still painful for him to remember the events of the past.

I poured him a hot cup of tea.

"It's a little bitter," I said. "It was produced here in Henan, in Xinyang."

Little Jade laughed, and his lips formed a tight circle to blow on the surface of the tea. "Xinyang tea is the only kind of tea in Henan," he said. "When my dad was still alive, he only drank Xinyang tea. He always said that Henan tea leaves were bitter in your mouth, but sweet in your heart!"

I raised my arm and our teacups met in a happy toast.

"Ah Qing told me about the two of you," I said to Little Jade. We were sitting face to face. "He told me that when you were together, he hated it when you flirted with other guys. He only went into the trees with that person in front of you to make you angry so you would go to the park less often. As he was dragging the bike out of the river, he was angry too, but he wanted to console that guy so you and him wouldn't get in a fight. That's the only reason he was willing to walk that boy home wearing soaking-wet pants, too. When he went back to the park, though, he couldn't find you. He figured you must have gone home, so he went home to look for you. You guys are too funny! Ah Qing looking for Little Jade at home, Little Jade looking for Ah Qing at the park, Ah Qing looking for Little Jade at the park, Little Jade looking for Ah Qing at home! Ah Qing and Little Jade looking for each other for an entire night. Ah Qing couldn't find you and he thought that you must have spent the night at someone else's place. He said he was quite distraught about the whole thing. The truth is, Ah Qing was being just as stubborn as you were. He said you should have apologized to him first. And yet, no matter how stubborn he was acting, when he saw you leave with someone else, he turned out to be very jealous! He said that when he saw you get in a taxi and leave with that comrade from out of town, his heart was completely torn to pieces."

I started to cook and Little Jade helped by washing the vegetables. When the food was ready, we continued to chat as we ate.

On the television screen there appeared a beautiful forest, which quickly gave way to snow-capped mountains, grasslands, and the vast, open sea. The masculine voice of TV-show host

Zhao Zhongxiang narrated as animals mated, reproduced, and killed each other.

"Do you like Zhao Zhongxiang's voice, Little Jade?" I asked. "I've always loved that show he hosts, *Animal World.* They changed the name to *Humans and Nature.*"

"Yes, I like it," Little Jade replied. "Zhao Zhongxiang came to Huaiyang County once as part of a TV production team. That's where I'm from."

Zhao Zhongxiang's voice faded, and I watched as a series of sick people appeared on the screen recommending that I purchase all kinds of unnecessary medicines.

"After living in Zhengzhou for a few years," Little Jade continued, "I didn't want to go back to my hometown and do farm work. But after I got to Xuchang, I didn't like Zhengzhou anymore. And after I got to Beijing, I felt that Beijing was the best!"

"If you visited New York City or Montreal, you wouldn't want to go back to Beijing," I said.

"I don't speak any foreign languages. If I went abroad I would turn into a mute!"

"If you do want to go abroad, you should start studying now. When you get there, find a job as a dish washer. You can make more money doing that than working in China!"

"In some countries, ignorant, narrow-minded people look down on the Chinese just like Beijingers look down on Henanese people here."

The topic made Little Jade's face grow red with agitation.

I pulled out a cigarette and offered it to him. He waved his hand to say no.

"There are so many poor people in China!" he lamented. "And so many corrupt officials—were they created by the system, or is there something fundamentally flawed about the Chinese? Why is Henan Province poor? If Henan were a colony, the people of Henan would be just as rich as people in Hong Kong, and all the people who look down on the

Henanese would be stumbling over each other to get there for work."

A swirling cloud of smoke poured out of my lungs. "I heard this joke from a Chinese guy I know who came back to China after living abroad. There was plane full of people flying in the sky. An American said, 'We Americans have a lot of money,' and he threw a leather suitcase full of cash out the airplane door. A Japanese said, 'We Japanese have a lot of computers,' and he threw out a computer. When it was the Chinese person's turn, he said, 'We Chinese have a lot of Chinese people!' and he grabbed one of his fellow countrymen and tossed him out the door. When I heard this joke, I thought it was disgraceful!"

3

When you were still inside your mother's belly, you had a three-year-old brother, but he died before you could even meet him. Your mother often blamed your father for this, saying that if he hadn't gone to the city to work, the boy would still be alive. Later, while still in the city, your father died, too. From that day onward, the very idea of the city filled your mother with fear; each time you went there to work, she went through another bout of sorrow.

She continued to work when she was pregnant with you, and she worked a lot. She had a strong and sturdy body. When your father was still living, it was only during holidays that he would come see the two of you.

On top of everything else that was wicked about your father being in the city, one very cold winter Mother heard that he had found another woman. Off she went to find him, her big belly sticking out and your older brother in her arms. You, being inside her stomach, had no idea what was going on. When your mother found your father, she didn't ask him a thing about what had happened, but just smiled and, along with your three-year-old brother, stayed in the city with him. A week passed and your father wanted to send the three of you back home. Mother wanted Father to come back with you, but he said that he couldn't leave his work. She, meanwhile, said that she couldn't leave him. When Father looked at Mother's big belly, he couldn't bear the thought of arguing with her. She pestered him for an entire month, and for an entire month your father lost his freedom, so in the end he began to argue with her. Mother cried, big brother cried. You had no idea what was going on, but if you had known that your mother and big brother were crying, you probably would have cried along with them.

Father told Mother that he had to go to his work unit for the night shift and that he couldn't come home.

The following day, he told her once more that he had to go to his work unit for the night shift. Upon hearing this, your mother sighed deeply. She knew he wouldn't be coming home that night, so she just lulled your big brother to sleep. A coal stove burned in one corner; it had no chimney, but a window was open and a frigid wind blew in, causing the air inside the home to grow cold. Mother sang lullabies to your brother to coax him to sleep, then started to knit you some wool clothing. She dreamed that growing inside her belly was a beautiful little girl.

One of Father's coworkers came by in the evening to borrow something from him. When your mother told him that your father was working the night shift, the coworker gave a look of surprise and said that the work unit was closed for vacation. He left, and your mother put on her big, cotton-padded overcoat and stormed out the door. The wind blew snowflakes in the air, pushing them through the window and into the house. Mother feared that your big brother, who was sleeping alone on the bed, would catch cold, so she closed the window and added a piece of coal to the stove. She walked all the way to your father's work unit, where she discovered that it was true: he wasn't at work. She was certain that he was with another woman.

Mother carried you—you were nearly nine months old now—in her belly as she walked sorrowfully on the road where falling snowflakes gathered. She went to the home of one of your father's friends to look for him, but he was nowhere to be found. That's when your mother fainted and collapsed, then gave birth to you on the snow-covered ground. The two of you were saved by a doctor who happened to be passing by, but your older brother, who was home alone, died from carbon monoxide poisoning.

Your mother said that you cried from the day you entered the world straight through till you were three years old and your sister was born. Mother had loved your older brother deeply. When the New Year came around, she burned joss-paper clothing for him.

After your brother died, your father asked for some time off work so he could come home and be with your mother for a few months. Mother wanted him to stay and farm, but Father said workers could earn more than farmers, so he returned to the city once more to work.

When you were seven, your father sent you to the village elementary school. Your childhood was full of sweetness—you ate all the candies that your father gave you. When you were thirteen, your father died in the city. Your mother said that he had died of illness, but behind your back, all of the grownups said he had been killed by a woman.

You grew bigger and bigger by the day. Mother didn't allow you to mention Father, and she didn't want to remarry. Anytime you were bullied, you thought of your father and of the older brother whom you had never met. This brother had died at the very moment you were born, leading your mother to state that it was decreed by fate that she should have only one son. You searched for that long-lost brother in your dreams. If you had found him, and if it really was true that Mother was destined to have only one son, you would have been willing to turn into a girl so that he could be your big brother forever.

"What was the woman who killed Daddy like?" You were as tall as your mother now.

"Your Daddy died of illness—don't believe what other people say!" Tears hung in her eyes.

You lowered your head. When standing before your mother, you always talked with your head lowered.

"How did you die, Daddy? Can you send me a message in a dream?" You looked at your father in a big, framed black-and-white photograph. He smiled at you from inside the glass; he was always smiling at you. Ever since you could remember your father had never hit you or yelled at you. If he and your mother were fighting and he saw you standing nearby, he would walk over to you with a big smile on his face. You loved your father. You loved your mother even more.

"Mom, I dreamed about Dad again! He gave me a pocketful of candy." You wrapped your arms around your mother's neck and kissed it.

Mother laughed. She said that you were growing quickly and would soon be as tall as your father. He always seemed to appear by your side whenever she spoke. When Tomb-Sweeping Day arrived, she wasn't going to forget to take you to your father's grave; when you got there, she asked you to kneel before his grave and kowtow. You didn't know how many times you were supposed to kowtow, so you just kept doing it.

"That's enough, Little Jade, you can stop kowtowing to Daddy." She started to pull you up.

A light drizzle fell as you and your mother left the cemetery. The soles of your shoes became caked with mud and you were suddenly taller than you had been just moments earlier. Mother's body suddenly seemed short and thin, and there were more and more wrinkles on her face. You held her coarse hand as the two of you walked home.

4

One Sunday evening you went to Xihaizi Park, where you met Mr. Bai.

The area of the park that was densest with trees was where it was the darkest, and where it was the darkest was where there were the greatest number of people. You walked ahead of Mr. Bai as he trailed behind you. You weren't attracted to him; you just wanted to get off. You slipped into a grove, where you saw a man and a woman locked in an embrace. You slipped further into the darkness, where you saw two more lovebirds holding each other. You were searching for a darkness in which there were no people. This Mr. Bai—the name meant "white"—was dressed in black from head to toe. He continued walking behind you, looking like a black cow in heat.

"Let's go to a friend of mine's house, we can fool around there!" Mr. Bai's forehead was drenched in sweat.

All you wanted to do with this old guy was get off. You certainly didn't want to sleep in the same bed with him. He was too fat. You were afraid he would crawl on top of you and crush you to death.

"I have to go back home tonight," you protested. "I work the early shift tomorrow morning." If it weren't for Mr. Bai's decent temperament, you would have lost interest in the whole thing by now.

The two of you made your way to a stretch of open space in the northwest corner of the park surrounded by verdant pines and cypresses. Enshrouded by darkness, you unzipped your pants and pulled out your cock for Mr. Bai to suck.

"What is this place?" Mr. Bai asked, pulling away and looking all around. "Is anyone going to see us?"

"Don't worry," you reassured him. "Cowards don't come here!" You lowered your voice and stuffed your thing back into his mouth.

"It's so cold and gloomy here! Seriously, what is this place?" He spit your cock out and asked nervously.

"You've never been here before? This is the burial ground of a great thinker from the Ming Dynasty! Don't worry, no one will come." You consoled the old man. He was going to make you feel good.

Mr. Bai had already unzipped his trousers at that point, but when his eyes adjusted to the dark and he saw the cement stele marking the grave, he became so frightened that he zipped back up and began to run. He immediately tripped and fell with a thud. Suddenly feeling a strong cold gust of wind, you zipped up your pants in a hurry and lifted Mr. Bai off the ground.

You and Mr. Bai stepped back into a lighted area, where you were able to see the huge, bloody gash on his forehead. From a distance, it looked like a budding rose. You covered your mouth and silently laughed, taking pleasure in his misfortune.

Two weeks later, you bumped into each other again at Xihaizi Park. The bloody welt on his forehead had disappeared; it was replaced by a thick scab.

"Let me take you to a bathhouse, Little Jade!" Mr. Bai looked at you affectionately.

"I don't want to go to a bathhouse. After it's completely dark out, let's go back to the cemetery and play there!" you said jokingly.

Mr. Bai's color changed and he took your hand solemnly. "Don't ever go back to fool around in that cemetery."

He held your hand tightly, leaving you with nothing to do but go along with this kind, eager Mr. Bai to a bathhouse.

"Which bathhouse are we going to, Mr. Bai?"

"Let's just go to whichever one is closest!"

"I thought you were going to take me to a gay bathhouse!"

"I've heard about gay bathhouses, but I haven't had the guts to go to one yet. I've heard that at gay bathhouses, there are hundreds of people who shower then fool around together. Sounds scary!"

You laughed loudly.

"Do you go to gay bathhouses often?" He seemed eager for you to describe in detail all that you had seen.

"I've been to two: The People's Bathhouse and Hanlin Spring." You went on to describe everything you had seen and done.

Mr. Bai wanted to see a gay bathhouse, so he flagged down a taxi and off you went to central Beijing. But when the vehicle reached Dabeiyao the traffic suddenly became congested. He didn't have the patience to wait, so the two of you got out of the car and he gave up on the idea of going to a gay bathhouse altogether. Instead, he took you to different one. It had an extravagantly renovated interior. It wasn't a gay place, though, and there weren't many people there.

"It's all rich people here, huh?" you asked, looking at all the big bellies.

They looked like a bunch of pregnant women as they lay on couches or stood languidly. Some of the men had breasts that were bigger than a woman's, and their skin was whiter than tofu. Their thighs were hairless and their legs had started to atrophy from all the years of driving around in cars, riding to and from work, and taking elevators. Their feet were the shape of pigs' trotters. You studied their penises carefully and discovered that the fatter the man, the smaller the dick. Some of their cocks had shrunken deep into their pubic hair—and yet, when these womanly males put their clothes back on, they were the wealthiest of all men! Did they have women? Were they able to make women climax? After achieving all that power and wealth, did they just go on to produce offspring who would atrophy even further? Did they have extramarital perversions, did they produce bastard children?

"What are you thinking about?" Mr. Bai placed a towel over your shoulder.

Something was making you feel heavy. What was it?

"I was thinking about what I've seen at gay bathhouses and what I'm seeing now," you laughed. "All the comrades at gay bathhouses have great bodies, faces and cocks, and yet they're not attracted to women! They don't like intellectuals, either; they say that intellectuals lack passion, that they only understand the refined culture of the literati. Lots of comrades like soldiers and migrant workers. They love their strong bodies and hard cocks."

Mr. Bai laughed.

"Mr. Bai, what's the biggest cock you've ever seen?" You stood under the faucet as the gentle water cascaded down your back and onto the floor.

"Nineteen centimeters!" He held his hands apart to show you.

Mr. Bai had lived through more mid-autumns than you, but he hadn't seen as many big cocks. In his time, people were afraid to even mention homosexuality, whereas for your generation, finding homosexual friends was the easiest thing in the world. Two people came to mind; you had met them when running wild in the parks and bathhouses. The first one was called Thirteen Spice because his cock was just as wide as a box of thirteen-spice powder. The other one was known as the Easy-Open Can because his dick was just as thick as any tin can. These two extremely well-endowed gay guys had come to Beijing from a poor and remote mountain region in Henan Province to excavate sewers.

"Different cocks give the flesh different sensations—the bigger they are, the better they feel!" Mr. Bai looked at your cock as he spoke and his medium-sized, sixteen-centimeter penis began to rise.

"You can't tell a man's cock size from his height!" you added with a laugh. "Some men are a hundred eighty centimeters tall, but their dicks are only fifteen centimeters long. Other men are only a hundred sixty centimeters tall, but their cocks are over twenty. Stupid women marry men with erectile dysfunction or men who prematurely ejaculate. If a woman really wants to marry the ideal man and if she's smart, she'd better consult a homosexual male!"

5

"Last night, I dreamed of our deceased friend Little Wave," Little Jade mused. "He was crying and he asked me if he could borrow some money."

"Then you should burn some joss-paper money for him!"
I said earnestly. "Wandering souls in the afterworld who've
died a wrongful death need to be pitied."

I went with Little Jade and paid ten yuan for a ten-
thousand-yuan spirit note, then we walked to an intersection,
where we burned it for Little Wave, who was in another world.

"Good people get good rewards!" I repeated several times
into Little Jade's ear.

I began to tell him a story from when I worked at the
crematorium.

One night, a pregnant woman dressed in white emerged from
a hospital. She hailed a taxi and asked the driver how much
the fare would be. The driver was a young guy. He asked the
pregnant woman where she was going.

"To the crematorium!" She opened the door and got in.

"Thirty kuai!" the driver said as the car flew forward.

They arrived at the crematorium in good time. The gated
entrance opened automatically and the taxi rolled into the
courtyard, then came to a standstill. The pregnant woman gave
the driver a one-hundred-yuan bill. When he looked at the
image of the old man on the banknote, he was satisfied that it
was legal tender, so he pulled seventy kuai in change from his
wallet and handed it to the woman. She took the money and
got out of the car, then disappeared in the blink of an eye into
the building. Just as the driver was about to put the hundred
yuan into his wallet, he suddenly shouted, then jumped out of
the car to go find the pregnant woman. Yelling at the top of
his lungs, he ran through the courtyard.

I was snoozing in the on-duty room at the entrance of
the crematorium when I was awakened by a loud voice. In a
rush, I threw on a jacket, then went outside to see what was
going on.

"Sir!" the driver started. "I just drove a pregnant woman
here from the hospital. She gave me spirit money and cheated

me out of seventy kuai! I saw her come in here." He handed me the hundred-yuan spirit note.

I looked at the image printed on the bill: it was Yama, King of Hell. Suddenly I felt a little annoyed. "The front gate is locked," I said, challenging his story. "How did you drive in?"

"It opened automatically," he replied. "That pregnant charlatan got out of the car, then came in here!" He pointed at the entrance.

I thought the driver was drunk and trying to cause trouble, but I took him inside, grabbed my keys from the on-duty room and went to open the door of the morgue. I turned on the light and waited to see whether this tedious driver had anything else to say.

"Take a good look," I said, pointing at the deceased woman lying on a bed. "Apart from her, there's nobody here."

"That's her!" he cried. "Sir, look—she's still holding my seventy yuan!" The driver's voice was becoming increasingly shrill.

"What nonsense are you talking? This woman died in labor and was brought here from the hospital over a week ago. Her relatives still haven't paid the cremation fee, so for now I have to leave her here." After saying these words, I noticed that there was indeed a small stack of RMB in the woman's hand, which hung off the side of the bed.

"I've worked in this crematorium for thirty years and this is the first time I've ever seen something as strange as this!" I said in a futile effort to console the terrified driver beside me.

The young man cried out once more, then ran out of the morgue and cremation room. His car was still parked outside, motor running, headlights staring into the darkness.

His car remained at the crematorium for two days. Nobody came to ask about it. Although the dead woman was holding seventy kuai in her hand, it still wasn't enough for the cremation fee, so she remained on the table.

My ex-wife divorced me because she was unable to get pregnant. She never remarried, but she did adopt a little girl.

During Spring Festival and other holidays I would go visit the mother and child. On a small street not far from the crematorium, this old lady—my ex-wife—opened up a little liquor and tobacco store. On one particular evening, an old drunk showed up; he had an oilpaper bag in his hand.

"Gimme a . . . pack of . . . Zhongnanhais!" the drunk commanded haltingly.

The old lady handed him a pack of Zhongnanhai-brand cigarettes, then took a bill from his hand. "Young man," she said sternly upon seeing the fifty-yuan spirit note he had given her, "don't you mess around with this old lady!"

When the drunk saw that he had given her spirit money, he was so startled that he sobered up right away. He shoved his hands into his trouser pockets and searched around until he pulled out three ten-yuan spirit notes.

"Fuck!" he shouted. "That stinking bitch who sold me roast duck tricked me because she knew I was drunk. She sold me a roast duck for twenty yuan. I gave her a real hundred-yuan note, and she gave me back eighty in spirit money! And there I had been thinking I was getting a good deal—twenty yuan for a whole roast duck! I was tricked! I'm gonna go find that stinking bitch." Though in a rage, the drunk was quite lucid, and didn't seem to be very drunk any longer.

"There's no roast-duck shop around here, young man . . . at least I don't think there is!" The old lady was perplexed and sounded uncertain. "Where did you buy that roast duck?"

The drunk pointed in the direction of the crematorium. "I got it at a shop over there!"

The old lady looked at him in surprise. She didn't dare believe that what he had said was true.

To prove to her that he was telling the truth, the drunk opened up the bag, but when they looked inside what they saw wasn't a roast duck, but a dead baby boy curled up in a ball. They were now so aghast that they began to shake.

The drunk was scared out of his wits. He threw the pack of Zhongnanhais to the floor and ran out of the store, shouting uncontrollably.

My ex-wife called me on the phone. With a trembling voice, she told me to get over there at once.

I helped her calm down, then took the dead baby with me back to the crematorium. When I opened the door to the morgue, the female corpse was still there, but what I saw nearly gave me a heart attack. Her belly had been cut open, her arms hung down beside her, and in both hands she tightly held two stacks of RMB!

To get credit in the next life for doing a good deed in this one, I parted with some of my own money to buy new clothes for the mother and son. After paying the cremation fee, I burned their bodies, hoping they would find peace and happiness in the next world.

TWELVE

1

Ceaselessly the rain fell. Seventh Brother was at home going crazy with boredom. "Fuck," he thought, "that black factory still owes Ah Qing and the others money. I should just go get it right now . . . and have a drink while I'm at it!"

He threw on some clothes and left the house. As he stepped through the entrance to the clothing factory, the boss's two sons warmly welcomed this "local ruffian." When the encounter was over, Seventh Brother took a portion of the money they had given him for Ah Qing and the others and bought two pigs' trotters, one jin of beef and a bottle of Siwu-brand wine.

Seventh Brother sat alone, drinking. Little Orchid was on the bed with Little Dragon, teaching him to walk. He heard the courtyard gate opening, so he put down his glass, opened the door and looked outside. Two disheveled beggars entered the courtyard.

"Seventh Brother—it's me, Ah Qing." Ah Qing's voice was hoarse and he was supporting Little Jade, who was in a delirious state, by his shoulders.

"Good heavens!" Seventh Brother cried in surprise. "Ah Qing, Little Jade! What happened to you? Little Orchid, come here, quick!"

They were taken to a clinic, where a doctor gave them a shot to bring down their fevers.

When Ah Qing awoke, he told Seventh Brother all that had happened. "Seventh Brother, hurry . . . you have to save Little Tough and the others."

The rain had stopped by now but the sky was still heavy with clouds. Seventh Brother went to the local police substation, where he found the station chief smoking a cigarette and reading the *Legal Daily*.

"Little Seven!" the chief called out. "What brings you here?"

"I'm here to report a case!" Seventh Brother replied. "My brothers were sold to a black factory by human traffickers!"

"Oh!" the chief exclaimed. "Is that right? Well, those brothers of yours—there's not a good one among them! Bunch of thieves and swindlers—human scum, every last one! They deserve to be sold to a black factory. Saves us a lot of trouble that way!"

Biting his tongue and swallowing his rage, Seventh Brother exited the substation. He considered talking to an officer in a police box outside, but it was no use. Everyone knew him, and everyone was likely to have the same response as the police chief. All he could do was go home.

"Fuck!" he raged. "Not a single one of them treats me like a human being!" Seventh Brother knocked over a teacup in anger. It fell to the floor and broke into pieces.

"How about I go report it?" Little Orchid changed her clothes and stepped out of their home.

A week later, Little Tough and the others were liberated from the black factory and, with the help of Seventh Brother and Little Orchid, Ah Qing and Little Jade returned home.

Only after she herself became a mother did Little Orchid realize all the difficulties that motherhood entailed. When she was a child and her own mother was still alive, Mother always held Little Orchid's hand tightly. She would ask her to be a good girl by taking care of her younger brother. At the time, she hated her mother and father for valuing boys more than girls. Now married and living in a strange and faraway place, Little Orchid returned to her natal home only once a year. Thanks to custom, it was not possible for her to remain by her parents' side and be a filial child; her younger brother, however—he still lived at home with their parents because he was a boy. She eventually forgave her mother and father for valuing boys more than girls, and was even consoled by the fact that she herself had given birth to a son.

Little Dragon slept beside his mother. Surely he was dreaming of something happy? Look! A smile as sweet as candy is written on his face.

Were those Seventh Brother's dirty socks under the bed? Little Orchid took a wash basin and laundry detergent, then turned on the water faucet and began to wash them. There was a washing machine in the room—she and Seventh Brother had bought it after they got married—but she never used it for washing small items. That way, she could save both electricity and detergent. Ever since she had married Seventh Brother and given birth to Little Dragon, Little Orchid couldn't bear to part with a single fen of money for makeup. One day she entered Sister Plum Blossom's Hair Salon and suddenly felt that she had grown old in the blink of an eye. It was frightful! Had Seventh Brother noticed?

She sometimes felt that Seventh Brother was still a child, even though he was already a little over thirty. Often her husband and son would make a terrible ruckus when fighting over which of them would get to have Little Orchid's breasts. At the end of the day, Little Orchid always preferred her own child, and she would hold him as they slept under a blanket. Seventh Brother would sit on the couch smoking and staring in Little Dragon's direction with hateful eyes; still, his clenched fists never came down on the child's body. How could a father be jealous of his own child? It was preposterous! When Little Orchid yelled at Seventh Brother, he would lower his head and grow quiet just like a child who had been caught doing something wrong. But it was never long before he asked for Little Orchid's breasts again.

"What on earth is this?" Little Orchid thought as she washed Seventh Brother's underwear. There, she found semen stains that wouldn't wash out no matter how she tried. Seventh Brother was a married man—did he still have wet dreams? Full

240

of questions and doubt, she continued washing his underwear in the basin.

Another month working as a maid for the old landlady. When Little Orchid got paid she wanted to buy some body lotion, so she called Little Lotus and together they went to Asia Shopping Center. Asia Shopping Center was no longer as bustling and prosperous as it had once been and the women who worked there were now old enough to be called "auntie" instead of "miss." In the early 1990s, Little Orchid and many other young women of the Central Plains region all dreamed of becoming Asia girls.

Little Orchid watched as Little Lotus bought body lotion, conditioning mousse, perfume, lipstick, and nail polish, spending two hundred forty yuan in total. That was how much Little Orchid made in a month! Little Orchid bought only a bottle of body lotion, spending six yuan seven mao. Little Lotus acted like a rich housewife. She walked ahead of Little Orchid, who trailed behind like a servant girl. "Come on, hurry up!" Little Lotus shouted, her eyes fixed on the body of a man before them wearing a Western-style suit and leather shoes. Little Orchid silently cursed her: "Bitch!"

After Little Orchid learned that Little Lotus and Little Chrys were prostitutes, she looked down on them somewhat. Later, she found out that Sister Plum Blossom from Sister Plum Blossom's Hair Salon was a prostitute, too. And the old landlady? Well, she had sung opera when she was younger, so she had probably once been a prostitute as well. Of all the women living and working in Courtyard No. 8, it seemed that Little Orchid was the only one who wasn't a prostitute! Although she looked down on prostitutes, she frequently felt a good deal of shame about her own identity as a maid. She saw the triumphant way in which the other girls took taxis and went to shopping centers, restaurants, and dance clubs. Her jealous heart began to ache! What's the big deal about being a prostitute? All she had to do was change into some pretty clothes and she could do it, too!

"If you don't make good money while you're still young, no one's going to be there when you're old to make up for what you *could* have made from your youth!" Little Orchid often heard these words ringing in her ears. Had marrying Seventh Brother been a mistake? Anytime he had grievances or was unable to make money, he would stay home in a foul mood. Little Orchid watched as other families made more and more money and her heart began to waver. Could a woman who had given birth to a child be a prostitute? Little Orchid looked at her son, who was growing bigger and bigger each day, and her heart ached. How would she provide for his education?

Little Orchid began daydreaming that she herself was a prostitute.

She stepped into Sister Plum Blossom's Hair Salon.

2

Another autumn harvest season had arrived. Farmers drove three- and four-wheeled tractors into their family fields to pick corn, soybeans, cotton, and other crops. Ah Qing was driving a three-wheeled tractor back home from the fields. Trailing behind him was a flatbed full of cornstalks, and on top of the cornstalks sat Ah Qing's father and younger brother. Little Jade, meanwhile, drove an identical tractor toward the fields. His mother and younger sister sat in the drawer-shaped bed at the back.

The yellow dirt road of the village wasn't very wide or straight, and vehicles kicked thick clouds of dust into the air when they traveled it. Little Jade drove the empty vehicle, its back right wheel perilously close to a shallow trench at the side of the road. It came to a standstill and he waited as a larger vehicle hauling something or other passed. Beads of sweat clung to Ah Qing's forehead. He smiled at Little Jade's family as he unhurriedly drove by.

A fifteen-watt light bulb shined down on a family that was sitting in the main room of their home. They were breaking husks from tufts of cotton while watching a fourteen-inch black-and-white television. On the TV screen, a celebrity danced and sang light-heartedly.

"Second Aunt! Second Aunt!" From outside, a little girl's voice could be heard calling out for her father's sister.

Little Jade's mother heard the shouting and quickly stood up. "Aiya!" she exclaimed. "It's Little Na! Come in and sit, come in and sit!"

Little Na stood the bicycle on its kickstand, then removed a basket of apples from the rack behind the seat. As she entered the house, Little Jade greeted his younger cousin with a smile as he took a heavy basket of apples from her hands. Little Jade's younger sister pulled up a wooden chair for her older cousin.

Full of smiles, Little Na adjusted the chair, then sat down and reached to the floor to pick up some cotton. There she sat with the rest of the family, watching TV, chatting, and breaking cotton husks.

Tufts of cotton, some white, some not so white, were piled up in two baskets. Their black shells were strewn carelessly about the floor.

"Does your dad's lower back still hurt?"

"He's fine! He was hauling bricks and tiles again today."

"It's not easy for us farmers to make money!" Little Jade's mother said as her hands paused their work. "All this cotton piling up here at home . . . we can never sell it at a good price!"

"That's right!" Little Na added animatedly. "Nothing we farmers have is of any value! My dad says we're not going to plant any cotton next year. He's agreed to let me go to Guangdong and work!"

"Little Cousin!" Little Jade said with a laugh. "Don't go out to some unfamiliar place only to suffer! You won't necessarily make any money by going out and trying to find work!"

"That's right, Older Cousin!" Little's Jade's younger sister added. "Whatever you do, don't let what happened to my older brother and Brother Ah Qing happen to you! Don't get sold by human traffickers to a black factory!"

"Little Na!" Little Jade's mother said with a sigh. "Don't go running around out there in the world, a girl all by herself! There are lots of bad people out there!" Little Jade's mother sighed.

Little Na gave Little Jade a sidelong glance and giggled. "I've already discussed it with my future cousin-in-law, Little Jade's fiancée," she said. "We're leaving after the fall harvest!"

"Aiya!" Little Jade's mother exclaimed with surprise and not a little nervousness. "Little Xiang is going with you? How can you girls be so bold?"

Little Jade grew pensive and quiet for a moment. "Ma," he said. "If Little Xiang wants to go to Guangdong I won't object. Maybe they'll have better luck than Ah Qing and I did!"

"Older Cousin!" Little Jade's younger sister said. "The two of you go first, then after you find a good factory I'll come down with you. I'm not going to school anymore!"

Little Jade patted his younger sister on the head and said, "Oh you, you're only fifteen! You don't have an identity card yet, and besides, factories don't allow child labor. Why don't you just stay here at home and keep Ma company?"

Little Jade's sister pouted in his direction. When Little Na saw how cute her little cousin looked, she started to laugh.

"Little Cousin," Little Jade continued. "Have you told Ah Qing that you're going out to work?"

"That's exactly why I came—to tell Ah Qing that after the wheat has been planted, Little Xiang and I are leaving!"

"Oh, children!" Little Jade's mother exclaimed with a face full of worry. "As long as you don't go hungry, what's so bad about staying at home? Do you really want to go out into the world and live a hellish life?"

Little Jade stood up and walked out the door.

"Little Jade, you—"

He didn't wait for his mother to finish. "Ma," he interrupted, "I'm gonna go get Ah Qing. I want him to convince them not to go out and live a hellish life!"

Ah Qing and Little Na were alone in the room. They sat, heads lowered.

"Little Na," Ah Qing began. "You really want to go out there and work?"

"After the wheat has been planted, there'll be no more work to do on the land. Am I supposed to just sit at home doing nothing for months?"

"I'm not telling you and Little Xiang not to go—it's just that I'm afraid something awful will happen to the two of you." Ah Qing raised his head and looked her in the eye.

"Little Xiang and I aren't little kids anymore! We can take care of ourselves." Little Na, too, raised her eyes and looked at Ah Qing.

At just that moment, Little Jade's mother pushed open the door. "Little Na!" she said. "You and Ah Qing are getting married in a year or two. Don't go running off to the outside world, okay?"

"Second Aunt!" she cried. "Ah Qing is twenty and I'm only eighteen! I don't want to get married so early." She blushed. "Besides, Ah Qing's dad hasn't built a house for us yet!"

"Little Na, my dad said he's going to build a tile-roofed house with three rooms for us next year." Ah Qing blushed, too.

"I want to wait another few years before we get married, Ah Qing."

He nodded as Little Jade's mother heaved an exasperated sigh.

Little Jade pulled a farm handcart filled with three large bags of cotton. His mother walked behind him, hands pressed up against the bags to prevent them from falling. Farmers squeezed into the courtyard of the purchasing station as a product-intake worker commanded everyone to open their bags. Then the product-intake worker began thrusting a hand into the bags, fishing around and pulling things out. Little Jade and his mother kept their eyes glued nervously to the hand as it moved from one bag to the next.

After the intake, the next step was for the cotton to be weighed. When it was Little Jade's turn, a weight worker instructed him to place the handcart on a metal weighing platform and then, using a calculator, subtracted the weight of the cart from the total weight. The weight worker then called out a number as the pay-slip worker filled out a pay slip. When all this was done, the handcart was removed from the metal weighing platform and the mother-and-son team pulled it in the direction of a warehouse. Little Jade and his mother removed one of the bags from the handcart and began to ascend a tall mountain of cotton-filled bags at the center of the room. Just as they were opening the bag, a group of young inspection workers came forward, finished opening the bag for them, looked inside it for a while, then went back down the mountain.

Little Jade and his mother returned to their handcart to remove the second bag, and then the third. At just that moment, a mother and daughter from the same village climbed up the cotton mountain with their own bag in tow. With lightning speed they opened up the bag and a stream of golden tangerines fell out. All of the inspection workers rushed forward to grab tangerines while the mother-and-daughter team laughed heartily.

Little Jade's mother counted the money, her face revealing a bitter smile. Pulling the empty handcart, Little Jade walked shoulder to shoulder with his mother as they drew closer to their village.

"Ma, next time we do this we have to learn a thing or two from that mother and daughter! We should hide ten jin of tangerines in every bag of cotton!"

"But if they confiscate them during the inspection, we'd really lose face!"

"Did you see all those young men and women on top of that big pile of cotton? They're all temporary workers and their wages are low. Either they take those tangerines or they lose out! If they get to eat a few, they'll keep their mouths shut. With ten jin of tangerines, we'll be able to sell our cotton for thirty or forty more kuai!"

"We'd better not take the risk!" his mother cautioned. "If they really do bust us during an inspection, that's an entire year of work right down the drain!"

"But Ma," Little Jade persisted, "we're losing so much from the way we've been doing things. The leaders pay us so little, yet they don't let us go out to the cities to sell. Seeds, fertilizer, and pesticide are all getting more and more expensive. And all the miscellaneous farming taxes we have to pay! Just growing a couple of fruit trees or melons means we have to pay a special local-product tax!"

His mother sighed but didn't reply. She just followed Little Jade and the handcart back home.

"Ma! Big Brother! Oh, it's just terrible! Little Xiang's mother hanged herself!" Little Jade's younger sister cried as she ran into the home they shared.

Gripped with fear, Little Jade and his mother rushed in the direction of Little Xiang's home.

There, Little Xiang and Big Xiang clung to their mother's lifeless body and wept; their father squatted in the courtyard, alone and silently crying. Little Jade just stood there looking at the corpse, dumbstruck and utterly at a loss as to what to do.

"Oh, Little Xiang's dad!" Little Jade's mother stepped forward with teardrops in her eyes. "What happened? Just yesterday everything was fine! How could she have suddenly hanged herself?"

"It's all my fault!" the father said after gaining composure. "Yesterday afternoon we went to sell cotton—we all hoped we'd be able sell for a few dozen extra kuai. It was my idea: hide ten jin of salt in there. I never thought it would be found during the inspection! They confiscated an entire handcart full of cotton! Little Xiang's ma cried all night, then just as the sun was about to come up . . . I never could have imagined that she would walk down that desperate path!" Little Xiang's father wailed as he recounted what had happened.

Tears fell from Little Jade's mother's eyes. She didn't know what words she could utter to console this destroyed family.

3

An early winter day.

Little Xiang is wearing a white flower in the long braid in her hair.

Little Na is wearing a yellow flower in the long braid in her hair.

Little Jade and Ah Qing carry the girls' luggage on their backs. They are seeing them off to the train station.

The train speeds toward the south.

In the window, two hair braids dance as they fly away.

Wintertime in the open country. Weak and delicate wheat seedlings raised their heads from the ice-frosted yellow earth. A few sparrows flew by, looking for something to fill their stomachs.

Two young men walked on a small road cutting through the land. Cigarettes costing one yuan five mao per pack dangled from their lips.

"Lots of people from the village have gone to sell blood, Little Jade—my dad has, too!"

"Yes, I heard! There's a rumor going around the village saying that whoever doesn't sell blood must be sick!"

"Our life is so boring now! We work hard all year round but we still don't have any money to spend."

"I want to open up a chicken farm, but my family doesn't have the capital to get it started."

"And I've thought about starting a pig farm or a chicken farm, but my family doesn't have the capital, either."

The two shadows moved through the wintery fields.

Little Jade and Ah Qing were at home, sitting together and watching a program on a black-and-white television set.

A fat man speaking non-standard Mandarin suddenly appeared on the screen.

"Little Jade, that's our county magistrate!"

"Look at that pathetic guy! What could he possibly do for the common people?"

The two of them laughed.

"Look, Little Jade, it's our county-town department store!"

"That's been on the county TV station hundreds of times! That department store is the only decent building in the entire county!"

"Little Jade, look! Your ma is on TV, too!"

There on the television screen, a reporter from the county TV station was interviewing Little Jade's mother in front of the county hospital. Behind her hung a banner on which was written in large characters: "It Is Glorious to Donate Blood to Party and Nation!"

"Ma! At this age, you're . . . " Little Jade's nose twitched and his eyes filled with tears.

Suddenly the TV screen was flooded with glorious farmers. Among them Ah Qing spotted his own father, whose dark and weary face smiled at them.

Ah Qing and his father sat facing each other.

"Father, Little Jade and I want to go sell blood, too!"

Father looked at Ah Qing earnestly. His son was already taller than him.

"Ah Qing!" he said. "When you do it, you have to drink lots of hot water!"

"Yes, Father, I know!"

Ah Qing arrived at Little Jade's house. As they were stepping out of the courtyard gate, Little Jade's mother began running after them.

"Children! Remember, drink lots of water! And don't pee before they take the blood. If you have to pee, just hold it till they're done!"

Little Jade nodded in his mother's direction. The boys left Dragon Gully Village and boarded a bus to the provincial capital. The first thing they did when they got there was go to a braised noodle shop, where they each had a bowl of braised noodles. Pinch by pinch, they each added salt to their meal.

"Ugh! So salty!" Ah Qing wrinkled his brow.

"Ugh! So salty it's killing me!" Little Jade grimaced.

The shopkeeper approached the two young men with a smile on his face. "First time going to the hospital to donate blood, eh? Well, when you're done with your noodles, just drink lots of hot water and everything will be fine."

They suffered through their unbearably salty noodles, then poured bowl after bowl of water into their bellies. When they got to the hospital, they stood in a long line which led to a registration room. Before long, it was their turn to lie on the hospital bed and allow the doctor to start drawing blood.

When it was over, Ah Qing got up from the bed, unrolled his sleeve and walked to the bathroom. When he unzipped his thick trousers to urinate, he discovered that the woolen long underwear beneath was completely soaked through with piss. Suddenly the bathroom door opened and Little Jade stepped in. Ah Qing pulled down Little Jade's pants and had a look.

"Little Jade, your pants are soaked with pee, too!"

Little Jade laughed, then reached into Ah Qing's trousers to feel his cock.

The two of them walked the road back to Dragon Gully Village.

"Ah Qing, are you going to give the money from selling your blood to your father?"

"No, this is my money from selling my blood! I'm not giving it to him. I'm going to sell my blood again and I want to save enough money to start a pig farm!"

"Ah Qing! Ah Qing!" Little Jade shouted as he entered the courtyard.

The door opened and his nostrils were hit by the scent of urine. He covered his nose with a hand.

"How can you still be sleeping, Ah Qing? It's already eleven o'clock. Come out and get some sun!"

On a pile of pillows were stacked a few books of poetry and a notebook. Ah Qing emerged from under the blanket, then languidly put on some clothes. He picked up the bucket he had pissed in the night before and started to carry it out of the room; the sunlight outside was so bright that it pierced his eyes! His body swayed and the bucket fell to the ground.

"Did you go sell blood again?" Little Jade laughed sardonically. "You can't go too often, you know. Once a month is enough!"

It was the season of warm spring blossoms. The two young men sat beside the river.

"Has Little Na written, Ah Qing?"

"She wrote one letter. She said she's no longer working at the toy factory."

"Where does she work now? Little Xiang said the same thing!"

"I don't care where she works! She can go be a prostitute for all I care!"

"Are you crazy? You wouldn't care if she became a prostitute? What kind of thing is that for my little cousin's fiancé to say?"

"Selling sex is still of form of selling. Selling blood is, too. Isn't it all just to make money? Isn't it all just to be able to live?"

"Ah Qing!" Little Jade said in shock. "Listen to you! Is this your idea of living a meaningful life? You've changed! You're losing your moral integrity."

Ah Qing said nothing in reply, but closed his eyes and inhaled the scent of rapeseed floating in the air. Little Jade turned to look at the plants, a large patch of bright yellow flowers, on the riverbank. Unexpectedly, he ran over, plucked a bunch of flowers and brought them back to Ah Qing, who was now lying down and appeared to be deep in sleep. When Little Jade placed the stems beneath his nose, Ah Qing entered the world of dreams inhaling the scent of flowers.

4

Little Xiang's and Ah Qing's fathers were smoking and chatting.

"Last night all of the village chief's stacks of wheat straw got burned up!" Little Xiang's father said.

"So what?" Ah Qing's father replied. "The village chief's family doesn't feed cows and wheat straw isn't worth anything anyway! It was only going to rot in the fields—may as well burn it!"

"But that's not what people are saying happened!" Little Xiang's father insisted. "I heard that the village chief went to the town head's house and reported that the fire was set by angry villagers! The town head agreed to the village chief's demand: two hundred kuai from the village finances to compensate for his losses!"

"Fuck!" Ah Qing's father retorted. "A few years back the paper mill still bought wheat straw, but nowadays it's hardly worth a thing! The paper mill won't buy it anymore and fewer and fewer families have cattle now. People hardly even use it for lighting fires anymore! A big stack of wheat straw will get you at most twenty kuai, so how can the village chief wheat straw be worth two hundred?!"

Little Xiang's father lowered his voice to a whisper. "I heard someone saw it. They say it was the village chief himself —that he set his own wheat straw on fire!"

Several nights of heavy rain fell in the village, causing the top of the two-room, tile-roofed house that Little Xiang shared with her family suddenly to collapse. Her father barely escaped with his life. Distressed and in tears, he sought refuge with his older daughter, Big Xiang, who had married herself off to a nearby town. Holding her baby girl, Big Xiang sat on a wooden chair beside her husband in the main room of the house and listened to her father tell the whole story of how the house had collapsed.

"Father," Big Xiang's husband began, "it's not that we don't want to take you in! It's just that our family has a lot of burdens, too! The Family Planning Office has notified us that we have to pay a fine because Big Xiang is pregnant again. If we don't pay it, they're going to force her to get an abortion!"

"Yes, that's right!" Big Xiang added. "And besides, Father, since you're sixty now and you've never had a son, you can apply to the village for the Five Guarantees. After you apply for the Five Guarantees, the village will help you build a new house!"

Little Xiang's father stepped out of his older daughter's house, then walked along an asphalt road leading back to his village. After some time, he turned onto a dirt road and walked another ten li before reaching home. When he looked once more at his destroyed house, he couldn't help but choke up.

He used wooden planks, tarps, tiles, and other materials to build a shed that looked like a doghouse.

Ah Qing's father stepped into Little Xiang's dilapidated house, where he saw a crude shed. "Old Brother!" he yelled. "Why are you living in a doghouse? If you don't have anyone to take care of you, go talk to the village chief!"

Dripping with snot and tears, Little Xiang's father went to see the village chief.

"Old Brother," the village chief said, "go back home! I'll be sure and let the town head know about this. As soon as he approves you for the Five Guarantees, I'll send someone to help you build a new house!"

Another rain fell, a lighter one this time, and Little Xiang's father, still dripping with snot and tears, returned to the village chief.

"Old Brother," the village chief said, "go back home! I've already let the town head know about this. As soon as he approves you for the Five Guarantees, I'll send someone to help you build a new house!"

Gradually the sky darkened, then lightened, then darkened once again.

Days passed and Little Xiang's father went back once more to the village chief's house, still dripping snot and tears.

"Old Brother!" the village chief said as he stood up. "Go back home! I've already let the town head know about this. As soon as he puts you down for the Five Guarantees, I'll immediately send someone to help you build a new house!"

Holding open a black umbrella, the chief of Dragon Gully Village stepped into Little Xiang's house. When he saw her father sleeping in a little shed that looked like a doghouse, he laughed. "Old Brother!" he said. "I have some good news for you! The town head has approved you for the Five Guarantees! And I have more news that's even better than that: The county magistrate himself has caught wind of all this and is coming tomorrow with winter clothes. He wants to personally deliver a little warmth to recipients of the Five Guarantees and to all families facing hardship!"

The following day, three cars from town made their way in the direction of Dragon Gully Village. It had just rained and the road was covered in mud; the vehicles were unable to enter the village and the drivers had to park outside the entrance. The village chief sent someone to keep watch over the leaders' cars.

Out of the first car stepped a reporter and a staff member from the county television station. From the second car stepped the county magistrate. And from the third car emerged the town head, whose arms were full of winter clothing. Laughing and smiling, the village chief and the team leader led the way for the entire group. They arrived in no time at the doorstep of Little Xiang's house.

"Come on out, Old Brother!" The village chief ran ahead of the others, shouting. "The county magistrate and town head have come to see you!"

Little Xiang's father came out of the shed. "I'm so grateful to the village chief!" he exclaimed, and was visibly moved.

"No, that's wrong!" the village chief said triumphantly. "You should be grateful to the county leaders!"

The county television-station reporter ran over and warmly took hold of Little Xiang's father's hand. "Uncle!" he cried. "Our station is doing some video interviews. Go ahead and say a few important words. Ready? Start!"

And so Little Xiang's father came out of the doghouse-like shed all over again, his entire body trembling from the cold. There he stood as the county magistrate removed a thick padded coat from the arms of the town head, then gracefully moved toward him, a big, warm smile on his face. A young cameraman was shooting the moving scene, but he suddenly lost his footing and the camera slipped from his hands and fell into the mud.

"Stop, stop!" the county TV-station reporter shrieked.

Little Xiang's father was just in the process of reaching out his arms to receive the thick, padded coat from the county magistrate, but when he heard the word "Stop!" he was so petrified that he stopped what he was doing and stood there rather stupidly, entirely unsure of what to do.

"Sir," the reporter said, "looks like the camera has fallen and is broken, so you'll have to wait a little while. The county magistrate will come back with some warmth again after we've fixed it!" And just like that, the entire entourage departed.

Ah Qing and Little Jade sat with their families watching TV.

"Ah Qing, come look, quick! Little Xiang's father is on TV!" Little Jade pointed at the black-and-white screen.

Everyone looked with wide-open eyes as Little Xiang's father emerged from the shed that looked like a doghouse. He stretched out his arms to accept something and the county magistrate stuffed a thick, cotton-padded coat into his arms. After that, a reporter stuck a microphone near his lips and, with great emotion and tears cascading from his eyes, Little Xiang's father gushed: "Thank you, Party! Thank you, County Leader! If it weren't for the Party's and the county leader's care and concern, I would have no today! If it weren't for the Party's and the county leader's fine policies, I'd have frozen and starved to death long ago!"

Ah Qing, Little Jade, and their entire families burst into laughter.

Half a year later, the chief of Dragon Gully Village sat in the town head's office, waiting for an order.

"The county leaders have given us a directive," the town head began. "They want our town to choose a Comparatively Well-Off Village. I've thought about it over and over again, and I believe that Dragon Gully Village fits the bill!"

"But Town Head!" the village chief replied. "It doesn't fit the bill at all! Almost all of the adult men and women in our village have gone to sell blood!"

"It's not *selling* blood," the town head explained. "It's gloriously *contributing* blood! Dragon Gully Village has been examined and verified quite earnestly. Your village has *three* households living in two-story homes, Village Chief, including your own family. In other villages, it's hard to find even one!"

And so the chief of Dragon Gully Village became the chief of a Comparatively Well-Off Village, and this chief of the Comparatively Well-Off Village soon appeared on television. His family and the other two families living in two-story buildings all appeared on television, too.

The chief of the Comparatively Well-Off Village assembled the villagers in a great meeting, where he asked them to pool funds to repair the asphalt road. Then he brought in the team leader and others, who went from household to household collecting funds for this project as more and more people left for the hospital to sell blood.

Later, the chief of the Comparatively Well-Off Village assembled all the villagers together in another great meeting, where he asked them to pool funds to construct a new, multi-story building for the well-off village's elementary school. Again he brought in an army of people, who went from household to household, forcibly extracting funds for this project.

5

"Girls—as soon as they go out into the world they start to learn to be bad!" Little Jade's mother sighed. "That Little Na, she's really pissing me off! If I were her mother I'd beat her to death when I found her. But Ah Qing—well, he's just wonderful! He's honest and capable, and so handsome too! But that damned girl Little Na has gone and married herself off to some old Hong Konger!"

"Ah Qing's fate is no good." Ah Qing's father sighed along with her. "He isn't lucky enough to marry Little Na!"

Ah Qing, for his part, just remained seated with his head lowered.

Little Xiang's father moved into a newly built tile-roofed house with two rooms. Little Jade's mother brought him a shoebox filled with eggs.

"It's been two years since Little Xiang has gone out to work!" Little Jade's mother said. "So many bad people out there, and she doesn't write often! Every time Little Jade receives a letter from her, she has a new address. Who knows what she's really doing out there?"

"When she was still at home she was a better girl than her older sister, Big Xiang," Little Xiang's father replied. "If she really has learned bad things out there, I wouldn't even recognize her!"

"The children are all grown up now. Little Jade is twenty-two! As parents, we should do something to get Little Xiang to come back soon so we can set up her marriage!"

Little Xiang's father nodded in agreement.

The fifteen-watt light bulb shined on Ah Qing, who lay on a bed reading a collection of poetry. He heard the sound of Little Jade knocking on the door outside.

"Ah Qing!" Little Jade said as he entered the room. "I have some news for you—it's just that I don't know if it's good news or bad news!"

"What news?"

"Little Xiang is coming back soon, and as soon as she does my ma and her dad are having us get married!"

"That's good news!" Ah Qing laughed.

"Ah Qing, will Little Xiang and I be happy after we get married?"

"Don't be stupid! How am I supposed to know if you'll be happy or not?"

Little Jade removed his shoes and jumped on Ah Qing's bed.

"You're about to be married," Ah Qing laughed, "and you're still going to sleep with me?"

"Before I get married, let me be happy one more time. Let me feel good one more time!"

Ah Qing held Little Jade tightly and kissed him.

"Little Jade!" Ah Qing said after a moment. "After I've drunk your wedding wine, I still plan to leave Dragon Gully Village, but this time I won't be going out for menial jobs like before. I'm going to learn a trade!"

"I want to learn a trade with you!" Little Jade exclaimed. "How about this: After Little Xiang and I get married, let's study hairdressing! Then after that, we can open a shop together. Opening a barbershop or hair salon doesn't cost much."

"You won't think I'm so important anymore after you have Little Xiang." Ah Qing grew sullen.

"Never, Ah Qing! We'll always be brothers."

"Is that all we are, Little Jade—brothers? Sometimes I myself don't get it . . . on the one hand, I can't stand the idea of you and Little Xiang getting married, but I also know that you and I can't stay this way forever."

"If two men could get married and have kids," Little Jade said, "I would definitely marry you!"

Ah Qing laughed as he rubbed Little Jade's nipple. "Little Jade," he asked, "when I touch you this way, do you feel anything?"

"Yeah . . . it feels nice. Do it a little harder." Little Jade closed his eyes.

Ah Qing took Little Jade's little nipple into his mouth, then poked and licked at it with his tongue.

"Ah . . . Ah Qing!" Little Jade laughed. "That tickles!" The words only made Ah Qing kiss him more.

In a wintery field, the occasional rabbit ran past one's eyes. Adjacent to the verdant fields of wheat, tombstones of varying heights and sizes sat nestled in the earth. Hand in hand, Ah Qing and Little Jade walked through the cemetery.

"Sometimes I feel so lonely, Little Jade, and when I do I go buy books. I've been reading a lot of poetry lately and have started to fall in love with it—it's becoming the place where I let my soul dwell! When I close my eyes, I always dream . . . and sometimes I dream of a woman in white. I always chase after her, crying 'Mama!'"

"Anytime you feel lonely, just come and find me, Ah Qing. I, too, am all alone at night and often have trouble sleeping!"

Little Xiang's father bumped into Little Jade's mother at the entrance to the village.

"That girl Little Xiang is coming back in a few days," the father said. "As soon as she does, let's get this wedding over and done with!"

"Yes!" the mother replied. "And when it's all over, we parents can finally take a deep breath and stop worrying."

On a winter's evening, Little Xiang descended a train carrying a leather suitcase. It felt heavier and heavier with each step as she walked through her small town under the swaying lights. She looked up and saw an old man on a flatbed pedal tricycle moving in her direction.

The old man slowed down as he passed her. "Ah!" he said. "You're Little Xiang! Big Xiang's little sister, right?"

"That's right! Where are you headed, sir?"

"I was at my eldest daughter's house today. I'm heading home now. You're out late, Little Xiang! Are you going home or are you going to your big sister's place?"

"My house is ten li from here and it's dark out, so tonight I'm going to my big sister's house because it's closer."

"I live close to your big sister's place. I'll take you part of the way!"

Little Xiang placed her leather suitcase on the back of the old man's trike. "Thank you, sir!" she said gratefully.

"It's nothing, nothing at all!"

Little Xiang climbed aboard.

"It must be hard going out and working, isn't it?"

"Yes, sir, but if it isn't hard you're not going to make any money!" Little Xiang laughed.

The pedal tricycle soon rolled into one of the town's villages. The sky was dark and the road uneven, and the old man pressed arduously on the pedals of the vehicle.

"You can drop me off here, sir." Little Xiang said. "My sister lives in that row of houses up ahead."

The old man came to a standstill and wiped the sweat from his forehead. "Thank you, sir!" Little Xiang said, sounding somewhat embarrassed about having put him through the trouble.

"It's nothing, nothing at all!" The old man waved goodbye.

Lugging her heavy, leather suitcase, Little Xiang stepped into her older sister's house.

A week later, the old man was riding his flatbed tricycle to town for the morning market when he suddenly caught sight of Little Xiang's father. He rode in the father's direction, then greeted him. "Little Xiang's dad!" he said. "I see you've also come to catch the morning market!"

"That's right!" the father replied. "Our Little Xiang is coming home soon and I want to pick up some of her favorite things to eat."

"Well, that doesn't sound right," the old man said, furrowing his white brow. "Little Xiang came back a week ago, didn't she? I gave her a ride to Big Xiang's house on my tricycle."

"She's back already?" The father's heart sank abruptly. "How is it that I haven't seen a trace of her?"

"Go to Big Xiang's house and ask—then you'll know!"

Little Xiang's father hurriedly lifted his vegetable basket, then rushed off to his older daughter's house. When Big Xiang saw her father approaching, she went outside and greeted him with a smile.

"Father, you've come!" she said. "We were just thinking of you—come in and have a seat!"

"Father, you've come!" Big Xiang's husband repeated. "We were just thinking of you—come in and have a seat!"

Little Xiang's father stepped into their house and sat on a wooden chair.

"You haven't eaten yet, have you, Father? Why don't you eat with us?" The old man's son-in-law offered a warm smile.

"I've come to ask you about something," his father-in-law replied curtly.

"Let's eat first!" he replied, ignoring what the old man had said. "You'll still be able to ask after we've eaten, right?"

Big Xiang came out of the kitchen carrying two plates of beef and chicken.

Little Xiang's father looked at his daughter and her husband skeptically. Was this really happening? They had never treated him this cordially when he visited. A pair of chopsticks was placed before him, but he didn't pick them up.

"I'm here to ask you: Has Little Xiang been in this house?" He looked at his son-in-law's face intently.

"Um, no—no, she hasn't!" Big Xiang answered for her husband. She looked tense. "Has Little Xiang been back?" she asked stiffly. "When?"

"That's right! We sure haven't . . . I mean, we haven't seen Little Xiang . . . not so much as a shadow!" The son-in-law stammered awkwardly.

Without a word, the father stood up, walked out of his daughter's house, and went to the police station.

"I never would have thought that Little Xiang's big sister and brother-in-law could be so cruel! Little Xiang—that was her blood sister! And it was all so that they could get their hands on the ten thousand yuan that she earned from her own hard work! To think they could actually kill their own little sister! To think that they could take their own little sister and throw

262

her down the well! Good god! My poor Little Xiang!" Little Jade's mother cried in anguish as Little Jade hung his head in silence.

A new tombstone was added to the fields that winter, and a father who had gone mad stood guard at the grave, calling out: "Our Little Xiang has come home! Our Little Xiang has come home!"

THIRTEEN

1

The day Ah Qing arrived in Beijing from Zhengzhou, he called me on the telephone to ask if I could help him find a place to rent. I gave him my address, then went out to buy groceries so I could prepare a meal for the newly arrived transplant. I was in my first month of retirement.

"Eat up, Ah Qing! Have some more soup. Do you like my cooking?" I filled his cup with alcohol and watched as his face grew redder and redder. I loved silently watching Ah Qing—was it traces of Xia Nanshan that I saw? Sitting across the table from him, I recalled the days of my youth when Xia Nanshan and I carried corpses together into the cremation room.

"Do you play, Uncle He?" Ah Qing eyed the piano at the foot of my bed with interest.

In his eyes I saw a brightness that shined like water, but it wasn't long before those same eyes were gripped by a new expression: part worry, part tipsy from alcohol.

Taking advantage of the kind of bravery that comes from alcohol, I played three songs for him: "Why Are the Flowers So Red?," "A Corner Left Unnoticed by Love," and "Troika."

"Have you written any songs, Uncle He?" He looked at me with devotion.

"Yes, I've written two, but they're dreadful!" I felt there was a generation gap between us.

We continued discussing music, and before long the conversation turned to poetry.

"That winter   Mama
Wearing white gloves you held me
At the train station rain began to fall
In the sky snowflakes began to flutter
Snowflakes and rain landed on your head
Gently you placed a sleeping me on the street

That winter has reached its end   Mama
Wearing soft gloves you held me tight
Willow trees sprouted light yellow buds
And around your beautiful face snowflakes flew
You forgot to see that spring is already here
After kissing me gently, you placed a heart on the street

That winter is gone forever   Mama
In the dark night I have grown up
I seek a mama who wears warm gloves
On the street it's still so cold
Why can I never see the spring
Why is my heart full of drifting snowflakes . . ."

Ah Qing gave me this poem after coming to Beijing. I promised him that I would write music to accompany the words.

He wanted to find a job in Beijing, and after staying at my place for a week, rented a small house in the outskirts of the city. He ran around for two weeks in search of a job, but finally set the hunt aside so he could start the lonely process of writing all alone in his six-square-meter space.

"Uncle He, where is Dongdan Park?" Ah Qing held a map of Beijing in his hands. I pointed to a patch of green the size of half a fingernail and Ah Qing circled it. It wasn't long before his shadow appeared on the ground there.

When I was lonely, I took the bus to go see Ah Qing, who was meeting more and more people at the park and as a consequence had fewer and fewer opportunities to see me.

"Ah Qing," I repeated into the phone each day, "If you don't find work, how are you going to survive?" The last thing I wanted was to see a talented poet like him degenerate into a money boy. I took him to bathhouses. I loved kissing him under the water faucet; the head of his cock would swell like a budding flower.

"Don't go to the park too often, Ah Qing, and be careful about STDs!" I myself was going to the park often even as I said this to him. My goal was to find a stable sex partner, for I often saw STD notices plastered on the toilet walls. Ah Qing and I had only had sex twice and after that he lost interest. On those two occasions, he never returned my kisses and I felt that he wasn't emotionally present. "Do you love me, Ah Qing?" I cried in my heart, though I knew that the person in his heart was Little Jade.

"Do you love that woman?" I asked.

"No!" he replied, growing impatient. "I've never loved her." He didn't like me raising the subject of Sister Plum Blossom.

"If you and she were to have a kid, it would definitely be smart and attractive!" I laughed, but Ah Qing just became agitated and annoyed. I kept wondering to myself: What would the child of a twenty-five-year-old homosexual and a forty-five-year-old prostitute be like?

2

You and Little Jade went to beauty school in Zhengzhou; you had learned of the place from advertisements on the radio. You enrolled in a short-term, month-long course that covered the topics of washing, drying, coloring, cutting, perming, and styling.

"Little Jade," you asked, "we may have graduated, but we've only given haircuts and perms a handful of times! Is that really enough for us to open our own shop?"

"If we don't open a shop right away, we're going to forget everything we've learned within a few weeks!"

The two of you went to the most prosperous area of Zhengzhou, but were scared away the minute you asked about rent. In the end, all you could do was look for a place in the villages surrounding the provincial capital. There in one of them, hidden in a remote little alley, you rented a space with a storefront and opened up a barbershop.

"Give me a haircut! Shave my beard!" A man demanded upon stumbling into the barbershop.

This was your first customer, and you and Little Jade welcomed him warmly. After Little Jade washed his hair, this Mr. Big Beard wobbled his way into a chair, where you wrapped a white towel around him.

"How would you like your hair cut, sir?" Little Jade pointed to the pictures of celebrities taped to the walls.

"Whatever, just a little short is okay," Big Beard replied.

"Let me do it, Ah Qing!" Little Jade said.

"No," you replied, "let me do it!"

You battled each other to see who would cut the first customer's hair. Finally, you won.

In your left hand you held a comb, in your right hand a pair of scissors. You began cutting as the Big Beard in the mirror closed his eyes and nodded off to sleep with a head that drooped downward. Suddenly you cut your left hand and blood started to ooze.

"Let me take over, Ah Qing!" Little Jade seemed startled by the accident. He took the scissors from you and began to cut the remaining hair with added caution. "His hair is already dry," he continued. "Hand me the spray bottle!"

You filled the plastic spray bottle half with hot water, half with cold water, then squirted misty pearls all around Big Beard's head. Beads of sweat clung to Little Jade's forehead, but he continued to cut carefully. Hairs from the customer that were as thick as grains of sand covered Little Jade's face. You grabbed a towel and wiped them away.

"What do you think, Ah Qing?" Little Jade asked. "Is it okay?"

You examined Big Beard's head from left to right and top to bottom. "Good," you replied. "Yeah, that works!"

"We still haven't shaved his beard yet, though," Little Jade lamented. "Our teacher never taught us how to do that!"

"This guy's beard is really thick, and there's a lot of it, too! How about we use the clippers first, then we can shave it with a razor." You reached out your injured hand to feel Big Beard's beard.

Little Jade grabbed a damp hand towel and wiped it across Big Beard's face. "Ah Qing," he said, "I think he's drunk!"

With a razor in your right hand, you used your left hand to push down on Big Beard's face to flatten his features. The blade revealed clean skin as it moved along the contours of his face; at the same time, tiny droplets of blood rushed out of his pores. You tried to stem the flow by pushing down with your fingers, but before long you ran out of fingers to push with. Little Jade tried to help by pressing down with his fingers, too. Then you used the damp towel to wipe the blood away. You handed the razor to Little Jade, who took over for a while, then he handed the razor back to you.

Little Jade patted the soundly sleeping Big Beard on the shoulder. "Mister," he said, "your hair is all done. Your beard has been shaved, too!"

Big Beard stood up from the barber's chair and stretched. "Ah, I fell asleep! How much is it?"

"Two kuai," Little Jade replied.

The man pulled a wallet from his pocket, and from the wallet two kuai, which he placed on the styling shelf before the mirror. He then looked at his watch. "Oh!" he exclaimed. "I've been asleep for three hours! Why didn't you wake me up?"

As your first customer stepped out of the barbershop and into the street, you threw your arms around Little Jade and laughed.

This is how you and Little Jade came to operate a small shop. Since your craft was not yet mature, however, the facilities were quite basic and you weren't able to charge much. Little by little, the number of your daily customers grew from one to more than twenty. After you paid all your expenses—rent, water, electricity, all the management fees levied by the Administration for Industry and Commerce, all the sanitation fees—the amount left over for income was only about eight or nine hundred kuai in total. But even this was more than you had made when you worked for someone else!

At ten o'clock each night after all the customers left, you and Little Jade closed the door of your barbershop and began to tidy up. You pulled a folding bed out from behind the second-hand couch you had bought, opened and set it up, then pulled out the bundle of quilts, bed sheets and pillows that were stored in a TV cardboard box during daylight hours. The two of you slept right there in the barbershop each night. The bed was very small, and you and Little Jade slept cramped close together.

A year later, your shop was demolished so the street could be expanded. You and Little Jade didn't mind taking a break, so for a spell you were not especially anxious to go and find a new shop front. Actually, your personality wasn't really suited for working in the service industry. All those grotesque faces! You weren't very good at putting on an act and presenting them with a fake smile.

When you were a kid you had gone to an outdoor screening of the movie *Shaolin Temple*, and from that day onward you had always yearned to go to the real place. After acquiring a little money, you and Little Jade took a trip to Shaolin Temple, where you stayed for two days. At a tourist spot you were ripped off by some local merchants, and you learned that the real Shaolin Temple was not the Shaolin Temple you had cherished in dreams for so long. The monks you saw there weren't shadowboxing. They were doing business.

Inadvertently, you and Little Jade stumbled upon a gay park. As happy as fish in water, you went there each night to go wild for several hours. A month later, the two of you had an argument at the park; in a huff of anger, Little Jade took off for the city of Xuchang.

You were alone now, and you didn't feel like opening another shop. Nor did you want to go back to the hiring site. You saw a sign outside Sister Plum Blossom's Hair Salon announcing that she was seeking skilled and unskilled labor, so you went inside and told her that you were very skilled at your trade! She knew that you lived in Courtyard No. 8 and that the two of you had a landlady in common.

Sister Plum Blossom looked at you earnestly and then, with a nod and a smile, became your boss.

3

"Do you have a girlfriend, Ah Qing?" Sister Plum Blossom was sitting on the sofa, her lips painted with crimson lipstick. When you were little, you often watched your adoptive mother dye baby chicks the same color and sell them as pets.

"Uh, not yet," you replied. You felt two eyes piercing into your face as you spoke.

"How old are you?" Sister Plum Blossom asked earnestly. She had asked you this question no fewer than six times, and each time it was with the utmost earnestness. Why couldn't she ever remember?

"Twenty-three," you reminded her in a loud voice as you resolved that this would be the last time you would answer the question.

You perceived a human figure moving outside the salon front door, so you stood and prepared to receive a customer. Sister Plum Blossom paid very little attention to customers, but always enjoyed chatting with anyone else who happened to be around. You sat in a chair and looked at yourself in the mirror, feeling rather uneasy. If no customers came in the morning, you'd feel anxious having lunch later on!

"Twenty-three . . ." Sister Plum Blossom repeated, unwilling to drop the subject. "You should really have a girlfriend by now! Do you want Sister Plum Blossom to introduce you to one?" She stood up, then sat down again, this time closer to you.

You started to feel awkward, so you stood and grabbed a towel, then began to wipe a window.

"How much is a haircut?" Finally, a customer entered the salon.

"Five kuai." Sister Plum Blossom remained on the sofa, not moving her ass one inch for the person who wanted a cut.

After the man sat down, you washed his hair and then, with a comb in your left hand and a pair of scissors in your right, started to cut. You liked easy-going customers, customers who handed their heads over to you so you could give them whatever hairstyle you wanted; with customers like that, you could make them happy and they'd be on their way. Most of the time, those two little prostitutes Little Lotus and Little Chrys didn't even come over to help wash people's hair! You silently cursed them, and you also looked down on yourself.

As you cut the man's hair, it fell to the floor; you felt the whole thing was filthy. It didn't matter how attractive a man or a woman was, all that falling hair always disgusted you.

When your adoptive mother was still alive, she got up early each morning and started making breakfast, always without washing her face first. Only after making the steamed buns would she then proceed to wash the sweat from her face and comb her hair, which looked like a chicken coop. Anytime you ate one of her steamed buns, you found a hair in it. "Ma," you would ask, "why don't you make them after you've washed your face and combed your hair?" You couldn't resist the urge to throw accusations at her. If you didn't eat, you'd be hungry; if you did, you'd be disgusted!

"That's not my hair," your adoptive mother would reply, hiding the truth without batting an eye. "That's from the brush of the flour-milling machine!"

After that, you no longer said that you had eaten one of her hairs; instead, you said you'd eaten the hair of a dog. She would get angry and scold you. She would say she regretted adopting a deviate son like you.

Were you a deviate son? Your adoptive mother was dead and you no longer bore a grudge against her. Now your hatred was directed toward your birth parents, who never should have brought you into this world! The scissors in your hand kept moving, but each time you gave a haircut you became distracted. Sister Plum Blossom said you were very meticulous in your work; she couldn't see that your mind was not at all focused on the customer.

"Done," you said as you swept up the garbage from the floor.

4

A hot summer night. The electric fan whirled endlessly, but the breeze it created was still warm. The instant one sat one's butt on the sofa, the sweat began to pour. What kind of desperate john would possibly come on a day as hot as this? Bills only flowed out of Sister Plum Blossom's wallet; they never flowed in, and for several days she was so distressed about it that she didn't even go grocery shopping. You got to work cutting customers' hair. As long as there was work to be done, you wouldn't have to live off anyone else.

"It's too hot, Sister Plum Blossom. Can I wear just a pair of boxers?"

"Sure," she replied.

You sat beneath the fan wearing nothing but boxer shorts. You didn't know it, but your testicles were hanging out, visible to anyone who cared to look. When Sister Plum Blossom saw them she started to laugh, enjoying the illicit show.

"How old are you, Ah Qing?"

"I've already told you a million times, Sister Plum Blossom!"

You grabbed a damp towel and started to wipe the mirror.

"Have some fruit, Ah Qing!" she called out. She, along with Little Lotus and Little Chrys, had been enjoying the fruit for some time before they finally asked you to have some.

You grabbed a peach and began eating with huge bites.

"Fuck! Where has everyone died and gone off to?" Little Chrys cursed. She got up and left the salon to go home and go to sleep.

Soon, Little Lotus got up and left the salon, too.

Feeling bored, Sister Plum Blossom went to find the old landlady to talk. When she returned she found you asleep on the sofa, your erect penis poking out of your boxers. She grabbed hold of it. You awakened suddenly, but she didn't release her grip.

"Let go, Sister Plum Blossom!" You were so agitated that your neck reddened.

"How old are you, Ah Qing? Do you think about having a girlfriend?" She looked at you with love and tenderness; saliva dripped from her mouth.

Sister Plum Blossom led you to the two-room apartment she kept at the back of the salon.

"Do you like me, baby?" She pressed down on you like a sow. When she spoke you could smell her foul breath.

"I don't know . . . " You got up and put Sister Plum Blossom on her knees, then entered her from behind. To you it seemed that the vagina wouldn't feel as good as the anus.

"Have you made love to a woman before, baby?"

"I've had anal sex with a few men!"

"What?!" she cried. "Anal sex with men? Ha ha! Does anal sex feel good, baby?" A white, sticky fluid dripped from her vagina as she spoke.

From the time you and Sister Plum Blossom first fornicated, she doted on you constantly. To avoid her, you took every opportunity you could find to run off to the gay park, where you ran wild. There you bumped into Little Tough; you told him all of your woes, but he just encouraged you to trade your flesh for Sister Plum Blossom's money!

"You've spent all your money again?" she would ask you. "Alright then, meet me at the usual place tonight!" She no longer paid you on time; instead, she made you use sex to get the money you needed.

The lock on the bathroom door was broken. Sister Plum Blossom peeped at you through the crack in the door as you showered, watching you like a hungry female dog.

"I'm done showering," you said as you hurried out of the bathroom, a terry cloth coverlet wrapped around your waist.

"I'm going to shower now, baby! Now, don't you try to sneak a peek at me while I'm in there!" She stepped into the bathroom fully dressed.

As if you would want to look at her! You didn't want to kiss her, had no interest in the breasts that languished in her bra, and you loathed seeing that black, crumpled up stuff between her legs.

The phone suddenly rang. Sister Plum Blossom was still in the shower.

"Wei? Hello, who are you looking for?" you called into the receiver.

"I'm looking for Sister Plum Blossom," a voice replied. "Hurry up and put her on the phone!"

"She's busy right now. Call back a little later!"

"You tell her to either pick up the phone right now or get back to the salon . . . hurry, something has happened . . . the police have arrested Little Lotus and Little Chrys!"

"What?!" You hung up the phone, ran over to the shower room, and pushed open the door. There was Sister Plum Blossom, fully nude with all of her fat flesh. Suddenly she turned around and—oh!—you saw that her chest was flat. She had no breasts at all—just two ugly scars.

If you exit Courtyard No. 8 through a winding, four-foot-wide passageway, then walk another minute or so, you'll arrive at a small alley where breakfast is sold. Seven cement-tiled sheds housing seven vendors line this nameless alley. Opposite every two sheds on average is a public toilet, three of them altogether. Inside these partially open-air toilets, the male and female sides share a single light bulb, which hangs from the ceiling and illuminates rows of piss buckets whose handles have been cut off. Near the toilets are two STD clinics, where the doctors are two middle-aged women who give anaesthetized abortions to local schoolgirls. Living in and around the alley are peddlers, prostitutes, cops, painters, thieves, poets, and unemployed workers, as well as a band of Falun Gong practitioners.

Morning is when the sun comes up. Morning is also when it's time to line up for the public toilet and line up to eat breakfast. Each day, the two lines quickly merge to become one. You hated waiting in line for the toilet, so you changed your crapping time from morning to evening. When the first toilet was full of people, you ran off to the second one. When the second toilet was overflowing with shit and piss, there was nothing to do but run off to the one that was farthest away and most hidden. When shitting all alone, you enjoyed looking at the dirty pictures and trashy limericks scribbled on the walls. Those degenerate words, those big round breasts and huge cocks! Together they called up a primitive power from your innermost depths—this is why you were never constipated!

You exited the toilet and returned to Courtyard No. 8, where you stopped by Sister Plum Blossom's Hair Salon.

"Sister Plum Blossom," you asked, "what are Little Lotus and Little Chrys going to do?"

"It's not that big a deal!" she replied. "Pay a fine and you can resolve anything!"

You assumed that Sister Plum Blossom would turn to the old landlady's Public Security Bureau director son for help, but to your surprise, Little Lotus and Little Chrys were released from jail the very next day.

"Ah Qing, have some chestnuts!" Sister Plum Blossom placed a bag of Chinese chestnuts on the table in front of you. "I've already peeled the skins off for you!"

You looked at all that white, skinless mush and felt sick. You didn't lift a finger to touch them.

"What—" Sister Plum Blossom protested, "—you don't like chestnuts? Go on, try one, they're good!" She gripped a chestnut with her long fingernails and stuffed it in her mouth, staring at you as she chewed. Saliva leaked from her mouth like vaginal fluid. She took hold of one of those white mushy things and popped it into your mouth.

"Ah Qing, your thing is so big!" Sister Plum Blossom said, and she began playing with your cock.

"Stop it, I can't stand it! Haven't you played with enough cocks already?" You hated having a woman's long fingernails come near you. "Sister Plum Blossom," you continued to dig at her, "were your breasts bitten off by a sadist?"

"Oh, stop talking rubbish!" She released her grip, and was visibly unhappy. "I had to get them cut off ten years ago because I had breast cancer."

Anytime you didn't want to have sex with Sister Plum Blossom, you brought up her breasts. The mere mention of them was like pouring a bucket of cold water on her erotic desire.

"Do you dislike women, Ah Qing? Was your mother good to you?"

"Stop asking questions! My head hurts . . . "

Again you went to the park, where you searched in the darkness. If you were to find a comrade who truly loved you, you would leave Sister Plum Blossom at once. You had no diploma, no education, no money, no home. You were poor, so poor that all you had was your own cock!

Your crotch started to itch; when you were out walking about, you couldn't help but reach into your trousers to scratch yourself. From your pubic hair you picked a crab louse that had bitten you, and then a second and a third. This was horrifying! In stealth you stepped into one of the STD clinics.

"Drop your pants for me to take a look," a middle-aged woman commanded soberly.

It wasn't easy, but you forced yourself to drop your trousers. Wearing latex gloves, the middle-aged woman inspected you, then gave you a topical medicine, which she instructed you to spread on your skin after shaving your pubic hair. Those crab lice really did look like little crabs; they bit into your flesh and held on tight. Day and night, those little hermaphrodites copulated and gave birth, leaving their hermaphroditic offspring buried deep in your pores. These annoying parasites were going through life with much more happiness than you were. You had no idea if Sister Plum Blossom had given them to you or if you had picked them up from some guy at the park.

"Sister Plum Blossom, I want to go study computers."

"Okay," she replied flatly. "I've known for a long time that something's been bothering you." She scratched herself as she spoke. Without doubt, her underwear was crawling with crabs, too.

For two years you lived with Sister Plum Blossom. They were two years that made you feel old. The twenty-five-year-old self whom you saw in the mirror was no longer recognizable. You went to the supermarket and bought a razor because Sister Plum Blossom had told you she liked you with facial hair.

"I want to give you a child, baby!" It was Sister Plum Blossom who wanted a kid, and yet she told you she was going to "give" you one.

"I don't want it. I don't want a child!" You pulled your penis from her womb.

"Why can't I get pregnant?" She constantly fretted about her age. "I'm going to go see Dr. Hua and have her take a look."

You had never met Dr. Hua, nor did you know what kind of medicine she had given Sister Plum Blossom. But two months later, Sister Plum Blossom rushed to the old landlady's home in high spirits and loudly announced, "I'm pregnant! I'm having a baby!" The old landlady congratulated the old prostitute with a feeble grin. When the two young prostitutes Little Lotus and Little Chrys learned of it, they congratulated Sister Plum Blossom, too. It seemed that within minutes, just about everyone who lived in Courtyard No. 8 knew that Sister Plum Blossom was pregnant. Her happiness was disgusting. It was enough to make one think she was carrying the descendant of an emperor.

She walked over to you to show you her belly, which was growing larger by the day.

"I don't want this child!" you said.

"Why, baby?"

"Because you're a prostitute and I'm a homosexual! We aren't qualified to have a child. We won't be able to bring it happiness. If you have this child," you continued, "I'm breaking up with you!" You were nearly in tears.

Sister Plum Blossom was quiet for a spell. But she was determined to have the child.

"Ah Qing, you're all grown up now, so don't act like a child! I can give you an adorable little baby who will laugh and play with you! I want to send our child abroad to study. I want him to get an official position that's even better than the one the old landlady's son has!"

"I don't want this child," you repeated, and you struck Sister Plum Blossom's stomach with a fist.

Perhaps she had never loved you. Perhaps she only wanted to borrow your young flesh so she could have the child of her dreams. Could a forty-five-year-old prostitute without breasts have a healthy child? When the child grew up and found out who his father was, he would surely look down on you, surely hate you . . . no! You could not let her have this child.

This society offered no sense of security; it wasn't worthy of receiving your child! You weren't a man, you were just human scum who had received more than your share of insults.

You stepped out of the drugstore and walked back to Sister Plum Blossom's place, where you put an abortifacient in her tea.

"Have some tea, Sister Plum Blossom!" You placed the teacup in her hand.

She took the cup from you and stuck out her big belly with a smile. Then she went over to the old landlady's place.

The instant she left, you packed your bags and boarded a train to Beijing.

FOURTEEN

1

A man staying at a hotel picked up the phone and asked Sister Plum Blossom to introduce him to a girl who would pay him a house call. She introduced Little Orchid to the john. Meanwhile, Little Lotus and Little Chrys stepped out of a bar and went back to Courtyard No. 8 just off Shangcheng Street.

"Little Chrys is back! Little Lotus is back!" the stupid boy stood outside the courtyard gate as he yelled.

Little Chrys patted him on the shoulder. "Go call Big Sister, Little Treasure. She'll give you some candy!"

"I don't want candy," the stupid boy replied. "I want milk!"

Little Lotus laughed. "Hey, Little Chrys! Hurry up and pull your milk out!"

Little Chrys laughed, too. "Hey, Little Treasure!" she said. "Big Sister Little Chrys has big boobs! You want 'em?"

"I want big boobs! I want big boobs!" Clapping his hands, the stupid boy jumped up and down outside the courtyard gate. Little Chrys quickly ran into the courtyard and Little Lotus followed behind her.

Inside the courtyard, a few old and dilapidated bicycles and tricycles were placed here and there. The old landlady sat on a small, wooden stool washing a curled-up bloody object in a pan.

"Grandma!" Little Chrys began to ask with curiosity. "What kind of intestine are you washing?"

"This?" The old landlady smiled. "It's something good! Something good that you've never eaten before! This is placenta—it's the best tonic! Eating it not only cures illness—it also promises longevity!"

Little Lotus moved a little closer. "Pig placenta or dog placenta?"

"Human placenta!" the old landlady replied. "Money can't buy this! My oldest boy went through someone he knows at the hospital to get it. I can tell you one thing, it sure wasn't easy!"

Little Lotus grabbed Little Chrys by the hand, then the two girls ran inside and darted upstairs. The old landlady called out: "Wei! When Grandma's done stewing it, I'll call you back down and you can try some!"

They ran into their room and shut the door.

"Oh, dear mother!" Little Lotus shuddered. "Disgusting! People will eat anything!"

When Little Chrys saw how disgusted Little Lotus looked, it made her laugh.

"Hey Little Lotus, did you know that Ah Qing split? And what timing! Sister Plum Blossom's stomach is growing bigger and bigger—when that child is born it's going to be a bastard now!"

"They weren't suited for each other to begin with," Little Lotus replied. "They've got twenty years between them! What on earth is Sister Plum Blossom thinking? She's forty-five years old—what's she having a kid for?"

"Well, with a child," Little Chrys reasoned, "at least you have something to rely on when you're old."

"Raising a child doesn't necessarily mean you'll be able to rely on it in old age. We should take advantage of our youth and make a lot of money for retirement!"

Waves of uncomfortable, itchy pain spread across Little Lotus's crotch. She was too embarrassed to tell anybody about it, so when Little Chrys wasn't home she shut the door, pulled her pants down and examined herself. When she touched herself and felt a lump, a piercing pain made her cry out loud. In terror she grabbed a mirror, studied herself in earnest, then silently began to cry.

She used rubbing alcohol and salt water to wash the infected area until it was as shiny as a crystal. And yet, the red growth seemed only to be getting bigger and bigger; eventually, it looked like a flaming cockscomb flower in full bloom. Little Chrys sobbed until her eyes were red; she hated everyone. Then she dried her eyes and went to Xinhua Bookstore, where she searched for medical books. She opened the books and looked inside, comparing her own ailment to what she saw until she finally understood what she had.

She went to the bank to withdraw money from her account. From how many johns' pockets this thousand kuai had come, she herself couldn't say. She didn't dare go to the pharmacy nearby, nor did she even know which pharmacy would have the genital wart medicine that she needed. She took a bus for half an hour, then went to a pharmacy. In the first glass cabinet she saw all manner of packaged aphrodisiacs for men and women; in the last glass cabinet sat all kinds of cold medicines. When the shop attendant warmly welcomed her and asked her what she needed, Little Lotus stuck out her chest and did her best to look like a healthy young lady. "I'm buying something for a friend," she said. "Do you have anything for genital warts?"

The salesperson recommended a big pile of medicines. Little Lotus didn't know which ones were effective, so she bought them all, swallowing the ones that were to be taken orally, smearing on her body the ones that were to be used topically.

Little Lotus feared that Little Chrys knew she had contracted an STD, so she locked the medicines inside her leather suitcase, taking them only when no one else was around. Evening came and it was time for another dose, but Little Chrys sat on the bed watching television for what seemed like

282

an eternity, so there was nothing Little Lotus could do but endure the pain. At last Little Chrys lay on the bed and went to sleep. Little Lotus got up from the bed, a shirt draped across her shoulders, and gently opened the leather suitcase full of medicine. Glancing at her watch, she saw that she had already missed a dose. Silently she grumbled a few words about Little Chrys, then took double the prescribed amount.

Increasingly delirious, Little Lotus returned to the bed, where she lay down just as her stomach began to churn. Quickly she got up, squatted beside the night bucket and vomited.

Little Chrys was awakened by the commotion. When she saw that Little Lotus was in pain, she started to joke around. "What's wrong, Little Lotus? Are you pregnant, too?" Little Lotus ignored her and, when she was all done throwing up, began to cry.

No sooner had Little Chrys put on her clothes and got up from bed than she smelled the foul odor of urine mixed with medicine rising from the urine bucket. "Are you sick?" she asked, dropping the jokes and draping a heavy coat across Little Lotus's shoulders. "What's wrong? Have you seen a doctor? Don't cry, Little Lotus."

The next day Little Lotus, accompanied by Little Chrys, went to a tiny, nameless alleyway, where she stepped into an STD clinic.

"What did you think of the man I introduced you to, Little Orchid? Was he generous?"

"Thank you, Sister Plum Blossom. He gave me a hundred kuai." Little Orchid reached into her pocket sheepishly and pulled out forty yuan. "Here's the agent fee I owe you!"

Sticking out her big stomach as she sat on the sofa, Sister Plum Blossom took the money from Little Orchid. "Is your child very naughty?" she asked. "I have no idea if the child in my belly is a boy or a girl. I want to have a naughty little boy!"

"Ever since starting kindergarten, Little Dragon has been really well behaved. He can already recite over ten Tang

Dynasty poems!" When Little Orchid spoke of her son, a brightness flashed in her eyes.

"Ah Qing doesn't want this child," Sister Plum Blossom continued. "Anyway, he left me. Very early on I felt that he wouldn't be reliable, but I still hope the child inside me is just as handsome as he is!" She rubbed her belly vainly. "But if I don't wise up, I may not have this child at all!"

"Why, what happened?" Little Orchid asked.

"Before Ah Qing left, he put an abortion medicine in my tea. I had long been cautious of his every move, so I poured the entire thing into the garbage can out in the courtyard. Ha! Serves that big speckled cat right. The old landlord lady tried to feed it fish and meat, but it wouldn't eat it. Next thing you know it's out there in the garbage can eating stuff with abortion medicine all over it. That cat was pregnant and lost its entire litter! Ha! That sure upset the old landlady for a few days."

Little Orchid laughed. "That old lady is so weird!" she said. "In the past when I was her maid, I saw her eat placenta many times. Her two sons would bring her fish and meat, but she'd always let it go bad in the refrigerator, then give it to the cat. One time I saw her boiling something I thought she was making for her cat. But when I fed it to the cat, she was really mad about it and gave me mean looks for two days. Later, you know what kind of soup I saw the old lady eating?"

"What kind of soup?"

"Dead-baby soup!"

Sister Plum Blossom's skin crawled as she tightly curled her arms around her belly.

2

Xiao An drove his motor tricycle for disabled drivers. He was going to see his younger sister.

"Little Lotus!" he exclaimed when he arrived. "You have to take care of yourself! I haven't seen you in a month and look how skinny you've become!"

"I'm fine, Big Brother!" she replied.

"You're fine?!" He pulled two hundred kuai from his pocket. "Here, take this money—and spend it!"

"Big Brother!" Little Lotus protested. "I'm really okay. I had a cold a few days ago but I'm fine now. I have money . . . "

"You're not working now—where would you get money from? Listen, Big Brother is giving you some money—now take it! I'll come back and see you in a few days." Xiao An let go of the money in his hand and limped his way back down the staircase.

When Xiao An got back to the place where he lived, he hauled out a cardboard box packed full of books from under his bed. The two books at the top of the stack were covered with a thick layer of dust: *Quotations from Chairman Mao* and *Selected Works of Deng Xiaoping*. The scrap collector he had seen when returning home was still outside the courtyard crying his wares. When the scrap collector saw Xiao An limping toward him, he retrieved a long string and a scale from the back of his flatbed tricycle.

"How much per jin for books?" Xiao An placed the cardboard box on the ground, then slapped the dust off his clothing.

"The price has gone up," the scrap collector replied. "Used to be 1.9 mao per jin. It's two mao now." He began inspecting the box to make sure there were only books inside.

The scrap collector departed and Xiao An's wife came home. She was with her elementary-school-aged child. "Well?" she asked. "Did you make a lot today?"

"Not much, just ten kuai!" Xiao An sighed. "How did selling cigarettes on the tarp go?"

"Not great. Selling fake cigarettes makes me so anxious! It's worse than shining shoes!"

As the family was eating dinner, they heard a knock at the door. Xiao An's wife answered it with fear in her heart because of the crime that she and her husband had committed. When she saw that it was married couple Seventh Brother and Little

Orchid, she smiled and welcomed them inside. Seventh Brother placed the gift he had brought on the table and offered candy to the woman's little girl.

"You're here so late; is anything wrong?" Xiao An accepted the cigarette that Seventh Brother offered.

Seventh Brother laughed. "We want to hear more about what Little Lotus has been saying: that there's a village somewhere in Hebei province where you can buy counterfeit money!"

"Don't do it!" Xiao An said ardently. "When we were there, we spent a thousand kuai on a gunnysack full of fake money, all ones and twos. We hadn't even gotten out of Hebei when two cops stopped and searched us. Our trike and the bag of fake money—confiscated! When they saw that I was disabled, they made us pull out the entire two hundred kuai we had on us, and wouldn't let us go until we paid a fine."

"We'd better not go, Seventh Brother!" Little Orchid exclaimed.

"If we don't make money, how are we going to send our child to school?" Seventh Brother sighed. "Teachers nowadays are so greedy, too. They don't teach kids how to become useful people—they're too busy thinking of ways to get them to ask their parents for money!"

"Yeah!" Xiao An's wife added. "Just today, our child came home and said their teacher is making everyone pay ten kuai as a fee for expanding their brainpower?!" Her face was always covered in fly shit. Lovingly she caressed her daughter.

"Well, we've come to ask you where that village is, the one where you can buy counterfeit money." The visitor gave Xiao An another cigarette.

Xiao An's wife received the gift that her visitors had brought, then explained in great detail, and more than once, how to get to the village.

Two weeks later, Xiao An and his wife learned from Little Lotus that Seventh Brother had been nabbed by the police.

Fearing that they might be implicated in the case, they packed up their belongings and left Zhengzhou.

"Why is my life so hard?" Little Lotus asked in despair, tears falling from her eyes. "As soon as my STD goes away, I get a tumor on my uterus!" Little Chrys sat by her side, comforting her.

Little Chrys wanted to help her friend, so she told Sister Plum Blossom everything. When the oldest of the three women went to see Little Lotus, her big belly sticking out, Little Lotus wiped her tears and gave Sister Plum Blossom a seat.

"It's not so bad, Little Sister Lotus—it's just a uterine tumor! I'll introduce you to Dr. Hua, a famous surgical physician. She's the director of Zhengzhou Hospital now!" Sister Plum Blossom rubbed her belly and continued. "Ten years ago I had breast cancer, and it was Dr. Hua who performed the surgery. The instant her knife touches you, the sickness is gone!"

"But in your case, it was your breasts that were cut off. I have to cut out my uterus! If I don't have a uterus, how am I going to have a child later on?" Her sobbing grew heavier and Sister Plum Blossom thought, "Thank goodness it was breast cancer that I had and not a uterine tumor!" She rejoiced knowing there was a child inside her womb.

"Let me carry the weight of your troubles, Little Lotus! When my child is born, I'm going to make you the godmother! If you're sick and have no money, I'll cover the expenses. Don't cry, Little Lotus, the most important thing right now is going to see a doctor!"

And so, together Sister Plum Blossom, Little Lotus, and Little Chrys went to Zhengzhou No. 1 People's Hospital, where they asked to see Dr. Hua. When they found her, Sister Plum Blossom quietly pushed a red envelope full of cash into the doctor's pocket. Dr. Hua personally examined Little Lotus, then made the decision to give her a hysterectomy.

Just as the surgery was about to begin, Dr. Hua's colleague Dr. Gou entered the operating room and injected Little Lotus with an anesthetic. Lying on the operating bed, the patient began to mumble incoherently as Dr. Hua put on a surgical mask and gloves, then lifted a scalpel.

Dr. Gou stepped out of the operating room, a pair of glasses perched upon his nose, and saw a pretty girl sitting in the hallway.

"Wei—hello, miss! Excuse me, you are . . . ?"

"Hello, doctor! My name is Little Chrysanthemum. I'm waiting for my friend Little Lotus, she's just had surgery."

"Oh! Well, I'm Dr. Gou. In addition to being a doctor, I'm also vice-director of the hospital!"

Little Chrys stood up and looked respectfully at the middle-aged man. She had temporarily stopped selling sex to stay by Little Lotus's side, but the main thing on her mind right now was seducing this Dr. Gou.

She returned to Little Lotus's room, where she sat beside the bed shelling five-spice melon seeds. "Sister Plum Blossom is usually so callous to us!" she exclaimed, "but she really stepped up at the critical moment! She's paying all your medical bills."

"Thanks, Little Chrys," Little Lotus said with emotion.

Suddenly the old landlady stepped into the room. "Grandma has come to see you, Little Lotus!" she said warmly. A package was in her hand. "Sister Plum Blossom told me you had surgery, so I stewed you up some Old Hen Soup! Come now, good child, do as I say and drink it while it's hot!"

Little Lotus took the soup. Then the old landlady left the room and headed straight to the office of the hospital director.

"My two sons mention you often, Dr. Hua!" the old landlady said with an ingratiating smile. "They say you're the best doctor in Zhengzhou! If it weren't for you, how could I have lived to be eighty? Thank you so much for the longevity tonic you gave me. Any aborted or miscarried babies lately?"

For several days in Zhengzhou, a major sanitation inspection had been underway; police and city management vehicles patrolled the streets. The vegetable and fruit peddlers strategically parked their tricycles at the entrances of small hutong alleyways, where they would be less conspicuous. An old farmer urged forward the donkey pulling his cart. Slowly it swaggered its way down the street.

"Stop right there!" a policeman suddenly shouted. "Do you know that we're doing a sanitation inspection? And here you are bringing an entire cart full of manure into the city? I'm fining you fifty yuan!" The police officer tore a ticket from a pad and handed it to the old farmer.

"I can't read, and I don't want that ticket! I don't have any money to pay a fine!" The old farmer laughed, revealing a row of teeth yellowed from tobacco.

"The boondocks really produce some unruly people, don't they? The poorer the people are, the less reasonable they are!" The policeman looked at the donkey pulling the manure cart. He couldn't make the donkey move any faster and he couldn't confiscate the cart, but nor did he want to just stand there and smell it. So he used his baton to hit the donkey on its rear. "Get going! Get going!" the cop shouted.

Startled by the blow it had just suffered from the police baton, the donkey barged about wildly in the street. In doing so, it suddenly crashed into a police vehicle that was driving by. The cart toppled and a mountain of manure fell to the ground. Tied to the cart and unable to run off, the donkey fell to the ground, too, where it started to bray in pain. All the small-minded people gathered around and gawked at the scene, laughing as they pinched their noses.

Little Chrys was walking past at this moment. She, too, enjoyed watching and laughing at the spectacle.

She went back to Sister Plum Blossom's Hair Salon, where she told Sister Plum Blossom and the old landlady everything that she had seen, making them hold their stomachs as they laughed. The phone beside Sister Plum Blossom rang and she picked it up. The voice on the other end told her that it was Little Chrys's younger brother on the phone, so she handed the receiver to Little Chrys, who listened for a moment, then hung up and sighed loudly.

"Did your little brother call because something's going on at home?" Sister Plum Blossom asked.

"He got into a prestigious county high school, but our family doesn't have the money for him to keep studying right now, let alone go to university further down the road!"

Little Chrys rode her bicycle to Little Orchid's place, where she found Little Orchid alone at home watering some plants and flowers outside.

"Is Seventh Brother out yet?"

"No, not yet."

"Where's Little Dragon?"

"He's at school."

"Oh." Little Chrys looked at her worried face, then gathered enough courage to ask another question. "Do you want to make some good money, Little Orchid? I met a movie director a few days ago. He's paying people a lot of money to be in a porn video!"

"What?! A porn video?" Little Orchid put down the watering can and her eyes widened. "If anyone saw it, you'd really lose face! How much is the director paying?"

"Around ten thousand yuan per hour!"

"Really?" Little Orchid lowered her voice. "And how do you know you won't be duped?" She took Little Chrys by the hand and led her into the house.

A few days later it was a bright and sunny Sunday. Little Orchid kissed her six-year-old son. "Little Dragon is a good boy," she said. "Little Dragon always listens. Mommy has something to do and is going out for a while. You stay home and do your homework. If you're hungry, have some crackers."

"Mommy, I'm afraid of being home alone!" Little Dragon lamented.

"Little Dragon is well behaved," she replied. "Little Dragon is a big man, he's a hero, he's not afraid of anything! When Mommy comes back she'll buy you some chocolate!" She stuffed a toy dog in her son's arms.

Little Chrys and Little Orchid met each other at the location where the movie director had instructed them on the phone to wait. An attractive, privately owned car rolled up to collect them, then sped off and took them to a large, luxurious house in the outskirts of the city. Together they entered the mansion and looked around: in the central room sat numerous attractive and marvelously adorned young men and women. The photographer, sound recorder, and other personnel had already done the preparations. The director entered the room.

"Are you all mentally prepared?" the director asked. "In foreign countries anybody can see movies like these."

"Director!" a girl bravely asked. "After the movie is shot, are you going to pay in cash? How will you be paying?"

"The compensation varies depending on the role of the individual and the type of film," the director replied as he cast his eyes around the room at the performers. Level Three movies are five thousand yuan per hour; Level Two movies are ten thousand yuan per hour; and Level One movies are twenty thousand yuan per hour!"

"Director!" a boy in his late teens asked. "With movies like these, what's the difference between the levels?"

"Level Three is heterosexual intercourse," the director replied confidently. "Level Two is homosexual intercourse; and Level One is human–animal intercourse!" Laughing, he looked around at all the money-hungry faces.

Sounds of disgust exploded from the performers.

"What level movie should we do, Little Orchid?" Little Chrys asked. Her mind flooded with wild thoughts and fantasies as she mused out loud, "Wow . . . human–animal . . . twenty thousand yuan an hour!"

The director divided them into three groups in accordance with their chosen movie types. Little Orchid was placed in the Level Three group. A young, unemployed worker was there, ready to have sex with her.

"Haven't decided yet, eh?" The director stood before Little Chrys and pressed her to decide. "Which level is it gonna be?"

Little Chrys clenched her teeth and the words burst out: "I'll do human–animal for twenty thousand an hour!"

4

Sister Plum Blossom's Hair Salon had been closed for several days when ownership of the space was transferred to another, younger, woman. The sign outside the salon now read "Sister Fragrance's Beauty Salon."

After Little Lotus left the hospital, she went to work for Sister Plum Blossom as a maid to repay her for covering her medical bills.

"Little Lotus," Sister Plum Blossom began. "Help me think of a good name for my child!"

"You don't know if it's a boy or a girl yet, right? I don't know what to call it, either!"

Sister Plum Blossom picked up a Chinese dictionary and started flipping through it, then began writing down name ideas in a notebook. She asked Little Lotus to look at the list and help her choose one.

"Future?" Little Lotus suddenly called out excitedly. "Yes, Future!" She pointed at the two characters written in the notebook: "Weilai."

"Yes, let's call the child Future! Whether it's a boy or a girl, if it's our child, then it's our future!" Sister Plum Blossom was getting emotional; she felt a twinge of pain in her stomach and two teardrops appeared in the corners of her eyes. "Oh!" she continued, rubbing her stomach, "as soon as the little one heard her name, she got happy and started jumping around in my belly!"

Little Orchid purchased a bag full of all of Seventh Brother's favorite things to eat, then went to the Kaifeng city prison to visit him. "Little Dragon always listens," she informed her husband proudly. "He's at the top of his class among all the first graders in the whole school. Seventh Brother, the child and I will wait for you to come home." She left the prison with tears in her eyes.

Little Chrys entered a shop, where she dialed a village's central administrative phone number from the shop's public telephone. "Wei!" she hollered into the receiver. "Hello, Uncle Village Director! This is Little Chrysanthemum. Would you please go find my little brother? Okay, I'll call back in half an hour." She hung up, waited thirty minutes, and then called the village again. This time, she heard her younger brother's voice on the other end. "Wei!" she repeated. "Hi, Little Brother! I've mailed you some money for tuition; be sure and keep an eye out for it. You have to make your big sister proud! You have to get into university! You have to . . . " Her voice began to tremble.

Little Chrys went to a clothing boutique, where she bought a skirt. She walked toward the bus station, humming a tune.

"Little Chrys!" It was Dr. Gou, who was suddenly standing right before her.

"Oh! You startled me!" Little Chrys laughed. "So, Dr. Gou was able to get out of the hospital and unwind a bit, eh?"

"I haven't seen you since your friend Little Lotus was discharged," the doctor said warmly. "Honestly, I missed you a little . . . still so pretty!"

With Little Chrys by his side, Dr. Gou hailed a taxi, which sped off to a motel. An hour later, they emerged from the room they had rented, and then went to a restaurant.

"Little Sister Chrysanthemum," Dr. Gou said, "let me help you find work!"

Tipsy from alcohol, she collapsed into the doctor's arms and fell asleep.

"Wake up, Little Chrys!" Dr. Gou repeated several times.

"Are you really going to arrange for me to be a nurse at the hospital?" Little Chrys asked when she opened her eyes.

"Yes!" he replied. "But first you have to hurry up and do two months of training. I've already found the instructor. After that, we can work at the same hospital and see each other every day!"

Her eyes filled with tears of gratitude as she wrapped her arms around Dr. Gou's big, thick neck.

Little Chrys went back to Courtyard No. 8 off Shangcheng Street and got to work arranging all of her clothes. The knowledge that she, a prostitute, would be starting all over again, left an intangible bittersweetness in her heart. She daydreamed of shedding her prostitute exterior like a shell and being transformed into a white-clothed angel! Yes! A nurse dressed in white, as beautiful as a swan.

Carrying her leather suitcase, she descended the stairs.

"Big Sister Little Chrysanthemum, are you leaving, too?" The stupid boy suddenly ran toward her, blocking the way. "Big Sister Little Plum Blossom has left," he continued. "Big Sister Little Lotus has left, Big Sister Little Orchid has left. Why does Big Sister Little Chrys want to leave, too? Aren't you all going to play with me? I'm not letting Big Sister Little Chrys leave . . . " He held on to her arm.

"Little Treasure always listens!" Little Chrys said in reply. "Little Treasure always behaves! Big Sister will come back to see you." She looked around at the big, multi-family compound that had taken her in six years ago; now, she suddenly felt reluctant to leave. At just that moment, a big, speckled cat leapt from the old landlady's window, landing on the ground outside just a few feet away from Little Chrys. It held a chunk of meat in its mouth.

"Damned cat, you drop that right now! Drop it right now!" It was the old landlady, who had come outside and was huffing and puffing as she chased the cat.

Little Chrys was able to see what the speckled cat held in its mouth: a thoroughly cooked human baby! No bigger than a pencil case, the baby's eyes were closed and it looked as though it were dreaming in paradise. The old landlady was like a big white cat in hot pursuit of the big speckled cat. But suddenly, the big white cat tripped and stumbled, causing a mouthful of white dentures to fall to the ground.

"Ha ha!" the stupid boy laughed. "Grandma fell! Grandma's teeth fell!" He released Little Chrys from his grip and excitedly began to clap his hands.

"Are you okay, Landlady Nai Nai?" Little Chrys said as she rushed over to lift the old landlady up.

"Yes, thank you, Little Chrys, Grandma is fine! A fortune-teller told me I'd live to be a hundred!" She pointed to her grandson. "You! You really are stupid, as stupid as can be! Grandma falls down and you start clapping? Now hurry up and pick up Grandma's dentures!"

The stupid boy laughed, then went to pick up the old woman's teeth from the ground.

Little Lotus carried a bowl of hot chicken soup to Sister Plum Blossom's bed. "Sister Plum Blossom," she said, "you and the child need your nutrition. Hurry up and drink this while it's hot!"

"Little Lotus," she replied, "I've been eating and drinking too much! Can't you see how fat I've gotten? I'm so fat that pretty soon I won't even be able to sit on a stool anymore!" She lay lazily on her bed, unwilling to lift a finger for the soup.

"Sister Plum Blossom, you're just lying there, but you should let me feed you. Do it for the sake of my godchild—for Future!" Little Lotus picked up a spoon.

The telephone suddenly rang. Little Lotus put down the spoon and answered it.

"Wei!" the old landlady's voice creaked on the other end. "Is this Little Lotus? Aiya, this is really bad! Ever since you girls left, this stupid grandson of mine has been crying and making a fuss from sunrise to sunset! I give him milk and he won't even drink it! He just cries out, 'Big Sister Plum Blossom, Big Sister Lotus, Big Sister Orchid, Big Sister Chrysanthemum . . .' But then last night, he suddenly disappeared! I've already asked Little Orchid and Little Chrys if they know anything about it and they both say they haven't seen him!"

"We haven't seen him either, Landlady Nai Nai! Sister Plum Blossom is going to be giving birth any day now and I can't leave her side! Make Little Orchid and Little Chrys help you!"

"Aiya!" Sister Plum Blossom started to cry out. "My stomach hurts real bad!"

Little Lotus hurriedly hung up the phone and then, thoroughly alarmed, picked it up again.

In the hospital emergency room, several doctors readied themselves for the women's arrival.

5

"Wei! Is this Landlady Nai Nai? It's Little Orchid. I found Little Treasure on Hero Road. He wasn't wearing any pants and he was sleeping with some crazy woman!"

"Thank heaven and earth, you found him! My Little Treasure! As long as nothing has happened to him . . . " The old landlady put down the phone and quickly dialed her eldest son's cell phone. "Wei! Son, it's me . . . *Me*! How can you not even recognize your own mother's voice? Listen, Little Treasure has been found! You have to go pick him up and bring him back! What? You're in a meeting? How can a meeting be more important than finding your own son? Wei? Wei? What? You want me to call Little Treasure's uncle? You want him to go and get him?"

Little Orchid was on Hero Road, where, along with a few heterosexual couples who were evidently very much in love, she watched the spectacle of the crazy woman and the stupid boy. The crazy woman was naked from the waist down, and filthy. On the upper half of her body she wore an old, worn-out men's military jacket and her haircut was appropriate neither for a man nor for a woman. She looked as content as could be, reclining in the sunshine and humming a tune without a care in the world. Suddenly she climbed into a dumpster, and from that dumpster she retrieved a brightly colored paper wrapper, the contents of which she poured onto the ground. Excitedly, she grabbed a sticky cucumber. She put it beside her mouth and kissed it.

Everybody thought the crazy woman was going to eat the cucumber, but instead she stuck it in her vagina, then started moaning someone's name. When the stupid boy saw what she was doing, he started to masturbate.

"Hey, stupid boy, don't masturbate—go stick your big cock in her cave!" A group of male and female hooligans shouted out to him.

"Don't do that, Little Treasure!" Now it was Little Orchid speaking. "Hurry up and go home, your grandma is looking for you!" Her face flushed crimson as she anxiously called out, but she didn't dare go near the boy.

A white car drove past and the stupid boy was grabbed and taken away.

"Grandma's good little baby is back!" the old landlady gushed with a smile. "Grandma will give you some Laughing Child milk to drink!" She stuck a straw into a milk bottle and handed it to the stupid boy.

"Grandma, I want to give this milk to the big sister on Hero Road!" the boy said as he lifted the bottle and ran out the door.

The old landlady ran after the stupid boy in a hurry, then grabbed hold of him. "Little Treasure listens," she said. "Little Treasure is Grandma's good grandson! We're not going to go look for that crazy woman, okay? Little Treasure listens, Little

Treasure is Grandma's good grandson, Grandma will find Little Treasure a pretty wife."

At that moment the telephone rang. The old landlady held on to her grandson with one hand and picked up the phone with the other.

"Wei! Little Lotus? My Little Treasure's come home . . . what? Little Plum Blossom is having a difficult delivery? My goodness! The important thing is to save her life! You tell that doctor that we don't want the child! What? They won't let you make the decision? Then convince Little Plum Blossom! The important thing is to save her life! . . . Aiya! How can she be so stupid? Alright, I'm going to come and try to convince her." The old landlady hung up the phone and prepared to leave the house. Just thinking about the fresh dead-baby soup she'd soon be drinking gave her a rush so great that she forgot all about her grandson. She shut the door behind her, then rushed out of Courtyard No. 8 and onto Shangcheng Street, where she extended an arm to hail a passing taxi.

"Are you a relative of the patient?" the doctor asked. "The situation is critical—we can only save one life. Please decide if it will be the child or the mother—and sign right here!"

Little Lotus shook from head to toe. She took the pen from the doctor's hand but did not dare decide who would live and who would die. "Poor Sister Plum Blossom!" she thought, "and our Future . . . " She thought of her own missing uterus and began to cry in agony.

"What exactly is your relationship to the patient? Speak up!" It was Dr. Hua herself, charging through the hallway in Little Lotus's direction.

"We're just friends. I'm afraid to sign!" Little Lotus continued to cry.

Rapidly, Dr. Hua entered the operating room.

"We're going to operate on you, Little Plum Blossom! I can't guarantee we'll be able to save the child—you've got to mentally prepare yourself!" Dr. Hua looked gravely at Sister Plum Blossom, who was bleeding heavily.

"No!" Sister Plum Blossom cried. "I want my child! Dr. Hua, I beg of you, you have to save my child first!" She struggled to get her heartfelt words out. "There's no more hope for me in this life, Dr. Hua! You've got to save my child. I've pinned all my hopes on her!"

Dr. Hua suddenly thought back to twenty-five years earlier, when she had abandoned her own child. Her heart ached with pain as she threw an admiring gaze at this great and mighty mother!

It just happened to be June 1st, Children's Day, and children in happy homes everywhere sang sweet nursery rhymes. The old landlady's feet moved quickly as she rushed through the main entrance to the hospital. When she arrived, she saw Sister Plum Blossom lying down with eyes closed, a faint smile lingering on her lips—and the baby she wanted to eat wrapped in a blanket, crying for its mother!

"Go, Sister Plum Blossom! Go and be at ease. I promise heaven that I will raise our Future to be a great person with an indomitable spirit!" Little Lotus wiped her eyes and gazed down at Sister Plum Blossom, this woman whom she both hated and loved.

Little Lotus held the child with all the warmth in her body and stepped out of the hospital, just like a real mother.

"Mommy, don't abandon me!" A child stood on the snowy ground, calling out to his mother.

Dr. Hua awakened from her dream and nudged her husband, who was asleep by her side.

"Nanshan," she said. "I had another dream about our child! He was standing in the snow, calling out to me." A tear fell from her eye and she began to choke up.

"Alright then, wife!" Xia Nanshan replied. "If you want a child, let's go to the orphanage in a few days and adopt one." He rolled over and went back to sleep.

Dr. Hua lay in bed tossing and turning, unable to fall back to sleep. When she closed her eyes the only thing she saw was Sister Plum Blossom's child. The likeness was uncanny! Truly, it looked just like him, looked just like her own child! Her mind returned to twenty-five years earlier when she had once held a fat, white baby in her arms.

Carrying a heavy gift, Dr. Hua went to the residence that Sister Plum Blossom had left behind. There she found Little Lotus holding the child in her arms, humming a folk song that her grandmother had passed down to her mother, and her mother had passed down to her.

"Little Lotus," Dr. Hua began, "you're not married. Why don't you give the child to us to adopt?" She held a thick stack of RMB before the young woman's face.

"I can't take your money, Dr. Hua. I promised Sister Plum Blossom that I would raise Future to adulthood! I already regard Future as my own flesh and blood, my own child, and for my child I would sacrifice everything!" She pushed the money back toward Dr. Hua.

Sighing heavily, Dr. Hua turned to look at the child once more, then picked up the weighty gift she had brought and departed.

The stupid boy left his grandmother's house and ran in the direction of Hero Road. He ran past Jiefang Road, past the hiring site and past the salvage station, all the while dreaming that he might find a beautiful, wonderful companion. As the sky began to darken, the stupid boy arrived at Hero Road, where he lay beneath a locust tree and fell asleep as his thick penis fell out of a split in the crotch of his trousers. Among the men who passed by, there were those who were impotent and those who suffered premature ejaculation. Some were able to get it up but couldn't keep it up, and some had small cocks. And some of them, of course, were hooligans of the first degree!

Early the next morning, the old landlady went to Hero Road, where she found her grandson lying on the ground, writhing in unfathomable agony. His genitals, both penis and testicles, were gone and his thighs were coated with dark red blood—blood that dripped onto Hero Road.

FIFTEEN

1

I was sitting with six angelic boys; on the table before us were all of our favorite fruits and other delicacies. We were drinking domestic alcohol: wine, beer, and baijiu; each drank so much that his face became like a spring peach blossom, making it easy for him to forget that outside the window yellow autumn leaves were falling.

"Come, sisters!" Little Fairy shouted. "Let us congratulate Uncle He! Always keep up the golden gun, now and forever staying young!" He raised a glass of beer above his head.

The six young men stood and raised their drinks in a toast. I listened to the sound of glass on glass and polished off my drink in a single gulp.

"Today is your sixtieth birthday, Uncle He," began Little Thing. "We six brothers have come to congratulate you on your long life—let's take a group photo to commemorate the occasion!" He pulled a camera from his bag and continued. "Alright, everyone, listen up! Uncle He, please have a seat. Little Fairy, you stand at Uncle He's left; Little Devil, you stand at his right. Ah Qing and Little Jade, you stand behind him, and Little Tough and I will squat in front of him." Little Thing directed everyone to take their positions.

"Wait a minute!" Little Devil left the room, then came back with seven bananas, which he distributed to everyone present.

"I'm a sixty-year-old man," I thought. "I'm not going to behave as outrageously as these young people!"

"Ah Qing, why don't you go grab my flute and I'll hold that instead of a banana?" I turned and patted him on the shoulder.

Ah Qing rushed to the other side of the room, but instead of retrieving my flute he lifted my guitar. "Let me be the flute blower, Uncle He," he said—jokingly, since he couldn't play. "Please, play the guitar and sing for us!"

I took the guitar from Ah Qing, then tuned the strings for a bit and started to play as I sang. "We love to eat big bananas! We love to eat big bananas!"

Little Thing set the timer function on his camera, then ran back to my side.

To the rhythm of the guitar, all six of them began to sing: "We love to eat big bananas! We love to eat big bananas!"

"Come, children!" I shouted. "Tomorrow belongs to you. To this beautiful day—cheers!"

The rousing sound of colliding glasses filled the room.

2

One Sunday, Little Orchid took her son Little Dragon to the park to relax and stroll about. There she spotted Little Chrys and Dr. Gou.

"Wait for me here," Little Chrys said to the doctor when she saw them. "I'm going to go talk to them for a minute, then I'll be right back!"

Little Chrys approached the mother and child. "Little Dragon is so tall!" she exclaimed with a smile.

"Hello, Auntie!" Little Dragon greeted her politely.

"Little Dragon is such a good boy. How old are you now? What grade are you in?"

"I'm seven years old, Auntie. I'm in second grade."

"Is that your boyfriend?" Little Orchid asked, peering at Dr. Gou from the corner of her eye.

"I'm going to be starting at the hospital as a nurse!" Little Chrys said proudly, ignoring the question. "And it's all because of him! He's the vice-director of the hospital, and he's also an outstanding anesthesiologist!"

Little Orchid snickered. "So are you his mistress now?"

"Mommy, what's a mistress?" Little Dragon inserted.

"You'll know when you're older, Little Dragon," his mother replied.

"He still has that goddamned woman at home," Little Chrys complained. "She won't stop wrapping her tentacles around him. If it weren't for her, we'd become husband and wife immediately!"

When Little Chrys finished talking, she returned to Dr. Gou's side.

"Uncle, Auntie, please buy a rose!" A little girl, filthy from head to toe, held up a withering rose for them to see.

Little Dragon looked at the little girl with pity. She was just around his age.

Having failed to make a sale with Little Chrys and Dr. Gou, the little flower girl continued on her way, hopelessly walking past one couple after another. Just then, a middle-aged woman appeared out of nowhere and stood before Dr. Gou and Little Chrys. She pointed at Little Chrys's nose and called her a tramp! Dr. Gou was so startled that he turned to run in the opposite direction; in his panic, he knocked over the flower girl. Her roses flew into the air and hit the ground along with two shiny coins that had fallen from her pocket. Panicked, the little girl got up from the ground and went to pick up the roses and coins, but at that very moment, a little ragpicker boy who happened to be passing by grabbed the coins and ran off. The little flower girl didn't chase after the boy, but instead collapsed to the ground and began to cry.

"Stop! You give that money back to her!" Little Dragon grabbed hold of the ragpicker boy, but the boy bit Little Dragon's hand and ran off.

"Who told you to go minding other people's business? Look at your hand—you're bleeding!" Angrily, Little Orchid grabbed her son to prevent him from chasing after the rag-picker boy.

304

"Mommy, Daddy is back!" Little Dragon charged through the gate and into the courtyard. A faint smile appeared on Little Orchid's otherwise quite bitter face. She wanted to go outside to greet her husband, but her feet hesitated for several seconds before she grabbed the watering can and went out to water the flowers and plants. She didn't know that Seventh Brother was already standing behind her, looking just as withered and dried up as a piece of firewood. He tried to raise his drooping head, but was unable to lift it more than halfway. He was waiting for his wife to scold him; somehow, this would make him feel more at ease.

"So you're back," Little Orchid said, setting down the watering can as she sat in an outdoor chair. "When do you plan on going back in?"

Seventh Brother knelt before her and burst into tears.

Rain fell all night long. When morning came the sun emerged from clouds that were as black as crows. It showed its face, which was the size of a baked sesame cake. Seventh Brother got up at the crack of dawn, mounted the family flatbed tricycle and left through the gate. At midday he returned with over a hundred empty penjing pots and began creating potted landscapes in the courtyard of his family home. Another spring was due to arrive and the strangely shaped plants were bursting forth tiny green hairs. When he was done potting the landscapes, Seventh Brother took them out to sell.

"Little Dragon, why aren't you in school today?" Little Orchid asked her son. He seemed a little off that day.

Lowering his head, Little Dragon stood in silence.

"What's wrong?" his mother persisted. "Good boy, tell your mommy." She squatted down to the boy's level and her tone grew warmer.

"Ma, the teacher wants my parents to go to school today!" Tears fell from his eyes.

"What on earth is going on? Did you get in another fight with a classmate?" When Little Dragon didn't answer, Little Orchid slapped him. "You tell me what's going on right now!"

In tears, Little Dragon told her what had happened. "There's a classmate in our class called Little Ming and he always bullies the kid I share a desk with and he thinks he can do it just because his dad is the director of the Bureau of Education. Little Ming always calls the kid a four-eyed dog because he's nearsighted and he wears glasses. I didn't like it so I went to hit him but I accidently stabbed him in the eye with a pencil."

"What?" Little Orchid cried in a panic. "How can you bring me such misfortune? Who told you to go minding other people's business?" She hit him again, this time on the behind.

When Little Orchid and her son came back from the boy's school, the young mother locked herself in her bedroom and cried.

"What's wrong?" Seventh Brother asked when he came home.

"Little Dragon got in a fight with a classmate and stabbed him in the eye with a pencil! The parents want a hundred thousand yuan as compensation—the dad is the director of the local Bureau of Education!"

"But they're just kids!" Seventh Brother reasoned. "It's normal for them to get in fights! Little Dragon didn't stab his eye on purpose, right? So what if his dad is the Bureau of Ed. director? If he doesn't let our Little Dragon stay at his school, we'll move to another city and find a school there!"

A month later, two cars pulled up outside Little Orchid and Seventh Brother's home; out of the vehicles stepped Little Ming's father and a school principal named Xia Nanshan. Inside the courtyard, a smiling Seventh Brother offered them a seat and a smiling Little Orchid poured them tea. Little Dragon clenched his teeth. His eyes were fixed on the strange and perverse penjing surrounding them.

"What do you think of this courtyard, Principal Xia?" the Bureau of Education director asked Xia Nanshan, who had recently been promoted from assistant principal to principal.

"It's quite big," Xia Nanshan replied. "Great geographical setting, too. The only problem is that the building is so old!" He offered the two sellers a smile.

"Go ahead, Principal Xia, name your price! My family has been in this house for generations; my father handed it down to me. As long as we're able to compensate Little Ming's dad, we're willing to sell it!" Seventh Brother tossed a cigarette butt to the ground gruffly.

"How about this, Little Seventh Brother: I'll go home and think it over, then come back with a reasonable offer." Xia Nanshan and the director of the Bureau of Education stood up from their chairs to leave, then got in their respective cars and nonchalantly drove off.

"Mommy, where are we going to live after we sell our house?" Little Dragon rubbed his eyes, which were bright red from crying.

"We'll have to move and go rent a house," Little Orchid replied. "Little Dragon, you have to behave from now on! Don't go minding other people's business. If someone bullies you, you just have to put up with it, and if you can't put up with it then run away. Study hard and one day you'll be a big official; we'll never be afraid of people bullying us again!" Little Orchid touched her son with sorrowful affection.

One week later, school principal Xia Nanshan bought Little Orchid and Seventh Brother's home for eighty thousand yuan. Principal Xia, his wife Dr. Hua, and their adopted child moved into the compound, and Little Orchid and her family went to live in an old, two-room house near the coal factory. The crisis thus resolved, Little Dragon was able to return to school.

When I wake up each morning, the first thing I do is remove from my pillowcase all of the hairs that fall out during the night. It seems to me that I have less and less hair with each passing day. I wash my face, but barely dare look myself in the mirror. Whenever I do, there appears before me a wan, lifeless face whose lips seem drained of blood.

At times like these, I pull my photo album out from a drawer and flip through pictures from my youth.

How wonderful it would be to stay young forever!

It's only when I remember that I still have my wonderful group of kids—Ah Qing, Little Jade, Little Fairy, Little Devil, Little Tough, and Little Thing—that my blood starts to warm.

I step outside and walk to a small park where old people exercise. There, I start to move alongside all those fat, slow-moving dinosaurs, hoping that I won't become a piece of waste too soon.

I'm still young—really! I'm still young because I still have the strength to love! I still have faith that one day I'll receive flowers and a standing ovation on the great stage of life!

I sit down to write, fantasizing that I can create a work even greater than *The Dream of the Red Chamber*.

I go to the vegetable market to buy fresh vegetables.

I go to the library to look for recently published books and periodicals.

I water my plants and flowers.

I wash my clothes. I wash my flesh.

I want to go see that group of kids! Do they have work these days? Are they hungry? Are they drunk? I have to go see them. I have to tell them to act as they should, to study well, to treasure their youth. I hasten the pace of my footsteps, moving forward like an anxious old donkey. By the time I enter the main gate of Dongdan Park, my entire body is covered in sweat.

I look for a bench or a stone to sit on.

I watch the young men as they move about in threes and fives, their bright eyes flashing in the shadows.

The night grows darker and darker. Young men with families return to their homes, while those who have no families but do possess a few dozen yuan go spend the night in bathhouses. Some remain in the park, pacing back and forth like ghosts between clusters of trees and the public toilet.

Tonight, I want to invite a young man to dinner. I want to let him eat until he's full, then take him home so I can hold him in my arms and kiss his red lips and tender feet.

A thin young man circles the park, then walks toward the public toilet. I can practically hear the sound of his stomach rumbling. If he likes me, if he likes this old man, I'll invite him out for roast duck and beer, then take him home to fall asleep with me.

There are only the two of us—one old, one young—in the public toilet.

He pulls out his soft cock and pretends to urinate.

I pull out mine and do the same.

I wait and wait until I cannot wait anymore, then reach out a hand to touch him. Suddenly he kneels and takes my soft, plush dick into his mouth, but spits it out immediately. He thrusts one hand in the air and grabs hold of my sagging testicles with the other.

"Hurry up!" he says. "Give me some money!"

4

Little Orchid asked Seventh Brother to pull the coal cart out to sell coal, but he was too thin and weak to make it budge, so he went to the hiring site to look for work instead. Zhengzhou's hiring site had been moved from the intersection of Erma Road and Jiefang Road to a courtyard nearby.

"Go in! Don't just stand there at the entrance! Go in! Go in!" a woman shouted repeatedly into a megaphone. The courtyard was packed with young working men and women; several migrant workers with backpacks clogged the entryway.

Seventh Brother squeezed into the hiring site as a few migrant workers asked him if he was looking for workers or for a job. He ignored the question; he just smiled bitterly and shook his head. The migrant workers' second guess was the correct one: he was there to find a boss.

Sweating profusely from being jostled about in the crowd, he sat down at a small tea stand, where he spent two mao on a sweet, colorful beverage made of saccharin and food coloring mixed with water. When he finished drinking it, he had to use a toilet, so he walked to the northeast corner of the hiring site, where an old man sat at the bathroom entrance collecting money. Beside the old man was a chalkboard with four crooked characters scribbled in white chalk: two mao per person, it said. Seventh Brother felt that a cup of a tea was worth two mao, but two mao to use a bathroom? Surely that was too much. He clenched his testicles and made his way out of the hiring site.

He ran along several streets until he came across a free public toilet hidden in a small hutong. It had been many days since the toilet was cleaned and the floor was covered in piss and shit. A young worker entered the bathroom carrying two bricks, which he placed on the sides of the pit beside Seventh Brother. Widening his stance, the worker placed a foot on each brick and squatted as a horde of flies lunged into the air. Seventh Brother swatted at his face with one hand and his ass with the other, but the flies wouldn't go away.

"Wei, brother, do you have any more of that paper?" Seventh Brother asked, looking at the newspaper in the man's hand. "I forgot to bring toilet paper!"

The young worker tore a piece of newspaper in half and handed some to Seventh Brother. "Fuck!" he exclaimed. "Look at all the old farts on this newspaper. Nearly eighty years old and their faces are as soft as a baby's butt! Compare that to our generation of young people from the countryside. We drop out of school early, drift around as vagrants, sell our labor and

310

get STDs. By the time we're eighteen we have hunched backs and wrinkled foreheads!" The young worker finished cursing and crapping, then rolled the colored newspaper into a ball and wiped his ass.

Seventh Brother laughed and wiped his ass with one of the familiar faces on the newspaper. Then he pulled up his trousers, picked up the two bricks that he himself had brought, and stepped out of the toilet. Just then, a youth with a backpack entered the public toilet and glued an advertisement for syphilis and gonorrhea treatment onto the wall. His poster covered up another STD advertisement from a different clinic.

Seventh Brother returned to the hiring site several days in a row, but not a single boss approached him. Anytime he felt hungry he would think of his wife and child. Each day, he walked to the hiring site to save the two mao it cost to park his bike at the bicycle lot. And each night, he walked back home to save the one kuai it cost to take a bus. The more he walked, the more his stomach filled with a fiery rage. He clenched his fists and felt an uncontrollable urge to punch someone. On the road up ahead he saw an old man selling roasted sweet potatoes. Seventh Brother approached him.

"Old man, how much for one jin?"

"One kuai."

Seventh Brother pulled a ten-RMB note from his pocket. "Give me three jin!"

The old man took the money and put it in his pocket, then pulled out a tray scale with a pleasant smile on his face.

"Three jin for three kuai!" The old man produced an oil-paper bag into which he placed the steaming hot sweet potatoes; then he placed the bag in Seventh Brother's hand. He began to retrieve his customer's change, carefully pulling the money out of his pocket and counting the bills one by one. "Here you go," he said, "seven kuai!"

"What?" Seventh Brother exclaimed. "You're confused, old man! I clearly gave you a one-hundred-yuan note. Why are you giving me seven kuai?" He raised his voice.

"That can't be right," the old man replied. "I distinctly remember that it was a ten-yuan bill!"

It took just moments for the conflict to escalate into a fight. More and more people appeared on the sidelines to watch the spectacle, but not a single person came forward to intervene. Seventh Brother punched the old man, who cried out, then pulled from his pocket a hundred-yuan bill earned by his own blood, sweat and hard work. He gave the bill to Seventh Brother, who took the money but ignored the sweet potatoes and slipped quickly out of the surrounding crowd.

An old john had a heart attack and died on top of Little Orchid. In alarm she got dressed. Not knowing what to do, she used the hotel phone to call Little Chrys.

"How could you do something so stupid, Little Orchid!" Little Chrys screeched from inside the nurses' work station. "You know what you are—don't report this to the authorities! Just get out of there!"

One week later, Little Orchid was arrested for prostitution and making obscene films. Her name appeared in a scandalous front-page headline written across Zhengzhou's evening paper. The following morning, the old dead john made the front-page headline of Zhengzhou's morning paper. But nothing scandalous was written now. Instead, the headline read: "A Noble and Prestigious Police Officer Who Had Battled Criminals for Many Years Suffered a Heart Attack in the Line of Duty, Gloriously Making the Ultimate Sacrifice whilst Positioned at His Work Station!"

"Daddy," Little Dragon asked as he rubbed two red, tearful eyes. "Why was Mommy arrested?"

"Your mommy was a bad woman, Little Dragon. Don't ever mention her again!" Seventh Brother replied in grief and indignation.

"I want Mommy . . . " Little Dragon raised his voice and began to cry.

"Don't cry! Hold it in for me!" Seventh Brother shouted, raising a foot to kick the child. "Cry again and I'll beat you to death!"

A police vehicle pulled up outside Seventh Brother's home. An officer approached the building, then knocked at the door and informed Seventh Brother that his wife, fearing punishment, had killed herself in prison.

With a blood-curdling cry, Seventh Brother lunged at the officer.

5

After my sixtieth birthday passed, I was retired forever. I wasn't used to having all those days without work, so I lay in my bed recalling the stench of corpses from days past. A single day in bed, however, made me feel that I was aging even faster than I already was; I wasn't going to just stay at home and wait for death! I squeezed onto a crowded bus and made my way to Dongdan Park.

I squatted inside a public toilet for hours thinking about the time Little Devil and Little Fairy stole a golden urn. This was not a place of auspicious feng shui; you'd be better off dying at home than sticking around there! The sky grew dark and I exited the toilet. Outside, I watched as two young men held each other and kissed among the shadowy trees. How wonderful it was to be young! I knew that I had lost many opportunities to be loved. I figured I would die soon, and that after my death two young people would lift me just as I had lifted so many others. They would lift me, and they would place me in a cremation chamber. Yes, let my ashes return to the ocean!

I returned to my lonely home. I wanted to ask Ah Qing to come and keep me company, but when I called his cell phone a recording informed me that it was disconnected for lack of payment. With nothing to do, I turned on my computer and entered the voice chatroom of a gay website. Twenty gay men with pseudonyms were engaged in private chat, while in the public chatroom someone by the name of Warm Spring Blossom was playing guitar and singing. These were the words of the song:

"I imagined myself a farmer
Growing wheat and cotton with my own sweat
But when I thought of natural disasters
And countless tax revenues
I no longer dared imagine

I imagined myself a worker
Creating wealth with my own intelligence and two hands
But when I thought of the boss's black-hearted deceit
And unemployment, or not being paid my wages
I no longer dared imagine

I imagined myself a prostitute
Trading my youth and beauty for money
But I want to have a warm home
And when I thought of AIDS
I no longer dared imagine

I imagined myself a thief
Robbing a bank with my own passion and vigor
But when I thought of danger, when I thought of death
When I thought of my own pitiable mother
I no longer dared imagine

I imagined myself an honest and hardworking person
But poverty, oh poverty
I am so poor that I have nothing
I can't stop imagining, imagining
I imagine that in a springtime
The moon casts its light on melancholy flowers . . .

I met President Jiang by chance in a WC
He fucked me ardently

And I shit out his semen happily
I took it abroad to auction
Even if sold for just one kuai per sperm
I can still become a trillionaire overnight"

Old He to Warm Spring Blossom: You sing so well—I love it! Was this song written by you?

Warm Spring Blossom to Old He: It's a poem that was written by a fellow netizen. I wrote music for it.

Old He to Warm Spring Blossom: We've chatted before, do you remember? I would like to meet you. Would that be okay?

Warm Spring Blossom to Old He: Yes, I remember. If it's decreed by fate, then we will meet.

Old He to Warm Spring Blossom: Can you tell me your phone number?

Warm Spring Blossom to Old He: I'm sorry, my life is unstable . . . if there's something you want to talk about, send me an email.

Old He to Warm Spring Blossom: I love music, too. I can play other people's songs with the guitar or flute, but I'm old now and can no longer write songs myself.

Warm Spring Blossom to Old He: Neither writing poetry nor music is an easy affair. Above all, a writer must have the power of insight. True art has vitality! Not only are today's musicians not progressing, they're going backward; things were better in the early 90s. The music and lyrics of today's popular music—the more they are written, the more pallid they become; the more they are sung, the more they stink. They moan and groan without cause. They are malformed, stupid, vulgar, and numb. They act like spoiled children. They show off. In this day and age, when consumption reigns supreme, the aesthetic judgment and connoisseurship of modern people has deteriorated. They are no longer willing to think. They regard cultural garbage as fast food for the soul!

Warm Spring Blossom played the guitar and sang once more:

"In this life I will be a vagrant
Go seek—a brilliant and stalwart father
He has a brilliant and stalwart mind
He is very lenient: lying
Fighting, stealing, drinking, leading a life of debauchery
Taking drugs and homosexuality
He is able, when his deviate sons are out of hope and
    commit suicide
To see them one last time

I will use this life to search, to be a vagrant
I will never be able to find it
So I can only live regretfully
And never be a father in this life again"

SIXTEEN

1

The roses in People's Park were in full bloom. Heterosexual couples walked about, then sat in chairs and discussed money. Two men holding hands walked about, then sat in a bed of roses. The top kissed the bottom's lips and they began to discuss love. The roses' faces flushed red as they scattered their fragrance upon the lovers' hearts.

At midnight, a black shadow jumped over the wall and into the park. The black shadow ran toward a thicket of roses, then pulled out a pair of scissors and began snipping the flowers, which the shadow then tossed into a cotton bag. Within minutes the bag was full. The black shadow threw the bag across its back, then jumped over the wall again and ran off.

When Seventh Brother returned to the dilapidated, one-room house he now rented, he saw that a light was on, pushing out the darkness. He opened the bag—he had made it from a bed sheet—and dumped its contents onto the floor. He gave Little Dragon some instructions and the boy began wrapping each flower individually in paper. Father and son were busy at work.

The following day, Zijing Mountain Park had one more child flower-seller.

"Uncle! Auntie! Why don't you buy a rose?" Little Dragon implored as he trailed behind a couple, sticking close to their heels.

After Little Dragon sold all of his roses, he walked home, where he emptied the money he had made from his pockets and gave it to his father.

"Daddy, I sold fifteen roses today! Some of the uncles gave ten kuai, some gave five kuai, and some gave one kuai!"

"Good boy, you did a good job! Daddy will fry you an egg." Seventh Brother patted Little Dragon on the shoulder.

One afternoon, Seventh Brother slipped once more into People's Park. He looked in each corner where roses grew but saw nothing but stems and leaves. So he left People's Park and went over to Zijing Mountain Park, but it was the same there: in the rose gardens there were no roses to be seen.

He sat on a street corner, smoking a continuous stream of cigarettes, ignoring the people coming and going around him. Little Dragon met him there.

"Daddy, let's go home. I'm hungry." Little Dragon took his father by the hand and led him home.

Inside their dilapidated house, father and son sat and ate noodles together. Little Dragon finished a bowl, but his stomach wasn't full yet so he went for a second helping. He fished around in the pot with a ladle for some time before finally salvaging a solitary noodle, which he grabbed with his chopsticks and put in his mouth. Seventh Brother, too, approached the pot with his empty bowl. He licked his lips and used the ladle to serve himself thin, watery soup.

"Did you get enough to eat, Little Dragon?"

"Yes, Daddy."

With a cigarette hanging from his lips, Seventh Brother was getting ready to go out when the landlord entered the building. "Time to pay this month's rent," the landlord said.

"Just wait two days," Seventh Brother said, compensating for his lack of money with a smile. "I still haven't got paid for last month's work!"

The landlord left and Seventh Brother heaved a big sigh. "Little Dragon," he said, turning to the boy. "Your mommy is gone and Daddy is unable to raise you. He's failed you, he's made you miss out on school. Daddy is going to find another home for you—a good home!"

"No!" Little Dragon cried. "I'm not going anywhere! I'm not going to school, I'm staying with Daddy. Wherever Daddy goes, that's where I'll go, too!"

Seventh Brother sighed again, then turned on his heel and walked out the door.

"Daddy, where are you going? I'm going with you!" Little Dragon stuck to his father's heels.

"Go back inside!" Seventh Brother said, reprimanding his son and feeling annoyed. "I'm going to the hiring site to look for work!"

Seventh Brother pushed open the door, a bag in his arms. "Little Dragon!" he called out with a smile. "Look at all the nice things Daddy bought you!"

When Little Dragon heard his father's footsteps, he quickly hid the second-grade Chinese-language-arts textbook that he was reading under his bed quilt. He looked at the new clothes his father had bought him and his eyes widened.

"Come, good son." Seventh Brother said. "Let Daddy put these clothes on you . . . Now let me see you . . . oh! My good boy! In these clothes you look like a little superstar!" The boy looked at his father and saw tears in his eyes.

Little Dragon looked at himself in the mirror. "Wow!" he exclaimed. "I'm not an ugly duckling, I'm Daddy's little swan!"

"Come, good boy," Seventh Brother continued. "Look at what else Daddy bought you: something nice to eat!"

"Wow! Chicken legs! I finally get to eat fried chicken legs!" Little Dragon squealed in delight, but his father lowered his head and in the blink of an eye the boy's smile disappeared. Timidly, he asked, "Daddy, why aren't you eating chicken legs?"

In the outskirts of the city, not far from where Seventh Brother and Little Dragon lived, a motor trike came to a stand-still at the side of the road. The man driving it was around forty years of age. In the passenger seat behind him sat a fat woman with dark skin. Back home, Seventh Brother mounted his pedal tricycle and began riding in the direction of the designated spot. Little Dragon was with him.

"Oh, this child is just adorable!" The woman reached out to embrace Little Dragon, but the boy ran around Seventh Brother and stood behind him.

"Don't be afraid, Little Dragon, these people will treat you well!" Seventh Brother tugged at his son gently, then placed him before the man and woman. "Brother, Sister," he said, "this child has had a difficult time! His mother died young. Please treat him well, let him go to school . . . "

"No! I'm not leaving Daddy!" Little Dragon began to cry in anguish.

The man stepped forward to take Little Dragon into his arms. "Don't worry, buddy!" he said to the boy's father. "We're honest, reliable farmers. We would never mistreat a child! A child who enters our home is like our own flesh and bone!"

"Daddy! Daddy, don't abandon me!" Little Dragon struggled to free himself from the man's grip.

Clenching his teeth tightly, Seventh Brother mounted his pedal trike and left his son, not once turning to look back.

Days, weeks, and months passed until Mid-Autumn Festival arrived and the full moon hung near the top of Zhengzhou's tallest building. A drunkard stumbling along the road collapsed to the ground and began to vomit on the asphalt.

"Daddy? Daddy?" A barefoot Little Dragon was suddenly standing at the drunkard's side.

Seventh Brother crawled up from the ground. "Get out of here—I'm not your Daddy!"

When Little Dragon saw that the drunk really was his father, he wrapped his arms around the man's leg and held tight. "Daddy! It's me, Little Dragon! I've come back!"

"Who told you to come back?"

"Daddy, I miss you! I snuck out and I came back all by myself!"

"Get out of here! I'm not your Daddy anymore!" With a single shove, Seventh Brother pushed his child to the ground.

The boy got up instantly and followed his father, limping slightly from the fall. The full moon set behind Zhengzhou's tallest building.

When they got home, Seventh Brother took a closer look at his son's swollen, festering feet. "What happened?" he asked.

"I was being careless . . . I stepped on broken glass."

"Does it hurt?"

"No," the boy lied, gnashing his teeth.

"Go back to your parents' house," Seventh Brother said. "I can't even take care of myself anymore. How could I possibly raise you?" He raised his bottle for another swig of alcohol, and then another.

"I'm not leaving you, Daddy, I'm never going to leave you! If there's happiness, we'll share it. If there's hardship, we'll fight it together!"

The father laughed bitterly. "What kind of a man am I?" he cried. "I'm worse than a pig or a dog! How could I have created a bold and fearless boy like you?" He took another drink but choked with tears as the liquid surged through his gullet and he vomited again. Little Dragon rushed to retrieve the chamber pot, which he brought to his father.

After his bout of alcohol-induced sickness subsided, Seventh Brother went out to buy his son some medicine to make the swelling in his feet go down. Just as he was passing a shopping center, he saw a child with no feet crawling on the ground. Pedestrians walking by bent down in pity to drop bills and coins into the cardboard box that the boy held. Seventh Brother watched the child for some time, becoming increasingly lost in thought until finally he gave up on the idea of buying his son medicine. Instead, he went to buy a heavy chopping knife.

"Little Dragon," he began the instant he entered the door. "Do you really think that if there's happiness we'll share it and if there's hardship we'll fight it together?"

"Yes, Daddy!" the boy replied, bubbling over with excitement. "No matter what happens, I'll never leave Daddy!"

"You really are a good boy!" his father said lovingly. "You know, people have feet so they can walk, but we no longer have a road to walk on. Come, drink with Daddy! After you've drunk, you'll be the one who raises me! After this, Little Dragon, you'll be *my* Daddy!"

2

Ah Qing passed a newsstand, where his eye was detained by a literary magazine with a date printed on the cover. The date was from two months earlier. He asked the salesperson if he could look at a copy, and when he flipped through it, he was overjoyed to find his own name. "Wow!" he thought. "My work has finally been published in a magazine with national circulation!" He pulled his bus money from his pocket and bought the printed item.

"Look, Uncle He, look at my work!" Ah Qing placed a sextodecimo-sized publication in my hands.

"A topnotch magazine with national reach!" I exclaimed. "Well done, you! Being able to publish on a platform like this! But look, only a third of a single page for two poems? And the layout is so cramped! Did they pay you?" Despite finding these flaws, I spoke cheerfully to project a positive attitude about his accomplishment.

"Not yet," he replied, "and I bought this copy myself. I've submitted my work to this magazine so many times and they never once published me! I even sent them these very two poems, but they didn't take them. Ha! It was only after I made it into a local city publication that they took me!"

"Ah Qing, this issue is from two months ago. Maybe they don't know your mailing address. Call them and ask for your author payment!"

Ah Qing found the telephone number of the editorial department printed inside the magazine. He used my home phone to call.

"Wei! Hello, editor shifu! This is Ah Qing. I saw my work in issue number five. I still haven't received a complimentary copy or payment!"

"Please contact the copy editor. The number is . . . " The editorial department hung up the phone.

"Wei! Hello, copy-editor shifu! This is Ah Qing. I saw my work in issue number five. I still haven't received a complimentary copy or payment!"

"Please contact the accounting office. The number is . . . " The copy editor hung up the phone.

"Wei! Is this the accounting office? This is Ah Qing. I saw my work in issue number five. I still haven't received a complimentary copy or payment!"

"Please contact circulation. The number is . . . " The accounting office hung up the phone.

"Wei! Circulation! This is Ah Qing. I saw my work in issue number five. I still haven't received a complimentary copy or payment!"

"Talk to the editorial department!" Circulation hung up.

Ah Qing was furious, but he wasn't about to let it end there. He picked up the phone one last time and dialed the number. "Wei!" he shouted. "Is this the editorial department? Go fuck your uncle!"

3

I had just taken off my clothes and gotten into bed when the phone rang.

"Uncle He!" It was Little Thing. "I got nabbed by the police when they were checking my temporary residence permit! I need you to send me a thousand yuan so they'll let me out. If I don't come up with the money, they're going to make me work on a construction site, then send me back to my hometown!" His voice choked with sobs.

In a hurry I threw on some clothes, then grabbed a thousand yuan to go and get him out of jail.

"Little Thing," I asked him when we were outside, "you've been in Beijing for so long now—why haven't you gotten your temporary residence permit yet?" My heart ached thinking about the thousand yuan I had just lost.

"I did get one!" Little Thing protested. "When they were searching me I pulled it out and showed it to them, but they grabbed it and tore it up!" His nose twitched as he aired his grievances. "I tried reasoning with them, but they said if they didn't do their job they'd get their squid fried! Once I fell into their hands, there was nothing I could do but grin and bear it!"

The following morning, I hadn't yet risen from bed when the phone rang once more.

"Uncle He!" This time it was Little Fairy. "I haven't paid my rent in two months! Can you lend me five hundred yuan?" he implored.

"I haven't even gotten out of bed yet! Come over here in a few days and I'll give it to you." I was getting annoyed.

"Uncle He . . . " Little Fairy continued to beg into the phone.

"Do you not even have money for food right now?" I sighed loudly. "Fine, come to my place this afternoon."

I was just about to go to the bathroom when suddenly I heard a knock at the door. There was Little Devil. He stepped inside with a big bag on his shoulders.

"Buy one, Uncle He!" He reached into the bag and pulled out a dildo that was at least thirty centimeters long.

"Ha ha!" I laughed the instant I saw it. "What a huge cock! Would it even fit?" I tousled his hair. "Are you trying to kill this old man, Little Devil?"

"There's medium and small sizes, too, Uncle He!" He suddenly turned the bag upside down, dumping its contents onto the couch. I watched as a hoard of dicks of all models and colors piled up before my eyes. "Use this vibrator, Uncle He!" he said, taking hold of a flesh-colored phallus. "Lots of single men and women have used this model and they all say it works well. When you stick it in, it won't lose its shape, the battery won't leak, and it won't transmit AIDS!"

In the end I spent a hundred kuai on a rubber dildo, size large.

"Little Tough is going to sell a kidney!" Ah Qing cried into the phone anxiously. "No matter how I try to persuade him, he won't listen. You have to figure out what to do!"

I threw down the phone and jumped into a cab, instructing the driver to take me to Luohe Hospital. As soon as I stepped out of the vehicle I saw Ah Qing and Little Tough standing outside the main entrance of the hospital. My heart fell like a stone.

"Little Tough, Ah Qing," I said. "Uncle He is taking you out for roast duck!"

I took those two unpredictable young men to a restaurant, where I ordered roast duck along with a few cold appetizers and beer.

"Come, Little Tough, have some duck!" With a smile on my face, I used a pair of chopsticks to place food on his plate.

He lowered his head in silence, but slowly began to chew.

"Little Tough," Ah Qing began, "you're only twenty-four! How are you going to live if you sell a kidney?"

"I don't want to get married and have kids," Little Tough explained somberly. "All I want is a place to live and money to spend. I can't take this anymore! I've been drifting as a vagrant and working since I was sixteen. I thought that as long as you worked hard you would have food to eat, a roof over your head and a place to call home! I don't want to keep living this life of a slave, this life of human scum. If I sell a kidney I'll make three hundred thousand yuan! I could collapse in the street from illness, but without any money no one would even notice me. I've drifted in the gay circle for several years now but I can't find anyone who truly loves me! I don't want to keep living this life—it's worse than the life of a pig or a dog!"

"Little Tough! If you want to make money, you can be a male prostitute like Little Jade!" There was exasperation in Ah Qing's voice. "After you've made some money from selling yourself you can start all over again! I mean, imagine losing a kidney! Won't your body fall apart?"

Setting down my glass of beer, I did my best to calm my aching heart. "Little Tough," I reasoned, "listen to me. If you have any difficulties, we'll help you!"

"I've already borrowed two thousand kuai from you, Uncle He. I can't keep involving you. I don't want to keep borrowing money from people and I don't want to sell myself! I can't stand the idea of going to bed with someone I don't love! I don't want to keep begging other people for help. All I want is to make some money and fulfill my childhood dream of going all over the country to see as much as I can. Once I've done that, I can die in peace!"

Ah Qing and I spent the entire afternoon and evening trying to persuade Little Tough not to sell his kidney. And yet, we were unable to change his hopeless heart.

I couldn't fall asleep that night, but tossed and turned, frustrated by my inability to change this helpless child's mind. The following day was Little Tough's day of surgery. To my surprise and dismay, I came down with a fever and had no choice but to go see a doctor. On the phone I told Ah Qing to nurse and take care of Little Tough as best he could.

Little Tough signed his name on the contract, thereby selling his own kidney to a wealthy, sixty-year-old man. With puffy, red eyes, Ah Qing watched his friend as he dressed himself in a patient gown.

"You're going to regret this, Little Tough." Ah Qing gripped his hand tightly.

"I'm so scared, Big Brother Ah Qing!" Little Tough's lips trembled. "We're brothers—you have to stay by my side. It's just selling a kidney—I don't want to die!"

"It's not too late for us to forget about this whole thing, Little Tough! We don't need that old guy's three hundred thousand! We're young, there's still hope! We'll make good money further down the road!"

"Thanks, Big Brother Ah Qing. When I get out of the hospital I'll be sure to reward you."

"Reward? Who wants your reward? Little Tough! Why won't you listen to me?"

With tears in his eyes and a faint smile on his lips, Little Tough was pushed by two nurses into the operating room. Ah Qing locked himself in the bathroom and burst into tears.

A month later, Little Tough emerged from the hospital. The first thing he did was buy a one-way plane ticket from Beijing to Zhengzhou. The flight was to depart in just a few days. Before it did, he and Ah Qing met.

"Thank you for taking care of me for so long," Little Tough said as he placed a wad of cash in Ah Qing's hand. "Just think of this five thousand yuan as your wages!"

"I don't want your money!" Ah Qing was on the verge of shouting. He pushed his hand back against Little Tough to reject the stack of bills. "What do you think I am? Are you my boss or are you my brother?"

"I'm sorry, Ah Qing. Of course, I know—we're friends now and we'll always be friends!"

Little Tough took Ah Qing to a restaurant, where the server politely sat them at a table and poured them tea. All at once, Little Tough started acting like a fat cat, furiously ordering a tableful of dishes and demanding that Ah Qing eat.

"Why aren't you eating, Ah Qing?"

"I can't eat."

Ah Qing clenched his fist tightly around the short, thin-blown beer glass in his hand, and in and instant—pa!—blood gushed from his fingers.

"Server! Server!" Little Tough shouted. "How can your glasses be this fragile? My friend just cut his hand!" No sooner had Little Tough finished saying this than his voice went soft. He pressed an anxious hand to his hurting stomach.

"I'm sorry, sir! I'm truly very sorry, sir!" The table server came running with a bandage for Ah Qing's hand.

Moving his attention away from Ah Qing's injury, Little Tough looked at the red braised carp on the table and began shouting all over again. "Server! Get the cook out here! Is this regular red-braised carp or is it red-braised *grass* carp?"

"I'm sorry, sir!" the server called out, running out of the kitchen to relay the message to Little Tough. "We don't have common carp here so we use grass carp."

"Send it back! We're not eating grass carp. And another thing . . . " On and on Little Tough went, finding problems where none existed, making things difficult for the server and the cook.

Unable to bear Little Tough's rant any longer, Ah Qing lifted his chopsticks and began to eat.

After dinner, the two of them went to the airport.

"I'm off, Ah Qing." With a wave of the hand, Little Tough boarded a plane.

Watching the plane as it flew into the distance, Ah Qing's mind went blank.

4

Little Thing stepped into the park as dusk approached. With brisk steps he passed shadows of trees and shadows of people, then climbed an artificial hill.

"What's the hurry? Can you talk for a while?" A middle-aged bottom suddenly blocked Little Thing's way.

Atop the hill there sat a pavilion whose shadow stretched lengthily beneath the evening glow of the setting sun. The two men sat in the pavilion facing each other, one half of their faces concealed in shadow, the other half shining like gold. Their lines of vision touched the stars in the night sky.

"Are you a top or a bottom?" The middle-aged bottom asked.

"Depends on you!" Little Thing laughed.

"I only like tops," the middle-aged bottom said with a laugh. "Do you have a friend who's a top? Let's find one with a big thing and the three of us can play!"

"My cell-phone battery is dead," Little Thing said by way of reply.

Little Thing used the middle-aged bottom's cell phone to call Ah Qing, whom he invited to join them. They had a few drinks at a restaurant, then proceeded to an opulent room that had been rented by the middle-aged bottom.

"This is a five-star hotel, you know!" the middle-aged bottom said triumphantly, pulling two Chunghwa cigarettes from a pack and handing them to Ah Qing and Little Thing. "I work at a county- and city-level government office. I'm here in Beijing mainly to enquire about literature PhD programs." The middle-aged bottom removed his clothes as he spoke.

"Working at a county- and city-level government office must be great!" Little Thing said enthusiastically. "If you want to slack off and have fun, you can slack off and have fun! If you want to be engage in graft, you can engage in graft! Why would you want to go do a PhD? That's so much work! And besides, after you get in, how much money do you get?" Little Thing peeled off his clothes.

"That's right!" Ah Qing added. "If you want to do scholarly work, you don't necessarily have to be in a PhD program for that, right? China has so many PhDs—they're flying around like locusts. And yet, not a single one of them is able to eke out a book or an essay of any value. China's true literature resides among the people!" When Ah Qing finished speaking, he went into the bathroom. Cold and hot water rushed from the faucets, making a splashing noise.

"The two of you don't understand!" the middle-aged bottom protested. "If you engage in too much graft, there's always going to come a day when you suffer the consequences! It's not that I have some great hope for Chinese literature. For me, doing a PhD is just a way of living in isolation." He grabbed Little Thing's cock as he spoke.

5

"I've still never been to Zijing Mountain Park!" exclaimed Little Thing. "Take me there to see it, Ah Qing!"

"There aren't many people there in the daytime," Ah Qing replied. "There's a lot of people there on Saturdays and Sundays. That's where Little Tough, Little Jade, and I all made our debut!"

Ah Qing took Little Thing to Zijing Mountain Park.

"How can there be so few gay guys here?" Little Thing asked. "Are there any money boys?"

"Yes, but not as many as in Dongdan Park!" Ah Qing took hold of Little Thing's hand. "Let's go to the northern bank of the river and watch the opera performers! Every day there are people there doing Yu and Qu opera."

Suddenly a child with no feet appeared. He was crawling toward them and in his small, blackened hands he held a box made of sheet iron. With begging eyes he looked at the people coming and going.

"Oh, how sad!" Little Thing said, pulling two coins from his pocket and placing them in the little boy's iron box.

Ah Qing pulled a two-yuan note from his pocket, then bent over to place the money in the box. When his eyes met the little boy's face, he exclaimed in horror: "Little Dragon!"

Having heard his name, Little Dragon raised his eyes to look, but the instant he saw that it was his own Uncle Ah Qing, he lowered his head in shame.

"How did you lose your feet, Little Dragon?! Where are your parents?" Ah Qing wrapped his arms around the boy and lifted him from the ground.

"My mom died!" came the child's hoarse reply.

"What?! Big Sister Little Orchid is dead?" Holding the boy, Ah Qing repeated the question again and again as his eyes welled up with tears.

"Let go of me, Uncle Ah Qing! I have to go keep begging for money. My daddy's coming back when it gets dark to take me home." Holding his beggar's box tightly, Little Dragon extricated himself from Ah Qing's arms and made his way back down to the ground.

"Let's go, Ah Qing." Little Thing tugged at his hand in an effort to lead him toward the park exit.

Just as the boys were turning to leave, they heard a woman cry out Ah Qing's name. It was Little Chrys. She ran toward Ah Qing and told him that Sister Plum Blossom had died and Little Lotus had adopted his child, Future.

"Wow!" Little Thing exclaimed as he gave Ah Qing a shove. "So all this time, Ah Qing has had a secret love child! Hurry up and take me to have a look! I want Future to be my godchild!"

Ah Qing beat his fists against his head in anguish.

Inside Zijing Mountain Park, the color of night grew darker and darker. A few silvery-white lampposts scattered their gentle beams among the quivering shadows of trees. Like ghosts, human shadows mingled with the shadows of trees and lampposts, fading in the darkness that belonged to them.

Little Thing paced back and forth until a middle-aged man entered the WC. Little Thing followed him briskly. Standing before a urinal, the middle-aged man pretended to urinate. Little Thing stood at the urinal beside him and did the same. They remained that way for a good five minutes, neither of them pissing. When Little Thing was certain that the man was gay, he reached out his hand and touched his cock.

"It's not safe here!" The middle-aged man pulled up his trousers and walked out of the WC and out of the park. Little Thing trailed behind him.

"Where are we going?" Little Thing asked the middle-aged man walking ahead of him.

"Come with me," the man replied, luring Little Thing onward. "You'll know when we get there!"

When Little Thing saw a police station up ahead he sensed that something wasn't right, so he turned around and began walking in the other direction. Suddenly, however, two tall young men lunged forward and took hold of Little Thing, punching him a few times in the process. At first he thought they were muggers, but realized that they were plainclothes cops when they dragged him into the police station. The middle-aged man who had seduced Little Thing followed the others into the station, but no sooner had he entered than another cop cast him a meaningful glance, signaling for him to leave.

"Everything on you—take it out!"

Little Thing pulled some money and a cell phone from his pocket and placed it on a table. An officer searched him, then yanked off the jade pendant of the Bodhisattva Guanyin that hung around his neck. One of the plainclothes cops who had punched him stepped forward; he, too, searched Little Thing until he found a wadded up ball of toilet paper. "Fuck!" he shouted, and he laughed. "Look how much tissue he's got for his period!" Another cop handcuffed Little Thing to the leg of the table.

"Tell us everything!" one of them demanded. "What were you doing?"

A number of gay guys in the circle had spoken of the way that plainclothes police officers seduced, beat, and extorted money from homosexuals. And so, without waiting for the cop to ask him again, Little Thing admitted that he was one.

"Have you ever prostituted?"

"No."

"How many men have you had sex with?"

"Between ten and twenty."

"How many?"

"Over twenty."

"*How many?*"

"A hundred and eight—that's the truth!"

"Fuck!" the cop laughed. "I haven't even fucked around with that many women! How do you guys do it?"

"Jerk each other off. Oral, anal."

"Does it feel good?"

"Yeah."

"Ha ha! Fuck! What's your phone number? I'm going to call your family and tell them to come pick you up!"

"My parents are dead!" Little Thing cried.

"Do you have any relatives? Rich relatives?"

"I have one. I'll take you to him."

"What does he do?"

"He's a lawyer," Little Thing replied, then stated a phone number, which the officer wrote down. He had suddenly thought of a gay lawyer he knew, and he thought that this connection might help him. The cops looked at the number for a moment, but instead of calling the lawyer, they unlocked Little Thing's handcuffs.

"Fuck!" one of the officers yelled. "Don't stay in here getting all warmed up. Go outside and squat down!"

Squatting outside the police station, Little Thing felt a cold wind blowing from the darkness of the night. He knew that the police officers were giving him a chance to run away. Slowly he stood up and walked in the direction of glowing streetlights.

After a sleepless night of soul searching, Ah Qing made up his mind. He purchased a box of powdered milk and went to the home that Sister Plum Blossom had left behind.

"Just take a look at how much Future looks like you, Ah Qing!" A smiling Little Lotus was dressed in clean, white clothes; in her arms she held a child who could not yet speak.

The child opened a pair of bright, black eyes and stared at Ah Qing with avid curiosity.

"Come here, Future, let me hold you!" Ah Qing stretched out his arms.

"There, you see?" Little Lotus exclaimed in approval. "It's different with blood relations! This child is usually so shy with strangers! As soon as someone approaches, this little one starts crying and won't stop!"

Ah Qing sighed audibly, then revealed his sexual orientation to her. Little Lotus comforted him with warm words, leaving him so moved that his eyes filled with tears.

"Not long after I was born, my parents abandoned me, and for a long time my adoptive parents neglected me, too. I'm twenty-six, but I'm always thinking about my childhood. It's not that I don't want to be responsible for this child, it's just that I'm not qualified to be a father!"

With eyes full of pity, Little Lotus watched Ah Qing as he left.

When Little Thing returned to Beijing, he told all the gay guys around him that Zhengzhou cops are a real bunch of bastards!

Night fell and Little Thing went to a gay bathhouse in Xinjiekou. Nearly every bed was occupied with guys whose lines of vision crisscrossed one another as their eyes darted about the room. In some corners, pairs of men were making love. While all of this was going on, several police officers suddenly charged in with colored felt-tip markers in their hands. They then proceeded to put a mark on the back of any man they saw having sex.

Little Thing was feeling pretty good when the pleasure machine up his ass was suddenly yanked out and his back was marred with a disgraceful mark. Over forty gay men were forced to get dressed, then hauled off to a police station. As he was putting on his clothes, Little Thing remembered the cell phone he had just bought. Taking advantage of a brief moment when the police weren't paying attention, he slid it inside his rectum.

After surrendering as a fine all the money that he had on him, Little Thing was released. The instant he stepped out of the police station, he ran like lightning to a public toilet, where he shit out the cell phone. He opened it and looked at the screen, then laughed. He had received a text: "Merry Christmas!"

SEVENTEEN

1

"Ah Qing!" I hollered into the phone. "I want to open a dumpling restaurant on Civilization Road! It'll face the crematorium at the north and the building-materials market at the south. Also . . . " On and on I rambled.

"That's great!" Ah Qing replied. "After you open it, I'll bring some friends and we'll have a celebration to congratulate you! Uncle He," he continued, "I bought a secondhand computer and I'm in the process of writing a novel."

"Oh!" I replied. "Are you still writing poetry? There are more opportunities to publish a novel than there are for poetry."

"A woman poet once said: 'Writing a novel is nothing but adding a bit of water to poetry!' If that's the case, I've added over a hundred thousand characters' worth of water to a single poem!" He laughed, then paused. "Uncle He, I emailed you a prose poem I wrote recently. Will you take a look at it?"

He hung up and I dialed up to the Internet. Once online, I logged into my free email account and opened the document he had sent me: *One Person's Hundred Dark Nights*. This is what I read:

As night begins to fall, I like to step into the park all by myself, my stomach rumbling with hunger.

At that most worried moment of the afternoon, my hair and face are washed as clean as Liu Dehua—and, of course, as clean as you. My ass, just before walking out of the door, is washed repeatedly. I use only cold water; my anus begins to tighten. Whether the soap is perfumed or not, my lower parts have no idea.

I bring only a stomach that hungers and a cock on the verge of going mad with hunger.

The dark night belongs to me and my loneliness. You, on the other hand, belong to strangers and to those with whom you are doomed to have failed relationships.

A bottle of beer will make my face ruddy; two bottles will make me look at you with love and tenderness; three bottles will make me consider going to bed with you. If I continue to drink, I'll slam my fist ruthlessly against your head.

If I hear a drunk singing deep in the park, I absolutely will not go near him.

Trees develop their strength in the light of lampposts, in the dark color of night.

In the darkest of dark corners, those whose breathing can be heard stick together. Please do not disturb them. Please take yourself away. May the police take you away, too.

I take myself away, walking on a path that you have walked.

I take myself away, and enter a WC that has you in it.

I take myself away, leaving you, your unfamiliarity, and your misfortune.

I am like one of a hundred Lan Yus, preparing a romantic tragedy for you.

My stomach starts to growl; madly, my desire grows. Hunger makes me even more sensitive. My aggrieved cock hangs limp. It does not understand what my heart thirsts for.

Stones are silent; after sitting on one, one can rest. You grow silent; no one takes you for a stone by sitting on you. Stones have been silent all along; after the person sitting on one left, you left too. You did not take me, just as you did not take this stone. Like a stone, I watch your back as you walk away, as you slowly blend into the night.

He has come. He doesn't belong to me; he belongs only to himself. Shoulder to shoulder, he stands at the urinal beside me, masturbating. Ah! What finally comes out is the fatigued sound of urine.

May I offer you a drink? As long as you don't come with someone who's impotent.

Music sounds in the distance; a man's man dances; a woman's woman dances joyfully, too. I dance alone with no need for music. I need nothing but sorrow.

A thin, dark face. Do you like it?

A plump, light face. Do you like it?

A guy walks by. He's either a migrant worker or a white-collar worker. You could be a money boy, twenty percent off just for tonight.

I like it when people take me for a money boy. In their eyes, I'm still somewhat youthful and handsome.

Tonight, please let me fall in love with you! At this moment I am a thousand times truer than Lan Yu. My cock hangs waiting for you, beautifully, poignantly tragic.

An old man I've seen in a hundred dark nights smiles at me. Politely, I return his smile. We shake hands in a friendly manner, and we talk. The moment he places a sexual demand on me, I reject him, and it's like rejecting my own grandfather. One day I will become someone else's grandfather. I'll go begging in the dark night with a face that could not be older or more shameless.

I ascend an artificial hill; there is no true emotion at the top. Oh, evergreens! I did not know that the sound of wind and rain could reside in your sexual orientation. My emotions stand tall and upright, just like the artificial hill.

Inside the darkness at my core, a hundred nights are on duty by turns.

Under a streetlight I begin to get lost. I mistakenly take your coldness for my hard food.

Are you hungry like me? Then swallow me! No preservatives have been added to my cock. Take advantage of its freshness and swallow me quickly. Sooner or later, the dark night will swallow me whole.

Sooner or later, the dark night will swallow me whole, leaving daytime with an unopened condom.

a says: I don't want to live with my boyfriend.

b says: My boyfriend is terribly unfaithful.

c says: At the end of the year, I will marry a woman.

d says: The men I love never love me; the women I don't love all love me.

e says: Have you learned how to use the Internet? Making love online is beautiful, exciting, transporting.

f says: I only want one-night stands. I love only strangers. I love parks. I love public toilets. I love bars. I love bathhouses.

g says: I'm afraid of AIDS . . .

o says: I only love men who are not homosexual, but I do not love my father. I'm glad he's dead.

The night's darkness is quiet. The sound of a pine needle falling to the ground can be heard, but no one can hear the dancing heart of a lover.

Person 1 and Person 2 walk, holding hands. It looks as though they've found the connection they were seeking; it looks as though they're searching for a quiet corner in which to make love; it looks as though they'll be sleeping in the same bed tonight, a bed that is big or small. Oh!

The joyful human shadows in the depths of the dark night are disappearing.

I pace back and forth.

Under lamppost lights, I cannot clearly see your handsome face. Under the moonlight, I cannot clearly hear your magnetic voice. I take hold of your flesh, your cold semen. I truly cannot say that I love you; my heart is separated from you by a hundred dark nights. In a hundred dark nights I search for you ceaselessly, persistently—ah! The lights have all died out, and the moonlight is weakening. A dark corner and an opening in my love overlap, forming the most complete part of the dark night.

Oh!

The lonely human shadows in the depths of the dark night are disappearing.

Little Tough arrived in Kaifeng, where he strolled about the streets for most of the day before deciding that his clothes weren't up to snuff, so he stepped into the city's largest shopping center. In the square outside, a red flag danced in the air as a flock of pigeons darted here and there. A child who had only just learned to walk held her mother's hand; in her other hand she held a piece of candy, which she tried to feed to the pigeons. After making his purchases, Little Tough left the shopping center and walked toward the square. He felt that the things he had bought were too heavy, though, so he opened up the exquisite boxes and changed into the leather shoes and jacket he had just acquired. Then he walked away, leaving behind a nearly brand-new pair of shoes and a blazer that hadn't even been washed yet.

Stepping out of a McDonald's with a fried chicken leg in his hand, he saw a ragpicker child carrying a garbage bag and a piece of chalk. On the wall outside the front door of the McDonald's the child wrote "shitting allowed here." The child's small, emaciated frame brought a bitter smile to Little Tough's mouth. He wanted to give the child the fried chicken leg, but the kid picked up the garbage bag and slunk off.

Little Tough took one bite from the chicken leg and threw the rest of it into a sewer.

Next, he went into a hair salon, where a young woman sat him down and began to wash his hair.

"Don't you know how to wash hair? You're scratching my scalp so bad it hurts! Don't you know how to cut hair? Look what you've done to it!" Little Tough slammed a one-hundred-yuan note down on the counter and walked out.

He went to an Internet cafe, where he used a computer to look up Kaifeng's gay spots, then left the cafe to go find them. He entered a public toilet, where he saw cocks and asses scribbled on the walls. He was only in the toilet for a minute before he turned to go back outside.

"Do you have a place, Big Brother?" A boy came toward him. Festering sores covered his mouth.

"No!" Little Tough eyed the boy with disdain, then turned and walked away, thinking "Not a single quality MB in this fucking place!"

Little Tough went back to the Internet cafe, where he looked at images of gay porn. When he tired of these, he entered a gay chatroom, where he began chatting with a user by the name of Bai Yu—"White Feather." After chatting for some time, they started having cybersex and eventually reached psychological climax. "I'll host tonight!" Little Tough typed on the keyboard, then gave the chatroom user his cell-phone number.

When Little Tough arrived at the agreed-upon time and place, he found himself face-to-face with the same sore-covered boy he'd seen earlier.

"Wait—*you're* Bai Yu? I would have thought you were Lan Yu!" Little Tough sneered. He didn't know whether the boy had caught the joke: that "lan yu"—"blue feather"—was a near-homonym both of "rotten feather" and of the name of a character in a gay Internet novel. "Was your mouth stuffed too full with huge cock, or what?"

"No, it's not that. My mouth has excessive internal heat! Big Brother . . . " White Feather lowered his head.

When Little Tough looked at this self-loathing young man, he felt that he was looking at himself a few years earlier.

"Fine, then! Since you're calling me Big Brother, I guess I'll treat you to dinner." Little Tough took hold of White Feather's hand.

After dinner, the two of them went for a walk in the streets.

"Are you a money boy?" Little Tough asked.

"Yes," White Feather replied, his face turning red.

"After drinking booze, does White Feather turn into Red Feather? What do you get into?"

"Let me suck your dick, Big Brother! I promise you'll like it."

"Your mouth is covered in sores and you want to suck me?" Little Tough sighed. "Let's do it from behind, okay?"

"I'm afraid it will hurt! But okay, Big Brother, if you stick it in slowly you can fuck me."

Little Tough took White Feather to a travel hostel, where they rented a room, took a shower, and got into bed. White Feather wanted to give Little Tough head, but Little Tough was disgusted by the boy's festering mouth so he refused. White Feather then switched off the light, got on his knees, and raised his ass for Little Tough. Little Tough felt his smooth skin, then moved his fingers toward his asshole. When he touched it, White Feather's body trembled. What Little Tough felt, however, made him suddenly want to turn on the light, and when he did he saw that White Feather's asshole was covered with a knotted mass of hemorrhoids.

"Why do you have so many hemorrhoids?!" Little Tough asked in horror as he reached for his clothes. "Why don't you get an operation?"

"I don't have any money!" White Feather cried. Crawling toward Little Tough, he begged, "I'm not afraid of the pain, Big Bother! Come on, fuck me! Afterward you can give me however much money you want!"

"I don't have the heart to fuck you," Little Tough replied. "Here, here's some money for you to get that looked at. Stay here and get some sleep tonight." He pulled a thousand kuai from his wallet, tossed it on the bed and walked out of the hostel.

At Baogong Lake in Kaifeng, the trees on the shore and the grass in the water were all a vibrant green, causing the water to look very green, too. Little Tough walked along the lakeside, noticing several anglers passing the time with their fishing lines submerged in the water. A carp bit; raised in the air, it looked like a dead pig! Why did it bite? Why not break the hook with its teeth? Little Tough suddenly recalled a fairy tale he had read when he was little: If a carp is strong and brave enough to swim upstream on the Yellow River and leap over the waterfall at Dragon Gate, then it will turn into a mighty dragon. The story was about working hard to achieve one's goals, but Little Tough no longer had any ideals. He felt he was now nothing but a lowly worm.

"So you've come to Kaifeng to have some fun, too!" Little Thing suddenly appeared before Little Tough's eyes.

"I've been here for two days," Little Tough replied. "How've you been?"

"Broke! I want to sell my kidney, too, but I can't find a buyer!" Little Thing continued in earnest. "You seem to be doing fine with just one kidney!"

They continued talking until suddenly they heard someone calling out for help!

"Let's go look!" Little Thing grabbed Little Tough by the hand and they ran toward a group of people on the opposite shore of the lake.

A woman was struggling in the water while the people on the shore stared as if they were watching a movie. By the time Little Thing and Little Tough reached them, the woman in the lake had already sunk. "She's committed suicide!" a woman in the crowd shouted as a car pulled up. Driving the car was the dead woman's man. He was the kind of guy who spoke very loudly because he had a lot of money.

"Who's gonna drag the body out of the water?" he yelled toward the crowd. "I'll give you a thousand kuai!"

Nobody stepped forward.

"Alright, two thousand, three thousand!" Before long the loud, rich guy said he'd pay five thousand kuai and Little Thing tore off his clothes and jumped into the water.

Racing through the water in search of the female corpse, Little Thing periodically rose to the surface for air, then went under again. When at last he found the woman, he wrapped his arms around her, struggled through the water, and pulled her up to land. The instant he plopped the dead woman down on the ground, however, the loud, rich guy walked up to her and pulled a diamond ring off her finger and two gold earrings from her ears. Then he started looking for something around the woman's neck.

"Come on, boss, give me the five thousand kuai!" Little Thing panted.

"Her necklace fell into the water!" the loud, rich guy said. "I spent eight thousand kuai on that thing! Go back and find it and I won't short you one bit of that five thousand!"

"You said you'd give me five thousand for pulling the body out of the water!" Little Thing protested. Then Little Tough got involved. "Go get the necklace yourself!" he shouted. "Now hand over that five thousand!"

"If I don't get that necklace, that body isn't worth five thousand kuai for you to haul out! If you guys don't go get it, I'm only paying a one-thousand-kuai salvaging fee!"

"Fine, I'll go get it!" Little Thing fumed, and he turned to go back into the water. Little Tough grabbed him by the arm and tried to dissuade him from going back in, but Little Thing ignored him and returned to the lake.

Standing on the lakeshore, Little Tough burned with impatience and anxiety as he waited for Little Thing to resurface. Five minutes passed, ten minutes passed. An hour passed and still no sign of him.

"I'm done waiting," the loud, rich guy said suddenly. "I've got business to take care of!" He handed one thousand kuai to Little Tough. "Here's your salvaging fee. I don't care about that necklace—if you find it, go ahead and sell it!"

From his wad of cash, the loud, rich guy pulled a few additional bills and paid two migrant workers to lift the woman's corpse and place it in his vehicle. Then he hauled her away.

"Help! Someone, please help!" cried Little Tough. His eyes filled with tears and he began to shout himself hoarse.

Little Thing never resurfaced from the lake.

3

Little Tough flew from Guangzhou to Zhengzhou, wondering while up in the air how much longer he had to live. The day he sold his kidney, he had it all planned out: if he spent thirty thousand per year, he'd live happily for ten years—that should be quite enough! He had eaten everything he'd ever dreamed of eating and worn all the clothes he'd ever dreamed of wearing. "So why is life still so hard for me?" he asked himself.

He walked along the streets of Zhengzhou, looking at all the construction projects built by workers who were paid only half of what they should be. Nothing had changed since he had arrived there to work at the age of sixteen. He noticed a dozen or more women sitting outside the entrance of a building. Behind them hung a long white banner covered in black characters: "Workers must eat! Money owed must be paid!" Little Tough watched them for a while, but he soon felt bored. Nor did he want to walk any further, so he raised a hand and hailed a taxi. "Take me to the hiring site," he said to the driver.

Little Tough was not going to the hiring site to look for work; he was going there for a barbeque restaurant nearby. Stepping out of the taxi, he saw all the young worker brothers and sisters looking for employment just as he had done in the past. Squatting or standing, they waited for a boss to come and pick them out like a head of cattle. Situated about fifty meters from the hiring site was the barbeque restaurant. Little Tough would never forget how, at the age of sixteen, he and Little Wave had walked past this very place, inhaling the appetizing scent of cooked meat. Back then, all they could do was swallow their hunger back down into their stomachs.

"Give me ten lamb kabobs, boss. Also, ten squid, ten chicken gizzard, ten . . . " Little Tough spoke very loudly. With a smile, the boss got to work filling the order.

Little Tough held an enormous bouquet of kabobs in his hands, but he didn't have the slightest bit of hunger. "Little Wave," he muttered to himself, "it would be great if you were still alive! I'd treat you to kabobs and you could have as many as you wanted!"

One by one, the streetlights came on; drop by drop, the rain fell. Little Tough entered Zhengzhou Railway Station, which was filled as always with homeless vagrants. He thought back to the time some years ago when he had slept in the ticket lobby of the station, how he had been pushed about by the police. He laughed bitterly, then felt the wallet in his pocket. No longer was he human scum! He could walk into any hotel in the city and be welcomed! At the ticket window he bought an express, air-conditioned berth ticket to Yangzhou. Walking away from the window ticket in hand, he passed a peaked cap and threw him a look of contempt.

At a gay bar in Yangzhou, a guy with a beer belly took a liking to Little Tough, hinting that he would pay a thousand kuai to have sex with him. "I'm buying, too!" Little Tough sneered, "but I'm not into you!" He paid the server and left a tip, then turned around and walked out of the bar.

On a bacchanalian dance floor, boys and girls placed their hands on their heads or asses and danced about wildly.

Outside, Little Tough pressed his hands against his aching stomach. He only had one kidney left, but it felt like he only had half a life left! It frequently occurred to him that he might die soon—so he may as well squander all his money! The many beggars he saw out in the streets—old, weak, sick, and disabled —he harbored vile thoughts about them. Puffing up his chest, he threw a coin into the gutter.

He knew that his body couldn't take any more alcohol, but still he got drunk and made his way to a hotel for the night. "Fuck!" he muttered to himself. "If I'm really going to squander money, thirty thousand isn't nearly enough for one year! Why live miserably for ten more years? Why not just live happily for one year?" Inside the hotel, he walked past a mirror, where he caught a glimpse of his ashen white face.

A dead man rose to the surface of Baogong Lake that night, eyes wide open as if he were plagued by an injustice that had not yet been redressed. His swollen, mud-filled mouth was open in a scream, but no sound came out. Frozen with rigor mortis, the corpse's cold hands reached out to grab Little Tough.

He awakened from the nightmare, then grabbed the bottle at his bedside, doing his best to forget the expression on Little Thing's lifeless face.

"Little Tough, Little Tough . . . " he heard the sound of a hoarse voice drifting faintly from the darkness.

"Little Thing!" he sobbed. "Your death wasn't my fault. Now leave me alone and stop tormenting me!"

Drunk, he rolled out of the bed and onto the floor, where he dreamed that he and Little Wave were walking with bare feet in a train station. Inside the building, snowflakes danced in the air.

At a bar, he saw two young people using drugs. He saw the state they were in and it was appealing to him, so he approached them to find out where he could get his hands on whatever it was that they had. One of them put him in touch with a dealer, and from then on, in a rented room at a bathhouse, Little Tough spent his nights lying in bed and getting high.

4

Little Chrys stepped into the office of the hospital vice-director.

"What is it, Little Chrys?" Dr. Gou could see there was something on her mind.

"My little brother is sick!" she said plaintively. "Dr. Gou, can you help him? He applied to university and didn't get in by just two points—now he's acting abnormal! He spends every second of the day cursing at people, and he went running naked through the streets twice!"

"Then you should take him to a mental hospital immediately so he can be cured!" Dr. Gou counseled.

"He won't go to a mental hospital!" Little Chrys replied. "He won't admit that he's sick. He says it's society that's sick!"

"Where is your little brother now? He's obviously very ill!"

"He's back in the village. Our grandmother is looking after him." She sighed, a vexed look upon her face. "Why is it so hard for rural kids to get into college?" she lamented, utterly exasperated. "If you're the child of a teacher or a cadre, you have all these opportunities to score additional points on the university entrance exam. Why are city kids' scores so much worse than the scores of rural kids, anyway? Why do they need to use family connections to inflate their results? The whole thing is just so unfair!"

"There's no use in talking about it, Little Chrys—the gaokao system is plagued with problems! But right now, the most important thing is for you to get your little brother to a mental hospital so he can be treated!"

"I've already been back to my hometown, but no matter how I try to convince him, he won't admit that he's sick! He says he'd rather die than go to a mental hospital."

A retired old man who was unable to receive his pension and whose children would not take care of him decided to sue. Walking along the road to the courthouse, he was suddenly struck and knocked over by a young man riding a bicycle. The retired old man gave up the idea of suing and went instead to the hospital, where he lay in bed for days as the young man stayed by his side. Each time the old man opened his mouth to announce that he was hungry or thirsty, the younger man would rush off and buy him some food or drink.

"Sir," the young man implored. "They've already done X-rays on you—your bones are fine! It's just a few scratches—why do you need to stay in the hospital?"

"I'm staying in the hospital!" the retired old man replied. "I have internal injuries. The doctor hasn't examined them yet, but I can feel them." He wouldn't let the young man leave.

"Sir," nurse Little Chrys intervened with a smile. "Bring some medicine home with you and take it there!"

"I'm not going home! If I die at home no one will even know about it!"

"Sir, you can't engage in this kind of extortion!" Her eyes grew misty as she turned to look at the kind and honest young man.

"I'm not extorting a thing," the old man pouted. "As soon as I've recovered, I'll leave!" A few minutes later he shouted, "I want a banana!"

"Yes, I'll go get some," the young man dutifully replied, and then went out to buy five jin of bananas. "Have some banana, sir!" he said upon his return.

"I want a tangerine!"

"Yes, I'll go get you a tangerine."

"I want an apple!"

"Yes, I'll go get you an apple."

On and on the old man continued.

"Sir, you should take some medicine!" The young man opened a bottle and placed a pill in the palm of the old man's hand.

When the old man put the pill in his mouth, he knitted his brow, then took a cup of tea from the young man and swallowed the pill down. "This medicine is too bitter," he said with a grimace. "Go get me some candied haw on a stick!"

The young man stepped out of the room, but before he could reach the hospital exit he heard Little Chrys calling out to him.

"Wei! Young man! What line of work are you in?"

"I'm a self-employed gas-range repairman."

"Well, you're not rich," Little Chrys continued. "You can't go on taking care of this old man for nothing!"

"I crashed into him," the young man said remorsefully. "I can't bear to leave until he comes out of the hospital! My grandma says that anytime you leave the house you should try to do good deeds—she says good people get good rewards! I feel terrible for this old guy—he's been in the hospital for two weeks now and his children haven't come to see him once!"

"Fine, then!" Little Chrys said. "If you feel sorry for him, then go ahead and keep taking care of him. But remember," she added, turning to leave, "there's no guarantee that *he'll* feel sorry for *you*!"

The old man remained in bed, doing almost nothing but eating until he came down with a case of diarrhea, an unfortunate occurrence resulting in him needing to go to the toilet a number of times throughout the night. Just before his ninth and final visit to the bathroom, a member of the cleaning staff began mopping the floor around his bed. When the old man placed his bare feet on the ground and stood up, he slipped, fell on his backside, and began to cry out in pain.

Another X-ray was taken. This time, the old man really did have an injury: he had fractured his pelvic bone.

"Ouch—it hurts, it hurts!" he howled from his bed.

The following day, the young man went to the hospital as usual. "Sir!" he said in surprise when he saw the old man in pain. "I thought you were getting better?"

"I'm staying right here in the hospital," the old man replied. "My illness has worsened!" He didn't tell the young man that he had fractured a bone from a fall.

Utterly confused, the young man went to the doctor to ask what had happened. But the doctor just said a few vague words about the old man not feeling well and did not mention the fractured bone. The old man remained at the hospital, taking his medicine and eventually being put on an IV. The young man continued to bring him food and regularly emptied the bedpan that the old man now had to use.

It was getting to be too much for the young man. "Sir," he begged, "I'm out of money. Go home and recuperate there!"

"No!" the old man croaked from his bed. "My sickness hasn't been cured and I can't get out of bed. When I can get out of bed and walk you won't have to look after me anymore."

As the days went by, Little Chrys watched with increasing animosity as the scenario unfolded. She went to Dr. Gou and attempted to reason with him.

"Little Chrys," he said after she had spoken. "A nurse's responsibility is to take care of the patient. And a doctor's responsibility is to heal the patient's sickness. Anything else is none of our business and we shouldn't ask about it."

Clenching her teeth, she left the vice-director's office.

At Zhengzhou People's Hospital, as the midnight hour struck and all the patients who were able to sleep slept, Little Chrys finished the evening shift and lay on a bed in the call room, her mind racing. When she was tired of thinking, she closed her eyes and fell asleep.

Little Chrys went sleepwalking that night. She got up from the bed, barefoot, and made her way to the patient ward, where she soon found the old man. Running her hands along the side of his bed, she felt his blanket, then moved her hands upward to touch his face. She lifted the blanket high and, covering the old man's nose and mouth, pressed down with all her strength.

5

Little Tough stepped out of the bathhouse and onto the street, where the sunlight was so bright that it pierced his eyes. Hunched over with shoulders that were weak and frail, he began to walk toward a dumpling house.

At Pingdingshan's number-one gay spot, guys stood near the WC entrance twenty-four hours a day, watching and following unfamiliar faces as they went inside. If someone saw you piss, he'd stand next to you and piss as well. If he saw you shit, he'd lower his head and look, wide-eyed, to find out your dick size.

The first time Little Tough went to this gay spot, an old guy who went by the name of White Peony gave him the following advice: "Eighty percent of the gays who come here are money boys!" he said. "Don't have sex with anyone lightly!"

"What about you, Grandpa? Are you a money boy?" Little Tough joked.

"I'm eighty years old!" White Peony laughed. "I've been here four generations—I'm a veteran! If you have any problems, you'd better come see me!" White Peony looked at Little Tough tenderly.

Little Tough noticed a young man giving him a look, so he picked up his bag and walked over to him.

"Don't pay any attention to that old Peony!" the young man vented. "Nobody here can stand him! He's so cheap he wouldn't give you an apple to eat if it was rotting under his bed. He can't get any dick, but he still hangs around the bathroom all day trying to get some cum down his throat."

Little Tough didn't like White Peony, nor did he care much for this boy who went around talking behind people's backs, so he went off and wandered around by himself.

"Good boy, come with me!" White Peony approached Little Tough again, and spoke to him with a soft and gentle voice. "My place isn't far from here." Raising a hand, he brought his thumb and forefinger together as if he were a female opera singer and continued. "One thing to know about the people here: if they have a backpack, they're selling; if they're holding a clutch, they're buying; if they've got a shoulder bag, they're neither selling nor buying; and if they're empty-handed, then they're a swindler or a thief! Anyway, you should come home with me. We'll cuddle up and go to sleep!"

Once again Little Tough politely rejected White Peony, then started chatting with a middle-aged guy who was standing near him. After a while, the conversation got boring and Little Tough turned to walk away.

"Wei!" the middle-aged man said as he grabbed Little Tough by the arm. "Stop right there! You haven't paid me a conversation fee!"

"You really are shameless!" Little Tough protested loudly. "Is it me who should be paying you a conversation fee, or you who should be paying me one? Now let go of me, you old pussy-seller!"

"Why is life so dark, ugly, and cruel?" Little Tough asked in despair as he walked through the city at night. The streetlights cast their glowing rays, yet he was unable to find the road home. He continued walking, his body so cold that he shook.

He was experiencing withdrawal symptoms. He returned to the bathhouse, where he lay on his rented bed and entered an illusory world.

He saw himself flying with outstretched arms. He flew all the way to Zhengzhou, where he discovered Ah Qing, Little Jade, Little Wave, and Little Thing squatting at the hiring site, waiting for a boss to pick them out like so many heads of cattle.

"My brothers and sisters!" he bellowed in a voice befitting a giant. "Come with me!"

All the young working men and women at the hiring site shouted "Big Brother!" as they cast off the millstones around their necks. They were free now, and they followed closely behind him.

"Brothers and sisters!" he called out again with great passion. "Stretch out your arms and fly like me!" The young working men and women stretched out their arms and rose up to the blue sky and white clouds like great eagles! "Look, everyone!" Little Tough shouted, turning his head to look back at planet Earth. "What is that black mass?" He reached to the sun and shouted, "Give us guns!" And then, into his arms he took a gun whose ammunition was universal love. He led his brothers and sisters to a black factory, where he opened fire. Bang! All the black-hearted bosses collapsed to their deaths, and the weary, suffering workers were liberated. Upward they flew, and Little Tough led them to a bank inside a big office building. Little Tough saw the police officers and security personnel guarding the place and he cried out, "Give us your guns and we won't shoot!" He led the way as his brothers and sisters gave the money that they had stolen from the bank to all the children who had been deprived of an education . . . ah! Little Tough is a hero! He was acclaimed by the whole world! He wrapped his arms around a trophy cup filled with flowers, and he listened to the sound of clapping and singing. Then he mobilized all the engineers of the world to build a great castle in the middle of the ocean. "I'm the richest person in the world!" he shouted. "Auntie Ni Ping will be my maid and I'll pay her 2,500,000 RMB per month. Uncle Zhao Zhongxiang will be my butler and I'll pay him 2,500,000 RMB per month, too. I'm also going to have lots of five-star celebrities come, and they're going to do things for me!"

Little Tough awoke from the dream, then crawled out of bed with difficulty. He washed his face and looked into the mirror, where he saw a young man who was now so thin that he was hardly anything but skin and bones. "Am I going to die?" he asked himself. "How much longer will I live? I can't die! I'm going to live another hundred years!"

He stumbled through the streets until he saw a slanted sign outside the entrance of a breakfast eatery. The sign read "Authentic Pepper Spice Soup from Xiaoyao Town in Xihua County." Little Tough thought of the hometown that had raised him and a tear fell from his eye. Slowly he approached the restaurant and ordered a bowl of the pepper spice soup he had loved so much in his childhood!

"This isn't authentic pepper spice soup! This isn't authentic pepper spice soup . . . " He stumbled away from the restaurant, mumbling to himself.

A light rain fell as several migrant workers curled up under the eaves of a shop to talk about the wheat and cotton harvest. Little Tough exited a bar and immediately placed his hand against a utility pole, then vomited. He leaned against a wall and called his drug dealer.

He took the drugs to a public toilet at the side of the road, then went into a stall and shut the door. There he entered his illusory world once more.

He saw himself driving a large truck which darted rapidly along a public highway. He approached a red light at an intersection, which he ran straight through without stopping. After that he approached a toll booth, which he charged right past. And then . . . oh! Up ahead he saw a vast ocean of human scum. Madly he lunged forward in the big truck, crushing each and every one of them until their cries and screams fell silent. He laughed ecstatically.

Little Tough resurfaced from the hallucination, then pulled up his urine-soaked trousers and stumbled out of the toilet.

He checked his bank balance and saw there was just ten thousand yuan left! He withdrew the entire amount, then gave his drug dealer another call. "I want ten thousand yuan worth of product," he muttered weakly.

He carried a tiny black bag packed with shimmering white crystal meth. He entered a cell-phone store. "Do you buy secondhand phones?" he asked.

"Let me take a look at it," the boss said.

Little Tough sold the cell phone he had been using for a year, then went walking through the dark and homeless streets. Just as he was looking for a cheap hotel, he suddenly caught sight of a fire up ahead. Hastening his footsteps, he moved toward the light. A large building had caught fire, and its crying, screaming inhabitants were desperately trying to crawl out to the street. A crowd of onlookers gathered around to gawk breathlessly at the sight just as casually as if they'd been watching a holiday fireworks display. When Little Tough saw the ocean of flames engulfing the building, he reached into his bag for his phone, but all he found was drugs!

"Mommy! Mommy!" a child's voice cried out and drifted into the street from the rolling sea of smoke.

Little Tough rushed into the burning building, where he began searching for the crying child. He found her in a corner on the second floor. Stretching out a pair of heroic arms, he lifted her, then rushed back downstairs and outside.

Safe and secure in Little Tough's broad, fatherly embrace, the child stopped crying. Little Tough, however, was in withdrawal, and his bag was nowhere to be found. He dropped the child to the ground and ran back inside.

Little Tough never did come back out of that building. Perhaps there, in the whirling sea of flames, he finally found a home!

EIGHTEEN

1

In the park I met two gay chefs, whom I hired for a total of one thousand yuan per month. Old He's Dumpling House was just about to open and some of my friends sent two big flower baskets to help me celebrate. Ah Qing had just finished his two-hundred-thousand-character novel and, despite being very busy, came to the restaurant to help me out. Black stubble showed on his face and his hair was longer than usual because he'd not had time to cut it.

"You've lost weight!" I remarked when I saw him. "Writing is hard work, eh?" I poured him some tea. "Drink!"

Ah Qing circled the forty-square-meter restaurant space, then asked, "How come Little Jade isn't here? His phone isn't working, either!"

"Let Little Jade worry about his own business," I replied. "Besides, we already have enough hands on deck!"

"Did he go back to his hometown?" Ah Qing persisted. "I haven't checked my email in over a month, so I don't know if he's sent me anything. Also," he continued, "I've written my own family a few letters. My little brother always wrote me back before he got married, but now that he has a wife he's forgotten all about his big brother!"

"Ah Qing," I said. "You should go back to your hometown for a visit. Hasn't it been five years since you've been there?"

"I don't have any money right now, Uncle He, so I'm not going to visit. After I publish my novel and get a little fame and fortune, I'll go back to Dragon Gully Village, the place that raised me!"

Suddenly Little Fairy stepped forward, a mop in his hand. "Don't just sit there talking, Ah Qing!" he yelled with a laugh. "Get to work!"

Ah Qing laughed and stood up, though he didn't know exactly what he was supposed to do. "Tell me what needs to be done, Uncle He!" he said.

"We're pretty much done with everything!" I replied. "All that's left is the sign. Let's ask Ah Qing, the great poet and writer of the future, to hang it for us!"

We all stepped out the front door and looked up at the front of the restaurant. "Miss!" Ah Qing laughed, "please bring me a table to stand on!"

Little Fairy and Little Devil went back inside, then immediately came back out with a table. Holding the "Old He's Dumpling House" sign against his chest, Ah Qing climbed onto the table, but it was too low and he wasn't able to hang it. I dragged a chair out and placed it on top of the table. The ground wasn't entirely even, but Ah Qing managed to step onto the chair as the table swayed beneath him.

As Ah Qing was hanging the sign, the string around his neck broke and a red, heart-shaped stone fell to the ground.

"It's up!" everyone shouted when the sign was successfully hung.

Ah Qing jumped down from the chair and table, unaware that he had lost anything.

As everyone was going back inside, I picked up the stone and looked at it for some time. For twenty-six years it had followed Ah Qing through his life. When I finally went back in, I said, "Ah Qing, leave this precious object with me. I'll take it home, and after I find a better string to put it on I'll give it back to you."

Fireworks weren't permitted in Beijing, but we lit a long string of firecrackers anyway and voilà, Old He's Dumpling House was open for business! This was the most exciting thing I had done since retiring from the crematorium.

One month later, however, the restaurant was cold and cheerless. Feeling agitated, I went to Dongdan Park to seek some distraction. As I was walking through the pedestrian tunnel that cuts under Chang'an Road, I heard a familiar melody coming from a guitar. Propped up with crutches, a young person with just one leg was singing and playing his stringed instrument:

"In this life I will be a vagrant
Go seek—a brilliant and stalwart father
He has a brilliant and stalwart mind
He is very lenient: lying
Fighting, stealing, drinking, leading a life of debauchery
Taking drugs and homosexuality
He is able, when his deviate sons are out of hope and
    commit suicide
To see them one last time"

Two people walking through the underpass dropped a few kuai for the singer. I stood quietly for a long time, watching and listening. The guitar playing ceased and I approached him.

"Hello, Warm Spring Blossom! Looks like we're destined to meet in person. I'm Old He."

I invited him to have a drink at a restaurant—not mine—and we chatted animatedly. "My greatest wish is to start a band!" he said.

The following afternoon I went back to the underpass to look for Warm Spring Blossom. I brought him back to my dumpling shop, where we had a bite to eat and I introduced him to Ah Qing, Little Fairy, and Little Devil. After Warm Spring Blossom looked at some of Ah Qing's poetry, he agreed to write music for it.

Penniless and frustrated, Ah Qing went everywhere looking for a publisher for his novel. He had no name for himself, nor had many people been paying much attention to his writing. After running in circles for several months, he started to lose hope in Mainland publishers and began looking toward Hong Kong and Taiwan. And yet, in Mainland China, almost all of the websites of Hong Kong and Taiwan publishers were blocked. There were a few Mainland-based avant-garde literature websites out there, but they were frequently shut down by the authorities. Ah Qing sent his manuscript to a few companies specializing in the promotion of culture, but each time he contacted them, these culture companies would reply saying that Ah Qing himself would have to pay the cost of publishing.

"Uncle He, what should I do? I don't have the money to pay for publishing. What I've written is no worse than works written by famous authors! Why isn't anyone willing to publish me?" He was nearly out of hope.

"Don't be upset, my good boy," I said in an attempt to console him. "There always comes a day when gold shines. At present your literary talent is buried, but one day it will be discovered."

"No!" he protested. "Times have changed. When gold is buried in dirt, it may as well be dirt, too. And when gold is thrown in the garbage, it too becomes garbage. Only when it's laid on the table in full view do people recognize it as gold." He lowered his head.

In the past I had dreamed of becoming a musician, and I tried to be a writer, but I failed—and there's no hope for me now because I'm old. I couldn't bear to see a young person lose hope like I had, so I became determined to do what I could to help Ah Qing publish his book. I handed over my dumpling shop to Little Fairy and Little Devil and, holding Ah Qing's manuscript tightly against my chest, went looking for that one-in-ten-thousand chance.

Every bus in Beijing was jam-packed with people and whether you took bus route 1 or 4, getting from Tomb of Eight Kings station in Chaoyang District to the Tomb of the Princess in Haidian was a real ordeal. In truth, I was very nearly squeezed to death, but no passenger died, for no one among them was a princess or a king!

After running around for a number of days and suffering looks from all kinds of disagreeable faces, I was certain that I had sprouted more than a few new white hairs on the top of my head.

All throughout my phonebook I had scribbled the phone numbers of publishers, culture companies, printers, and even book counterfeiters. Those futile numbers, I scrawled a hex over each and every one! I was just about to lose hope when I dialed the last number on my list; it was the phone number of a culture company.

Dragging my weary bones, I stepped into the office of Red Sun Culture Communication Company.

"Please have a seat, Mr. He," the boss said politely. "We've read the manuscript that you sent—not a bad work! However, the writer has no name for himself. Nowadays, competition in the culture market is quite fierce, and many publishers are only able to sell books at a loss. If a title doesn't sell more than ten thousand copies, we don't make any money!"

"You won't lose money with this book," I asserted confidently. "After publication, you will most definitely sell more than ten thousand copies!"

"Even if we do publish it, the author won't necessarily receive any royalties. If an author isn't well known, their book will only find a market if they themselves put up the funding. Now, if it was a famous author, then we would consider it!" The boss continued. "May I ask: Does the author want to publish this book for fame or for money? If it's for fame, I'm afraid there's not much we can do. But if it's to make money, I think we can help him."

"How can you help him make money from it?" I pressed to know more.

"Sell the work to another writer!" The boss paused as if wishing to gauge my reaction, and then continued. "If the two of you are in agreement, I can help you find a buyer who will pay a handsome price."

Little Jade went to meet a boss who was interviewing prospective male prostitutes.

"Not a bad-looking guy!" the boss said, patting Little Jade on the shoulder. "How old are you?"

Little Jade had not forgotten to shave a few years off his age to appear a bit younger. "Twenty," he replied with a smile.

He descended a staircase which led him to a basement lined with small rooms where male and female prostitutes had sex with their clients. A bright electric light shined twenty-four hours a day, and yet Little Jade felt he was in darkness. He went to lie down in the break room. Was that perfume he smelled? Cologne? Flatulence? There was no air in this place! All that mattered to him was making some money. He started imagining who his first client would be—would it be a man or a woman?

Time to receive clients. Wearing numbers on their chests, the prostitutes formed two rows, male and female, as they did their best to force out a fake smile. A woman with heavy red lipstick and an ashen white face drew closer, then walked along the line of men, an unlit cigarette between her fingers. She filled Little Jade with terror and he lowered his head. There was one thing he remembered hearing from all the grownups who had gossiped about his parents when he was a child: the woman who had killed his father smoked cigarettes!

The woman smoker cast Little Jade a look of disdain, then came to a standstill before the male prostitute standing at his left. She popped the unlit cigarette into her mouth and the young man produced a disposable lighter with a practiced hand. After lighting her cigarette, he picked up a condom and the two of them disappeared into one of the adjacent rooms.

An old man came in next. His mouth cracked open in a lecherous smile as he leered at Little Jade, who saw an incomplete set of big, yellow teeth. Feeling quite disgusted, Little Jade lowered his head once more. A woman who looked like a corpulent pig came in next. She accepted a piece of chewing gum from one of the young men, then went into a room with him.

After the two boys standing at Little Jade's sides were selected by clients, there were only a few male prostitutes remaining; with heads hanging dejectedly, they returned to their beds to go to sleep. All they could do was hope that they would have better luck tomorrow.

Anytime Little Jade stood with the other male prostitutes, his head hung low and he did his best to avert his eyes from the lustful glances of the men and women who approached him. He fidgeted constantly with the lighter in his hand, but he never raised it to light a prospective client's cigarette.

At lunchtime on his third day in the basement, Little Jade went to get his vegetables and rice.

"We've been feeding you for three days now, and still no clients? Someone get over here and help Number 108 wise up!" The boss took the food bowl from Little Jade, then waved a hand and one of his thick, strong hatchet men stepped forward.

Little Jade endured a beating, then lay in bed and silently cried, his empty stomach growling.

The following day, the still hungry Little Jade did his best to stand up straight. Anytime a client entered the basement he put a big, fake smile on his face. A foreigner, a black woman, took a liking to him. She took the piece of chewing gum from his hand and placed it in her big mouth and began to chew. Little Jade picked up a condom and led her to a room.

"Oh, baby!" the woman said in Mandarin. "Please hold me! Let me kiss you!"

She placed her body on top of Little Jade's and caressed him as if she were his mother. Unable to get hard, Little Jade started to cry.

"Oh, baby! Don't cry! If there's anything wrong, you just tell me all about it." The black foreign woman kissed his tears.

Little Jade took hold of his semi-erect cock with one hand while forcing himself to fondle the woman's body with the other. She opened her thick, heavy thighs; still he was unable to get fully hard. She placed his hands on her breasts, which swelled up like two basketballs.

When it was all over, the foreign woman closed her thighs, then gave Little Jade five hundred yuan and left. He gave half the money to his boss and placed the remaining two hundred fifty yuan in the small zipper pocket lining the outside of his underwear. He zipped up his pants and got ready to greet a second client, and a third.

3

Little Jade looked at the old woman lying on the bed. Three centimeters of gray hair sprouted at the root of her dyed hair and her sagging breasts hung down as long as a ruler. Her pubic hair was like withered grass on a patch of barren land, her buttocks were covered with vitiligo, and everywhere Little Jade looked there were wrinkles, lines, and age spots. She opened her greedy legs to welcome Little Jade's cock, but it was no harder than a soft and tender cucumber!

Little Jade sprayed an erectile-enhancement tonic on his semi-flaccid cock and it quickly doubled in size. In haste he grabbed a large-sized condom and unrolled it down the shaft.

"Fuck me to death!" the old woman cried with a serpentine mouth. Her feet ensnared Little Jade at the waist, piercing his tender and delicate skin like demon claws. "Yes! Fuck me to death!"

She gave Little Jade a thousand yuan, then gazed at him lovingly as she gathered her belongings and departed, wiping saliva from her lips as she walked out the door. Little Jade divided the money into two parts and went to the boss. "That old woman gave me five hundred yuan," he said. "Here's the part that I owe you."

Lying on his bed, Little Jade downed a glass of alcohol, then placed a hand against the bulging wad of cash tucked away in his underwear. He fell asleep, but when he woke up the money was no longer there! He shouted that he'd been robbed and the boss came running over to ask how much was missing. Little Jade was afraid that his boss would find out that he had been stashing more than his share, so he mumbled a vague answer. Then he lay back down on the bed and placed a hand against the empty underwear pocket as the tears began to flow. "That was my hard-earned money!" he thought, engulfed in rage. "Ten thousand yuan earned by my own blood and tears! Which shameless bastard took it? A month of work —down the drain!" His heart ached as he cursed.

After a while, Little Jade wiped his tears and returned to receiving clients. He still hid the money that he earned in his underwear, but now when he slept he wore the underwear both inside out and backward so that the small zipper pocket was touching his skin and the money was pressed against his backside.

"Oh, my precious!" a foot fetishist exclaimed. "I love your feet!" The person put Little Jade's toes into their mouth and licked, sucked, sniffed, and chewed on them.

"Oh!" a client who was like a sow in heat cried out, "hurry up and fuck me! And I don't want a cock with a rubber on it!" Little Jade removed the condom and stuck it in. At this point he couldn't even distinguish between male and female clients.

"Do you like to be abused?" a male client asked.

"Abused in what way?" he answered with a question. "How much will you pay for it?"

"A leather whip," the client replied. "Ten kuai per lash!"

Little Jade undressed and the client proceeded to bind his hands. The man produced a leather whip from his bag and Little Jade clenched his teeth as he endured a series of lashes. The impotent old john whipped him until he was tired out, then placed ten thousand yuan on the table and left.

Little Jade went to the bathroom to urinate, and when he did he felt pain in his urethra. He urinated again a few hours later and the pain was almost unbearable. While showering, he noticed that his body was covered in red marks—they were different from the ones caused by the whip—and he knew at once that he had contracted an STD. There was nothing he could do but go to the boss and ask if he could take leave from work in order to seek medical treatment.

Little Jade went to a public toilet, where the walls, he knew, were always plastered with advertisements from STD clinics. He got on a bus and went to one of the locations.

The clinic doctor took Little Jade's five yuan and examined him. "What you have is syphilis and gonorrhea!" he announced dramatically. "This type of illness is very serious, second only to AIDS! If a person doesn't get it looked at in time they'll die. You'll have to come here for a shot each day. It's quality, imported medicine and it's only one thousand yuan per shot." He held a package of medicine before Little Jade's eyes and continued. "As a doctor, I must observe medical ethics. I have never swindled a soul, and as you know I took only five yuan for the examination fee. If you were to go to a big hospital, the registration fee, examination fee, and lab tests would add up to hundreds!"

"Doctor, when will my illness be cured?" Little Jade implored.

"Listen to me carefully," the clinic doctor said sternly. "From now on, anytime you get sick, don't go running around looking for a different doctor. I will heal any illness that you have!"

Ah Qing didn't have a stable address after arriving to Beijing. A poet friend let him use his mailing address, so each time Ah Qing received mail he would go to the friend's place to collect it. "Another one of your works has been published!" his friend said, pulling some printed matter from a desk drawer. "Here you go. They sent you a copy of the publication and a money order."

"Just thirty kuai for two poems?" Ah Qing laughed bitterly as he looked at the money order. "I can't even cash this! When I sent them my manuscript, I used my legal name in my mailing address! Those turtle spawns at the magazine company put my pen name on the money order because they know I won't be able to cash this."

"That sort of thing happens all the time!" his friend said. "One writer gets thirty kuai, ten writers get three hundred kuai . . . a hundred writers, a thousand writers . . . on and on it goes." The poet friend paused and continued. "Ah Qing, the fact that you've been published is fantastic in itself! So many publications nowadays want the writer to pay for page space. If you don't have connections with the editor, it doesn't matter how good your writing is, no one will pay attention to it. I used to do odd jobs at a well-known publisher, and each editor would only open mail that was addressed to them directly. If a writer addressed a manuscript to the editorial department, it would go straight to the trash without anybody looking at it, then get sold to paper recyclers! Publishers today are mini-fiefdoms where selfish editors exchange manuscripts among themselves. They don't want progress, they stick stubbornly to outdated aesthetic standards, and they repress the power of newly emerging culture. If a publication does all that, it's going to lose its readers, and if it doesn't have any readers, it may as well shut its doors for good!"

Ah Qing went to the vegetable market with the magazine that had published two of his poems tucked beneath his arm. Although he hadn't made anything from this release, he had still published his work, and after thinking about it for a while this was enough to make him happy. At the market there was man named Mr. Zhang; he was from Ah Qing's hometown and operated an outdoor vegetable stall. Ah Qing took the two poems, which he'd written for all the people at the bottom of society, and gave them to his fellow villager. Mr. Zhang read the poems, then smiled warmly, grabbed Ah Qing by the hand and dragged him off to have a drink.

Mr. Zhang's son Xiao Hui was a soldier stationed in Beijing. He was around twenty years of age, and when he came to the vegetable market dressed in an army uniform to see his father, he met Ah Qing.

"So you write poetry, Brother Ah Qing? That's great! Listen, there's something I'd like to ask your help with." Xiao

Hui gripped Ah Qing's hand tightly. "I have an injury . . . I'll be better in another year, but right now I don't want to go home and till the land! And I don't want to sell vegetables in the street like my dad, either. I want to stay in the army but I'm just an ordinary solider. I want to render meritorious service but I don't have the opportunity! If there's a war, I'll be the first to rush to the frontlines, even if it means losing an arm or a leg! As long as I can render meritorious service, I'll do whatever it takes. Brother Ah Qing! You have to help me! I don't want to go home and till the land, and I don't want to sell vegetables in the street like my dad, either . . . "

"How can I possibly help you?" Ah Qing asked anxiously. "I'm just a poor poet that no one respects!"

"Write a poem for me, Ah Qing, a eulogy! Write a poem that will be moving to my leaders!" Full of emotion, Xiao Hui held Ah Qing's hand tighter. "In the army, each year we have a cultural activity on New Year's Day. This year I want to read a poem for all of our leaders, something that will be so moving that they'll give me a promotion! Then, after I get promoted, I'll be able to stay in the army. I don't want to go home and till the land, and I don't want to sell vegetables in the street like my dad, either!"

"I can't help you!" Ah Qing insisted. "I don't know anything about army life, and I don't know anything about your leaders' achievements!"

"I can tell you all about their great deeds! You can also think about some things you've seen on TV or read in newspapers. All you have to do is mention a leader's name in a poem and they know it's dedicated to them!"

"Xiao Hui," Ah Qing tried to reason, "it's not that I don't want to help you. It's just that I've been writing poetry for ten years and I've never written a eulogy! I've never learned the art of singing someone's praises."

"Ah Qing—my Brother Ah Qing! You can't watch someone dying and not save him! Your brother begs you, please say yes! Just help me this one time! I don't have any other way out." Xiao Hui's eyes were red and his voice trembled. His calloused hand continued to hold Ah Qing's. "In the army, it doesn't matter how hard or dirty the work is. Since I haven't read many books and I can't write well, I'm always first in line for the grunt work! And yet, I just can't get a promotion from the leaders! An army buddy of mine who enlisted at the same time as me got a few eulogies printed in a tabloid, and because of that he's constantly being promoted, and now he's even a military commander! During Spring Festival and other holidays, all my war friends give the leaders gifts! One of the cadres in the platoon has a child—that kid gets over a million yuan in New Year money every year!" Xiao Hui was beginning to choke up, but he continued. "My mother died young, and it's not easy for my dad to run a vegetable stall all by himself. Our family doesn't have enough money to give the leaders presents."

At this point Mr. Zhang intervened. "Help your brother Xiao Hui out, Ah Qing!" His eyes were moist.

"Okay, Xiao Hui, let me give it a try," Ah Qing finally relented. "If you like what I've written, you can use it."

"That's wonderful, Brother Ah Qing! I don't understand poetry, but I still remember reading 'Premiere Zhou, Where Are You?' in school. The teacher forced all the students to read it out loud! Brother Ah Qing, if you can write a poem of that caliber, that would be great!"

Xiao Hui wrote down the names of his leaders, then handed the list to the poet, who was feeling far from inspired but in the end was able to use his imagination to put together a heroic song of praise! Three days later, Ah Qing returned to the outdoor vegetable stall, where he handed the work to Xiao Hui's father. Mr. Zhang went off to buy meat and alcohol for Ah Qing to thank him for his help, but Ah Qing just wandered off with a smile on his face before the man even returned.

4

Unable to get through by phone, I hopped on a bus to go tell Ah Qing about the Red Sun Culture Communication Company boss's idea of selling his book manuscript.

"I'm not selling my manuscript, Uncle He! I . . . " Whenever Ah Qing's temper flared, he would start to stammer. Now he lowered his head, too.

"Ah Qing," I said, trying to persuade him. "You don't have a job or any income right now. You should just sell it!" I looked at this impoverished, dissatisfied young man, thinking that if he were to sell his manuscript I would no longer have to lend him money. I loved Ah Qing, but his becoming famous was the last thing I cared about. All I wanted was for him to have a stable life; this alone would put my heart at ease. "You're still young!" I continued, trying to console but also reason with him. "If you sell your first novel, you'll still have the chance to write a second one and a third. Your life is hard enough as it is—why go chasing vanity? As long as the book is out there, you'll have made a contribution to society!"

"Uncle He," Ah Qing said, "if I were to sell my first novel, I would never be able to write anything again. If I were only doing this for the money, I'd have no reason to put all of my emotion into my writing. But writing is my religion! Without it, would I even have the confidence to keep living?" His eyes filled with tears.

I sighed deeply and suddenly felt ashamed of what I had just said.

"Don't worry, Ah Qing!" I tried to reassure him. "You still have me by your side. If you have any troubles further down the road, you know I'll be here to help you!"

Ah Qing started to make me a meal, but although I was hungry I stood up and told him that I didn't feel like eating. Part of the reason I had gone to Ah Qing's place to begin with was precisely because I didn't want to take him out to eat. Indeed, if he were to sell his manuscript, surely we'd go out and enjoy a wonderful feast together! This guy—he just didn't get it. In fact, all the young people in my life were quite hopeless: I couldn't even get an invitation to a restaurant from one of them! I left and walked along the road with an empty stomach, full of resentment toward Ah Qing. I had endured so much for him. "Forget it," I thought. "May as well return to my dumpling restaurant and eat there!"

Holding his manuscript in both hands, Ah Qing sat and stared into space, just as distracted as if his soul had wandered off. The kettle on the coal stove came to a boil; the water inside it howled.

Ah Qing rushed from the small, one-story house he rented and found a phone booth, where he shoved an IC card into a slot. He dialed a number but hung up before it even began to ring. "I can't do it! I can't sell my own manuscript!" he cried, utterly on the verge of madness. "I'll starve to death before I sell it! I'll burn it before I sell it!"

Dongdan at dusk was the Dongdan of wild ghosts and wandering souls. Despondent, Ah Qing paced back and forth in the little corner of the park that was theirs.

Suddenly he heard a voice rolling downward from the top of one of the artificial hills. "Ah Qing! Ah Qing!" It was Little Jade.

"Little Jade!" Ah Qing exclaimed. "Where did you die off to? I haven't seen you in nearly a year!" With a big smile he went to hug him, but Little Jade skirted to one side. "What's wrong?" Ah Qing asked. "I haven't seen you in this long and you don't let me hug you?" He reached out to take hold of Little Jade's hand.

"Don't touch me, Ah Qing, don't touch me!" Little Jade choked up. "I have an STD!"

Ah Qing pulled his hand back. "Have you seen a doctor? It couldn't be AIDS, right?"

"I went to an STD clinic on-and-off for three months, but they didn't cure it! Then I went to a big hospital and they said

I had stage-two syphilis! I don't have the money to get it looked at!" Tears streamed down his cheeks.

Ah Qing reached out a hand to wipe Little Jades tears, but suddenly changed his mind and recoiled. "Little Jade," he said, "I don't have any money to help you. Let's call Uncle He! He'll help us."

"How was business today?" I asked Little Fairy and Little Devil when I returned to the dumpling restaurant. "A little better?"

"So-so, Uncle He!" Little Fairy replied.

"We didn't lose or make any money," Little Devil added.

We began to eat dinner and the phone rang.

"Wei!" I shouted into the phone. It was Ah Qing. "What it is?"

"Uncle He," he began, "I urgently need money! Please— lend me two thousand kuai!"

"Aiya!" I exclaimed. "Ah Qing, in the three months since I opened this little place I've been losing money nonstop! I don't have anything to lend you; you're going to have to think of something else!"

After hanging up the phone, I no longer felt like eating. In just a few minutes, however, the phone rang again, and once again it was Ah Qing.

"Okay, Uncle He, I've figured it out!" He spoke rapidly. "Help me sell my manuscript, and the sonner the better. Sell it tomorrow, or even tonight if you can!" Urgency flooded his voice.

"Ah Qing," I laughed, "is the landlord pressing you for rent again? Make him wait a few days! If you don't have money for food, come to my dumpling house and eat."

The following day, I hadn't even risen from bed yet when Ah Qing called to ask about his manuscript. "This child!" I thought. So hungry, so starved into madness, that he was finally willing to give up the vanity of the writer. Shaking my head and laughing, I returned to Red Sun Culture Communication

Company, where I handed Ah Qing's work to an agent who would negotiate the sale.

Two days passed, then three, four, five . . . again and again I told Ah Qing on the phone: "Wait one more day! I know I'll get ahold of this money soon!"

"We can't wait any longer, Little Jade!" Ah Qing opened the door to his home and the two boys stepped inside. "I'm going to go look for a poet friend of mine so I can borrow some money, and I'll get as much as I can! Just stay here and wait for me; don't go running off anywhere. I'll be back as soon as I get it." Ah Qing dug through his pockets and pulled out all the cash that he had. He left everything with Little Jade, taking just twenty kuai with him for bus fare.

He took a bus to the southern outskirts of the city. The previous night he had spoken to a poet friend who sold pre-fabricated houses. At the end of the conversation, the poet friend agreed to lend Ah Qing five hundred kuai. After a long bus ride, Ah Qing arrived at the building where his friend lived, but when he called him on his cell phone, the poet who sold prefabricated houses said that he wasn't home!

"I'll wait for you to come back!" Ah Qing hollered into the phone.

"Don't wait for me," the poet replied. "All my money is in my wife's hands!"

Again Ah Qing took the bus, this time to the northern out-skirts of the city, where another poet friend—someone who represented writers working in the Misty Poet tradition—had also agreed to lend him five hundred kuai. On the phone, he and this Misty Poet representative had agreed that Ah Qing would arrive to his home between the hours of three and five. Ah Qing squeezed onto an unbearably crowded bus which barely moved forward, crawling at a snail's pace in an ocean of vehicles of all sizes. Up ahead, a red light flashed and the bus came to a standstill; when the light turned green, the bus didn't move an inch. Ah Qing's heart leapt from the window.

At five o'clock on the dot, Ah Qing arrived at the home of his friend, but the man wasn't there so Ah Qing called his cell phone. "I'll wait for you!" he said. "And I'm going to keep waiting until you come home and lend me this money!"

Ah Qing began to lose faith in the second poet. He had been friends with this "teacher" for more than a year, but neither Ah Qing's poetry nor his actions were enough to move him. The Misty Poet representative had agreed to lend Ah Qing money on the telephone, but when push came to shove he wasn't willing to see the promise through.

"What's the use of continuing to write poetry?" Ah Qing agonized. "And why doesn't anyone believe me when I say that if I borrow money from you, I will pay you back! I can't publish my poetry collection or my novel! Why . . . why am I so poor? Why must I live without face? This is an age without a Bo Le, a time when no one is able to detect hidden talent. This is the age of pedantic scholars who suppress the power of new life!" It was only at this moment that Ah Qing truly understood why the poet Hai Zi had killed himself!

Ah Qing walked through the streets—not a single person wanted his poetry! Peddlers sold their cheap goods, unemployed workers held job advertisements real and fraudulent between their fingers, but not a soul had any desire for Ah Qing's work.

5

Waiting for Ah Qing to return, Little Jade did his best to endure the pain. To him, each minute felt like a year. He looked at the palm of his hand and saw red spots that resembled the petals of plum blossoms. The flowers bloomed across his body.

He went outside to a public toilet, where he squatted down with clenched teeth. He squatted for over an hour, but still the feces wouldn't come out. Each day's shit was torture to him. Finally, he pushed as hard as he could and a searing pain tore through him as blood and excrement fell out.

He went to a bookstore, where he consulted a book about STDs. Then he went to a pharmacy and bought all kinds of medicine with the money Ah Qing had left: erythromycin, roxithromycin, tetracycline, oxytetracycline. He also bought hemorrhoid treatment pills, iodine tincture, an anti-inflammatory and a pain reliever. Little Jade swallowed everything that could be swallowed and immediately vomited all of it back up. His stomach spasmed, his liver and kidneys hurt, and his intestines felt as though they were being torn apart. His blood vessels may as well have been crawling with insects biting at his rotting flesh.

"How much will we get and when will we get it?" I asked the agent with a smile.

"The author is reading the manuscript as we speak!" he replied. "As soon as he's done reading it, he'll decide whether or not to buy it. This is a famous author, you know! If your work doesn't meet his standards, he wouldn't take it even if it was free. But if he likes it, he'll dish out a lot of money for it! We all have to keep our word! None of us can go back on this."

"Don't worry," I said earnestly. "As long as we can make some money from it, we won't go back on it."

Ah Qing never was able to borrow any money from his poet friends, and the small amount of money in his possession had already been spent. He didn't go back to Little Jade that day. Instead, he paced through the streets with an empty stomach. Finally, he stepped into Dongdan Park.

The telephone rang; it was Ah Qing.

"Did you sell the manuscript, Uncle He?" His voice was weary on the other end of the line.

"Very soon!" I replied. "Ah Qing, it will do us no good to worry about this. I assure you, there's a writer who's reading your manuscript at this very moment. He'll only decide if he wants to buy it after he finishes it."

Without a word, Ah Qing hung up the phone.

Little Jade returned to Ah Qing's home. To avoid the need to defecate, he hadn't been eating much. Instead he just mixed various medicines together and swallowed them on an empty stomach; but each time he did this, he vomited them back up. In the darkness he lay waiting for Ah Qing's return, eyes dry from having cried until there were no tears left.

The sky gradually lightened, and with great effort Little Jade got up from bed. When he saw the empty medicine boxes around him, his heart turned to ash.

He found a pen in Ah Qing's desk and wrote two suicide notes, one for his mother, one for Ah Qing. He washed his face and combed his hair, then put on the shoes that his mother had made for him five years earlier. He stepped out of Ah Qing's little house and into the street.

At Dongdan Park, Ah Qing bumped into a money-boy friend of his.

"My good brother," he said, "can you lend me some money? After I get some I'll pay you back immediately!"

"I've never lent money to friends in the gay circle!" the money boy said. "If you really need some cash, though, I can help you find a john."

Through the introduction of the money boy, Ah Qing met a Japanese man.

"Alright," the Mandarin-speaking Japanese man said the instant Ah Qing walked into the rented hotel room. "You can take off your clothes now. We'll calculate the cost by time. Do you want Japanese yen or Chinese RMB?"

"I want Chinese RMB!" Ah Qing quickly removed his clothes.

"Not bad!" the Japanese man remarked when he saw Ah Qing's physique. "With a body and cock like that, I can tell with one look that you're a male prostitute!" He continued, "I like a Chinese guy without any meat on his bones! I'll give you a thousand yuan an hour."

Little Jade walked through the streets until dusk fell. He climbed to the roof of a hotel and looked down at the cars and people busily moving below. As he watched the world beneath him, he recalled that he hadn't been home in five years. For five years he hadn't seen his mother. He thought about the day he left home to go find work; he was only seventeen and his mother had run to the front gate with tears in her eyes. He thought about the last time he had received a letter from her; it was a year ago. In that letter, his mother had said that she missed him very much. "Mama," he thought, "do you hate me now? I've written you ten letters this year, but not a single one has come from you. Mama, I called the village chief but his phone wasn't working! I really want to hear your voice right now, Mama. Mama . . . " He repeated the word out loud.

"How are you doing, Little Jade?" Ah Qing thought, closing his eyes to avoid looking at the Japanese man he was with. "You have to get through this until I come back!" He felt nothing but numbness.

"Talk dirty!" The Japanese man shouted as he slapped Ah Qing's ass. "Don't just lie there like a corpse! Tell me how much you want it!"

"This ten thousand yuan is advance payment," the agent said. "After the book is published I'll give you the remaining seventy percent."

I took the ten thousand yuan and left Red Sun Culture Communication Company.

I wanted to relay the good news to Ah Qing right away, but as always his cell phone was disconnected for failure to pay the bill. All I could do was go straight to his house and tell him the news in person. I started to feel anxious, and couldn't decide if I should take a taxi or ride the bus.

But I already had the money, so what was there to be anxious about? For days I had been running myself ragged. I should rest my feet a bit! I stepped into a supermarket that had just opened. They had all kinds of things: foods, beverages, household items . . . I bought myself a huge piece of cake which I decided to enjoy right then and there.

"We're the best of brothers, Ah Qing!" Little Jade cried out loud. "If you had been able to borrow money, I know you would have come back. If you weren't able to, I won't hate you for it! We're brothers, Ah Qing! After I die, you have to take good care of my mother! Mama . . . Mama . . . " Tears fell from Little Jade's eyes.

Ah Qing lifted his head and looked at the clock on the wall. He knew that he had already made a thousand kuai, but he wasn't ready to get dressed because a thousand wasn't enough to cure Little Jade's illness. He wanted to stretch out the time as long as he could. He needed to make more.

The Japanese man rinsed off in the shower, then came back out and sat on the couch. With a knife he began to peel an apple, his belly as big as a pregnant woman's.

"Why haven't you gotten up and put your clothes on yet? You want me to keep fucking you?" the Japanese man looked at the clock on the wall. "I'm done with you, so hurry up—get dressed and get out of here. You Chinese money boys are so greedy!" He grabbed a calculator and started punching buttons. "Okay, you were here for one hour and twenty-eight minutes."

The Japanese man pulled a wad of cash from his wallet and tossed it to the floor.

Ah Qing got up from the bed, then dressed himself and picked the money up off the floor. As he was about to exit, he grabbed the knife from the couch and stabbed the john in the stomach.

After finishing the cake and downing a big glass of milk, I had much more energy, so I went to go look at all the products on the shelves. Wow! Delicate little kids' toys, gorgeous, youthful T-shirts . . . So many lovely things!

I came across a collection of little gift items tied to red strings tacked to a wall. They made me suddenly remember Ah Qing's red stone heart, which was still in my desk drawer at home. I bought a jade figurine of the Bodhisattva Guanyin and removed the string; it was just the right size to fit through Ah Qing's stone heart.

By the time I came out of the supermarket, the sun was about to set. Time to go find Ah Qing and make him buy me a drink! I was walking along the street as happy as could be when up ahead I saw a crowd of spectators. What were they gawking at? I walked toward them.

"Wei, Big Sister," I said to an elderly lady. "What are you all looking at?"

"Performance art!" she replied. "Who knows how long this youth is going to stand there?"

After stabbing the Japanese john, Ah Qing rushed out of the hotel and into the street. He froze when he saw a group of people standing outside the front door because he thought they were staring at him, but when he realized that they were looking up at something, he continued forward to see what it was.

I looked up and saw a young person standing on the roof of the hotel—he was about to jump! Who was this person? I could see the vague outline of his silhouette and it looked so familiar! When I realized who it was, my chin dropped.

Ah Qing looked up and saw a young man standing on the roof of the very hotel he had just exited—he was about to jump! It couldn't be Little Jade, could it? When Ah Qing realized who it was, his chin dropped and his heart turned to ash.

"Wei! Hey you! On top of the building!" a man yelled from the crowd. "You gonna jump or not? If not, I'm going home for dinner!"

Laughter erupted from Little Jade's lips. Then he jumped.

From the foot of the building came an explosion of cheers and applause.

NINETEEN

1

The silent autumn rain fell, coldly.

"We're going home, Little Jade!" Ah Qing stepped out of the crematorium holding an urn with Little Jade's ashes tightly against his chest.

"We're going home, Little Jade!" He entered Beijing Railway Station with the urn full of Little Jade's ashes pressed tightly against his chest.

"We're going home, Little Jade!" He boarded a train. It wailed and sped off.

The damp autumn air flew past the window. Outside, withered leaves and crop plants swayed in the wind.

Ah Qing's body, and even it seemed his mind, was so cold that he shook. Trying to stay warm, he continued to grip Little Jade's ashes. "Do you remember, Little Jade? We escaped from that black factory and went into the cornfields. We ate cornstalk shoots when we were hungry, and when it rained we took off our clothes and hung them over the cornstalks for shelter. It was so cold that we held each other to stay warm. Little Jade, are you still cold? Don't be afraid, don't be afraid of anything! I'll be with you forever. We're going home together . . . we're going home together."

Ah Qing's voice was hoarse from crying, his lips so dry that blood seeped from the cracks. Again and again he called out Little Jade's name as if he were afraid that the heartless autumn wind would blow his friend's soul away. He was determined to take this soul back to the hometown they shared. "Little Jade," he repeated, "we're going home together!" The train stopped at one station, and then another. Ah Qing feared that Little Jade's soul would be crushed by the passengers. "We're going home together, Little Jade. We're going home together . . .

"Do you remember, Little Jade? When we were little, our families were so poor that we we couldn't eat vegetables, so we carried bamboo baskets on our shoulders and went into the fields to dig up wild herbs. You said you loved the tender shepherd's purse plants that we found in the fields of wheat seedlings. 'Let's go dig them out together!' you always said. You said you loved elm seeds in the springtime; together we climbed the trees and picked whatever we could find. Do you remember, Little Jade? While we were cutting grass we found a wild melon the size of a fist and scrambled to see who could get it first. I won because my P.E. class was better than yours! We sat beside the river and ate that bittersweet melon together. Do you remember, Little Jade? When we went swimming in the waterhole, I cut my foot on a piece of broken glass and you carried me on your back to the village clinic. Do you remember, Little Jade? When the flowers of the pagoda trees were in full bloom, we sat together at an outdoor movie theater and watched a film. A scary scene left you so afraid that you didn't want to walk home alone, so you made me walk with you. After primary school we entered middle school together, then we dropped out and went to places far from home; we drifted, we became vagrants, and we worked. Do you remember, Little Jade? You said that as long as you were with me, you would be happy! Well, I'm with you now! We won't be apart after this, Little Jade. Let's go home together. Let's go home together." Ah Qing's tears fell like the autumn rain outside the window. The train wept its heartbroken cry and continued to race forward.

The train stopped at Zhumadian and a sea of black umbrellas began moving along the platform.

"We're almost home, Little Jade. Time to get off the train and go home!" Ah Qing alighted the train, holding Little Jade's ashes against his chest.

Rainwater soaked Ah Qing's head, face and entire body. Fearing that Little Jade would get wet, he gripped the urn tightly and moved rapidly through the streets, which were washed by the rain until they were shiny. On those streets, Ah Qing saw no loved ones.

"Let's get on a bus and go home together, Little Jade!" He boarded a local bus that serviced towns and villages in the area.

The bus coasted through the rain as Ah Qing watched the blurry streets. Those streets bore the footprints of him and Little Jade.

"Have you ever seen a train, Ah Qing?" Little Jade had asked him when they were kids.

"Only in the movies!" Ah Qing laughed.

When they were kids, Little Jade would take hold of Ah Qing's hand and they would go running along the road connecting their village to a bigger town. They promised each other that when they grew up they'd go to the city and see how the trains raced along the tracks.

"Have some candy, Ah Qing! My dad gave me this!" Little Jade popped a piece of candy into his mouth and broke it in two.

"It's so sweet!" Ah Qing said, and then he shouted excitedly. "I envy you, Little Jade! You have a dad who works in the city!"

When they were kids, a barefoot Little Jade took hold of Ah Qing's hand. "Let's go catch cicadas!" he cried.

"Time to get off the bus, Little Jade! Just ten li and then we'll be home!" Ah Qing got off the bus and began walking through the muddy streets.

The hometown autumn rain fell relentlessly, callously. It soaked Ah Qing through.

Up ahead was Dragon Gully Village. Ah Qing saw long stretches of bleak, desolate fields, farmland that seemed not to have been cultivated for a very long time. He saw the tile-roofed houses, but he heard no barking dogs or crowing roosters. In the cemetery just outside the village, there were a number of new tombstones. This was his first time back in five years. How could so many villagers have died? He hastened his footsteps.

"Halt! What are you doing?" Two police officers stood at the village entrance.

"I'm going home. My home is here in Dragon Gully Village!" Ah Qing eyed the officers suspiciously as they looked him up and down.

"What's that you're holding?" one of them asked.

"Ashes," Ah Qing sobbed. "Little Jade's ashes! Little Jade, he . . . " His voice faltered.

"Alright! You can go in!" The officers stepped aside and let him enter Dragon Gully Village.

Not a shadow moved in the village. The muddy, rain-soaked streets were carpeted with withered and yellowed leaves.

"What on earth has happened here?" Ah Qing felt as though he had entered a village that was deep in sleep. It was a deathly silence. He ran through the mud, fell down, got up again.

"Little Jade, we're home," Ah Qing sobbed. "We've made it to Dragon Gully Village! From now on, your mother is my mother. Let's go see her together."

"Ma, I'm home! Ma!" Ah Qing cried as he entered Little Jade's house.

It was dusk outside and an oil lamp flickered inside the dark house. An old woman with disheveled hair and looking as withered as tinder sat up in her bed. She looked at the urn in Ah Qing's arms with empty eyes.

Ah Qing prostrated himself before Little Jade's mother's bed and sobbed.

"Little Jade has come home! My Little Jade has come home!" The old woman's lips twitched as a final tear fell from her eye.

Ah Qing left Little Jade's mother and ran toward his own house. When he pushed open the door, he saw a younger brother who was on the verge of death and a younger sister whose entire body was covered in lesions.

"Big Brother, you've come back!" his sister cried. "I thought I would never see you again! Everyone in the village has AIDS from selling blood! So many people have died—our dad died a month ago, too! Big Brother, I'm so glad to see you're still alive! Why did you come back? Don't stay in this village, hurry up and get out of here! We could infect you . . . "

"How is this possible?" Ah Qing asked. "The entire village has contracted AIDS and I didn't know about it? Why haven't there been any TV or news reports?" His cries echoed through the dark room.

"Hurry up and leave, Big Brother!" his sister shouted. "Little Sister is begging you to go! Never come back here again!"

Her lamenting voice rang in Ah Qing's ear. Utterly broken-hearted, he knelt on the floor and looked at his sleeping brother, who he knew would soon be reunited with their father.

Outside the village there stretched a vast expanse of tomb-stones. Ah Qing walked through the darkness toward the train tracks.

He hopped on a freight train headed north.

After arriving at his destination, he exited the train station, where a pair of handcuffs awaited him.

2

The Japanese man whom Ah Qing had stabbed was taken to a hospital—he didn't die—and Ah Qing went to prison for prostitution. The manuscript he had sold was published and placed on bookstores' most conspicuous shelves. The title of the novel and the names of characters were changed, but the content was not otherwise touched. The name printed on the cover of the book was that of a famous author who was no longer able to produce like he used to.

Old He's Dumpling House went out of business. Again Little Fairy and Little Devil were out of work, and again they began drifting in the park.

I tightly held Ah Qing's stone heart, that vivid red stone heart, that silent stone heart, the heart on which was written the word "love." I opened my photo album and flipped through the pages. These young friends—one by one they had all left me.

Ah Qing and Xia Nanshan . . . How was it that when I looked at their pictures they seemed to be one and the same person? Could it be that Ah Qing was the very child that Xia Nanshan and Dr. Hua had lost so many years ago? Tightly I squeezed the red stone heart in my hand.

"Ah Qing!" I said out loud. "You have two years of prison ahead of you—two years of torment! You have to keep on living." Tears streamed down my cheeks.

I bought a bag of sweets and went to visit Ah Qing in prison, where we were separated by walls, separated by bars, separated by glass.

"Ah Qing, you have to keep living! You're still young and this society needs you. I'm in the process of preparing the manuscript for your collection of poetry. I'm going to use the money from selling your novel to pay for it to be published."

"Thank you for coming to see me, Uncle He," Ah Qing smiled weakly. "I don't want to publish my poetry collection. No one needs poetry anymore. Take the money from my novel and give it to Little Lotus and her child. I'm living pretty well here in prison; everything is reliable here. I no longer have to worry about things like food and shelter! When they tell me to work, I work. When they tell me to sleep, I sleep. I've found a home here! Prison is the best place for me."

With heavy steps and a heavy heart, I left the prison.

I took a train to Zhengzhou, carrying the red stone heart that Ah Qing's birth mother had given him.

When I got there, I bought a package of baby food and went to Little Lotus's house. "I'm Ah Qing's Uncle," I said, introducing myself. "Ah Qing made some money from the manuscript of a book he wrote; he wants me to give it to you!" I removed twenty thousand kuai from my bag and placed it in Little Lotus's hands. I also informed her that Ah Qing was in prison.

"Thank you, Uncle He! Is Ah Qing doing okay in prison?" She held little baby Future, who was one year old now, in her arms. "I want to take the child to see him."

"Ah Qing's mental state is not very good right now," I cautioned. "He's had a lot of difficulties and suffered a number of blows." I pulled the red stone heart from my undershirt pocket and showed it to Little Lotus. "Ah Qing's birth mother left him this stone. He's always worn it around his neck, and he's been looking for her ever since. If it turns out that Dr. Hua is Ah Qing's birth mother, wouldn't it be wonderful? A mother's love would truly be the warmth that he needs."

"Dr. Hua? Director Hua? How could she be Ah Qing's birth mother?" Little Lotus was perplexed.

"It's just a hunch!" I replied. "It's because Ah Qing looks so much like Xia Nanshan. If they were to recognize this red stone heart . . . " I placed it in the palm of Little Lotus's hand.

We went to Zhengzhou People's Hospital and straight to the office of Director Hua.

"Hello, Dr. Hua, do you remember me?" I asked with a smile.

"Oh, Big Brother He! When did you get to Zhengzhou?"

"Earlier today. Dr. Hua, I'd like to show you something." I pulled the stone from my pocket and placed it on her desk.

She picked it up and I watched as her eyes widened. I could see that her mind was racing back to a memory.

"Brother He!" she exclaimed. "Where did you find this?" She grasped my hand and I could hear the emotion in her voice.

"You remember this? Why, that's wonderful, Dr. Hua!" I, too, was getting emotional.

"My child!" Dr. Hua cried out as her eyes filled with tears. "Where are you now?"

I told Dr. Hua everything: about how Ah Qing had been forsaken by his birth parents, how he had been raised by adoptive parents, and how he later left his village to drift as a vagrant and a worker. She listened to me tell the story and it wasn't long before she began to weep.

"Ah Qing, my child! Is he still suffering in prison?" She picked up the phone on her desk and dialed Xia Nanshan's cell phone. "Nanshan!" she cried, "we've found our child!" She hung up the phone and the four of us—Dr. Hua, Little Lotus, Future, and I—went to the doctor's home.

After hearing us out, Xia Nanshan put on a serious face. "Ah Qing is not our child!" he said sternly. "Our child, the child we adopted, is in middle school now."

"But he really is our child, Nanshan! Look at this red stone heart—don't you remember it? After we got married and went to the seaside for our honeymoon, we found this stone heart on the beach! You yourself carved the word 'love' into it, and you put a red string through it and gave it to me to commemorate our marriage." Her voice shook as the maternal love that had lain idle for so long welled up in her heart.

"Enough!" Xia Nanshan was growing impatient. "We do not have a son who's in prison! You've found the wrong person, Old He. Now hurry up and get this stone heart out of here!" Flustered and frustrated, he was beginning to raise his voice.

"My, what a noble and esteemed school principal *you* are!" Little Lotus said with a sneer. "You won't even acknowledge your own flesh and blood!"

"Let's go, Little Lotus!" I pulled at the indignant young woman's arm and we left the director's home.

Xia Nanshan and Dr. Hua sat on their bed, feeling glum and disconsolate.

"Let's go to the prison and see our child, Nanshan!" Dr. Hua pressed.

"Are you out of your mind?" he replied. "You're the director of Zhengzhou People's Hospital and I'm the principal of Zhengzhou No. 1 Middle School! To even think that we would let anyone know that we have a child who's in prison! Even if we had any face left, would we dare show it in public? We already have a child, a child who's outstanding both in behavior and in school! We have to be mindful of how we look in the eyes of others!"

Days passed. I knew that if I was going to be able to console Ah Qing's aching heart, the heart that had been forsaken by his own family, I would have to convince Dr. Hua to bring her child back into her life. But when I returned to the hospital, I found the director's office door shut.

"Excuse me, is Dr. Hua here?" I inquired in the office of the vice-director.

"Dr. Hua hasn't been to work for a several days now!" replied Dr. Gou.

I left at once and went to Dr. Hua's home to look for her.

"Please leave, Brother He!" she said with red, swollen eyes. "We already have a child!" She lowered her head and her nose twitched.

I took a deep breath and began to speak:

" . . . That winter has reached its end   Mama
Wearing soft gloves you held me tight
Willow trees sprouted light yellow buds
And around your beautiful face snowflakes flew

You forgot to see that spring is already here
After kissing me gently, you placed a heart on the street

. . . That winter is gone forever   Mama
In the dark night I have grown up
I seek a mama who wears warm gloves
On the street it's still so cold
Why can I never see the spring
Why is my heart full of drifting snowflakes . . . "

With a hoarse voice I recited the words as tears streamed down
Dr. Hua's cheeks. "Ah Qing wrote this poem for his mother!"
I said. "This is a poem about Ah Qing's search for a mother's
love!"

"Tomorrow I'll go with you to see Ah Qing, to see my
son!" Dr. Hua's voice choked.

I took Dr. Hua, Little Lotus, and Ah Qing's child Future
to the railway station, where I bought three tickets for an
express train. The three adults sat quietly in the waiting room
listening to the child's joyful laughter.

Suddenly Dr. Hua's cell phone rang. It was the hospital
calling: they said there was a patient who urgently needed surgery and that she alone had to perform it. She rushed back to
the hospital and never again attempted to see the child she had
abandoned twenty-six years earlier.

3

In autumn two years later, an anthology of Ah Qing's poetry—
selected, edited, and financed entirely by me—was published.
On the day he was released from prison, I went to meet him
and bring him home. I held a copy of his book under my arm.
At this point, I regarded Ah Qing as my own son.

"I'm not leaving!" Ah Qing protested at the prison gates.
"I'm not going anywhere! Prison is my home . . . " He was
determined not to budge.

"Ah Qing, my good child! Come home with Uncle!" I put my arms around him and did my best to coax him into leaving the prison. "Look, your book has been published—it's beautifully printed!"

I held Ah Qing's hand as we walked through the autumn streets. He squinted at the bright sunlight, which pierced his eyes. During the years he had spent as a vagrant, working odd jobs, and writing poetry, he had become as thin as a pencil. Two years of living and eating in prison, however, had made him gain a good deal of weight. No wonder he was unwilling to leave!

"My good child, what do you want to eat? Let Uncle buy it for you!"

"I don't want to eat anything."

"Uncle will buy you a persimmon, a big persimmon!" I led him by the hand into a fruit shop. "Hey boss," I called out, "how much are persimmons per jin?"

We left the shop and again I took hold of Ah Qing's hand, this time to take him home. In my other hand I held a red persimmon.

"Ah Qing," I said when we got back to my place. "Uncle needs to update the software on his computer. Can you help me upgrade from Windows 98 to Windows XP?"

"I've forgotten how!" he said. "I've forgotten everything." Absentmindedly he flipped through his book of poetry for a while, then threw it aside and lay on the bed to sleep.

"Come on, Ah Qing, don't just lie in bed all day! Go out and walk around, enjoy life!" I tried dragging him outdoors a few times, but he refused, wanting only to crawl back under the blankets and stay there.

Little Lotus phoned from Zhengzhou to ask how Ah Qing was doing. "Ah Qing!" I called out. "Come pick up the phone. Little Lotus and Future want to talk to you!"

"I don't want to talk on the phone. I don't want to see anybody!" He poked his head out of the blankets long enough to say these words, then disappeared again.

To coax Ah Qing into a little happiness, I played guitar and sang for him until I was out of breath and covered in sweat. Then I remembered the red, heart-shaped stone in my desk drawer, so I went to get it. I opened the drawer and touched it with both hands. "Ah Qing, your stone!" I exclaimed. "Uncle's going to return it to you now! You know, your birth mother—" I shut my mouth before finishing the sentence. I hadn't meant to tell him about her.

"Uncle He! Have you seen my birth mother?" His eyes widened, and they sparkled.

"No!" I lied. "If I had seen your birth mother I would have made her come and claim her poet son!" My face reddened and my heart ached. "Child," I continued, "so many people love your poetry! Do you remember that musician named Warm Spring Blossom? He's written music for a number of your poems." In saying this, I hoped that I might awaken his numb memories.

Ah Qing walked through the streets, endlessly it seemed, and alone. He seemed to want to go to Dongdan Park, but his footsteps inexplicably turned in the opposite direction.

"Ah Qing—are you Ah Qing?" A blind fortune-teller sitting on a street corner called out.

He halted his footsteps and looked at the blind fortune-teller incredulously. He didn't think he had ever seen this person before. "Shifu," he said, and he stepped forward. "Are you calling me?"

"You've already addressed me as 'shifu,'" the blind fortune-teller replied. "The person I am looking for is you."

"But shifu, why don't I recognize you?" Ah Qing reached back as far his memory would go, but the blind fortune-teller remained unfamiliar to him.

"Child, have you just returned from prison? And you were abandoned by your birth parents when you were little, yes?" The blind fortune-teller described nearly everything that Ah Qing had experienced.

"Shifu, are you telling me my fortune? Everything you've said is so accurate! Let me give you some money." Ah Qing reached into his pockets, but they were empty. His face turned red. "I'm sorry, shifu, but I forgot to carry money on me today! I'll come back tomorrow and bring you some."

"I knew long ago that you would have no money today!" The blind fortune-teller laughed and continued. "Child, the day I've been waiting for has finally come! You are the person I am looking for—you are the one who must inherit the craft of divination described in the *I Ching*!"

"What?!" Ah Qing laughed cynically and shook his head. "Shifu, are you telling me that you want me to be your disciple? You're blind—what could you possibly have to teach me?"

"I wasn't always blind, child. After my shifu taught me the *I Ching*, I started telling people's fortunes. My eyes went blind after the very first time, and it's all because I divulged the mysteries of nature!" The blind fortune-teller continued. "Now I want to show others the way."

"Shifu, if you teach me the fortune-telling of the *I Ching*, will I also go blind?" Ah Qing pressed him to know.

"What goes blind is only our bodily eyes," the fortune-teller explained. "It is only when our physical eyes can no longer see that we can open up the eyes of our soul! Child, you must come back on the ninth day of the ninth lunar month. I will wait for you here!"

Ah Qing nodded, then turned to walk away, but he only went nine steps before he regretted having agreed to the request. Not wanting to lose his sight, he turned around to speak to the blind fortune-teller once more, but the man was nowhere to be found!

"I met a blind fortune-teller on the street today, Uncle He," Ah Qing said. "He wanted to take me as his disciple."

"Don't believe what those rip-off artists say! They can't even support themselves and they want to show others the way?" I laughed and patted Ah Qing's shoulder. "Good child, just keep writing your poetry. You can use it to show more blind people the way!"

Somebody knocked on the door outside. Ah Qing went to see who it was, and in walked Little Devil with a big backpack.

"Wow, Little Devil!" I tousled his hair and laughed. "Long time no see! Have you come to sell more dildos?"

"Nope! I've become a Christian, Uncle He, and I've come to give you the Bible." Gently Little Devil opened his backpack and pulled out a thick copy of the Bible.

Holding the heavy book in both hands, Ah Qing began silently reading the psalms inside.

"You and Little Fairy have really turned over a new leaf!" I said. "One of you has become a Christian, the other a Buddhist!"

Ah Qing put the book down and looked at me. "Has Little Fairy become a monk, Uncle He?"

"After you got out of prison, my dumpling shop was unable to stay afloat, so I shut its doors. Little Fairy was out of work again and went back to being a vagrant in the park. One day—it was a snowy lunar New Year's Eve—he encountered an old monk. The old monk didn't say a word to Little Fairy, but just took him by the hand and led him away. The last time I saw him was last year at a temple fair on Tomb-Sweeping Day. He was wearing a monk's robe and beating a wooden fish drum."

Little Devil left and Ah Qing resumed flipping through the Bible. "Uncle He," he asked, "do you think it's better to be a monk or a Christian? On the ninth day of the ninth month, should I go back and see that blind fortune-teller?"

"Don't go indulging in flights of fantasy, Ah Qing!" I replied. "I've invited a famous literary critic to come over. Let's ask him to write a review of your book of poetry! It won't be long before you're a great, renowned poet!" I tried to console Ah Qing with love, and warm him with sincerity.

The famous literary critic came over and Ah Qing and I invited him for a meal at a high-end restaurant. After looking through Ah Qing's book of poetry for a while, the famous literary critic slammed his hand on the table. "Great poetry!" he shouted. "A real talent!"

After the famous literary critic left, Ah Qing was so excited that he couldn't sit still. He wanted to take his poetry collection and go find some writers to become friends with.

A group of people were holding a poets' symposium in Tianjin. They invited Ah Qing to pay a membership fee and attend.

"Uncle He, they want me to pay a fee and join," Ah Qing said. "What do you think? Should I go?"

"Go!" I replied enthusiastically. "Go and meet some poets! Go interact with them!"

To help Ah Qing's heart learn to live again, I encouraged him to go out and see the world. I couldn't let him continue feeling so dejected and dispirited. "Go, good child!" I said. "Bring some good news back to me!"

Ah Qing boarded the train to Tianjin with a smile.

4

Little Chrys married the self-employed gas-range repairman who had waited hand and foot on the old man at the hospital. They honeymooned, and then they both returned to their respective jobs.

It was right around the time Xia Nanshan was fighting his way to the chairmanship of the municipal branch of the Chinese People's Political Consultative Conference that he suddenly collapsed to the ground. He was rushed to Zhengzhou Hospital, where he was examined by each of the physicians until finally he was diagnosed with cardiac necrosis.

"We're preparing to give you a heart transplant, Nanshan!" Dr. Hua consoled her husband, who lay in the hospital bed.

"Don't you worry—we'll find a donor! I've already contacted a few prisons."

Little Chrys came by the room, a dextrose solution in her hand.

"Little Chrys, please take good care of Principal Xia!" said Dr. Hua.

"I will! Please, Director Hua, don't worry!"

That night Little Chrys lay in bed with her self-employed gas-range-repairman husband. "You seem exhausted, wife!" he remarked.

"Our hospital director's husband is sick," she replied. "Cardiac necrosis! We're getting ready to give him a new, young heart, but he's almost sixty! Why not just let him die?" Little Chrys slurred her words somewhat, as if she was talking in her sleep.

Little Chrys went sleepwalking again that night. Barefoot, she slipped out of the home she shared with her husband and made her way to the hospital patient ward.

"Why on earth are you barefoot, Little Chrys?" the night-duty nurse asked in surprise.

Little Chrys did not answer the question, but continued to make her way to Xia Nanshan's bed. She reached out and slowly began to feel the heavy cotton quilt covering him. Xia Nanshan wanted to cry out, but Little Chrys cuffed her hands tightly around his neck before he could speak.

"Someone come! Someone come!" screamed the night nurse as she pounced on Little Chrys.

Little Chrys was diagnosed as a somnambulist: during her night walking she had killed twenty-eight old and sick patients. After being convicted of her crimes, she changed out of the white angel's clothing of a hospital nurse and into the attire of a mental hospital patient.

Ah Qing went to Tianjin to participate in the poets' symposium. On his third night there, he dreamed of the blind fortune-teller.

The man took Ah Qing by the hand and they walked until Ah Qing turned around to look behind them and saw Little Lotus leading Future by the hand. "Little Lotus! Future!" he called out. Future waved at him and smiled. Ah Qing released the blind fortune-teller's hand to go embrace his own Future, but the child turned to a pile of stones and Little Lotus quickly did the same. "Shifu!" Ah Qing cried, but the blind fortune-teller, too, was gone in the blink of an eye.

Ah Qing awoke from the dream and went immediately to the long-distance bus station. At a newsstand inside the station, he bought a copy of the *Southern Weekly*; in the supplement section he saw the review that the famous literary critic had written. Ah Qing's poetry, he wrote, was a pile of dog shit! Ah Qing recalled something that the famous literary critic had said over dinner: "In this day and age, having a lasting reputation is synonymous with having a name that stinks to eternity!" Ah Qing laughed and put the newspaper in his bag, then bought a bus ticket to Zhengzhou.

The bus broke down halfway through the journey, so all the passengers had to find other modes of transportation. When a freight vehicle approached, Ah Qing waved his arms in the air and tried to stop the driver.

"Where are you going?" the driver asked.

"To Zhengzhou."

"Give me money for a pack of cigarettes and I'll take you!"

Ah Qing pulled a bottle of liquor from his bag and handed it to the driver through the passenger window. "This is for you, shifu!"

When the driver saw the bottle, he smiled and reached across the passenger seat to open the door and let Ah Qing in. The vehicle continued racing down the road.

"This goddamned weather!" the driver shouted. "It's only the ninth lunar month and already it's this cold?"

"It sure is!" Ah Qing replied, and then suddenly realized that it was the ninth day of the month. "I wonder if that blind fortune-teller really will return to the same place to meet me!" he thought. "Now I want to go, but I can't."

"Hey fella," the driver said, eying the label on the bottle that Ah Qing had given him. "That's not bad booze! Open it up and let me have a few sips to kill this cold!"

Ah Qing was cold and wanted a few sips, too, so he opened up the bottle. The driver took a couple of swigs, then passed the bottle to Ah Qing, who also took a few swigs before passing it back to the driver.

Zhengzhou was approaching rapidly as the vehicle rushed past a long stream of villages in the outskirts of the city. Suddenly a motorcycle was coming straight at them. The driver of the freight vehicle turned the steering wheel and slammed on the brake, causing the wheels to spin and the vehicle to fly into a ditch on the side of the road. Hundreds of apples in the back of the truck rolled out onto the ground.

A group of farmers who had been the crossing the road ran into the ditch and began madly snatching up the apples that had fallen.

Red blood marks spotted the face and hands of Ah Qing, who struggled to crawl out of the vehicle. The driver was covered in even more blood. He was trapped inside the car and couldn't get out.

"Someone help! Someone help!" Ah Qing's cries were drowned out by the yelling of people scrambling to pick up apples.

A farmer who lived nearby approached the scene carrying a basket and two empty bags that were normally used for chemical fertilizer and pig feed. He began picking up the apples that were still in the back of the vehicle and hadn't rolled out. Before long, every last apple had been taken.

An old man gnawing on one of the stolen apples stepped up to Ah Qing. "Hey fella," he said, "where did you get these apples from? They're real sweet!"

"Sir, please help us!" Ah Qing said desperately with a voice that was growing weaker.

Some of the people on the road walked up to Ah Qing, but when they saw he wasn't anyone they knew, they turned back around and walked off without a word.

"Sir, please help us!" Ah Qing repeated, and he stretched out a bloody hand to the old man.

"Hey fella," the old man said. "You have any money? If you don't have any money, I'd be taking you to the hospital for free!" The old man sighed and continued. "Give me a hundred kuai and I'll find a motor trike to take you to the hospital!"

With all the effort he could muster, Ah Qing pulled a one-hundred-kuai note from his pocket and handed it to the old man, who then shouted for two young people to come and pull the driver from the truck. The two injured men were placed on a flatbed full of pig manure hitched to the back of a farming motor trike. Then they were rushed off to Zhengzhou People's Hospital.

"We're ready for surgery!" Dr. Hua shouted to the hospital staff after giving Ah Qing a blood test. "Nanshan!" she continued to her husband, "we found someone to save you!"

Ah Qing and Xia Nanshan were both rolled into the operating room.

"Doctor," Ah Qing said weakly, "I want to make a phone call . . . "

She leaned into Ah Qing's ear. "All you have to do is sign your name right here," she whispered.

With a trembling hand, Ah Qing signed his name as Dr. Gou injected him with an anesthetic. Dr. Gou looked at this young person's face and his hands began to tremble.

Clenching her teeth, Dr. Hua gripped the surgical knife and cut open Ah Qing's chest. Out came a red heart and a hoarse voice cried out, "Mama! Mama!"

When Dr. Hua heard the familiar cry, her mind raced back to a cold, snowy night twenty-eight winters ago. Then she saw another heart near Ah Qing's chest, a red stone heart that had fallen behind the patient's neck during surgery.

"Ah Qing! My child!" She fainted and collapsed to the floor.

The surgery failed and Ah Qing and Xia Nanshan died at the same time in their respective beds. Only the driver of the freight vehicle was saved.

In the dark night, a madwoman repeated again and again: "I killed my child . . . I killed my child . . . "

I flip through my old photo album, looking at all the pictures. I light a candle and burn Xia Nanshan, burn Ah Qing, burn Little Jade, burn Little Tough, burn Little Thing . . . Finally, I burn myself, laughing as the wax tears of the candle drip.

"Our dumpling shop is open for business, Uncle He!" Ah Qing ran toward me, then kissed me on the cheek. Little Jade, Little Tough, Little Thing, Little Fairy, and Little Devil ran toward me, too. We held the string of cracking, popping fireworks and welcomed customers as they stepped into Old He's Dumpling House. In the blink of an eye, a forty-square-foot restaurant became a four-hundred-square-foot restaurant, a four-thousand-square-foot restaurant!

An old coworker called out to me. "Old He! Our director is dead, the vice-director is dead, and the vice-vice-director is dead, too. We invite you to go to the crematorium to serve as our new director!" I threw on the Western-style suit that I normally reserved for celebrating the New Year, then shined my leather shoes until they glistened. I stepped into the crematorium, where I saw Little He and Little Xia carrying corpses, which they placed one by one into the cremation chamber. When they saw me—a leader!—they greeted me deferentially. I was delighted!

"Uncle He!" Ah Qing said, running to me. "The customers don't like pork dumplings!"

"I know what to do!" I replied. "From now on we're not selling pig-meat dumplings, we're only selling human-meat dumplings! Little He! Little Xia! Prepare the kitchen knife!" I took hold of the knife and stepped into the morgue—damn! Bodies everywhere, I'm rich! I stripped off their trousers and began slicing fatty meat from their asses. Unrelentingly I cut ten jin of meat from each one! If anyone's buttocks were too thin to provide ten jin, I sliced meat from their faces to make up for it! I put the fatty human flesh into a grinder and ground it into a five-spice meat stuffing, then wrapped it all up in holiday dumplings! Ladies and gentlemen! Welcome, customers one and all, to Old He's Dumpling House! Today we present to the public an alternative five-spice pork stuffing for the twenty-first century! Not only tasty but also cheap—just five RMB per jin!"

I stepped out of Old He's Dumpling House and made my way to the crematorium.

"Old He!" an old coworker greeted me. "Long time no see!"

"How dare you call me Old He, you bum! I'm your director! Now get to work for me! Each person has to cut a thousand jin of meat! Hurry up and pull down those dead people's trousers."

"Old He, are you ill?" my former coworker asked with concern. "You're retired now—why not just enjoy life at home?"

"I'm your director! I haven't retired! I'll never retire. I'm going to keep living and I'm going to live well. I'm going to sell even more human meat and make lots of money! I'll make it to eighty years old and I won't die—hell, I'll make it to a hundred and I won't die! I'll be a vegetable and I still won't die!" As I was screaming and yelling, a white car rolled its way toward us. Surely they wanted to invite me to the great meeting for the election of a village chief for the United Nations Global Village!

Little Lotus had lost all faith in the future! Once again she entered the red-light district to sell sex, and continued to do so until she caught another STD.

She took Future with her as she walked through big streets and small alleyways; she was intent on finding the child a warm, safe home. They walked past a child with no feet; they walked past a child selling flowers; they walked past a child picking rags from garbage piles.

"Little Lotus! Long time no see!" It was the old landlady, who called out to her at the vegetable market. "That big speckled cat gave birth, eight kittens all at once! Little Lotus! Should I buy pig liver for the cat, or cow liver?"

Little Lotus left the vegetable market empty-handed.

On Christmas Day, a circus troupe from America arrived in Zhengzhou to give a performance.

"Mommy, let's go see the circus!" Five-year-old Future looked up at Little Lotus.

"Alright!" Little Lotus replied. "Mommy will take Future to the circus!" Using the money she had set aside for antibiotics, Little Lotus bought two circus tickets.

Two American clowns, one male, one female, walked onstage, greeted by the sound of laughter and clapping.

"Now," the Mandarin-speaking female clown said, "I want to find a *very* naughty child—the worst of the bunch! Let's get 'em up here to do a number with us!" Scanning the faces in the audience, she moved her heavy, costume-encumbered body across the stage. Suddenly she spotted Future smiling up at her from Little Lotus's lap. The female clown jumped down into the aisle and took Future by the hand, then led the child back to the stage.

Little Lotus watched as Future happily performed the act with the two clowns. All throughout the audience roared the sound of laughter, clapping and cheering. That's when Little Lotus grabbed a pen and a piece of paper from her bag. "Dear Mr. Clown and Ms. Clown," she wrote. "Thank you for choosing my child from a thousand children! Please, Mr.

Clown and Ms. Clown, adopt my child. Signed, a mother who has lost all hope!"

She asked a member of the audience to give her suicide note to the two clowns.

With tears in her eyes and a faint smile on her lips, Little Lotus left the circus and disappeared into the night.

5

Beijing in the springtime. Tiny, fragile buds burst forth from willow trees; a heavy snow falls in the cold and desolate wind like banknotes from the afterlife. When dusk comes, the earth gleams with a brightness that looks like morning sunlight. From the second floor of a mental hospital, a pair of gray eyes peers through the glass, attentively watching the snow-buried world.

A thin, hollow face rests beneath an old man's white hair; on it lingers an imbecilic smile. The mouth is askew, but the teeth remain intact. He is waiting to die in the line of duty.

The wind sobs outside the window. Cold that clings to glass is moved to tears by the heater inside the room.

Hoarsely the old man sings:

That winter   Mama
Wearing white gloves you held me
At the train station rain began to fall
In the sky snowflakes began to flutter
Snowflakes and rain landed on your head
Gently you placed a sleeping me on the street

That winter has reached its end   Mama
Wearing soft gloves you held me tight
Willow trees sprouted light yellow buds
And around your beautiful face snowflakes flew
You forgot to see that spring is already here
After kissing me gently, you placed a heart on the street . . .

The singing voice floats to Zhengzhou on a sky of dancing snowflakes. A child with no feet crawls along the road, begging as passersby bend down low to offer a bit of compassion.

Dancing snowflakes float to Beijing on the sound of singing. A youth with just one leg leans against his crutches. He is standing in the square outside the train station, plucking at guitar strings as he sings:

That winter is gone forever   Mama
In the dark night I have grown up
I seek a mother who wears warm gloves
On the street it's still so cold
Why can I never see the spring
Why is my heart full of drifting snowflakes

That winter   Mama
Wearing gloves you left me forever
On streets, icy snow graves move
There is only my crying as I search for my own Mama
Why can I not grab hold of spring
It's because the sound of singing in spring has buried Mama

That winter has reached its end   Mama
Your gloves are wet with tears
You've walked a long and weary road
Your feet, swollen and cold
Your lonely silhouette leaves me, moves toward death
And my fragrant dreams suddenly wither

That winter is gone forever   Mama
I've lost twenty-three springs
Like a snowflake I search for Mama's embrace
Search for Mama's gloves
A stream is sadly flooded with my tears
Black clouds in the sky are tired, too

That winter   Mama
Wearing gloves you stepped into the dark night
On streets, icy snow graves move
There is only my crying as I search for Mama
Search for my own unfortunate Mama
Why can I not hold on to your sorrow
Why am I not the gloves on Mama's hands

Why can I not forget the direction of falling snowflakes?

TRANSLATOR'S ACKNOWLEDGMENTS

I am grateful for the generous assistance of my literary agent Jayapriya Vasudevan, who saw something in Mu Cao's book that was worthy of sharing. Thanks also to Susan Harris of *Words without Borders*, who published an early draft of an excerpt of this translation. Additionally, a number of individuals helped in ways big and small in the realization of this project. John Balcom, Hongwei Bao, Sam Wukui Bao, Miguel Bejarano, Xiaochuan Cao, Cui Zi'en, Fan Popo, Angela L. Gibson, Jessica Goldblatt, Ivo, Lucas Klein, Skye Savage, Susan Su, Jeffrey Tharsen, Trudy, Nina Ventra, Jerry Junqi Wang, Remy Wei, Xiaogang Wei, Jenny Man Wu, and Zheng Lianjie: thank you. Above all I am grateful to Mu Cao himself, who gave me a copy of his book when we first met at the 7th Beijing Queer Film Festival. His work continues to fill me with love and rage each time I read it.